PRAISE FOR TIF MARCELO

"M   rama and sweet
mo   lture, language,
and   . The endearing
protagonists, dramatic sibling rivalry, and idyllic coastal setting make
for a feel-good romance that readers won't want to miss."

—*Publishers Weekly*

"Readers will yearn for more stories about these compelling characters."

—*Booklist*

"Another home run for Tif Marcelo! This time as she takes us behind the
scenes of a family-run romantic couples resort on the eve of its grand
reopening—complete with sibling rivalry, long-held family secrets, and
a slow-simmering can't-take-your-eyes-off-the-page romance between
two family friends determined to try to keep a lid on the burn. With
her signature style and deftly drawn characters and setting, Marcelo
takes us on a storytelling journey of family and love and second chances
and explores them with a fresh new lens, reminding us how it feels to
escape—and, more importantly, how it feels to finally come home."

—Amy Impellizzeri, award-winning author of *I Know How This Ends*

"Compelling family tensions, a captivating second-chance romance,
and an evocative beachside setting come together beautifully in Tif
Marcelo's gem of a book. I fell in love with Heart Resort and the Pusos,
and I can't wait to return to this world in the next installment!"

—Mia Sosa, *USA Today* bestselling author of *The Worst Best Man*

In a Book Club Far Away

"Marcelo captivates in this endearing story about the bonds of friendship . . . Making good use of army life as the backdrop, Marcelo skillfully layers the narrative with the three women's points of view, capturing both their singular and collective worlds. Themes of friendship, forgiveness, and women's independence make this propulsive, feel-good story a gem."

—Publishers Weekly

"Fans of book clubs will enjoy the discussions of the popular reading that Adelaide's book club favors . . . Told in a straightforward style, this story of women's friendship and commitment to the army lifestyle will appeal to fans of Kristin Hannah, Debbie Macomber, or Sarah Pekkanen."

—Library Journal

"With a wonderfully diverse cast, tantalizing descriptions of Filipino food, a realistic portrayal of the challenges of being a military spouse, and a hint of romance, Marcelo's latest will charm readers and could lead to a fruitful book discussion."

—Booklist

The Key to Happily Ever After

"Marcelo movingly portrays sisters who love each other to death but also drive each other crazy. Give this to readers who like Susan Mallery's portrayal of complicated sisters, or Jasmine Guillory's sweet, food-focused city settings."

—Booklist

Lucky Streak

OTHER TITLES BY TIF MARCELO

Heart Resort Series

It Takes Heart
Know You by Heart

Journey to the Heart Series

North to You
East in Paradise
West Coast Love

Contemporary Fiction

In a Book Club Far Away
Once Upon a Sunset
The Key to Happily Ever After

Young Adult

The Holiday Switch

Anthology

Something Blue
Christmas Actually

Lucky Streak

TIF MARCELO

Montlake

Text copyright © 2022 by Tiffany Johnson
All rights reserved.

Published by Montlake, Seattle

www.apub.com

Amazon, the Amazon logo, and Montlake are trademarks of Amazon.com, Inc., or its affiliates.

ISBN-13: 9781542038355 (paperback)
ISBN-13: 9781542038348 (digital)

Cover design by Eileen Carey
Cover photography by Regina Wamba of ReginaWamba.com
Cover images: © brizmaker / Shutterstock; © Amanda Carden / Shutterstock; © f11photo / Shutterstock

Printed in the United States of America

To J.R. and Racky, my steadfast, funny, stoic, and gentle brothers.

"Then I defy you, stars!"
—*Romeo and Juliet*, by William Shakespeare

CHAPTER ONE

Las Vegas, Nevada
Five Years Ago

Today's affirmation: I trust my instincts.

Three signs—that was what it took for Beatrice Puso to pay attention.

Three was her good luck number. She was the third out of four Puso siblings. Her mother, Marilyn Puso, a spiritual woman and also a third child, had waxed poetic about the magic of threes. Beatrice had learned that when threes came a-knockin', she'd better come a-runnin'.

Beatrice had other *inclinations*—her mother had possessed those too—and all these things had been so distracting that Marilyn had taught her at a young age to choose a daily affirmation to help her focus.

So, when Beatrice's phone rang from somewhere in the dim hotel room during a hot and heavy make-out session, and it was followed by a text notification and the trill of a FaceTime video request, she knew it was serious.

Serious enough to disentangle her lips and limbs from the man on top of her.

Beatrice palmed his bare muscular chest. It was physically painful separating her underwear-clad body from his. *"Jackson."*

Above her, Jackson the motorcyclist and champion of the hottest kisses, as he would always be known, propped himself on an elbow, groaning. With his thigh cradled in between her legs, he readjusted so the weight of him lessened.

Beatrice mourned it immediately. Her body temperature had been climbing at such an astronomical rate that she was on the verge of lust. Recently, these moments of inhibition had been fewer and further in between with her increasing responsibilities. Her weekends of fun, of being reckless, of taking risks had been shortened and bookended by being the maternal figure in her family despite being third born of four siblings.

So she cupped her hands around the back of Jackson's neck. She ran her fingers against the perfect fade of his military haircut one last time and gazed into his ocean-blue eyes. Goodness, she could've gotten lost in his eyes. They reminded her of the Atlantic in the Outer Banks on a steamy summer day.

She swallowed her need, and said, "I'm sorry. I'm being summoned."

Summoned by reality, she continued in her head. What happened in Vegas stayed in Vegas, after all.

"Back into your boa and tiara?" His gaze darted to her stray clothing on the floor, a cookie-crumb trail of evidence of their instant attraction to one another. How they had gotten up to his room from the MGM casino floor, Beatrice didn't know. She had been simply high on need after their first introduction. He hadn't had a drop to drink either.

She grinned at the purity of it all. At what she knew wouldn't end with regret because there wasn't a beer goggle in sight. "Yeah, I *am* the wedding planner. Though honestly, right this second? I kind of wish I hadn't volunteered for this position."

He grazed her cheek with a thumb. "Damn. I had a few more things in mind for us to do." He hovered his lips over Beatrice's before touching them lightly, tongue darting out for a brief taste.

"Like winning our money back?" Beatrice attempted to keep her composure, though her heart was surely betraying her. They'd met at the blackjack table. She hadn't been able to keep her eyes off him from the moment he'd taken a seat across from her. Jackson was White American, broad shouldered and lean, and he had greeted the table with a humble nod. He, however, shared her mediocre card-playing skills, and they'd both lost their hands to the third person. "I don't know . . . you're pretty bad at it."

"I wouldn't say that. You're here, aren't you? Seems like I'm the one that got lucky. But no, no cards on the agenda." He plied her with another kiss. "Just you. And me. Naked."

It was her turn to groan, and she bit her lip. If she didn't somehow wriggle herself from under him, she was bound to ignore every phone call and text and the wedding altogether.

The temptation gave her a thrill. *"Jackson."*

"Tricia." His hand migrated down to her décolletage, to the sensitive area between her breasts.

Her eyes rolled back in their sockets. *Bless the reliability of available men here in Vegas.* Unlike her home in Heart Resort of the Outer Banks, where everyone was friend or family.

This one was sexy, beautiful, and sweet, not to mention gentle and communicative. And he was good with those lips, with his hands, and she could only imagine what could've happened if there had been more time.

But at the mention of her fake name, Beatrice cooled, like the first chill of late fall in North Carolina. She reached up to his descending hand and clasped it, linking her fingers through. "I've got to wrangle the wedding party. I suspect they've gotten into some kind of trouble."

"Okay. I get being the responsible one." Understanding flitted through Jackson's expression, and he smiled. A real one, though slightly regretful. He carefully slid off her, helped her to sitting and then standing, a gentleman through and through.

Apparently, he was making it hard for Beatrice to want to escape. "So, um, what are you doing the rest of the night?" She honestly couldn't remember if he'd mentioned it, except that he was here on leave with army buddies. She belatedly realized her faux pas. "Not that you need to tell me."

They'd turned away from one another without fanfare to dress. It was the most unromantic moment. Anticlimactic, where Beatrice, who preferred noise over the angst, found herself in her head.

Rustling sounded from behind. "My buddy Gavin—his kid's in a high school basketball championship at the Vegas Convention Center. So Marcus—that's my other buddy—and I drove up from Fort Irwin to meet them. Game starts in a couple of hours."

"Oh my gosh, how sweet." The thought warmed Beatrice. The guy wasn't here to party—though they'd ended up doing their own version of it. She turned to look at him. Jackson had his gray T-shirt back on— it had been the softest—and he stood to button up his jeans.

He faced her, eyes trailing down her body. His lips quirked.

"What?"

"I think *you* are the sweetest, Tricia. For volunteering to plan your brother's wedding, for going all out by wearing a tiara, and for this tiny snafu." He neared, then tugged at the collar of her shirt and trailed his fingers down to the buttons, and started to undo them. His fingers were deft, and her breath left her lungs, only for her to realize that she'd missed a button and he was fixing it for her.

Her cheeks warmed. This felt more vulnerable than actually being in bed with him. She laughed. "I'm a mess."

"Nah. You're not a mess. I'm just a little 'dress right, dress.'"

"What's that mean?"

"Army term for everything in its place. But you are perfect just the way you are. Tiara and all." He finished buttoning her up, righted the tiara on her head, and picked up her purse from the bedside table and handed it to her.

"You do keep a clean room." She led him to the door, turning back to glance at his motorcycle helmet perched next to his backpack on the desk. Running shoes lined up underneath the hotel table. Wallet and phone beside the television's remote control at the bedside table. Her hotel room, on the other hand—it looked like a tornado had hit it. It was the hub of all the wedding planning; it was probably good they hadn't ended up there.

"I'm also called the neat freak, always turned to as designated driver and the elected timekeeper. The old man in the group. Now if that doesn't set me up for getting your number, I don't know what will." He dipped his head down in a blush, then opened the squeaky door. The hallway was bright, and it caused Beatrice to squint. "Which leads me to the ever-awkward topic of . . . I'd love to keep in touch."

Her heart did a little somersault. Jackson had done and said all the right things tonight. Not one moment had she felt uncomfortable, nor had there been a single proverbial red flag. Tonight had been perfect; she would remember it and him for a long time.

But she didn't want to ruin it. There was a touch to these things, a precarious tightrope of balancing or bailing. Beatrice had never had an issue with attracting nice-enough men, but keeping them was another question. And there was more to her than what she'd shared in this room.

A thought back to how they had been minutes ago set her face aflame. She cleared her throat to keep from grinning. "I don't know. It's just that . . . you understand, right?"

Disappointment flashed across Jackson's face, but it disappeared just as quickly. He clasped her hand and brought it to his lips. "Well, thank you for tonight. This was . . ."

"Absolutely amazing. Safe travels, Jackson."

"You too. Break a leg, or whatever wedding planners do." His gaze was intense yet playful.

Caught in it, she pointed at the helmet behind him. "You . . . don't . . . break a leg. My other brother rides, and . . ." What the heck was she doing? She was stalling. "Yep. Well. Goodbye."

She spun on her two-inch wedge and headed down the hall, turning once to see him watching her. He raised a hand in a wave, and she wiggled one back, biting her cheek. She committed his smile to memory: another man placed perfectly in her life when she needed it. A little fun, a moment of joy without anything remotely stressful attached to it. Just as she liked it.

She made the elevator her target and set off.

While waiting for the elevator, Beatrice fiddled with the strap of her purse, still buzzing with energy. She'd been gone an hour judging from a quick glance at her phone. The elevator alcove filled with guests meandering from their rooms. She readjusted her tiara, nose in the air, hoping she looked somewhat decent. Her eyes wandered to the decor in the alcove, to the lights above the elevator door, and then to the number next to the door, which read **3**.

She was on the third floor.

Warmth filled her just as the elevator doors opened. She was enveloped with the memory of her mother holding her hand at the very edge of the surf as the tide rolled in, jumping the waves at the perfect moment. She remembered the exhilaration, the feeling of safety with her grip.

At Jackson kissing the top of her hand.

It was a completely unrelated thought, and yet, it made enough sense for her to stop in her tracks. People brushed past her, some grumbling at her indecision. She took out a scrap receipt and a pen from her purse. As she walked back to the hotel room, she scribbled her number, fully intending to hand it to Jackson, but she knocked on his door to no avail.

Then, her phone began to ring.

Choices. There were so many that occurred in one's day, and Beatrice had learned to lean into her instincts rather than logic. And the ringing? It sounded much too urgent. So, in a last-minute decision, she slipped the piece of paper under his door, infusing it with all her good vibes.

If it was really meant to be, their paths would cross again.

♡

Yes, all kinds of things happened in Vegas, but Jackson Hill hadn't expected for any of it to happen to him. He'd gotten into enough trouble as a boy before he'd donned his uniform for the first time, but now he was about reliability and safety—and that included the ways in which he was introduced to women. Which meant that he'd met women through mutuals, at work, and via wannabe matchmakers like his mother. He'd gone at a snail's pace each and every time in romance, and sometimes to a woman's frustration.

But not so this time. This time, he'd thrown all his usual inclinations out the window. He hadn't been able to help it. The moment he'd spotted Tricia across from him at the blackjack table in her getup with this infectious smile, he'd been hooked. She was of Asian descent, and the way she'd played her losing hand, biting her bottom lip, had been adorable. And when they'd had their first kiss in a darkened corner on the casino floor, he'd been sunk.

Jackson pressed a white plush towel against his face, drying off from his quick shower. It was more to reset him than for actual cleanliness. Somehow, he would need to feign casualness when his friends showed up at his door, even if his insides screamed that this Tricia was the woman he was meant to spend the rest of his life with.

He guffawed at this thought. "That's just ludicrous, Hill."

Again, like most things in Vegas, that didn't happen to him, nor did he believe in fate, so why even entertain the notion? Logic. Science.

Dress right, dress. *Those* things were what made sense and facilitated his world turning. He was probably just taken in by her refreshing attitude, her playful nature, and those sincere brown eyes.

He was rubbing the towel roughly against his high-and-tight haircut when a knock sounded on the door. He stilled for a moment, considering. What if Tricia had returned? What if she'd decided to leave her number after all?

Jackson scrambled out of the bathroom with his jeans on, and he was throwing on a shirt when he opened the door . . .

To his two best friends.

"Took you long enough." Marcus Layne, his battle buddy all the way from basic training, sauntered in and went straight to the view of the strip outside his window. He hummed an appraisal. Jackson had done the same when he'd first arrived. From the third floor, there was a lot to see.

"I was just getting ready."

"You showered, so that must mean something, eh?" Marcus stuffed his hands in his pockets, and his lips quirked. He was of Italian descent and kept his dark hair a little longer up top, and for tonight he'd spiked it up like one jagged peak. "How did it go?"

"Fine."

Marcus had been on him about letting loose while in Vegas, and he coaxed Jackson for more information with a hand.

Gavin Drake, whom he'd met at Basic Leader Course years ago, remained at his side, arms crossed. He was Black with close-cropped hair and was built like a tank, which was perfect because he actually did drive tanks. "He'll tell us when it feels right. Give him some space."

"Okay, but this is all so new, and I'd like for us to guide him if we can. First with his promotion to sergeant first class, and now this. He's growing up so quickly."

"I am . . . right here . . ." Jackson shook his head.

The two laughed. They'd known each other too long—and had seen one another in their toughest moments—that Jackson knew he would have to give them something.

"She was . . . gorgeous," Jackson started, chest warming. "And sweet. She had this laugh."

"But did you get her number?" asked Gavin.

His body cooled with disappointment; he shook his head. "I asked. She said no."

"Damn." Marcus perched on the bed.

"Well." Gavin grounded him with a hand on his shoulder. "That's the cards. It's Vegas. Sorry, man."

Jackson shrugged, because what else could he do? "We'd better go."

"Yep. Team's warming up in a half hour."

"I'll grab us a rideshare." Jackson picked up his wallet and keys and stuffed them in his pockets, then thumbed the rideshare app on his phone. As he turned to the open doorway, Gavin held out a piece of paper.

"This was on the floor. It was right under my foot. Hope you didn't need it."

"Nah, that's not mine." Jackson kept track of everything. Still, he scanned the receipt, which was crumpled and marred, the pressure-sensitive paper darkened by the heavy sole of Gavin's shoe. He turned it over to something written in pen. *Tricia.*

His jaw fell open, heart thudding.

"What is it?" Marcus looked over his shoulder.

"Tricia's number." Jackson lifted the receipt by the corner, disappointment replacing his excitement. "Except there's not much of it to read."

"Oh man, I'm so sorry. I swear I didn't see it until now." Gavin checked the underside of his shoes. "Dammit."

"It's like one of those signs. That it isn't meant to be," Marcus supplied.

"Or maybe that it is?" Gavin countered, ever the optimist.

But what was in front of Jackson was the hard truth. He still didn't have a number. "It's all right." He tossed the receipt in the garbage with a little more force than necessary, because it would be of no use to him, but *damn* . . .

"You sure?" Marcus pointed at the can.

"We can try to trace it somehow?" Gavin said belatedly in the hall-way after he'd closed the door.

"Nah. It is what it is." He shrugged with extra effort to force the moment forward. Because that was all he could do, right?

His friends let the subject drop, and they resumed their banter about basketball and the Triumph Bonneville, Jackson's intended promotion gift to himself, parked out front of the local motorcycle shop. Usually, talk of a new ride would have taken Jackson right out of his thoughts, but the fact of the matter was nothing would ever make him forget about this night, and what could have been.

CHAPTER TWO

Present Day
Nags Head, North Carolina

Today's affirmation: I know what I'm doing.

"Just put it anywhere." Beatrice waved in exasperation at the general vicinity of what had been her living room when asked where she wanted her packages. She lived in a first-row beach house, though one wouldn't have been able to tell, with boxes piled up next to the windows.

The deliveryman, Cal, entered. He was Mexican, and his brown ball cap was tipped to the back while he carried a tall box. Grunting, he set the box down among the others he'd delivered yesterday. "Pretty soon you're going to need a whole new building. You're running out of room." He pulled out his handheld device for Beatrice to sign, which she did with a flourish.

"From your mouth to the universe's ears." She grinned up at him, though she didn't want to say more to jinx her newfound success. Her subscription fashion-box business, Beachy, had blown up the last few months thanks to viral social media, but she wasn't counting all her eggs yet. Though, she *did* need to make moves soon, physically—since the current Beachy office brimmed with stock, hence her house being the secondary storage location—and emotionally, with expanding.

But that would entail dealing with her real full-time job with Heart Resort, the Puso-owned private couples resort.

"You'll keep these deliveries on the DL, right?" she reiterated to Cal, then backtracked so as to not seem suspicious. "I want all this to be a surprise to customers."

"Oh, of course. It's part of the job. Trust me—people get a lot more strange things delivered to them. But yes, your secret is as good as mine. Marla's a Beachy customer, and she can hardly wait for that yellow box to be delivered every month. Wouldn't want to ruin that."

"Thank you. I appreciate it. And it thrills me that Marla loves her monthly box."

"That is an understatement."

Cal's wife was a bona fide social butterfly. Marla had a dress shipped to her every month, and Beatrice had seen her around town wearing them. The last thing she wanted was for Marla to tell all of Nags Head that Beatrice had a home in town, when she hadn't yet told her three brothers.

It was a precarious thing to live in a small town when one was trying to keep a double life.

Okay, so it wasn't a double life more than that Beatrice had come upon a crux in her road. She'd bought her beach house after she'd had one of her *feelings*, even though she lived and worked at Heart Resort as the director of client relations. When her side hustle, Beachy, had grown, along with her fervor for business rather than hospitality, she'd spent more time at her beach house.

Her brothers had assumed she was spending nights at Beachy. And she hadn't had a chance to correct them.

What could she say? She had yet to find the perfect time to tell them.

"I'll be seeing you soon, Bea," Cal said, heading out, only to be pushed aside by her best friend, business partner, and one-week brand-new sister-in-law, Geneva Harris Puso, barreling through the door. "Holy . . ."

"Sorry, Cal . . . Bea! Why aren't you answering your phone?" Geneva, wearing a sundress with an orange swirl pattern, threw off her worn leather messenger bag. She was getting ready to set it down at her usual spot, then halted. A dark eyebrow rose. "Where's the couch?"

Beatrice gestured to it, pushed against the other side of the room. "I had to make more space."

"And where's my baby? She usually greets me at the door."

"She's had it with all this, I think." Beatrice pointed to Roxy, her rescue terrier, lounging in a dog bed at the kitchen bay window. "She's been giving me the side-eye all day."

"I don't blame her. This is getting out of control. Which makes my news timely. Sit . . . somewhere."

Beatrice popped up on the kitchen stool, amused at the sight of Geneva, who was usually the calmer of the two of them. She was out of breath, cheeks pink, and her highlighted brown hair was in a low sagging bun. She was mixed-race Filipino American, and today she was glowing. Marriage looked good on her.

Geneva spoke with her hands. "I was driving around town, and there I was at a stoplight. It felt like the longest light in the world. Then this family of tourists started crossing the street—slowly, mind you—and then . . . I saw it."

Beatrice raised her eyebrows, giggling. "Saw what?"

"A for-lease sign on the corner shop on 12 and Bryan."

Highway 12 was the most sought-after strip of commercial real estate as the main road through almost the entirety of the Outer Banks. "Where the soap shop was?"

"Yes. And I made a call to the listing agent. I also sent some pictures to your phone. And a long text, which you didn't answer—"

Beatrice patted her back pockets for her phone.

Come to think of it, she hadn't seen her phone all day.

"This is a great opportunity." Geneva paced, though not very far. She sidestepped a box. "Look, your vision board has Beachy opening a brick-and-mortar retail establishment. We've already moved toward that direction. You've added private retail appointments. You've partnered with a couple of local businesses for the boxes. And, we need a bigger storage area. I mean, look at this house, Beatrice."

In the almost year since Geneva had joined Beatrice in this endeavor, Beachy had gone from a subscription-box model to a lifestyle brand. They'd designed homewares that were now being carried in select boutiques; their website had expanded to fashion blog posts that were being shared through viral marketing.

This shop on 12, if it all worked out, could be the flagship Beachy retail shop.

There was only one hitch.

"I *do* want to expand. And God, I want my house back. In fact, I have a new neighbor, an older woman, who moved in a week ago. I've seen her a few times beachcombing, and she seems so sweet, and I wanted to invite her over and really can't with this mess." Beatrice heaved a breath. "But. I can't expand without telling my brothers. And if I tell them how quickly Beachy is expanding, then they're going to question my dedication to Heart Resort, and I'm not ready for that conversation. Especially since it was me that suggested buying the resort in the first place."

Beatrice winced at her complicated dilemma. Seven years ago, while on vacation in the Outer Banks, she'd come across the sale listing for the peninsula, and all the siblings had contributed to its purchase using their inheritance money from their parents' will, all on the basis that she'd had one of her feelings.

But what if her feelings had been wrong? What if she'd put too much stock in these unexplained emotions?

Her brothers needed her. They would fall apart without her. All three wouldn't have married had she not been part of the planning committee; at the very least, their then fiancées would have left them at the altar if she hadn't been in the background twisting her brothers' ears toward their partners' wishes.

They'd needed a mother, and she was it.

But Beatrice couldn't ignore the siren call that kept her up at night and woke her early in the morning: Her ambition for world freaking domination. Specifically, to have her Filipino American brand be recognizable to the fashion-loving woman.

"So what do you want to do from here?" Geneva asked. "I hate to put pressure, but Bran and I leave for our honeymoon in three days. If you're interested in the space, I want to see it with you."

"I need to check my calendar. I might have left it in my car. Hold on." Beatrice frowned, now wondering how many emails and phone calls she'd missed from Heart Resort too. She popped off the stool and maneuvered her way out of the house and down the steps to her Tesla parked in the carport underneath. A quick peek revealed that she indeed had left her things there.

Beatrice unlocked her car door and grabbed her phone. Notifications riddled the screen, mostly emails from Kim Jones, her executive assistant at Heart Resort, and "Where are you?" texts from Gilbert, the second Puso sibling, who had recently ascended in the Heart Resort hierarchy as second to Christopher, the eldest and CEO. Gil had once been the mediator in their birth-order dynamics but had proven in the last year that he had more underneath than a chill exterior—so much so that whenever his face flashed on Beatrice's cell, her heart rate sped up. Hearing from him equated to accountability.

When Beatrice finally exited her car, a sound took her attention. Her new next-door neighbor, a White American woman with wispy, shoulder-length gray hair, who looked to be in her mid- or late sixties, was walking next to her bicycle as it squeaked. It was an odd sight.

And her mother had always told her to key in on her instincts.

Beatrice approached the woman, daring a wave. Closer, she noticed the bike had a flat tire. "Hi. My name's Beatrice, your neighbor."

The woman halted. "Hi. I'm Cathy Hill."

The name and the stunning stone pendant on her neck struck a chord, but Beatrice pushed it aside. "Is everything okay?"

"I'm fine, but my bike's not. Leave it to me to run up against a curb and break the spokes." She looked behind her. "Luckily I didn't get too far away."

"Oh no. Can I help?" Beatrice, however, didn't wait for an answer and took the bike from her.

"Thank you. I appreciate that."

"I saw the moving truck last week. Where are you coming from?"

"San Diego. I'm just visiting, to help my son settle in. Are you a local?"

"You could say that. Funny, I was telling my sister-in-law a few minutes ago that I was hoping to invite you over. But my house . . . we're in a little bit of a transition too."

"We?"

"Me and my business. Long story." She smiled.

"Tell me about it," Cathy replied. "I'd love to know what magic happens next door."

The idea that magic was happening within the four walls of her beach house made Beatrice beam, and she filled Cathy in on the basics of Beachy. "But the magic is truly the customers. I hope that they feel comfortable in the clothes we send them so they can do what they need to change the world." She bit her lip; only few understood her passion, and she feared she'd said too much. "I know that sounds cheesy."

"It's not cheesy. That's your mission. Be proud of it."

She looked at Cathy squarely, at the sincerity in her blue eyes. It bolstered Beatrice to turn her back on her doubts, which seemed to always linger in the periphery. "You know what? Thank you. You're right."

They'd gotten to Cathy's carport, where a motorcycle was parked.

Beatrice was hit with a wistfulness and an image of Jackson riding up in his motorcycle to whisk her off her feet. It was followed by a flood of warmth for what could have been.

It was silly. First, Beatrice wasn't even a motorcycle kind of girl. She had clear knowledge that most everyone took safety on the road for granted. Second and most relevant, their encounter had been five years ago. Jackson hadn't contacted her like she'd hoped, and she had nothing to go by, not even a last name. Nothing, except for how that night had made her feel—a kind of freedom.

"Looks like my son's home," Cathy said.

Beatrice stood Cathy's bike next to the motorcycle; there wasn't a second bicycle in the parking space. "Do you have a car?"

Cathy shook her head. "Oh, no. I prefer to bike when I can. It gets me to exercise."

"Ah . . . you know, it might take you a while to get another bike. The bike shop down the street always has a waiting list, and who knows how long it will take them to fix your wheel. How about you use mine in the interim?"

"Oh no, dear. That's too generous."

"It's no problem. Wait here." Beatrice jogged to the dark corner of her parking space and pulled off a tarp, uncovering her cruiser. It was yellow with a brown leather seat, tassels hanging from the handlebar, and a basket. She walked it to Cathy. "Here you go."

"Ah, she's *so* pretty. It's exactly my kind of bike. Are you sure?"

"Absolutely. Use it for as long as you need. I thought I would have more time to bike, but work always seems to take my time, so it hasn't really been used. Not that I'm complaining—about work, that is." Beatrice was babbling again, but it was because Cathy's vibe was so warm, and she'd missed speaking to someone who clearly was so wise, who could be old enough to be her mother.

And how she missed it. How she missed *her*.

"Work is important. Especially if the work fills you up. I remember those days. I'm not quite as productive as I used to be, but I remember that rush and urgency." Cathy smiled. "How about coming over at your next break? In a couple of hours? I make a mean chili, and it's been in the Crock-Pot all day. I want to thank you for loaning me your bike."

"Really? Homemade chili sounds so good, actually . . . will your son mind?"

"Nah. He's in and out for work. You can keep me company and tell me more about Beachy."

"Yay, okay." Beatrice was gleeful. Then, her phone buzzed in her back pocket. "Dang, I'd better run. I've got my business partner waiting for me . . . I'll come by in a couple of hours? Oh, wait." Her mind was all over the place. "I have a dog, Roxy. Can I bring her over?"

"Absolutely. I've seen you with her on the beach, and I love dogs. See you, dear."

Beatrice said a final goodbye and then climbed her stairs, optimism growing with each step. You never knew when you needed a sign, and she had been handed one by the name of Cathy Hill.

What she was doing for Beachy mattered. She couldn't be ashamed or shy about her ambition.

Beatrice burst into her house, to Geneva attempting to rearrange the living room—her friend couldn't sit still if she tried. "Let's see this property tomorrow morning. And I'm going to make a plan to tell my brothers everything."

♡

A couple of hours later, Jackson entered the beach house, grumbling as he fiddled with the lock, then popping the door open. All at once the frustration of the day melted away with one sniff of the air. Chili. His mother's version: all beef, no beans, spicy, chock full of veggies, topped with a heap of cheddar cheese.

"Son, is that you?" Cathy Hill called from the kitchen.

"Yep." He kicked off his shoes, caked with dirt from work; set down his backpack; and unloaded his pockets of his wallet and keys onto the nearest side table.

"You're home early." She peeked around the corner; she was wearing an apron.

"Today didn't go as well as it should have, but I really don't want to talk about it," he grumbled.

"Which is just fine, seeing that you haven't really told me anything."

"Mother—" he started.

"Jackson James Hill." Her voice dipped into an accusatory tone, and it clawed against Jackson's insides. "I've been here unpacking your boxes and cooking your most favorite meals. I think I've been pretty patient and respectful of your privacy. I keep waiting for you to fill me in."

He should have anticipated the frontal attack for information. It had been a week since they'd moved in, and through some miracle she hadn't nagged him about it. But he chose redirection, grabbing a soda from the fridge. "Is that dessert I smell?"

"Don't change the subject. I have kept up with every hustle, job, and duty station you've had. Retirement from the military doesn't mean you're excused from running it all past me. This job—is it illegal?"

Jackson threw his head back to laugh. "Not illegal."

"Then tell me you picked up a seasonal job here in the Outer Banks. That this job has nothing to do with your father."

He sipped his soda to buy himself some time. He had to tread carefully around this most sensitive topic in their two-person family. "Why do you think this has anything to do with McCauley?"

"Jack, you requested any duty station in any other state except North Carolina your entire army career. And now you're here, in the

Outer Banks. Where Dillon McCauley the third and I met. Where I know he lives." She peered at him with those eyes that could see right through him. She pressed her lips together, accentuating the lines around her mouth. She was still a mama bear at sixty-three.

His mother had protected him in every way, though she'd never lied about who she was to the old-money, North Carolina McCauleys. At the age of thirteen, he'd been told two truths: Cathy Hill wasn't McCauley's chosen love, and Jackson was a by-product of an affair.

Pros: Tell my mother everything so I can get it off my chest, because this opportunity is huge.

Cons: Keep my mouth shut. I don't want to say. I also can't say exactly what I'm doing for my father since I'm bound by a legal nondisclosure agreement.

But could he really withhold everything from her?

Oh, who was he kidding? "Okay, yes, this has something to do with Willow Tree."

"Jack." Her voice became a whisper. Worry flickered across her features.

Willow Tree Incorporated ran adult resorts around the country and was headed up by his father. "I have full understanding and control over this. I weighed the risks, and it will be fine." He braced himself for a comeback, something similar to a "You can't trust him" or "Don't rely on him," and prepared to stand his ground.

What his mother hadn't realized was that his curiosity about McCauley had multiplied in spades over the years. Despite despising him, Jackson wanted to know this man more than anything in the world. Jackson had counseled young soldiers throughout his army career, and he'd often wondered why he hadn't had anyone speak to *him*. Sure, he'd had his mother and his grandparents. But a father—that was entirely different.

McCauley also had offered him a job after retirement when Jackson had had nothing in the wings. This job was immediate, lucrative, and temporary. His salary and his army pension would set him up for his later plans, whatever those were.

And it was easy: all he had to do was represent Willow Tree in buying a piece of land for an adult summer-camp resort.

The risk was worth it, for now.

Surprisingly, she said, "I suppose you should do what you think is best."

Jackson's eyes rounded in surprise, though he said in a truthful jest, "I mean, I *am* forty."

"That can't be, because I'm only thirty-five."

Her answer eased the tension between them, allowing him to relax. He looked out the window to the distance, to families at play on the beach. At the people seemingly without worry.

He didn't know what he wanted for this next stage of his life, but . . . he wanted that. Not necessarily the kids or even the marriage but that freedom of knowing that things were settled, that there was someone, or people, by your side. That there was something concrete in his future.

It had been a while since he'd felt that zest.

Vegas was a time, his conscience reminded him. More good things had happened since then, of course, but his mind always defaulted to Vegas. It had been when his career was at an all-time high—he'd been promoted around the time of the trip, he'd purchased his bike outright, and he'd met Tricia, who'd given him a taste of bliss.

"I just want you to be okay, son." His mother's voice edged him from his thoughts.

"I *am* okay." Technically, he was all right, though currently frustrated because the person he was tasked to partner with in his new job, his only sibling, his half brother, Lonnie, hated him and had just stood him up for their planned meeting.

Welcome to the family.

"Wait a second." His mother peered at him. "Is this house . . ."

"McCauley's? Yes." He looked away to hide his remorse.

She snorted. "Then I guess I'll keep a faucet on drip and the lights on all day."

"Ma, I'm sorry. I hope you don't mind staying here or that I can't tell you what I'm doing. The NDA is a bear, and it's real, and I don't have any doubt that McCauley would enforce it."

"Maybe it's good I don't know." She sighed.

"Believe me; it's tedious. It'll be a miracle for us to actually get this job done."

"Us?" She said with a raised eyebrow. "When did *you* become an *us*?"

Jackson tiptoed around this land mine.

His mother braced an arm against a kitchen countertop. "Who else are you working with?"

Jackson took his time to word his answer and set his gaze upon her. "Dillon the fourth. Lonnie."

Her eyes shut. "You're playing with fire, Jack."

"Yes, but the potential burn will be worth it." Because he was going to be rich afterward. And he had survived worse being paid less.

"Is it, though?"

"I gamed it out," he insisted. He'd thought about it for days; he'd run it by Marcus and Gavin. He'd emotionally prepared to protect himself from his father and his half brother, determined to not become attached. But he didn't want to keep talking about it. "Speaking of fire . . . something is definitely burning."

His mother leapt to attention and turned. "Gah. My apple streusel!" Her limbs were like octopus arms as she managed the exhaust and the oven. In between, she was mumbling a recipe to herself, and Jackson considered himself scot-free.

It gave him a chance to check a new text message that contained a web link to another property for a viewing late tomorrow.

"What are you doing tomorrow, Ma?"

"Stuff." She tested the cake with a toothpick and inspected it. "Ah, it's perfect."

"Stuff?"

"Yeah . . . I wanna head into town to see what's changed. Spend time under the sun. And work." She grinned.

"Work, huh?" It had been a while since Jackson had heard his mother say the word *work* in this hopeful tone. He glanced at the shells she'd collected since she'd arrived, laid out on the coffee table in rows, as if ready for inspection.

When he was a kid, there'd been nights when he'd woken to the sound of The Cathy Hill, then a renowned jeweler, drilling holes into rocks or hammering designs into silver.

"Yep. I met our neighbor today. She owns a boutique, and I got to thinking about how much I miss working."

"Wow." He looked up from his phone. "Are you thinking of getting back into it?"

"No . . . there used to be a time when I was on top of my game, for lack of a better term. And now? I'm not so sure. What do they say? It's an honor just to be nominated."

He didn't like how she was underestimating herself. Though it had never translated to outright riches, his mother was known for her artistry and craftsmanship. "You are The Cathy Hill. You weren't only nominated. You won."

Her face softened. "Then *maybe* I'll think about it." She smiled, giving the chili a good stir. "Anyway, we got off topic. Tomorrow I'd also like to tool around with those shells. So I'm parking my butt right here in town. What's your plan?"

"Work. But the schedule can be flexible. I just feel like you haven't seen enough of the Outer Banks, and I'd like to take you around."

"Honey, you know me. You're like me. We're independent." She winked. "If I wanted to explore much further, then I would have asked. Heck, I would have scheduled myself on one of those senior citizen

23

tourist trips." She shivered. "Speaking of exploring . . . your neighbor's also lending me her bicycle to use."

"A bike?" Jackson was distracted as he sorted the rest of his emails, one from a hospital medical center in Georgia. He'd sent in an application to the risk management office over four months ago.

"A banana-yellow cruiser. Isn't your neighbor so generous?"

The first line: *Thank you for your inquiry. Unfortunately . . .*

"What neighbor?" Jackson placed the phone facedown on the counter; he didn't need to read the rest. He took a sip of his soda to wash down the bitterness rising up his esophagus.

People had painted such a pretty picture for him and his postmilitary-retirement future:

You're going to be so marketable when you retire.

You're going to get the first job you apply for.

The transition will be seamless.

They'd all been wrong, because there were always reasons:

You have a fairly soft bachelor's degree.

Is that college an online school?

Benefits aren't included in this package.

In the background, his mother prattled on, and it pulled him from his thoughts.

"Sorry. You were saying?" he asked.

"Really?" She leveled him with a glare and came around with a stack of plates and bowls. "Go set the table."

A second later a knock sounded on the front door.

"Can you get that for me too, honey?" A sticky-sweet smile appeared on his mother's face. Then, in a slow clip, it all came together. The dinner, the streusel. He looked at the stash of dishes in his arms. There was indeed an extra place setting.

"Who's coming over?"

She sighed, "Our neighbor. I invited her over for dinner. She's the one I was telling you about? The one that owns the boutique. The one who lent me her bicycle, for as long as I need it?"

He frowned, pulling the strings of his thoughts together. "It's the same person."

Cathy cackled. "Yes, Jackson. And she has a dog! Anyway, there's just something about how she looks at things. It's hard to describe. Have you met her?"

Jackson pressed his fingers on the bridge of his nose. Cupid Cathy was back. "No, Ma, I haven't met her."

"You'll like her."

His mother was a lovely woman, but she was a nag when it came to this, to him dating.

Jack cursed under his breath as he set down the dinnerware on the dining room table on his way to the foyer. Quietly, because his mother would not have hesitated in twisting his ear. Then, he opened the door to a petite woman holding a covered dish in one hand and a leash with another.

He gasped. *It can't be.*

He took in the woman's pink glossy lips and golden-brown skin and the plunge of her dress.

Tricia.

CHAPTER THREE

Today's affirmation: I open my heart to possibilities.

"Holy . . . champion of the hottest kisses." Beatrice's legs buckled, and the cold dish in her hand wobbled. Because she'd time-traveled to five years prior, and she was at the MGM Grand. Instead of slipping her number under the door, she'd knocked, and Jackson had answered, and their romance had continued.

Jackson looked different but stunningly the same, though she couldn't parse the details just yet, so overwhelmed with his actual presence.

Because this was a dream, right?

Roxy pulled at her leash.

"Tricia. Oh my God." Jackson closed the gap between them, first taking the dish from her hand, and linked an arm around her waist. At their proximity, and giving in to his hold, she was lifted to her toes, her heart soaring in turn.

"I can't believe this. The motorcycle in your carport. I was just thinking of you," she whispered. "Literally."

"Same," he said into her hair. "I'm sorry; I know I should have asked before hugging you . . ."

She clutched on to his neck with one arm. "No. Don't let go." Beatrice shut her eyes.

"I won't."

She dropped the leash, knowing that Roxy would not be going anywhere, and wrapped both arms around Jackson's neck and breathed him in. She'd thought of this hug, even yearned for it at times. She knew it was because she'd placed him and their encounter on a pedestal, but now that it was happening, it was even more epic than she'd imagined.

Because, in his tight grip, it was obvious that her feelings were reciprocated.

She didn't know how long they were standing there, not until Cathy's voice and footsteps from afar interrupted them. "Jackson, is that Bea . . . *oh* . . ."

Jackson eased his hold, setting Beatrice back on her feet, the act waking her from her shock. Still they locked eyes—yep, he still had the same soulful eyes—and when she finally tore herself away from their ocean blue to take him in, she clocked the changes five years had brought.

He now had lines of maturity across his forehead, some around his eyes. And he had hair. A full wavy head of it. Long enough to be raked back but still clean cut around the ears and neck. Which made him stunning, like he'd grown into his spirit.

Cathy appeared at their side. "Clearly this is a reunion, or my son needs a good talking-to on how to introduce himself to strangers."

Jackson rested a hand behind his head. His cheeks bloomed pink, eyes never veering. "It is most definitely a reunion. What a coincidence."

Fate was the word that came to Beatrice's mind, and in the overwhelming feeling that followed, Beatrice burst out in a giggle. "I can't believe this. Cathy . . . you . . ." She looked at Cathy, whose grin was wide and sincere, then to Jackson. Holy moly . . . *Jackson*. "You're her son?"

"Yes—unlucky for her, I am that person . . . whoa." He stepped back. Roxy was circling and sniffing his legs.

"This is Roxy." Beatrice picked her up. It seemed only fitting that they should get a formal introduction. "Roxy, this is Jackson."

"Nice . . . to meet you." Curiously, Jackson's smile slipped a little.

Cathy swooped in to take Roxy. "Come here, cutie-pie. I've got a treat for you." She ran a hand down Roxy's back. "And, you two, come all the way in. We're letting the AC out. Not that it matters—we should really run the whole bill up—but I don't want Roxy to wander out." She waved the air around them and headed toward the kitchen. "Carry on; you can keep hugging. I'll get the food ready."

Beatrice caught only half of what Cathy had said but hopped to it, with Jackson easing her presence inside with a gentle touch on her lower back. It was so instinctive and sweet that her cheeks warmed. She glanced with what she knew was without a lick of chill, but she didn't care. She wanted to know everything about him, including why he had never reached out.

Except there was a short circuit from her brain to her lips, and instead of that, she said, "I made a fruit salad."

"It looks . . . delicious. Even if I actually didn't look at it . . ." He lifted the dish, and a giggle bubbled out of him. Apparently he didn't know how to go about this either.

"It's Filipino-style, so it's a little different, super sweet, but refreshing. But if you don't end up liking it, it's okay." She breathed out the last of her words, because she wasn't done being awkward too.

He winced. "This is weird, right?"

She nodded, relief pulsing through her. "Yeah."

"Weird but awesome," he added.

"It is. Awesome."

"Goodness, you two are like two middle schoolers." Cathy was by their side once more. "Here, give me that dish, Jackson, so I can keep it chilled. Beatrice, you sit here. Jackson, you sit next to her." She spoke like a kindergarten teacher, and thank goodness, because they both needed clear and concise directions. Beatrice could focus only on her words. "I'll be back with appetizers; then I want to hear all about how the both of you met."

Jackson pulled out Beatrice's chair for her to sit, and when he took his place at her side, an eyebrow arched. "So . . . *not* Tricia."

Her face erupted in flames. "Yeahhhh, I suppose we should meet formally. I'm Beatrice Puso." She offered her hand.

"It's okay. I get it. No judgment." He half laughed, taking her hand. "Jackson Hill. Puso, you say?"

"Yep."

Cathy placed a bowl of dip and cut veggies in the middle of the table. "Soooo . . . tell me how you know one another."

"Vegas," he said.

"This is the woman from Vegas?" Cathy picked up a carrot stick, though she didn't take a bite. "The one who turned you down when you asked for her number?"

Beatrice choked on her own spit and took a sip of water.

"Ma." Jackson cleared his throat and turned to Beatrice. Their knees touched, and the fact that he didn't scoot away sent a thrill through the lower half of her body. "I swear I don't tell my mama everything."

"He's lying. He calls me every day. And he told me about how much he was smitten by you."

"Ma!"

Beatrice relaxed into her seat; Jackson and his mother were so much like her family that the last of her awkwardness fell away. "Gosh, if he liked me so much, then why didn't he call me?"

"So you *did* have her number, Jack."

"I slipped it under his door." Though she shrugged casually, a tinge of disappointment ran through her. What would have happened had they tried to make it work? Because the chemistry between them? It was there with the press of his knee against hers.

"No, no, no. Hold up." He stood and bounded to the foyer, then snagged his wallet. From it, he fished out a piece of paper. Sitting, he tossed it on the table between them.

"Is that . . . ?" She was stunned just by the thought of the possibility that it was . . .

"*The* receipt. My buddy Gavin stepped on it when he walked in my room. The only thing that's legible is your name. But your number? I couldn't read it. Of course you really can't see anything now."

Beatrice was still stuck on the fact that Jackson had kept the receipt. So much so that when she opened her mouth, nothing came out.

Cathy stood. "Oh, look, Roxy's just yearning for a walk outside. I'll be back. You two keep talking."

But despite Cathy's swift and somewhat noisy departure, Beatrice could not form thoughts. Not till the front door shut.

He frowned at the receipt and fingered it. "This probably makes me look like a creep. I threw the receipt in the trash at first but fished it out before I checked out. I don't hang on to a lot of things, but I wanted to remember the night. That night was . . . great."

Great was the least of it. Memorable. Epic. *Romantic.* "It was really great. And you're not a creep at all. I keep everything. I bet I could find a random receipt from five years ago that has no special meaning except for the fact that I hadn't gotten around to shredding it. But you . . . you're usually dress right, dress, right?"

"That's right. You remembered." His face broke out into a smile.

"I remember everything about that night." She bit her cheek to pull herself back from the ledge, because her woo-woo feelings were tugging at her. They were telling her that Jackson was something, was special, was *it*, and that couldn't be.

"I . . . ," he started, then, as if recalibrating, shifted in his seat. "Are you . . . seeing anyone? Because I'd like to ask you out. And before my mother walks back in here and asks you out for me."

A rush of warmth overcame her. He was so straightforward, though no part of him was intimidating. "I'm not seeing anyone. And yes, I'd like to go out with you, and not just because your mom is actually such a nice woman."

"Great. Tomorrow?"

"Tomorrow." She nodded, though the voice in her head continued with, *And the day after that and the day after that . . .*

It was official. She was in trouble.

♡

After his mother returned with the dog, and when he knew Beatrice was fully consumed by her storytelling and getting the food on the table, Jackson wandered to the back room, where he could catch a breath.

What he needed right then was some support. His mind swirled with too many thoughts, and there were only a few people with whom he could talk things through.

He texted his group chat with Marcus and Gavin. You won't believe who I just ran into.

Marcus:
Dude that could be anyone.
Gavin:
We've been places

Jackson:
True true
Jackson:
I'll give you a hint. Vegas

Marcus:
Vegas was wild.
Gavin:
Remember that drunk guy we had to help out?

Marcus:
We need more info.

Jackson:
Tricia

The phone buzzed in his hand with a group video chat. Jackson escaped farther into the house and pressed the green button. The faces of his friends appeared on his phone.

"*The* Tricia?" said Marcus without pretense.

Jackson kept his voice low. "The very one. The one with the receipt that Gavin stepped on? Get this—she's my neighbor."

"Hold the phone." Gavin was on the move, the noises on his side of the world lessening, and his image darkened as he likely ducked into a closet. He was a new grandfather. That high school basketball player they'd all watched in Vegas had grown up, gotten married, and had a baby.

"That's what I'm doing. Holding it, my breath, everything. I'm kind of in shock. This is wild, right?"

"I say it's fate, but I know you don't believe in that. Anyway. All that doesn't matter," Marcus said. "You asked her out, right?"

"I did."

"And yet you sound hesitant," Gavin said. "Don't be."

"Right," Marcus added. "What's the worst case? What's the risk?"

Jackson settled the cogs in his brain. "That nothing comes out of this. That she isn't who I made her out in my head to be." There was more too. Her last name, Puso, rang a subtle bell in his head, but he couldn't put a finger on the note.

"Look at it this way," Marcus said, the camera now tilting up toward the ceiling—the guy really needed lessons on camerawork. "This is all part of the jump start of the next chapter. The job, a new place to live, a first date. That's all this is, anyway—one date. Low risk."

"You're right." He laughed to himself; he was in his head as always. "Why do I feel like a kid?"

"Because everything feels so new right now. You've only gone on a handful of dates since your divorce. And I felt what you're feeling now, when I retired," Gavin added. "Army life had been go go go. We were given orders to follow. And now . . ."

Jackson finished his sentence. "Now it's back to being brand new."

"It's okay to not know what comes next. It feels risky, but we've got to face the fear of the unknown."

Was it fear he was feeling? He was three years postdivorce with Emily, though they were still friends. He'd learned some lessons from their one-year marriage—namely, that he shouldn't jump into something just because it seemed like the next step. And his entire career had been about the mitigation of fear. By rationalizing situations, by preparing for contingencies.

"But you should go, Jack," Marcus prompted.

"Right. Okay. I'm going. Thanks, guys." After a final goodbye, Jackson hung up, then stuffed his phone in his pocket and wiped his hands against his jeans.

He walked out to the dining room, and Beatrice, who was setting food on the table, turned her face up to him with a smile. All at once, his current doubts skittered away. He couldn't get over how gorgeous she was, and what he wanted more than anything else was to surround himself with her presence. She had a lightness around her, and she brightened up the hesitant parts of himself. So much so that he wanted to kiss her right then and there.

But he passed Roxy, who side-eyed him while nestled in the cushions of his favorite side of the couch. And his mother walked into the room holding a bowl of chili in each hand. Both were as effective as a bucket of ice water thrown in his face.

Cheeks burning, he sat down as the two women did the same, then picked up his spoon when they did. "So what did I miss, besides my mother probably making fun of me?"

"Oh my God, Cathy just admitted to me that she is The Cathy Hill!" Beatrice all but yelled.

"She told you, eh?" Impressed, he turned to his mother with arched eyebrows. Cathy rarely disclosed this information.

"I was gushing over that pendant she had on. The Cathy Hill was my mother's most favorite brand of custom fashion jewelry."

"Eh." Cathy waved a hand. "Those were the days when I was all right designing and making jewelry into the night. It's a tough business world out there, and this old lady needs her sleep."

"You're not old—you're mature. And your jewelry was gorgeous. *Is* gorgeous." She gestured to his mother's neck. Admittedly, Jackson hadn't noticed the pendant. She had so much jewelry from her career that an entire walk-in closet in her condo in San Diego was dedicated to it. "Anyway, I was telling The Cathy Hill that I would put anything of hers in my online catalog."

"I *actually* suggested earlier that I thought she could get back into it," Jackson teased.

Cathy peered at him. "I see what's happening here. You're turning this conversation around on me."

"Abso-freaking-lutely." Jackson darted his eyes to Beatrice. "I think it's time for The Cathy Hill to come out of retirement. What do you think?"

Beatrice clapped. "Yes, yes, yes!" Her eyes lit up with joy, and Jackson's entire body warmed at the reaction. She was so . . . happy. "And my shop's growing, too, so perhaps there are more opportunities for me to bring you into Beachy. Unique pieces from The Cathy Hill in some subscription boxes? That would be epic."

"Beachy, huh?" Jackson took a bite of his chili, and damn, it was delicious. "That's a play on your name."

"Totally. I'm so thrilled you put it together. Not many people do." She wiped the corner of her mouth with a napkin. "And it's going super well, actually. We're planning to expand. My business partner and I think the next step is to open a retail brick and mortar. Though I'm feeling some growing pains."

"Growing pains are inevitable, but it might be worth it, Beatrice," his mother said.

Everything was moving too quickly for Jackson—he was still processing Beatrice's presence—especially as Cathy and Beatrice volleyed ideas about expansion across the table. The two ate and chatted like they'd known each other for years rather than hours; he marveled at their chemistry—his mother was kind but was not nearly as forthcoming with strangers.

What he also absorbed was that Beatrice was proud, a success, but was undecided in her next step. He could relate.

"I know who can help you parse the pros and cons." Cathy pointed the tines of her fork at him. They'd moved on to the apple streusel. "Jackson."

"Really? Why's that?"

"I'm in risk management." He cleared his throat. "Was. When I was in the army."

Her eyebrows lifted. "Was?"

"I'm retired. Recently."

"That's such an accomplishment. Congratulations."

"Thanks."

"That explains the haircut."

"Or the lack of one? Yeah. I'm still getting used to it." Among other things, really.

"I like it. I liked it the other way too . . . but this way you can see your highlights."

"Those are . . . gray hairs."

"Huh." She peered, laughing. "You're right."

With a glance, Jackson noted that his mother was drooling all over herself. She was probably already sizing Beatrice up for her wedding dress. He had to wrangle this conversation to the straight and narrow. "Anyway, I was in hospital risk management."

"Though I'm sure there's some kind of overlap for your industry, Beatrice. Safety, process, and plain old gut check can span the spectrum. And Jackson's the best," Cathy added.

"Ma . . ." His mother was really laying the Cupid on thick.

"Actually, I'd love to talk about this more." Beatrice took a bite of her dessert and eyed him mischievously. "When you finally take me out."

In front of him, his mother squealed and clapped. "Oh, you are a mother's joy, Beatrice."

He shook his head, chin dropping into his chest. "Let it be known that it was you who released the beast that is my mother."

"I think I can handle it. Now, can you?" Beatrice shrugged and sipped from her glass.

Jackson caught the tease and the double meaning in her eyes but answered with full sincerity, "You can bet on it."

CHAPTER FOUR

Today's affirmation: I can have it all.

The next morning, on the corner of Highway 12 and Bryan, Beatrice cheered as she spun in the empty retail shop. At her feet, Roxy was doing her version of a dance with her leash in her mouth. "Oh my God. This is perfect."

The possibilities were limitless in this new shop. The white walls were a blank canvas that wouldn't take much to dress up. The space boasted three hundred square feet of floor space (already a wood laminate, to boot), plus a two-hundred-square-foot storage area behind a set of double wooden doors. And as a corner shop in a strip mall, with large front windows, the view was of the ocean (across a four-lane road, but she wasn't going to be picky about that).

"This is it, don't you think?" she called to Geneva, who stood at one of the windows, hunched over her phone, texting. Her face sported a frown, left cheek sunken as she bit against it.

Since a bitten cheek meant stress, and the only things that stressed Geneva were personal matters because she was a queen bee entrepreneur, this meant that it had everything to do with Brandon and their upcoming honeymoon.

"Geneva?"

"Oh, what? Sorry. Just more changes to our plans. Bran wants to take a look at an investment property while we're in Nashville." She looked up, expression slightly disheveled, though she was, as usual, effortlessly beautiful. Geneva was the perfect Beachy customer—she wore Beachy dresses every day. And just as Beatrice was pulled in so many directions, Geneva had other commitments too. Thank goodness that they took turns at being distracted.

Beatrice had woken up this morning committed more than ever to expanding Beachy. Last night's dinner with Cathy and Jackson had bolstered her.

"The space. What do you think?" Beatrice joined Geneva at the window and spied the cars rushing past on the highway and the dip in the sidewalk that was the wide entrance to the parking lot. It was a far cry from Beachy's current space, which was off the beaten path.

Geneva seemed to snap to and straightened. "That you're going to need customers, and being right here where the action happens is priceless." She looked up at the ceiling for a beat. "Not priceless. We'll be paying for it."

Beatrice snorted. "Yeah, we will, partner." She lifted her hand for a high five, and at the contact of her best friend's hand upon hers, her resolve strengthened. "This place is going to be hot."

Geneva gestured to herself. "I mean, you only have the best designer working with you. It's going to be more than hot. It'll be sizzling. On fire." Then she pointed at the different corners of the space. "Register here, counter back here, dressing room to the left. You can make space for a dais and mirrors for your discerning guests. Then, a dedicated housewares section to the right, and an area in front where we can feature a local artist, like you've wanted."

"We can have room for everything." Beatrice's imagination took flight and the space transformed before her eyes. The dreams that had kept her up at night and launched her out of bed in the morning materialized in front of her as if someone had drawn it in pencil and brought it to life with a painter's brush. And with Geneva by her side, Beatrice was convinced that everything she had envisioned would come to fruition.

"But." Geneva cut through Beatrice's thoughts.

The word snuffed out the picture like water being spilled on paper, and what was left was soggy and a pure mess. "But what?"

"Might I remind you that we have a huge obstacle ahead of us. And it has nothing to do with money."

Beatrice stuck her bottom lip out. "You're going to be a killjoy, aren't you?"

"Afraid so." Geneva dragged her gaze down. "The S-word." She tsked.

Secrets.

"I was thinking about what you said yesterday about being ready to tell your brothers about expanding and focusing on Beachy, but I don't know, Bea. I'm not going to believe it until I see it."

"Are you saying I'm a fraidy-cat?" Beatrice joked to ease the moment that had seemed to delve right into the serious and the dark.

Months—it had been months—of Beatrice sneaking around, but it was all to help what had been a tumultuous year at Heart Resort: first, the rebuilding of the resort after a hurricane; then a social media war against Willow Tree Incorporated; Chris's five-year wedding renewal to Eden; and Brandon and Geneva's wedding.

Beatrice was exhausted just thinking about it; she certainly hadn't wanted to saddle her brothers with more changes.

Life was too short—she knew this to the marrow of her bones— and she wanted everyone happy and at peace.

Geneva's expression softened. "You haven't exactly rushed to tell them . . . honestly, I don't know how you keep it all straight." She gestured to their real estate agent, Fiona Li, perched on the hood of her Mercedes outside the front door. "I'm shocked no one knows what's going on, with how small this town is."

Fiona looked up, as if hearing them, and gave them a thumbs-up.

"Well, I think I'm ready, Gen."

"How about this?" Geneva asked. "How about we don't sign the contract until you are a hundred percent ready to tell your brothers. I want this next step, too, but only if you're truly in and don't just *think* you are."

Ouch. Beatrice inhaled at the dig. Then again, she couldn't blame Geneva because she was right. She'd asked Geneva to be a partner for this very reason—her straightforwardness and business acumen. "All right. Let's hold for now. I'm heading into the resort after this. I can start there."

"Sounds good. We can revisit the topic after Brandon and I get back from Nashville. I'll be sad if we lose this place, but it will work out better if you have buy-in from your brothers. Yes, this is *our* business, but we need to be transparent. Our personal and business lives are so entwined."

"Okay. I guess we should update Fiona." Beatrice pushed the glass door open and was greeted by the warm wind. Though it was late September, it was still a tepid seventy-five degrees. The sound of Highway 12 reached her ears with the familiar rumble of a motorcycle engine, followed by a pack of leather-vested motorcyclists on shiny bikes rolling by. On one motorcycle was a couple, with a woman seated a little higher in the back, long hair trailing from under the helmet.

For a beat she wondered how she would look behind Jackson on a motorcycle, with the engine under her and his body nestled in between her thighs.

Her heart rate spiked.

"Uh-oh. You're thinking of the legendary Jackson Hill, aren't you?" Geneva whispered behind her. "With the way you went on last night over text, I'd better meet this guy before it gets fast and furious quick."

"We're going on our first date tonight, and we're just having dinner. Certainly not fast." *Unfortunately,* she added to herself. She hadn't been able to stop thinking of Jackson all night, and especially with how close he was in proximity.

"It's not about what you're doing but how you're talking about him. I've known you a million years, and I can tell you're really into him. You might end up picking up from where you left off." She pressed her hand against her chest. "I think it's so romantic. What luck, right?"

Beatrice fought back a cheesy grin because Geneva was giving voice to the thing that had nagged at her the last twelve hours. That maybe this was something else. Something different. Something meant to be.

She watched the bikes go at the green light. Motorcycles were everywhere this morning, like the world was teasing her by putting one at her every path. "It's like time didn't pass. It felt . . ." She sighed.

"Mm-hmm," Geneva mused. "Just don't make any rash decisions, like fall in love, while I'm on my honeymoon."

"There is zero chance I'm falling in love." It wasn't that Beatrice didn't believe in love—she was free with the word and never hesitated in showing affection—but her love was right here, in front of her. Namely, Beachy. "I just found out his last name. I don't even know if he has food allergies. What if he hates Filipino food—that would be a hard pass for me."

Geneva waved the notion away. "Small potatoes. Most importantly, you already know what he looks like naked, and you had zero complaints."

"Half-naked." Face burning, Beatrice pretend pinched her friend, and Geneva squealed in jest.

"I'm just saying—"

"*I'm* saying that yes, I'm swooning a little—okay, a lot—but Beachy is my real and true love. Beachy is what gets me up in the morning; it's what I think of right before I go to bed. My happily ever after is Beachy twenty-four seven."

At their arrival, Fiona stood from her Mercedes with a hopeful expression. She was Chinese American with fair skin and dark eyes, and she raised her sunglasses to the top of her head, pushing back her long fringed bangs. "So . . . what do you think?"

"I mean, it's perfect," Beatrice said. "I bet we can make it work with our budget. Location's prime."

"Shall we go over the lease?"

"I need to clear a few things before we commit." Beatrice briefly glanced at Geneva. "Do you think it will go fast?"

"I don't have any other leads, but I can't guarantee that someone won't swoop it up." She smiled. "How about I let you know if I hear anything at all? And I can poke around with the owner to see if she'll budge with the cost of the lease."

"Thank you, Fiona." Beatrice hugged her. "We'll get back with you soon."

And hopefully with good news.

♡

Jackson looked up from the list of North Carolinian island properties provided to him by his real estate agent. "I had no idea there would be so many islands for sale."

From across the table, Peter Holshbach of Outer Banks Elite Realty clasped his hands on top of his desk. He was an older White gentleman with long gray hair pulled back into a ponytail. According to their earlier small talk, he was a veteran agent but new to the Outer Banks.

He also wore a satisfied grin on his face, and Jackson could see why, with how expensive all these properties were. The guy was going to make bank if they moved on with a purchase.

"What do you think of what's listed, Lonnie?" Jackson turned to his half brother, hoping to entice him into some kind of conversation. As it was, they'd arrived separately to Outer Banks Elite Realty this morning, and they hadn't exchanged but a "Morning" with one another.

"When can we head out to tour these properties?" Dillon McCauley IV answered, though not to Jackson directly. His expression was stone cold. It gave nothing away. It hadn't given anything away since Jackson had showed up at their father's doorstep a week ago.

Jackson couldn't blame him. He and Lonnie were nearly the same age, with Lonnie younger by a few months—that alone had been a knife in Jackson's side because it was a reminder to the both of them that their father had not been faithful to either one of their mothers. It also didn't help that despite Lonnie being the legitimate child, Jackson looked more like their father with his blond hair and blue eyes, when his half brother was warm complected with brown hair, taking after his late mother's Cuban ancestry.

But Jackson had a job to do; he wasn't to be deterred. While his brother's mission was to make him feel uncomfortable, Jackson had his own. He was there to get a job done and get paid.

"We can get started on tours first thing in the morning," Peter said.

Lonnie frowned. "Why not now?"

"We have to make appointments to view these properties, and because I didn't get your . . . choices yesterday, I wasn't able to give the current owners a heads-up. I also have another client on their way here. I apologize." He scrolled through his tablet sitting faceup on the table. "Looking out to the schedule, I've got all day tomorrow, and really the rest of the week."

"I need to be out of town tomorrow. Can we tour at least one property today, to get an idea of what the landscape is? Surely there's another agent that can help us?"

"I'm sorry. There's only two of us in this office, and my partner, Fiona, is gone for the day."

Lonnie swung his eyes to Jackson, a rarity. "We can always go elsewhere."

Jackson reined himself in to keep from giving his brother the death stare. Everything about this transaction needed to be done in confidence. McCauley required them to deal with Peter, and Peter only. "I think it's best that we keep the circle close, don't you think?" Jackson steadied his voice. "I'm here tomorrow and can tour what's possible, and we can pick up from where we leave off when you return."

"Yeah . . . no. That's not an option. We're partners in this. You'd better believe that I'm in on everything."

"And yet, we also have a timeline." Jackson shifted in his chair, refraining from reminding him that it was he who'd canceled on Jackson yesterday. "We can parse out our priorities by this afternoon."

"Dad's not going to like this."

Jackson still winced at the word *dad*. He hadn't called anyone *dad* growing up, and his mother had remained largely single. He had yet to move past calling their father McCauley. Which also meant he wasn't afraid of him, unlike Lonnie, who in their short interactions had shown himself to be nervous and skittish. "I think I can handle it."

"Fine." Lonnie stood, perturbed, his irritation steaming off him. Holding out his hand to shake Peter's, he said, "I'll be on my way. Jackson, I'll see you at the pub." His chair squeaked as he brushed past Jackson and then out the office door. With a buzz, the front glass doors of the office opened and shut. Jackson watched as his brother's shadow became a blob down the sidewalk before he turned the corner.

"Well then." Jackson heaved a breath, face warming at the embarrassment. Peter looked about as shocked as he felt. "I apologize for that. I wish I didn't have to claim him, but we indeed share DNA."

"I truly did not intend to upset him."

"It's not your fault." Jackson grinned for his benefit. "Though I didn't know him at birth, I have a feeling he graced the family with that same attitude from day one."

Peter smiled tentatively. "We are . . . still seeing each other tomorrow to tour these properties?"

"We most definitely are. Our father said that you can be counted on for privacy."

"Absolutely. We have a small office, and you're listed as the interested party, and not Willow Tree."

"Great. I'll text you with our choices later on today, and I'll be back first thing in the morning."

"I'll have my comfy shoes on." Peter led Jackson out of the office and opened the front door.

As soon as Jackson stepped out, he checked his phone for the time. Five more hours until his and Beatrice's date.

At the thought of her, the negativity that had invaded him bled out. He had everything planned for the evening; he wanted it to be a proper date, with no pressure for more. Undoubtedly, their chemistry was still through the roof, but getting to know this woman slowly, intently, was his goal. He didn't want to pressure Beatrice, despite the temptation he'd faced last night to knock on her door for a nightcap and Vegas part two.

The job, a date. That's all this is anyway—one date. Low risk.

Marcus's words returned to him, and Jackson heaved a breath to center himself.

He scoured the parking lot for his bike, then remembered that he hadn't driven but walked from the beach house. It had been only a month since he'd retired from the army and about a week since his arrival at Nags Head, and he at times forgot where he was. He'd get up in the morning thinking he was running late to army physical training; he'd open his closet and wonder where his uniforms were. And, like right this second, he'd expect a commute home on his bike.

Jackson had assigned his entire identity to the army, and now he was like a kid in a new school, looking for a friend to take him in.

He joined the pedestrian traffic, the majority heading toward the break in the dunes that led to the beach. The sun was high in the sky—it was shy of eleven o'clock, and Nags Head was bustling.

One street over was Beachside Pub, where tourists milled outside as they waited for tables. It had been his and Lonnie's prearranged meeting spot for their meeting yesterday, which he'd ended up at on his own. Jackson now greeted the waitstaff at the front and gestured to the bar, where his brother was already seated, spine straight, and nursing a beer.

Jackson hopped up on the worn padded stool and waved the bartender down. "Coffee, black."

Lonnie snorted. "Classic. Is the prodigal son too good to day drink?"

"The coffee's for my migraine after dealing with your disgruntled attitude." The coffee was set in front of Jackson, and he blew against the hot liquid. "Look, Lonnie. We've got to help each other out here."

Lonnie took another sip, and at the snub, Jackson slapped the list of properties on the bar between them. "Twelve properties, Lonnie. Twelve that we can't see in one day, so we'll need to prioritize. I've got a list of what McCauley wants, but you know how he feels, what his pet peeves are. I, personally, don't want to get to know the guy, so I need your help."

Lonnie blew out a breath. "Right. As if you're not trying to weasel your way into the family will."

Jackson was speared with a pain, not from hurt but from anger. At the assumption that he was there to be a gold digger, at the preposterous idea that he was even in the realm of someone who would be considered family. Because he was neither one of those, and the reminder was a double-edged sword. No, he didn't want to be a McCauley, but he was one and was now acting in the public as one, even though he'd been denied his lineage all his life.

He snorted at his brother's comment. "I've lived the last forty years without McCauley's hand over me, and I plan to live the next forty free as a bird. Yes, I'm here to get paid, but only when I—correction, when we find the right property for him. So the faster we do that, the faster I'm out of your hair."

Lonnie sized Jackson up. "So this is temporary."

"Yep." But when he said it, his voice wavered. Had he really signed up for a temporary job, when temporary wasn't his style? He usually approached his commitments full throated.

But beggars couldn't be choosers, especially when none of his employment options had panned out.

And when Lonnie crawled his fingers to snatch the sheet of paper, Jackson felt the sharp edge of that sword dig deeper into his chest.

His brother wanted him gone.

Complete the mission; then you walk away, he told himself, though now he wished he had something stronger than black coffee.

Lonnie asked for a pen from the bartender and proceeded to number the properties on the list, citing a myriad of reasons. Jackson listened intently to keep up: *travel by boat might take too long, this one's a little too close to civilization, too far from the Pusos.*

Pusos. The bell clanged in Jackson's ear now. Beatrice's last name. He'd heard it in passing from Lonnie once before.

"What's with the Pusos?"

"They own Heart Resort, Dad's public enemy number one." He continued on with the list, taking a swig of beer, clearly intent on getting Jackson out of his hair, totally oblivious to Jackson's growing alarm that he'd been parachuted into unstable territory.

Jackson had not been briefed about Heart Resort, but *public enemy number one* sounded like fighting words.

After Lonnie finished, Jackson bid him a haphazard goodbye, all but running back to the beach house and taking the stairs up by two. The bells were now in surround sound.

Calm down. Think for a sec.

Jackson refocused and jogged up to his room. He powered up his laptop and clicked onto the search engine, then typed in "Heart Resort." The first link was to their website. After taking a deep breath, he clicked on "About us."

Of course he had put it together that Tricia, that Bea, was Beatrice Puso. But to see it on the screen made it real. She was the only woman in this four-pack of siblings, and the only person smiling.

It made sense now—Beatrice had been hesitant with expanding Beachy because she worked for Heart Resort too. Scratch that . . . she *was* Heart Resort.

Then Jackson explored the rabbit hole of available online information. He checked out Beatrice's social media and the resort's history, from its purchase, to its opening, to its grand reopening. His eyes popped out of their sockets as he tracked their involvement with Willow Tree. In the last year alone, the two companies had had public beef, leading to the CEO of Heart Resort and his wife participating in their own retreat to prove their legitimacy. When staring at the screen had become too intense and he needed a break, Jackson printed out the articles written about Heart Resort. All the while, a ball of tension formed in his gut.

Somehow, without him knowing, he was on team Willow Tree. Which was inconvenient, with how much he was already attracted to Heart Resort's director of client relations.

CHAPTER FIVE

Heart Resort, North Carolina

Current affirmation: I will be honest with my emotions.

That afternoon, after a working lunch with Geneva and changing into her Heart Resort uniform—a black embroidered polo, which she paired with white linen pants—Beatrice drove her Tesla over the resort's land bridge. At the entrance, in front of the security arm, was a newly erected sign that read, **Voted number one couples resort in the United States**. Ironically, while it was a resort that promised couples their versions of a happily ever after, the Puso family members themselves had their own issues in their romantic relationships.

It was one of the reasons why she'd slowly felt disconnected from Heart Resort. While she'd been the catalyst of the land's purchase, Beatrice had since learned her own happily ever after had nothing to do with romance and everything to do with where she belonged in society, and what she could contribute to society with *her* gifts: her love for pretty clothes, her want to give people joy in what they wore, and in helping the community.

And somehow she was going to have to admit all this to her brothers.

As the arm raised, she waved at Sal Medina, the head of security, who happened to be manning the gate, and parked her Tesla in the employee parking lot. She unbuckled Roxy from her back seat and carried her into her designated golf cart and took every bit of advantage of the ten-miles-an-hour speed limit on the short way to the headquarters and family home, named Puso. Every home had a Tagalog name assigned to it, including the tiny cabins guests stayed in, the restaurant, and the yoga studio.

At a little after one in the afternoon, the sun was punishing, perhaps appropriately, because she was, once more, late. Sure, she was always on Filipino time, but she'd wanted to be at her Heart Resort apartment before the meeting—each sibling had their own living quarters—so as to not make a scene by driving up. Her brothers always made such a fuss regarding her whereabouts.

But she and Geneva had been transfixed with work. They'd crunched their numbers and confirmed that they could afford the bigger retail space. They'd concluded that they could save money by doing the move themselves and waiting on purchasing merchandising displays. They could lean heavily on their community relationships and social media and hold off on paid advertising.

Now, it was her turn to come through with her part of the deal.

"I'm not going to hold back," Beatrice said aloud to Roxy in her arms, though she was filled with trepidation. "I'm going to tell them the truth."

But which truth? The controversial—that her business was growing large enough to warrant a bigger space? To the horrible—that she'd bought her Nags Head beach house without telling anyone, and it was now her default storage space. And the absolutely terrible—well, terrible for everyone except her—that she was likely leaving Heart Resort so she could focus on her business.

Her tummy swirled with apprehension.

She parked next to the other golf carts in front of Puso. By the looks and count of it, all her brothers were here. Her heart rocketed and lodged itself in her throat. Showtime.

As she turned the golf cart off, she was startled by surround sound hyena-like yelling. Which meant only one thing—technically, two.

Looking to the right, she felt the nervousness in her body melt away. Her nieces bounded down the front step. Eight-year-old Izzy and six-year-old Kitty were in swimsuits. Kitty clutched on to a plastic bucket. The girls surrounded Beatrice and talked over one another. Beatrice, as usual, passed out Pixy Stix, because a little candy never hurt anyone, and if she was going to be a single auntie, then she was going to take advantage. Her nieces took turns petting Roxy, who lapped up the attention, and relayed in a chaotic banter that they were off to the beach with their mom.

It prompted Beatrice to look up to Jessica Puso coming down the stairs of the house. She wore a wide-brimmed hat to shade her alabaster complexion from her Irish American roots, though her curly black hair cascaded around her shoulders. In one hand she carried a cooler and in the other a beach bag.

And, of course, it wasn't a Beachy beach bag. Nor was the cover-up she was wearing.

Beatrice was glad to have sunglasses on so she wouldn't have to hide her disdain. Jessie and Gil had had a long friendship and an eight-year marriage that had ended in divorce, though somehow Jessie was back in her brother's and everyone's good graces.

But Beatrice *hadn't* forgotten, and she surely hadn't forgiven.

"Hi, Bea," Jessie said. "We missed you at lunch."

Her first thought: *Lunch?*

Her thought and a half: *Oh, crap.*

She slapped a palm against her forehead. "Dammit."

Chris had sent an email before she'd toured the Nags Head retail space. She'd spied the notification on her phone and promptly forgotten about it altogether. Someone really needed to invent something that solved that problem.

It wouldn't help her at the moment, though, because she was in trouble.

"Bea, is that you out there?" a voice called from the inside. Chris.

"Yep. Coming, Kuya." She heaved a breath, brushing past Jessie. The upside was that she didn't have to feign small talk with her.

Entering the foyer of Puso, she was met by the drastic dip in temperature from the AC and her executive assistant, Kim Jones. She was mixed-race Thai and Black American, and she bent and whispered in Beatrice's ear, "I tried calling when I noticed you weren't here for lunch."

Beatrice gritted her teeth as she dug through her purse. She looked at her phone screen and groaned. "My phone was on silent. Geneva and I were deep in the throes of stuff." Gah. She had to get it together.

"There's something up, though I'm not sure what's going on."

Beatrice nodded. "Thank you for the warning."

Voices filtered in and echoed, coming from the boardroom. She plastered on a smile and donned an armor of nonchalance.

"Hi, hi, hi!" she cheered, walking into the boardroom.

"Ah, she shows!" Her youngest brother, Brandon, stood, arms up in welcome. His hair was recently close cropped from the wedding, and against dress code, he wore his Heart Resort polo untucked and over jeans. "It's a damn miracle. Where have you been?"

Out in space apparently. "Oh, you know me . . . just grinding." She scanned the room, and it teemed with staff. Chet Seiko, the director of programming; Mike Strauss of maintenance; Gil; Tammy, their publicist; and Chris's and Gil's assistants.

"You're just in time for a very important meeting." Christopher Puso—the CEO of Heart Resort, eldest brother, and proclaimed head of the family—was sitting in a tufted leather chair; on the ottoman in front of him were his devices and a planner turned to the monthly calendar. "We've got great news."

But by his harried expression and the way he scrubbed a hand against his short, full beard, Beatrice could tell that this news was going to entail a lot of work. "Oh gosh, what?"

"Leila made retreat reservations. Six weeks from today."

Beatrice frowned; this was all levels of confusing. "That's not possible because we're booked out through spring, and who's Leila?" Along with the silence, she was met with stares and mouths agape. "What?"

"You know. *Leila.*" Gilbert, second brother and director of employee relations, raised his dark eyebrows. Next to him, Brandon stood and mimicked a familiar dance.

An image materialized in her head of a Guamanian woman with thick curly hair dancing on a stage. "Leila the talk show host? *The* Leila?"

Chris's smile was like a billboard in Vegas. "Yes, *the* Leila. She and her partner are coming for an R and R. They've already chosen the retreat program. Sorpresa."

It was the same retreat program that Chris and Eden and Brandon and Geneva had gone through in the past year, where clients were provided a customized experience based on a survey of their wants and needs.

But Leila? At Heart Resort?

Beatrice had to sit to process the magnitude of it all, and Roxy lay down at her feet. They'd had VIPs come to stay at the resort in the past. Many had been wealthy, but Leila would be their first commercial celebrity. "But wait. Did we have a cancellation?"

"No," Chris said. "You'll need to reschedule Papadakis."

"That's not cool. She and her husband have been scheduled out since last winter."

"Their schedule was the easiest to modify." Gil took his seat next to Chris. "I'm sure there's something we can do to help compensate for the reschedule."

"I mean, I guess." She winced at the anticipation of having to endure the awkwardness the next time she and Michelle spoke. "I can look at options before I let them know. They might not even care since it's Leila."

"Uh-uh." Chris shook his head. "We're not allowed to say that Leila's going to be here. You'll need to come up with a solution and run it by us. As for Leila—everything about her stay has to be perfect. This might be the ticket to really catapulting our resort."

"It's already in the freaking galaxy, Kuya Chris. What more do you want?" Beatrice blurted out, then bit her lip to keep her frustration from bursting forth. She really should have been consulted prior to them picking Papadakis. Perhaps she could have made an alternate suggestion.

Chris scoffed. "We can't rest on our laurels. Willow Tree or other competing resorts are around the corner, ready to bring us down. And what's better armor than a celebrity endorsement?"

At Chris invoking the name of their nemesis, Willow Tree, the collective mood plummeted. Since Heart Resort Exposé, they hadn't heard much from Willow Tree's CEO, Dillon McCauley III, but they were all still reeling from the shadow it had cast over the business, despite the fact that in doing the retreat, Chris and Eden had saved their then-rocky marriage.

Chris stood and held out a stapled packet. "This is a starting list of Leila's must-haves, to include her dietary preferences and fitness routine. Leila is . . . particular."

Beatrice grumbled as her head spun. Leila would be taking her limited spare time. When would she be able to move Beachy, should they sign the lease?

"What's wrong?" Chris asked.

She was going to tell him about Beachy. She was going to say that she needed a break. She was overwhelmed. But when she opened her mouth, what came out was, "Nothing. Sounds great. I'll get right on it." Then she gritted her teeth together into a smile. Because anything else would have caused a ripple effect of worry and discussion, and she just couldn't do it right now. Especially with Leila's arrival on the table.

The meeting ended when all the directors were given a set of their marching orders. The office cleared except for Gil. As Beatrice stood to leave, he said, "Can we chat?"

He crossed his legs and inspected the ironed crease on his linen pants. Beatrice was still amazed at the 180 Gil had executed in a year. From a downtrodden just-divorced former actor who could barely remember what day it was to ironed creases and hair products that did magical things to his tresses so they could withstand the coastal winds.

"Sure, Kuya, what's up?"

"Do you mean besides the fact that you've been dropping the ball?"

"Dropping the ball?" She crossed her arms, appalled at what he was saying. Never mind her previous thought—he was still the same cross person from a year ago.

"Yep. I'm apparently the only one who'll call you on it. There's no pretending around me, Bea. You're barely sleeping here on the resort. Your voice mails are chock full. You don't know what's up versus down. Just because you have Kim doesn't mean that you can disappear. She was hired to help with your workload, not take it on altogether."

Beatrice felt a pain that started in her temples. Had he called her a pretender? If there was anyone who was pretending, it was him. Just because he'd been appointed second to Chris didn't mean he was allowed to boss her around.

"First of all, Kim is an *executive* assistant. She is capable and thorough and doesn't need to be micromanaged. She fit right in the first day we onboarded her, and she is excellent at her job. Second, I work as hard as all of you in this resort, and you know it." She steadied her voice. "I'm the one who holds the hands of our clients. Sometimes, it's me who makes the final sale, or the one who encourages the word-of-mouth referral. None of you can do that because all of you are just how you're being right now—rude. Might I remind you I just planned and executed Brandon and Geneva's wedding a week ago? And that maybe I'm still recovering from that?"

She reined in her temper—the conversation was running away from her, and she redirected it to the bottom line. "Look, Kuya Gil. I know you're upset that Jessie and I aren't all up in each other's business."

Saying his ex-wife's name ramrodded her brother's spine straight. It was his defensive posture, like he was ready for a fight or a photo shoot. But he'd donned the boxing gloves first.

"You can't get me back for not liking your ex." She focused on his dilated pupils. "You can't call me out because I haven't welcomed her with open arms. If you remember, she hurt you. She hurt all of us."

"You cannot . . . and I won't let you continue to blame her for something I had fault in." He shook his head, and it was clear that Beatrice had struck a chord. Heck, she'd always been the one to protect him, to shield him. She'd even covered for him, so intent on keeping the family together in light of his partying. Then, she'd been sideswiped by the fact that Jessie had had her own indiscretions.

Gil might have been older than her, but he was soft.

Who was she kidding? All of her brothers were soft, but Gil's exterior was sheer and brittle, despite how polished he appeared to be.

And she was tired of holding everyone up.

She was tired of being a mother, which she wasn't.

She was a sister. A sister who wanted to explore her own dreams.

"Beatrice." He held her by the elbow. "Look at me. I was not innocent in our divorce. I am an alcoholic. You know that, right? The rest of the family can call it something else. You can continue to say that I partied too hard. That I got a little out of control. But it's code, absolute code, for the fact that I used and abused alcohol during our marriage and especially after Mom and Dad died. I will always be one, even in recovery. Jessie had to live with that. She had her affair, and alcohol was mine. So I beg of you. Just stop. Because if she and I are willing to forgive one another, then you have to also."

"I'll do what I damn well please. I am my own person." And yet, she growled in remorse. She growled because she also didn't mean to drag this conversation right down to personal drama. Gil was absolutely right. She knew their story; she'd lived through their story. "Argh. I'm sorry."

He heaved a breath. "I'm sorry too. That we're fighting—but not about me and Jessie. I don't know what else to tell you, Bea. We're walking into our relationship with our eyes open. I know it's hard to believe, but despite all of my faults, I can still make decisions. I'm not who I was five years ago."

"Kuya Gil, I didn't mean . . ." She lowered her gaze to the floor at the mention of his absolute low, also a Vegas memory.

"It's fine." He sighed, moving the moment forward, and for that Beatrice was grateful. It was enough fighting for the day. Gil leaned in to give her a hug. "I get it; it's stressful right now. And you did a great job on Bran's wedding."

"Thanks." She shut her eyes at the comfort of his hug. "There's just a lot going on."

He stepped back. "What's up? With you not sleeping on the resort . . . I know that's none of my business, but is everything all right? Besides Heart Resort stuff?"

If he only knew that *that* was the problem. Everything was going swimmingly. She should play the lottery—she had everything she wanted, to include a reunion with an old flame. "Everything is totally all right."

"Okay." He set both hands on her shoulders. "Look, I'm here, even if we're upset with one another. I know I have the girls and Jessie, but just as you've been there for me, I want to be there for you."

She nodded, though inside, she understood that people said that all the time. In truth, everyone had their own priorities, and being single meant that no one had her as first. But Beachy was her first, and she intended to grow it and make it the best it could be.

Now if only she could finally admit that to everyone else aloud.

♥

Jackson raised a nervous finger to press Beatrice's doorbell at four o'clock without a real plan for how to admit who he was. All he knew was that this first low-risk date suddenly had astronomical stakes—if not for him, then for Beatrice.

But before his finger made contact with the button, the door flew open to Beatrice wearing a colorful, casual dress that tied around her neck. She was glowing; her smile was radiant. "Hi, you."

"Hi . . . ," was all he could say, captivated by her energy. "You look . . . wow."

Really? Are you a high schooler on your first date?

"Thank you. *Beachy*." She beamed, striking a pose. Then, she pulled him by the wrist and tugged him inside. "I've been looking forward to this all day long. Come in for a second, and grab a seat. I've got to send one last email."

"Oh . . . sure." She had him with *looking forward to this all day*, and he let himself be dragged in. Except, when Jackson entered, there wasn't a seat to be found that didn't have a box on it. He followed her to her kitchen, to her laptop set up on the island, where a couple of sketch pads and pens and a myriad of sticky notes resided. He hopped onto the only empty stool and, upon sitting, took stock of the open-concept house, which was riddled with boxes.

While he'd had an inkling at how busy Beatrice was from their conversation last night and his research about Heart Resort, this house was the evidence.

At the moment, Beatrice's fingers were flying on the keyboard, and her face seemed to contort with emotion as she composed sentences.

It was endearing and adorable and at the same time a turn-on, because this woman? She also exuded *boss*.

He deflated at the reminder of their situation—that this relationship could end before it began.

He busied his nervous brain by taking in the house and all of its details: pictures in frames perched on surfaces, school-made pottery on the windowsill, and trinkets everywhere in between. She really did keep everything. Then, he spotted a set of boxes in a corner that was precariously stacked, and he stood to fix it.

"I'm almost done here, I swear," she called, though she didn't look up from the computer.

"It's all right. Take your time." Also, he could use another few minutes to figure out what to say. He read the contents of the boxes: *Muumuu, Sundress, Crossbody*, and so on. "I just want to make sure this doesn't topple over and hurt you or your dog. Speaking of . . ." He looked around surreptitiously, and there was no Roxy to be found. He exhaled a breath.

It wasn't that he didn't like dogs . . . he just didn't prefer them.

But . . . back to his task. He proceeded to arrange the boxes by type in low, safe stacks.

"Are you sorting those boxes over there, Mr. Dress Right Dress?" she said.

He stilled. "Sorry. That okay?"

"I don't mind at all." A smile graced her lips. "That's been on my list to do, but I haven't gotten to it."

So he rolled up his sleeves and continued doing his thing with gusto, if anything to get himself ready for when he revealed his identity. He tried to be as quiet as he could, keying in to the clack of the keyboard, and his curiosity piqued at how her entire business worked, at how she managed her time. He'd always been interested in the inner workings of things—of groups, processes, people.

He'd sorted through the boxes in one corner of the living room when he said, "Done!" When he turned, she was walking toward him with ice water. "Thank you. You're amazing just jumping in like that."

"And now you can see right out to the beach." He took a sip. "But it's nothing." *Especially when you have to hear what I have to say.*

"It *is* something. You could have literally left ten minutes ago, so thank you for being patient." Her face screwed into a grimace. "I love Beachy, but sometimes I lose track of time with all I have to do. Apparently having a business partner and an office manager isn't enough."

Jackson took a sip of ice water to settle the growing unease in his throat, and despite the cold AC blasting through the vents, he started to sweat. "Beatrice."

"Yes?" She stood straighter.

Just say it, Hill. "My father is Dillon McCauley the third."

Beatrice's face stilled, though Jackson could read her thoughts in the minute changes in her expression: shock, confusion, and then the slow rise of understanding. Then he realized that he should provide more context. Words plopped out in chunks. "But he was . . . absent. My parents never married. He and my mother had a fling. I just started working for him, and I had no idea of your connection, but you told me your last name, and it sounded familiar, so I looked you up."

"Wait." She shook her head. "You are Dillon McCauley the third's son?"

"Yes. And I work for Willow Tree."

Beatrice speed walked to her front door and opened it.

"Bea." Jackson, despite his plea, walked to the foyer, now lit by the sun streaming through the doorway.

She looked out, a signal for him to leave.

Dammit. "I'm sorry." Then he crossed the threshold and watched the door close in his face.

He was still holding on to his ice water.

CHAPTER SIX

Current affirmation: I stand in my own decision.

Beatrice stared at the front door after it clicked shut.

Oh my God.

Then she shook her head to loosen her thoughts, like a vending machine with her much-craved Snickers bar clutched in its spiral claw. She played the scene once more, from seeing the most handsome man at her front door wearing a short-sleeve button-down and navy shorts perfectly fit over his trim body, using said trim body by taking the initiative to move some boxes, to imagining herself peeling off said clothes at the end of what would've been their perfect first date, and then to hearing him say the words: *My father is Dillon McCauley the third.*

Dillon McCauley III, the CEO of Willow Tree Incorporated.

No. She covered her mouth with a hand. *Oh my God.* She'd almost had sex with a McCauley. She was living next to a McCauley.

She shut her eyes and braced a hand against the door; she leaned her back against it.

Jackson Hill was a McCauley.

I like Jackson Hill.

Her body teetered with the grief.

"What kind of luck is this?" she said aloud to the room, to her mother, who she wished was here.

Then Beatrice started to cackle. It was either that, or cry. Of course, of *course*—for all the success in her business, for all the gifts of the woo-woo she'd been bestowed, she couldn't seem to get love right. She hadn't seen this one coming.

"Bea." A muffled low voice sounded through the door and her body, sending shivers through her. "I'll go, I promise. But I just wanted to make sure you knew . . . that I had no idea how our families were connected. And I hate it. I hate it because we finally . . ."

At his pause, she finished the sentence in her head. *Finally found each other.*

Curiosity nudged her hand to the doorknob. For the short time she'd known Jackson, not once had he shown malice or greed. Yes, she hadn't known the details of who he was (obviously!), but his vibe was of gentleness, goodness.

She turned the knob and popped the doorway an inch. Peeking out, she found Jackson still on her front stoop. He met her eyes. "So you had nothing to do with—"

"With anything up to last week? Absolutely nothing. I . . . I'm sorry about everything that happened earlier this year with the exposé and all that bad public beef. I feel horrible about it."

She assessed him; she really took him in. His shoulders were slumped, face crestfallen, lips turned down into remorse. "I believe you."

He seemed to fold into himself. "Thank you."

But questions arose the longer she stood with this new revelation. "Work. You said you worked for him, and you'd heard my last name. What context was it under? What kind of work are you doing for your father?"

His gaze dropped. "I can't say. I signed an NDA."

Her eyes narrowed. "Really."

"Really. But." He shifted his feet. "I can tell you that nothing underhanded is being planned for Heart Resort. I hope you can trust me."

Now it was her turn to deflate from relief. With certainty, she said, "I trust you."

He nodded. "Well, I'd better go." He offered the glass that she hadn't noticed he was holding.

She accepted it; the glass dripped with condensation. Their fingers brushed, and at the contact, something sparked inside her. It triggered a yearning, and as she watched him turn to walk down the stairs, her heart felt like it was being pulled out of her chest. As if it was attached to him. She encountered that same moment of decision she'd come to in Vegas: either enter the elevator and leave, or return and give him her number.

"Jackson. Don't leave." Her voice came out like a panicked yelp. Then, unsure how to proceed, she defaulted to what was true and solid in her life. Her work. "I . . . I need more help with these boxes. Would you lend me a hand?"

"Of course," he said without a second's pause, a hesitant smile on his face. "Put me to work."

♡

What did you get when you mixed two people in a situation they couldn't fix, a slew of emotions they couldn't put words to, and a houseful of boxes?

A staggeringly organized space.

Jackson grunted as he pushed the sofa that had been previously moved to the side back to where Beatrice was standing in the living room. She'd since changed into a tank and shorts from the couple of hours of sorting through every box in the house. She'd even unpacked a few of them and consolidated inventory.

Jackson was fine with all of it. More than fine—he absorbed every minute with her. He didn't know how long she would allow for them to hang out. From the looks of it, she hadn't quite made up her mind about what to do with him.

Beatrice nudged the couch just so, then brought over its pillows. "Perfect."

Jackson plopped down into the cushions and blew a breath up to his forehead. He was covered in a thin layer of sweat and remorse, but he had to admit the physical work had eased the tension. He'd learned a little more behind Beatrice's business processes, which had taken his mind off their present conundrum. She was so easy to work with; it solidified how much he liked her company, despite it all. He half laughed at the irony that the woman he found amazing in every way also detested the very essence of who he was. "This wasn't quite what I planned for our first date."

She snorted, looking down on him. She was clutching a pillow to her chest. "Do you mean the inventory management or the part where we're smack in the middle of two warring clans fighting for precious resources?"

"I would laugh if it wasn't all true."

"You can't make this stuff up." Beatrice sank down into the sofa, leaning back. She was comfy looking with her ponytail skewed. "It's a shame."

"It sucks," he said at the same time.

They turned to face one another. It was the same face he remembered gazing at in Vegas: vulnerable, open, and beautiful. It was the face he searched for in his memory when he wanted to conjure joy. And by God, he didn't want to let go of it yet.

"We make such a good team too," she said. A hint of a smile graced her face, breaking another layer of ice between them. "Look at what we got done in such a short amount of time."

"More hands mean light work. Even better when you're working with someone who's got their stuff together."

"Ha. If my brother could hear you now."

"Which one?"

"Gil."

He thought back to the website. "Director of employee relations."

"The very one."

"So how does that work? With Heart Resort and Beachy? How do you do both? At our dinner you didn't mention Heart Resort once."

"Heart Resort is the family business. Beachy was my side hustle. At one time, it was clear where my priorities were, and now, it's flip-flopped. The reason why you probably don't hear me talking about the resort is because, to my brothers' chagrin, Beachy is my passion."

"It's no wonder you're busy."

She nodded. "I have assistants. Kim for the resort, and Giselle for Beachy. And I've got an apartment on the resort, which is where I stay sometimes." She grimaced. "They don't know I have this house."

Jackson sat up. "What?"

"Yeah." She drew out the word. "Or that I have plans to expand. I have good reasons for this. But, you see how you telling me who you are makes all this worse." She inhaled, chest rising.

This is it, Jackson thought. This was when she was going to show him the door.

"Jackson, I know this was weird for me to invite you back to help move boxes, but I wasn't ready for you to leave, and work helps me think." She looked away. "I'm just going to come out and say it, even if I'm going against everything Puso. But I wish there was a way we could do this."

Jackson had been fully prepared to walk away—this, he hadn't expected. It was a joke, right? "Why, did you come up with a list of things for me to muscle through?"

She grinned mischievously and, in a sultry tone that stirred the need in Jackson's belly, said, "In a heartbeat. In more ways than one."

His jaw dropped. "You're serious about this."

"I am." She picked at a tuft of fabric between them. "You weren't part of any of the things that happened last year. What's between you and me is completely separate of our family businesses. And, I like you. So why not?"

"Why not?" And now, saying it aloud, Jackson questioned his own assumptions. He took her hand into his, and they interlaced their fingers. At their connection, clarity descended. Maybe this wasn't a big deal after all. Maybe what he'd read online had been an exaggeration. Perhaps—

"We just couldn't tell anyone."

His train of thought screeched to a stop. "We'd have to keep it secret?"

"Yeah. Just for now." She tugged his hand gently, and he inched closer. "We're just at the beginning and . . ."

"Secret's not really my thing, Beatrice." That wasn't how he lived his life; he refused to hide from people. He also heard the underlying message in her words: that this thing between them was casual, and he wasn't sure how he felt about that.

Then again, he *had* wanted to take things slow, and had he really expected a serious relationship from the jump? He also had an NDA—he would be navigating his own family dynamics and needed space to do that. He shelved his hesitation. "But okay, I'll do it. I like you, too, and it makes sense while we're still getting to know each other."

It was the quintessential adult thing to say, but it still left a horrid taste in Jackson's mouth. But if this was the only way he was going to be with Beatrice, he would relent.

She inched closer, and he drew her into the crook of his shoulder. She wrapped her arms around his waist, and the relief of that physical contact assuaged his doubts. Her feelings for him were palpable in their physical affection. "I don't know about you, but I'm starving."

"I could go for some chow." Her enthusiasm gave Jackson a jump start. "Though we missed our reservation at the Crab House."

"I love the Crab House. That would have been delicious, but . . . are you open to trying something new?"

"Yeah."

"Great. I know just the place. Not in town, since we can't be seen together."

Right. Jackson willed the unease away. "Sure . . . anywhere you want."

"Yay! I'll go change real quick, and I'll drive us."

"Where are we going?" He took out his phone, ready to research.

"It's a surprise."

"Oh."

An eyebrow rose. "Jackson, do you not like surprises?"

"I do. It's not that. I like to be prepared." Preparation was the name of his game.

"The only thing you'll have to be prepared for is to get your lips wrapped around something delicious."

Now it was Jackson's turn to raise his eyebrows. As innocently as she'd said those words, his body took it sinfully. "All right then."

Beatrice's cheeks turned pink, and she straightened, perching at the edge of the couch cushion. "I'm gonna go before I say anything else incriminating."

"Hold up. What other incriminating things did you have to say?" He tugged her back toward him and to the rush of his libido; she knelt in between his legs and rested her hands on his thighs.

"That I still can't get over that you're here. And I don't want to let you go," she said, breathless. "And part of me doesn't care about anyone else."

Jackson's last bit of hesitation gave way to this unexplained feeling that this time wasn't to be wasted. "Let's agree to be honest with each other. Always." It was his bottom line.

"Absolutely."

He brushed the hair off her shoulders and cupped a hand around her neck. It was warm to the touch, and he had the need to splay his hands all over her body.

Beatrice shut her eyes; she leaned in. Her lips parted, and he captured them with his. It was their first kiss after five years, and it was exactly as he'd remembered, and everything he'd imagined it would be. With every lap of her tongue against his, slow and sweet, his worry about this secret relationship left him. Because this—this was right.

After, when her eyelids fluttered open, she whispered, "Wow."

"Damn, girl."

She giggled. "I'll go get dressed. Don't go too far."

He nodded. "I'll be right here."

Except now he had to calm down. While she was gone, he hefted to his feet and went to the kitchen and splashed cold water on his face. While there, he spied the refrigerator door, filled with photos secured by random magnets. On a side table was a stack of photos next to a half-complete scrapbook page.

Not only did Beatrice keep everything, but she kept them treasured. A burning desire rose within him to be part of a family like hers, like the army family he'd left.

A few minutes later, with Beatrice back in her halter dress, they climbed into her car. On the drive north on Highway 12, where conversation flowed, he spoke of the army; she gushed about Beachy. They were like friends catching up rather than strangers getting to know one another.

After they passed the city limits for Kitty Hawk, Beatrice turned into a beachside public parking lot. She placed the car in park and shot him a wicked expression. "Do you have any food allergies? Or extreme dislikes?"

"Nope."

"Let's go, then."

They got out, and she led him by the hand down to the sand, where they both took off their shoes. It was too early for sunset, but the sky was a clear dark blue. White streaked across it, and the total picture was enthralling. With his phone, he snapped a few photos of the horizon, then swiped through to make sure he was satisfied. When he looked up from the phone, Beatrice was ahead by a few steps and was looking at him.

She was a pretty outline against the background, captivating with the long flowing skirt and her hair swept up by the wind. How he was going to keep her a secret when he wanted to shout out that finally, *finally*, they'd found one another, he didn't know.

"What is it?" Beatrice asked.

He took her side and sought for a more neutral topic, focusing on the give of the sand under his feet. "Your dress. It's aerodynamic."

"That's a new way to describe it."

"I noticed that Beachy carries so many styles."

"Because there are so many different occasions, for so many different body types. What I'm wearing right now, for example—it's versatile, so I can use it from day to night. Some of the styles are more formal. Some styles accentuate curves just the right way. I try to pick styles and sizes that are inclusive. I want women to feel beautiful in their outfits." She looked down at the ground as they strolled the surf, hair flying at a random gust of wind. "Listen to me; I'm totally rambling."

"No, don't stop. The way you love your business—it's, I don't know, inspiring."

She seemed to appraise him. "Thank you. You don't know how much I need to hear that. I don't doubt my passion for it, but I wonder if it's the right time to go for it."

"I get what you mean—" he started as relief pulsed through him. She'd gotten to the heart of what he'd been feeling about working for Willow Tree, especially after his day with Lonnie and after finding out about Heart Resort. Doubt, that he'd jumped the gun and retired too early. That maybe he should have prepared even more. "But you can only make the best decision at the moment, you know? And sometimes the right time follows the deed rather than the other way around."

"That's true." She looked up to the right, and a smile graced her face. "Here we are!"

They'd gone down about a couple of blocks, and Jackson squinted at a tiny beach house on stilts closer to the road. A vinyl sign hung from the deck that read **SWEET BIRDIE**.

Beatrice was already rushing toward the house, so he chased after her, then up the house's white steps, and the scent of sugar reached his nose. Beatrice threw the front door open, and they were met with a plexiglass counter that covered tubs of ice cream.

Behind the counter looked to be a full kitchen, complete with a deep fryer. An employee fished out a waffle from an iron and molded it around a tube.

"How about chicken-and-waffles ice cream?" Beatrice placed a warm hand on his forearm.

It all came together. The name of the business, the smells, the way his tummy was growling. "Oh, let's serve it up."

To the apron-clad employee behind the counter, she said, "Two orders, please."

Once they got their orders, they sat side by side, sharing a small round table overlooking the ocean. In his paper bowl was a bowl-shaped waffle filled with deep-fried chicken breast strips and two scoops of vanilla ice cream. "I think my soul has been awakened."

Beatrice laughed. "This surprise was a good thing, then?"

"With you that always seems to be the case."

She blinked up at him with an expression he couldn't place. It made every part of him hum, more than the sugar rush that was sure to invade him.

Later, and by the time he'd walked Beatrice to the front door of her house, Jackson couldn't feel his face because he was smiling so much. They'd talked their lips off on the way back home, about their favorite desserts (hers: ube cake; his: banana pudding), favorite holidays (hers: Christmas; his: Thanksgiving), and the last show they'd marathoned (hers: *Tidying Up with Marie Kondo*; his: ESPN's *30 for 30*).

Important stuff.

"I had an amazing time." She spun on her heel after she unlocked the door. "Would you like to come in?"

"Of course I want to." And he would, but there was more in their relationship, namely their families, and he needed things to go slow, now more than ever. He stuffed his hands in his pockets. "But it might be wise to take a rain check for today. Can I see you again?"

"I mean, you're my neighbor. We're always going to see one another." She arched an eyebrow. "And after that kiss earlier . . ."

She wanted a status check; she wasn't going to let him get away with being neutral.

He loved that she wasn't afraid to ask for what she wanted. "What's your schedule like this weekend? For you and me, and another getaway."

She beamed then, and it was all the answer he needed. Whenever she was available, he was going to make room, come hell or high water. "I can do this weekend, but I'll need to check my schedule for an exact time."

"Sounds good. You can always let me know by yelling out your window." He turned to look at his front door, just feet away.

"Or you can take your flashlight and send me Morse code messages. So that we don't wake The Cathy Hill."

He snorted. "She's literally probably watching us. A resourceful one, she is."

As she laughed, strands of her hair caught her eyelashes. She reached up to brush them away at the same time as he instinctively did, and their fingers touched. It was accidental on Jackson's part, but she cupped her palm against his wrist, encouraging him to finish the job.

The contact drew them closer; she turned her face up to him. "Maybe we could give her a show?"

He winced, playfully. "Only if we stop talking about her."

"Not one more word. I promise." Beatrice rolled on her tiptoes.

At the press of her mouth, Jackson's eyes shut. He savored the leftover sweetness from her ice cream. Her kisses were light, traipsing across his heart much like their date had, with sunshine despite the darkening sky.

The kiss ended with her falling back on her heels and Jackson slightly woozy.

"See you this weekend, Jackson." After stepping back into her doorway, Beatrice leaned against the door.

"You can bet on it," Jackson replied, turning away, knowing it wouldn't be soon enough.

CHAPTER SEVEN

Heart Resort, North Carolina

Today's affirmation: I will stick to my to-do list.

Jackson:
Have you ever had matcha affogato?

Beatrice:
That is a silly question

Jackson:
Southern Shores has a place

Jackson:
Thought of you

Beatrice:
I know all about that place

Beatrice:
I like that you think of me

Jackson:
I'll add it to the list

Jackson:
I've had practice thinking of you

Beatrice set her phone down and bit her lip, leaning back against the office chair. It tilted backward, and her gaze went to the ceiling as she remembered their kiss a couple of nights ago.

She sipped in air to slow down her racing heart, because if she thought she was in trouble keeping her beach house and Beachy's expansion from her brothers, she was surely on the wide road to excommunication.

She was attracted to and pursuing the enemy. Instead of letting him leave and ending what had been a brief reunion, she'd opened her house to him. Not only that, but they'd gone out on their date anyway. And they'd kissed. Twice.

The kisses had been sweet but seductive. Their date had been that same way—so simple but foundation building. It felt easy but meaningful, precursors of what could be, like their nonstop texts since then, showing crumbs of his personality.

The worst and best part of it all? Her attraction to him grew by the text. He was a listener. Open to change, albeit a mega planner. Thoughtful and helpful.

And in the last day, she had been tempted to knock on his door.

This was bad. So bad.

But so good.

She cackled at her warring thoughts.

"What's so funny?" Kim lifted her dark eyebrows in concern, drawing Beatrice's attention to the present. They were in her Heart Resort apartment on the second floor of the Puso building. Her living room had been converted to her Heart Resort office.

"Nothing." Beatrice straightened, and the chair popped back into place. Their desks faced one another, and it was obvious who was right versus left brained. "So where were we?" She pressed her fingers against the bridge of her nose to refocus. As she did, she was reminded that that was something three out of her three brothers did whenever they needed a second of peace.

Oh gosh. Not only was she wearing this drab Heart Resort polo like the rest of them, but now she was doing the bridge pinch of the nose.

What had her life become? A mess, that was what.

"Are you sure?" Kim frowned.

"Absolutely." Beatrice shook herself to get with the moment. *First things first*, she told herself. They'd completed a recap of all the resort clients and all their immediate concerns. On her computer screen was a beautiful color coded to-do list from an app that Kim swore by, populated with current guests, previous guests, forthcoming guests, and the communications they'd had with them. All the boxes had been checked off for most of the clients, with tasks that ranged from sending the welcome packet to reviewing feedback they received during and after their stay. "Looks like you're on the ball, as usual."

"I also scheduled calls between you and the clients coming in this week."

"Ah, thank you. I'll look at that schedule now." But when she clicked onto their shared calendar, her heart dipped into her chest. In seeing the shaded areas of each day, she realized how little time she had for Beachy.

For what she wanted.

"Bea? You're doing that pursed-lip thing again. What's wrong?" Kim said.

She fixed her face. She'd spent the majority of the last couple of days in Heart Resort and sleeping here at Puso—she was feeling just a little claustrophobic. "It's not you, or any of your work. You've been amazing. The schedule's just been so full."

"It's really picked up. Even in the last six months . . . we went from houses going about three to four days in between clients to one to two days."

Beatrice was thunderstruck by this. "I'm definitely feeling it. Did that come out at the meeting?"

"Oh, no . . . I did my own data analysis. It was easy."

She said it so coolly that Beatrice grinned. Kim had been her hire; she'd had a strong résumé. But what had impressed Beatrice most was her inquisitiveness. Her energy, an energy that Beatrice had been lacking for Heart Resort. "Have I told you enough that I appreciate that you're here?"

"I mean, it's you who hired me."

"But you chose to apply. And you do above and beyond anything that's asked of you." She smiled. Though in the pause, she circled back to her discontent in the lack of time she had for Beachy.

At the beginnings of Heart Resort, Beatrice had been excited. She'd thrown her entire self into it—her thoughts, her ideas, her processes. But in founding Beachy, it had become clear to her that *that* was her passion, her life.

"Do you want me to reschedule some of the calls?" As if reading her mind, Kim tapped on her mouse. "I know that you prefer to work on Beachy in the afternoons. How about I move that ten o'clock on Monday to . . . oh, wait, you have that community luncheon you have to attend. Hmm . . . I wish I could take some of these calls for you, to free you up."

The idea snapped Beatrice out of her thoughts, and she tilted her head to look at her assistant. Like, really look at her. Kim Jones, twenty-eight. Right out of her MBA. She was always in the correct uniform (unlike Beatrice). Organized. She had a fun side to her that came out when they caught lunch together at the resort café. But she was often-. times exactly like this—even keeled, helpful. "Kim."

"Mm?" She met Beatrice's gaze.

"How *do* you feel about taking on some of these calls."

"But . . . it's not allowed."

Chris had been specific about having directors being up front and center and involved with clients. He'd wanted personal communications to come straight to Beatrice.

"You're perfectly capable, especially for the postretreat phone calls." She woke her computer screen and scanned the names. "You can start with the Fullers and Kirkpatricks."

"Really?"

"Yes." She smiled. "I'll send you the document of my usual script and the form I type into during the conversation."

A knock sounded on her front door, and it opened a second later. Geneva entered, with Brandon behind her. Just beyond the doorway were two rolling suitcases. "All right. We're off!"

Beatrice and Kim stood; then came the circle of hugs.

"Enjoy Nashville. And make sure it's a honeymoon, Bunso." Beatrice arched an eyebrow at her baby brother, invoking his nickname. The guy always came off like a joker, but when it came to houses—the building, the renovating, and the selling of them—he was unstoppable, and a little bit of a workaholic too. Aside from the resort, he also co-owned P&C Homes with his best friend.

"I promise, Ate Bea." He kissed her on the cheek and stood at the doorway.

A grin spliced across Geneva's face, and she whispered, "He doesn't know about the boutiques I want to visit while I'm there."

Beatrice rolled her eyes. "You're just as bad as he is, I swear. You both need to rest."

"We will. Promise. So long as you promise to keep out of trouble while I'm gone."

"Who, moi?"

Kim snorted, taking a seat once more in front of her computer.

"Hey, I sign your paychecks, lady." Beatrice chuckled.

"Why do I feel like I'm going to come back and find out you're engaged?" Geneva linked an arm around Beatrice and whispered into her ear.

Oh my goodness. Beatrice all but dragged her to the other room because Brandon was right there. Geneva herself didn't know Jackson's identity. It had been hard enough to give Geneva the most generic of information about their date at Kitty Hawk. "First of all, it was one date—"

"Technically, it's your third date. The first being your almost-sex night—"

"Gen, shhh."

"Oh my gosh, another secret, I swear." She pressed her lips together for a beat. "And then, the second-date dinner with his mom, and then the third was your chicken and waffles."

Third. Three.

She swallowed this revelation, not sure what to do with it. "I want to keep it on the DL just until I can figure out where things are going."

"Because you like him?"

"I do," she said truthfully. *Even if I am committing a cardinal sin.*

"I knew it," Geneva whisper-screamed. "Dammit. I can't leave now."

"Geneva, I promise, if anything comes up, I'll text you." A glance up at her brother, who was checking his watch, showed that he was raring to go. So, Beatrice led Geneva back to the living room.

The final goodbye was so chaotic, as usual, that it took Brandon to pull Geneva by the hand to take her away.

With one final look, Geneva yelled, "Beatrice, no decisions without me, got it?"

"Promise!" Beatrice quipped back. And yet, with so many things in the air, her conscience warned her that this might be a promise that would be hard to keep.

♡

Jackson was halfway up the back stairs of the house after his beach run when he received another text, prompting him to speed up. On his deck, he peeled off the Velcro phone armband and looked at the sender, the smile on his face a classic Pavlovian reaction.

Beatrice:
Do you like Asian cuisine?

They'd been texting back and forth since their date, and today's topic seemed to be food. And since their date, Jackson had made his own deductions about Beatrice. As gregarious as she was in person, over text, she was less so. And, as honest and transparent as she appeared to be, there were things she kept to herself. It wasn't hard to notice that her beach house had been empty the last couple of days; it remained dark, and his mother had commented on her absence.

She was most likely at Heart Resort, but she wasn't forthcoming with that information either. Beatrice had another life, and he wasn't yet privy to it.

Jackson was perfectly fine with that—he trusted her and respected her boundaries, seeing that he had his own life to manage—yet, he yearned to one day be on the other side of that wall.

But that would mean traversing their family situation. Which, after thinking on it these last couple of days, he admitted would be harder than he'd initially thought. He hadn't liked that he and Beatrice were a secret, but at the moment, it might be their only option.

He leaned against the deck railing as he took deep breaths. The horizon was gorgeous, and he'd run farther and faster than his normal beach pace. And though he knew he should be stretching, he couldn't *not* respond to Beatrice. His legs could wait.

Jackson:
Yes I do. I ate my way through South Korea when I lived there
Jackson:
Want to get out of here? We can hit Tokyo en route
Beatrice:
Don't forget Manila

>   **Jackson:**
>   Never

A grin returned to his lips. Their texts were like little escape pods in which he could get away from reality.

> **Beatrice:**
> I know a place that makes hand pulled noodles
> **Beatrice:**
> A little hole in the wall near Hatteras
>
>   **Jackson:**
>   I'm down
>   **Jackson:**
>   This weekend?
>
> **Beatrice:**
> I can do Sunday. Saturday I'm meeting a vendor
> for Beachy at Ocracoke Island

Jackson weighed the pros and cons of his next question. Then, in the midst, thought—*what the hell, just go for it.*

>   **Jackson:**
>   Need company for Ocracoke?
>   On the way up we can do noodles?
>
> **Beatrice:**
> on your motorcycle?
>
>   **Jackson:**
>   If you want

She shot him a heart emoji—and what did that mean? And without the sight of text bubbles on her end, he set the phone down on one of the outdoor chairs.

A date, this weekend. As he stretched, groaning with relief, his mind wandered to where else she would want to go. If she didn't feel comfortable riding, he could grab a rental. It wouldn't be as fancy as her Tesla, though . . .

His cell phone rang, taking him out of his thoughts and his current stretch. At the sight of Lonnie's name, a foreboding feeling descended. It flipped his mood inside out—they had plans to meet with their Realtor, Peter, in forty-five minutes.

"What's up, Lonnie?" was Jackson's greeting when he accepted the call.

"I can't do this today." His brother's voice was hoarse.

"The only way you're getting out of this is if you're sick, and if that's the case, I'll be there in ten minutes with a thermometer."

"Just not feeling it, man."

"We've only had a few showings. You can't bail now."

Jackson walked in circles on the deck partly to cool down but mostly to temper his impatience from Lonnie's hot-and-cold attitude. Canceling on Peter was a nonnegotiable.

"McCauley will want an update soon," Jackson reminded him. "We can't show up empty handed."

His brother groaned.

"Lonnie."

"Listen, you go view the properties, but I'm keeping my butt right here in this house." He hung up without a goodbye.

Frustration coursed through Jackson, though his conscience tugged at him. Something with Lonnie was amiss.

Jackson entered the back door, passing the increasing amount of jewelry being made and displayed on his kitchen table, and spied the clock. Forty-three minutes remained to get Lonnie to the real estate office.

He was in and out of the shower and the house in ten minutes, and he took his motorcycle to the other property their father owned.

Lonnie's car was parked outside; Jackson climbed up the stairs and pounded on the door, sighing.

No answer. Two could play at this game. Jackson peeked into the windows, spotting a shadow in front of the big screen. "I see you in there. Open up."

Jackson had no issues making morale checks. It was a leader's and an empathetic human's role. But Lonnie resented him, which didn't make this a pleasant trip.

After a few seconds, the shadowed blob moved to the door, and finally, it popped open.

Lonnie was wearing joggers and a T-shirt that hung askew on his torso. "What are you doing here?"

"Is this the way to greet your big brother?"

Lonnie cocked a head at him. "You should leave."

"Nope. Not leaving." Jackson crossed his arms. "You're stuck with me, so either you let me in, or I'll park my butt at your front door."

Finally, after a beat, Lonnie stepped aside with a grumble.

Jackson entered. Nothing seemed awry, except for the fact that Lonnie looked like he hadn't slept. Under his eyes were dark shadows; his face was unshaven.

"All right. You're here, now leave," he said.

"Look, you not showing up today'll affect my bottom line." He turned up the lights; Lonnie squinted at the shock. "Get some clean clothes on. Let's go."

"Does our father know that your mother's staying with you?"

"I don't know what you're talking about." Jackson took a wide stance. There was no relaxing with this guy.

Jackson could deal with shy. He could even deal with hesitant, with stubborn, but a jerk?

Damn, did he need a for-real escape hatch that would take him straight to Beatrice.

At the thought of her, Jackson warmed a smidge. She was the light at the end of this week's tunnel. He simply had to get his brother moving.

"I dropped by the other day," Lonnie continued. "I wanted to invite you for a drink but stopped short when I saw her enter the house. Why would you bring Cathy Hill here?"

The sound of her name on Lonnie's tongue made Jackson bristle. "Careful, Lonnie," he warned. Because Jackson wouldn't have his mother be disrespected.

"You're the one who needs to be careful. Our father's the worst." Lonnie sank into the couch with a whoosh. That was when Jackson detected what looked like sadness in Lonnie's eyes. "My mother died a lonely woman because of him. How could you bring your mother into the situation?"

Jackson ran a hand through his hair, surprised at Lonnie's vulnerability. "Not that it's any of your business, but I didn't exactly have a choice. Cathy Hill answers to no man." Jackson drew his eyes down to the carpet. "What's going on, Lon?"

"I'm . . . in a rough spot. I'm pissed . . . it's been a lot lately, with you showing up. Imagine if you were in my shoes."

"Imagine if you were in mine," Jackson countered. He tolerated only so much of *woe is me*, even from himself. If he'd lived his life hanging on to what could have been, he wouldn't have been able to get up in the morning for work. "Imagine knowing you had a family out there but fully understanding, as a child, that you weren't a part of it."

Lonnie's shoulders slumped. "I know. It's all levels of messed up."

Jackson backed up and perched on one of the kitchen chairs. His brother's face was contorted, as if he was working through a problem. "Look, Lonnie. I'm not trying to take your place. I needed a job, bottom line. Other than that, I had gotten used to being invisible." Bitterness rose in Jackson's throat, and he swallowed it back with pride. He was forty, dammit, and he'd told himself a long time ago that he wouldn't allow people to hurt him. He didn't have to like Lonnie to get what he needed from him. "I'm trying to work my way through this too. And that means making sure that you're doing fine."

"What is *fine*, anyway?"

"Now you're worrying me."

"Heather and the kids left Grandview yesterday. She's staying at our time-share in Florida."

Grandview was the McCauley estate on Carova Beach, where their father spent his time in between his visits to the Willow Tree resorts. The property was large enough that it was what Lonnie and his family called *home*.

Jackson exhaled, taken aback. "Sorry, man. Can I ask why?"

"Let's just say that she's been living with our dysfunctional family and wants a break from it. And . . . she wants *me* to do the same . . . of course I said no."

Jackson eased his expression. "She wants you to leave Willow Tree?"

"Yeah." He half laughed. "I don't know why I'm so surprised that she left me. When we met, I wasn't involved with Willow Tree at all. But, like you, it was time to get a job, and our father was hiring. And then it became my life."

"What are you going to do?"

"What can I do?"

"You can fight for her."

"I have been." Lonnie shook his head. "Have you ever been married?"

Jackson nodded, though he wished he was the kind of person who could lie. His married life hadn't been his best moments. "Married a year. Been divorced for two."

He raised an eyebrow. "Really? What happened?"

"I jumped in, both feet, with a woman who it made sense to be with, but it wasn't enough. And she left me." Jackson stiffened at the memory at how he'd gotten it all wrong. He and Emily had checked off the boxes in their relationship in perfect order, only to realize that there'd been gaps in between. Gaps made by him.

"And now?"

"Now what?"

"Have you found someone new?"

"Yeah," he said, then realized that with Beatrice, it was the other way around. They had checked zero boxes and were considered wrong by both their families, but their connection was solid and real. "But this isn't about me. Why are you sitting here and not going after your wife?"

"Because I can't choose, and I won't."

"I hate to tell you, but you'll have to eventually." In his pocket, Jackson's phone buzzed. It was his five-minute warning to get to the real estate office. "Go get some clothes on. Let's take these tours, and then you and I can figure out what you're going to do about Heather."

"I don't need your help."

He arched an eyebrow. "Your mirror would object."

Sighing, Lonnie pressed both palms against his knees and stood. "All right." But before the guy walked into his bedroom, he looked back at Jackson. "Why are you being so nice to me?"

Jackson shrugged. "I mean, I feel like we're in this together. Might as well team up, right?"

Lonnie paused as if to think on it, then nodded, shutting the door.

CHAPTER EIGHT

Duck, North Carolina

Today's affirmation: I can do new things.

On Saturday morning, while sitting in her car and staring out the windshield to a storefront she'd parked in front of, Beatrice ruminated on her most recent decision. She shouldn't have agreed to invite Jackson to Ocracoke Island, and travel on a motorcycle no less, for four reasons. For one, they couldn't be seen together. While she was relieved to take a second person to the vendor meeting, what if someone recognized them and put the pieces of their secret together?

Second, she and Jackson would be together for at least six hours; this trip would be a crash course in getting to know one another. What if as they got to know the intricacies of each other's personalities, the magic between them went poof, and they decided that their whole secret relationship wasn't worth it after all?

The beginnings of relationships were sublime because of the excitement of the discovery. This close proximity would speed things up. At this rate—and if she took her romantic history into account—they'd know everything about each other by next week, and they would be broken up.

Was she being dramatic about this? Not in the slightest. She believed in love, in long-lasting love, but it was not as if their relationship was set up for success from the jump.

Oh, and third, Beatrice had never ridden a motorcycle. She had mixed emotions about them—the instability of being on two wheels, the exposure of not having layers of metal protecting them from the outside, the peril (gah) of going very quickly, but also the sexiness, the temptation, the romantic danger—and was she truly willing for her first experience to be an almost two-hour ride, plus navigating a ferry, each direction?

And, fourth and just as dire—she had nothing to wear. Nothing for riding, anyway. Her closets were filled with dresses and outfits made of comfortable fabrics, some delicate enough to be hand-washed but none able to withstand an accidental trip of her own feet.

"But I can do this, I can," Beatrice said aloud to no one as she unlocked her car door, because despite her inner discussion, she wanted to see Jackson. She wanted time with him, alone and apart from her family and distraction from her work. To see him for who he was.

The sun was bright, and she squinted at the impressive business signage in front of her. **BIKERS HAVEN.** It was made even more striking by the gleaming motorcycles on the front lot.

Once inside, she hurtled herself toward the first employee, because she was going to need help.

"Excuse me." She trailed him. "I was wondering if . . ."

"Yes, ma'am." The man turned. No, it was practically a boy who looked not a day older than eighteen, and could he really outfit her?

"Um, yes. I was wondering if you can help me pick out a riding outfit."

"I mean." He gestured toward the side of the shop that had a **WOMEN** sign hanging from the ceiling. "Take your pick."

"Great. Thanks."

Beatrice heaved a breath. She would have to figure this out herself. On her phone, she did a quick search on Pinterest, which brought up a myriad of outfits. It was overwhelming, because what style should she commit to? Cowboy, or grunge, or metal, or sexy?

She walked along aisles and pulled random clothes from racks. She sifted through pants (leather or chaps?), jackets (thick denim or leather?), gloves, and shoes. There were so many options that her head spun. She was in the clothing business. This wasn't supposed to be hard.

She paused next to a mannequin that looked to be a size triple zero—and how was that even realistic? Maybe this was a sign that her focus was on the wrong thing. Her trip to Ocracoke was for work. She could very well take Jackson in her car and wear absolutely normal clothing and not have to think about how hot he would look straddling a bike.

Yet, now with all these clothes in her arms, Beatrice had to follow through. She went to the dressing room area. There were only two stalls; both were occupied. While she waited, Beatrice scrolled through her phone with one hand and went to her bookmarks that she'd set aside about Leila. In the last couple of days, she and Kim had done research about this multimedia star.

One article's heading: Leila and her love for her menagerie of pets. Another: Leila finds love away from the spotlight. Then another: Leila around town without Kelsey. Are they over?

She screenshotted the website and sent it to Kim via text and with the message: Let's keep a close eye on this.

Then, because Beatrice still had to take care of the couple who Leila had displaced, she texted: Also, send me options for future dates for Papadakis.

Kim:
Ok to all

The click of the dressing room door snagged Beatrice's concentration, only to face the last person she'd expected this morning: Jessie Puso, with clothing draped across her arm.

They both seemed to freeze at the sight of each other. In the six or so months since Jessie had moved to the Outer Banks, they'd never been alone. Last night at the family's Friday dinner at their usual location, Salt & Sugar, despite sitting across from each other, they'd barely spoken.

"Um. Hi." Jessie broke the silence.

"Hi," Beatrice said, clamoring for an excuse as to why she was at a bike shop. Jessie had a reason because riding was a passion she shared with Gil.

Jessie's gaze dropped to what Beatrice was carrying, and her expression turned curious. "You going riding?"

"No." Her answer was like a snap of a whip. No one could know about Jackson. And even if he hadn't been a McCauley, Beatrice rarely brought anyone home. The last time she was close to introducing a love interest had been a couple of years ago, but days before the meeting she'd found out that he'd cheated on her.

Jessie's eyebrows plunged. "Really? Is that why you're standing in line for a dressing room in a motorcycle shop."

"Nope. I'm just doing . . . research." She inwardly winced.

"Oh, okay. Enjoy your *research*, then." Jessie turned and hung half the clothing in her arms on a rack. She looked over her shoulder. "Or you can, I don't know, simply ask me."

"I'm fine, thanks." Beatrice raised her nose in the air. But as Jessie headed to the register, logic became a traitor and took over her vocal cords. If there was anyone who could help her at the moment, it was Jessie. "W . . . wait."

Jessie turned. "Yeah?"

"I do . . . need help, I mean." She bit her lip and tamped down her pride. "What would one wear if they were a passenger on a motorcycle ride a couple of hours down and back?"

"What size would this hypothetical person be? Because if this is their first ride, it wouldn't make any sense to buy these very expensive clothes when some could be borrowed." She paused. "And I have a closetful."

All at once, Beatrice remembered Jessie digging through her closet when she'd visited during the holiday season. They shared the same size, and Jessie needn't even have brought her suitcase.

They had been sisters by marriage once. More than that . . . they had been sisters by choice.

Were they still?

"Forget I asked," Jessie blurted out, digging into the clothes in Beatrice's arms. She picked out the leather jacket and thick denim pants. "These should do. Use your best leather gloves, and any kind of hiking boots if you have them. The most important safety gear is your helmet, and you can rent one from this shop. Get a full-face helmet. Got it?"

Beatrice nodded, a frisson of guilt running up her spine. Jessie was helping her despite everything.

"Is this person an experienced rider?" Jessie asked, voice firm.

"He is."

"I haven't heard Gil say a thing about you seeing someone, so this person . . . he's new?"

The question was so loaded, and Beatrice answered with a squeak. "Sort of."

She nodded. "Make sure you leave your location info with Geneva. I know she's on her honeymoon, but it's good to send occasional updates. Roads are dangerous. Oh, and here, I'll message you a little cheat sheet on what it's like to be a passenger." She pulled out her phone, and after a protracted minute, Beatrice's phone buzzed in her pocket with the text. "Make sure you read it, okay?"

"Okay."

"Who's taking Roxy?"

"My neighbor."

As a pause settled in between them, a rush of emotions overtook Beatrice. Gratitude for all this information, nostalgia for the kind of sisters they once had been. Then this swirling abyss of regret, all compounded by this complication that she was sneaking off with Jackson. Topped by a wish that she could tell Jessie about it.

In Beatrice's heart, she knew Jessie could commiserate. She could advise. And she would do so without judgment. But it was no longer the same between them.

"Well, good luck." Jessie headed to the register.

"Thank you," she said belatedly, left with remorse—it didn't have to be this way.

♡

"Breathe, son; it's an afternoon ride." Jackson's mother watched him through the reflection in his bathroom mirror as he finished up shaving. It reminded him of when he was a teenager, when she'd catch him in the mornings before he left for school.

Pressing a hand against his cheeks to double-check the job he'd done, he exhaled and silently begged to differ. This was a secret afternoon ride. A ride with a woman who could decide that whatever this was between them had lost its luster after she'd gotten to know him more. Or, the opposite; she'd decide that involving herself with a McCauley was too messy. "I want for her to have a good time. It's her first ride."

"I've no doubt you both will have the time of your life." She patted him on the back, turning. After hanging his towel on the rack, he followed her to the kitchen.

His mother had been busy since the early morning. Piles of shells were scattered on the dinner table, and her tools were parked on random surfaces. It was The Cathy Hill's way, this slow reallocation of space. His heart swelled seeing his mother's renewed interest in something that had fulfilled her so long ago.

A knock sounded on the front door, and Cathy beamed, rushing past him. "Yay."

Yay? Had his mother said *yay*? But when she opened the door to Beatrice wearing a tank top, slim jeans, and ankle boots and carrying a helmet and a leather jacket, the actual word that came out of Jackson's mouth was "Damn."

Beatrice was sexy. Hot. And she was going to be sitting behind him. Her arms would be around his waist, and his body was going to be pressed against hers.

Jackson steamed up despite the AC on full blast.

And she heard him, returning a grin that lit up her entire face. It was disarming, jump-starting the moment. Jackson wrapped an arm around her and breathed her in. Beatrice smelled of a floral, sweet perfume, and when she clutched him around the waist, warmth invaded every cell in his body.

She blinked up at him. "Do you like?"

"I more than like," he said into her ear, kissing her earlobe. "I want."

"Jack," she whispered in a playful warning.

"Yes, Jack, your mother is still in the room," Cathy said, which took his need down by a notch.

He felt pressure against his right knee. Roxy was propped against his leg, mouth open into what he thought was a smile—he couldn't tell.

"Aw." Beatrice's gaze dropped to her dog. "She's warmed up to you."

"Can I pet her?"

"Yes, it's what she's asking for."

"O . . . okay." Still, Jackson hesitated. Roxy was a small dog, but one couldn't be too careful. They still had teeth.

But when he scratched Roxy behind her ear, her jaw dropped farther, and a pink tongue lolled out. Roxy was cute, actually. "Good dog."

"I packed a little something for the both of you." Cathy produced two lunch bags, like she was sending them off to school. "Have fun, kids. Roxy and I are going to work all day today. I'm brimming with ideas."

They were all but shoved out the door, and Jackson ran a hand through his hair. "You can see who's in charge around here."

Beatrice giggled as she walked down the stairs. When she was at the bottom, she turned to wait for him.

Alone now, he slung an arm around her shoulder, tucking her close. It had been out of instinct, and without missing a beat, Beatrice wrapped an arm around his waist, hooking a thumb on a belt loop. "I think she's sweet," she said. "And it's nice to have a parent around."

"To be honest, I don't mind at all. If I could have her live close by, it would make me feel a ton better. She's always been so independent, though. Didn't matter how many invitations I sent for her to live in all the places I moved to, she respectfully declined." When they got to his bike, he broke off to undo the leather saddlebag to store the lunch bags.

"She's so proud of you." She fisted the left handgrip as if testing it out; Jackson's insides fluttered at her curiosity. "At our dinner, when you were in the kitchen, she gave me the CliffsNotes on how accomplished you are."

"Cupid strikes again." He grinned, stuffing the lunch sacks in the saddlebag.

"She also told me that you're the best man she's ever known." She ended up at his side once more, and watched over his work. "May I?"

"Be my guest." He stepped aside for her to rethread the straps, and he couldn't tear his gaze away from her nimble and strong fingers. "Anyway, my mother said that because she hadn't exactly met the best men." His cheeks reddened despite his attempt at aloofness, both from the compliment and the reminder that his mother deserved more than what she'd been handed in life.

"Ta-da!" she sang with the final slip of the leather into the buckle.

"Well done." He took one of her capable hands and pressed it against his lips. It was overkill, but he couldn't seem to get his emotions in check with this woman. Everything she did turned him on. *Ease up, buddy.* "Anyway, wanna take a look at the drive plan?" He let go of her hand and fished out his phone, then zoomed in on the map, on Highway 12 south.

"It's just one straight road."

He nodded. "It should be a leisure drive. But it's mostly one lane each way, and it may feel intimidating as your first experience."

She seemed to stiffen, and it gave him pause.

"Are you still all right riding?" When she didn't answer, he turned to her fully. "Because we don't have to. We can take your car instead."

"You'd do that?"

"Absolutely."

But she ran her hand on the leather seat and said, "No, I want to. If . . . I ask to stop to rest, we can, right?"

"Of course. As I mentioned . . . the drive plan? It has us stopping at every scenic stop or town. I intend to take pictures. See?" He showed her his phone and clicked on the photos app, and scrolled and scrolled. "I'm a sky-pic kind of guy."

"No kidding. These are such great photos, Jackson." Her voice switched from worry to awe, so Jackson pushed on.

"The sky reminds me of what's possible. That things are limitless. These days, when I ride and take in that open space . . . it leaves me feeling hopeful, you know?" But as Jackson said these words, he blushed. He'd been in his head for so long, since preparing for his retirement a year ago. For other people, he had simply left a job, but he'd retired from an entire lifestyle, and what was in front of him these days was both overwhelming and beguiling. "Anyway, you ready?"

"As I'll ever be." She shrugged on her coat, then zipped it up. She was going to look so good on his bike, with him, and that thought washed away his serious mood. "Jackson?"

"Yeah?"

She fussed with the helmet's opening. "I know that feeling, that rush of possibility. It's like potential, but more."

"That's right." He breathed out relief.

"And I think that in whatever you decide that is, that hope? I believe that you should have it, and you should go for it." Then, Beatrice put on her helmet, as if her words had been casual advice.

But it meant more to him than that. It felt like a wish made in his honor.

And for the first time in his life, he considered that he could believe in that little bit of magic too.

CHAPTER NINE

Current affirmation: I will hang on!

At first, being a passenger on a motorcycle going a high rate of speed wasn't as easy or as romantic as depicted in all of those photographs and how-to guides Beatrice had consulted prior to her ride with Jackson. She had to remain focused; all her muscles were engaged. Aware that she didn't have a seat belt or protection aside from her helmet and the thick fabrics she was wearing, she held on, literally for her life.

But she got into a groove. She leaned into Jackson; she breathed deeply and slowly, and she took in the sights of the water rushing past, of the road up ahead, of what Jackson had described earlier as *possibility*. Then, slowly, fear switched to exhilaration.

They'd stopped at every beach town along the way: Rodanthe, Waves, Salvo, Avon, Buxton, and Frisco, and as promised, Jackson took a million photos.

All the while, Beatrice lost herself in this soft-spoken and kind human, who was so different from so many men she'd met. He was fully aware of his faculties but didn't enforce or express them, and he moved in this confident manner that turned heads.

Star quality. It had been what her father had called a person's undeniable quality that rose above the rest. It was as subtle as it was pervasive.

And she had to admit, there was something in the way Jackson wrangled his bike—she fully trusted him. Under gloved fingers, she felt his strength and his intensity. He made split-second decisions against reckless vehicles; his fearless nature and competence at times left her boneless from adrenaline.

By the time they parked and dismounted from the bike on the Hatteras–Ocracoke Ferry, Beatrice's attraction for him was at full throttle. She wasn't sure how she would be able to keep it together the rest of the day. What she *was* certain of was that as soon as they were indoors and alone, she would tear his clothes off.

The lunch bags that Cathy had handed them earlier were crinkled when Jackson retrieved them from the saddlebag, but after they sat on a bench for a quick lunch and dug into their sacks, Beatrice found that inside were perfect triple-decker sandwiches made with white bread.

She ditched her libido in exchange for nourishment. "Oh my God, this looks so good."

"Turkey and cheese. My fave." Jackson all but inhaled three-quarters of the sandwich at his first go. Then, as if belatedly realizing that she was there, he laughed, wiping his mouth with the back of his hand. "Sorry. Starving."

"No, same." She took a bite, and sure enough, it was the best sandwich she'd had in forever. "It just hits different when someone else makes it, right? Like none of the food I make is as good as my mom's, even if I use the same recipe."

"Do you get to see her often?" Chewing, he licked a stray crumb from his finger.

"No. She passed away."

His hands lowered to his lap. "Shit. I'm sorry."

"Thank you for saying that." She inhaled slowly. "My parents were together when they died. A car accident, a drunk driver."

"Beatrice." He took her into his arms, forgetting the sandwiches in between them. And though it surprised her at first, she shut her eyes at the contact. She'd been holding him for the last couple of hours, and now, with the tables turned, it felt good.

"It's weird," she felt compelled to say after they settled back in their seats, then halted. "Never mind."

"It's okay, Bea. Say it only if you're comfortable."

She looked at him; she decided she *was* comfortable. "It's been eight years. And I think a part of me got used to it, to knowing my parents are gone. When you hugged me just now, I realized how big of a thing it is. I don't know if I'm explaining myself well."

He smiled. "I get it. My dad wasn't a part of most of my life—it was his choice. And when I meet people who don't have that experience, I'm surprised when they're shocked by it. That what happened to me wasn't normal."

"What *is* normal, anyway?"

"That's a good question. Maybe there's no such thing. Everyone has something to deal with. But we spend all our time making decisions toward whatever we think that is." He shrugged.

Beatrice took him in. This man was speaking to her as if he knew exactly what was in her heart. Her recent life had been all about the decisions she'd made to live up to whatever was expected of her. Where did responsibility end and individualism begin?

But with the somber mood settling in, she straightened and blasted a smile on her face. "Sort of like deciding to come along today. What spurred that?"

"Well . . ." He looked away, lips pursed for a beat in thought. "It came down to one thing, really . . . I've been incessantly dreaming of . . . those hand-pulled noodles."

The no-nonsense tone in his answer brought her to laughter.

Then, he smiled so big, cheeks reddening.

She tapped his leg with her foot. "Well, because of you, I'm no longer a motorcycle virgin, even if I thought I was going to die those first few miles." At the concern on his face, Beatrice backtracked. "I'm fine now, I swear. And, you were right about the sky. It was scary and exciting to ride off into what felt like the horizon. It felt like freedom—"

The wind swept up her hair and splayed the strands across her face. She attempted to palm them away. "Oh jeez."

"Your hair's getting into the mustard." Jackson laughed while trying to assist in the endeavor, and when his fingers grazed against her cheeks, her breath hitched. She melted at the methodical way he tucked the strands behind her ears, all the while gazing into her eyes. "There you go."

"Thanks." Beatrice swallowed against the lump of need in her throat from that sweet moment. Her feelings for Jackson ping-ponged from an innocent crush to an all-out hunger to a desire to talk to him for hours. She wanted him; also, she *liked* him. "Jackson, what do you think would have happened if you called me back then?"

He shook his head. "I don't know. I'm not really the kind of person to think about *what if* . . . you could go down too many roads, you know?"

"Yeah . . ." She looked away from him.

"But I did think of you a lot in those years."

"Really?"

He nodded, folding his napkin. "I often wondered where you were, what you were up to. I thought of you often up to when I got engaged."

Beatrice sucked in a breath. "You were married." Her tone was sharper than she'd intended, following a deep jealousy that came from the unknown. She checked herself: she had no ties to him.

Still.

"For a year. We're still friends." He half laughed. "And she's married to one of my best friends."

"Wow . . ." Beatrice was afraid to ask. "Is that awkward?"

"Oh my God, no. Not anymore. Though I didn't fully realize what was missing in our marriage until we spoke as friends and not as exes—I was pissed when she left me. But after the dust settled, I understood that I wasn't all in in the way she had wanted and expected. And she's with someone who I respect, and they're both happy."

This conversation they were having—it was serious. In early dates of previous relationships, Beatrice hadn't touched the topic of commitment. It was taboo. But this didn't scare her. "Well, I'm sorry that you had to go through that pain, but also I'm not sorry at all."

He burst out in a laugh. "Me too, Bea. Me too."

Beatrice was sure she was blushing now. "I thought of you too. A lot. I wondered why you didn't call. But I also had this peace that at least for that small moment, our time together was perfect." She looked beyond him, to the upcoming darkening land. An announcement broke over the speaker that they would be docking in ten minutes. "I had such a good time on that trip. It was largely uncomplicated."

"Uncomplicated is a gift." He nodded, understanding flitting across his face that she wasn't just talking about them but life in general. "Especially now with the whole warring-families detail."

"Booo." She gave him a thumbs-down.

"Too soon?"

"Too real. But"—she took a cleansing breath—"we have Cathy on our side."

"You're right." He raised his water bottle. "Here's to Cathy Hill, and chili, and apple streusel."

"To *The* Cathy Hill, and turkey-and-cheese sandwiches." She bumped her water bottle against his. "And Roxy. We can't forget her. She gave us her blessing."

He raised his eyebrows. "To Roxy." He bumped her water bottle.

She detected some hesitancy. "I'm sorry; I didn't even ask. Do you like dogs?"

A sheepish smile graced his face. "Um, certain? I was bitten by a dog when I was a kid and since then, well . . ."

Her jaw dropped; remorse filled her. "I'm so sorry. That must have been horrible."

"It was accidental. I was at the neighbors' and was petting the dog. The doorbell rang, and the dog barked . . . right into my face."

She winced.

"The bite wasn't huge, but it was enough that I've since been skittish. And though my mom wanted a dog, we were renters along the way, and our landlord didn't allow pets. I've gone through life avoiding dogs, I guess." He squirmed. "Not to say that Roxy isn't great. She is."

It touched Beatrice that he was trying, despite his fear. "Well, now I know. And I do feel that it's just as important for the human to get used to a dog as much as it is the other way around. We should plan to spend more time together. The three of us."

"I'm down." He grinned.

They were interrupted with a five-minute warning announcement that they were soon docking.

"Since we're starting our final leg," Jackson started, "for this vendor meeting, what can I help with?"

Anticipation rushed through Beatrice; she loved talking business. "Breezy Bandanas has a total of four employees. They sew matching pup and owner bandanas, monogrammed headbands, and custom fabric face masks. I love their stuff, but before I carry them for the subscription box and our online catalog, I want to make sure that their employees are working in a safe environment and that they're being treated fairly. Geneva, my business partner, is on her honeymoon, and she's usually so good at providing another point of view."

"I'll do my best to be an adequate replacement," he said. "But I like that you care about how a vendor runs their business. It's commendable."

"I'm trying." Beatrice shrugged. "It's hard to find the balance between having a sustainable business and making sure I'm doing what I think is ethical." He was looking at her so intently that she asked, "Is that too much to ask of a company?"

"No. Not at all. You want them to live up to their commitments, but you also want to make sure that you're working with ethical proprietors. You're a good person, Beatrice."

"Thank you." She splayed a hand against her heart, and it beat a steady drum. Some people would render her too much of an idealist. Jackson seemed to understand her, but the compliment was almost too much, so she changed the subject. "You are too, which makes me wonder why you're working for Willow Tree." She grimaced.

"Ouch. I thought it was too soon?"

"Honestly, it doesn't make sense to me. It's incongruous—how you are with me, and how Willow Tree has been with Heart Resort."

"My dad reached out at a time when I needed a job."

"You said he was relatively absent. How are you getting along now?"

"Let's just say it's been kind of a complicated, slow roll to get to know one another."

"What happened with your dad and Cathy . . . if you don't mind me asking? You'd mentioned an affair. I would have never thought . . ." Then, she realized where her thoughts were running to . . . and regretted saying it aloud. "I'm sorry."

He frowned. "What did you mean by that?"

She pressed her lips together. They weren't at the island yet, and already she was starting to ruin things. "I . . . I guess I have an opinion of people who get involved with committed couples. I've been hurt, so . . ."

"To make it clear, my mother didn't know she was the other woman. Not until she showed up at his door and encountered his wife."

Beatrice shut her eyes. "Ugh. I'm so sorry. And I apologize for my assumption. What I said came from a place of bias, and anger still."

She remembered returning back to Heart Resort after being betrayed and heartbroken. Her sister-in-law Eden had been there, thank goodness, to pick up the pieces, but it had taken weeks of deep cleaning her apartment, of being dragged around town, for her to finally open up with her pain.

"I see," Jackson said. "And I completely understand. When you're hurt and deceived, sometimes it's hard not to put it on everybody you meet."

Beatrice nodded. "Exactly. And whew, are you telling the truth." Beatrice had pent-up anger still wanting to unleash itself. It fueled her suspicions of Jessie. He looked away, allowing Beatrice to take a breath. "So, okay, no questions about work."

He laughed. "Unfortunately no, but as I've told my mother, it is not an illegal operation."

"The Cathy Hill . . . she gets right down to the heart of it."

"That she does." He paused. "Speaking of, thanks for being so enthusiastic about my mom's work. It means a lot to her. And it means a lot to me. She hasn't made anything in a while, and you've given her hope."

"I mean, c'mon, it's The Cathy Hill. How could I not gush?"

"That's what I'm saying! But the moment she stopped making jewelry, she began to retreat back into the background. To see her work is to see her happy, and you had a hand in that."

The ferry blew its whistle, signaling their arrival at Ocracoke Island.

"Here, let me get that." Jackson went to dispose of their trash, leaving Beatrice a moment to breathe in the ocean's air. It was refreshing; it cleansed the moment. It came with a feeling of lightness as well as the memory of her as a child, when she'd learned to float on her back on the soft waves of the sound. With the tips of her mother's fingers and her reassuring voice buoying her, Beatrice had found relief and confidence in the water.

She felt this relief and confidence now—in Jackson. Eyes shut, she smiled against the warm sun.

Hi, Mom. I know. He's sweet.

"Beatrice?"

Jackson's voice eased her eyes open, though that small bit of joy didn't lift. On the contrary, it was enhanced by his presence.

He was smiling too. He was a foot away—and when she didn't answer, he touched her wrist with a finger. "Ready?"

"Yeah," she said, meaning it, as people started their vehicles. Then the mad rush to exit the ferry began, and as Beatrice climbed on behind Jackson and wrapped her arms around him, she finished her thought. "I am so ready."

♡

Jackson assessed Breezy Bandanas as closely as he had with any of his projects, with a discerning eye. He took notes on his phone as Leon Breezy, a sunburnt man wearing a rolled-up tie-dyed bandana around his forehead, introduced them to his employees and showed them their production facility.

In that modestly sized room, sewing machines and sergers whirred, and packages were being packed, and Jackson was in awe of all of it. He'd become a soldier the day after high school graduation, when he'd boarded a plane for basic training. Besides Willow Tree, he hadn't worked in any other industry but the military. Small businesses were fascinating.

"Do you have a good feeling?" Beatrice whispered as they were led out of the room.

"Yes, I do," he said.

"Any concerns?"

"I would say their production capability. How many customers do you have currently for your subscription box?"

As she told Jackson, it set off a slew of equations in his head, estimating a conservative percentage of customers who'd like a bandana in their box. "With their current output and orders, you'll have to ensure that they prioritize Beachy."

"I agree with your assessment." She blew out a breath, eyes darting to the left. "Okay. Do you mind waiting while I take a quick meeting with him?"

"Not a problem. There's a whole sky waiting for me."

She nodded, her face serious. But as he walked away, she tugged him back by the arm. "Thank you."

"Glad to help." Pride filled him as he walked outside, down the steep stairs, and then to the edge of the sand. He took off his boots and socks and became engrossed in the enormity of his surroundings.

"Damn, this is beautiful." He was on a tiny island surrounded by water. Yes, he knew that was the definition of the word *island*, and yes, he'd visited a handful for McCauley since he'd arrived. But he hadn't stopped to take it in—being with Lonnie had dampened the experience.

But, with Beatrice . . . Beatrice seemed to change the game for him in every way.

Jackson dug his toes deeper into the sand and took another panoramic photo with his iPhone. At this rate, he would run out of cloud storage.

What a day it had been.

Something had changed between him and Beatrice, though Jackson couldn't put a finger on it. Was it normal to feel invested, to empathize so much in such a short amount of time? To sympathize? It was one thing to help, to assist, to be available for people, to be attracted to them, but wholly another to care. He cared about his mother, about a select few. Because one couldn't just give that care away, could they?

Especially when they belonged to families who hated one another.

He finished up the panoramic photo and was examining it when the phone rang in his hand. Lonnie's name popped up.

Jackson answered it. "What's up?"

"Wanna grab a beer?"

Jackson looked at the phone, confirming that this was, in fact, his half brother. "What's the catch?"

He chortled. "No catch. I figured your boring butt was sitting at home on a Saturday. And since my loser behind's doing the same thing . . ."

This was . . . nice. "Yeah . . . sure. I don't get back until later, though."

"Where are you?"

"Out."

"Okay? Is this with the girl you're seeing? Tell me more about her, man."

"Eh . . . it's kind of on the DL right now, so . . ." Silence settled in where Jackson didn't offer any more information. Guilt and trepidation warred; Jackson wanted to share this news with anyone who cared—and yet, he couldn't.

His brother cleared his throat. "You know what? I'm actually busy tonight."

Dammit. "Lonnie—"

"I'll see you at the showing tomorrow. And take it for what it's worth, as if I'm in a functional relationship at the moment, but when something's on the DL, you've gotta wonder how far this thing's gonna go." Then he clicked off the line.

Jackson grunted in frustration, trudging to the edge of the surf, and lifted his phone to snap another photo. The sky had clouded over since the beginning of Beatrice's meeting, though streaks of pink and orange bled through.

But no matter how he tilted the camera, or how he attempted to set the focus on different parts of the sky, he couldn't quite get the colors right. There was really nothing like real life, where the hues were that much richer.

A surge of emotions rushed through him, surprising him out of his thoughts. He had no real hold of his current reality. Without the army, his constant was no longer. What had been a reliable life had been disrupted, and everything he'd known as true was being challenged. Such as:

That the only DNA that mattered was his mother's.

That he would never allow his father into his life.

That secrets were evil.

And that instant love was a farce.

Love? Why in the hell was he even thinking about that?

Jackson shook himself out of his thoughts.

He was still adjusting, right? It had to be what all this was. His life had been under a schedule, a routine. He'd known where in the formation he stood. And now, he was all kinds of confused. He was all kinds of lost.

"Jackson!" The wind swept what sounded like his name, and he turned. Beatrice was running toward him, sand kicking up in her wake. She was alone, and when he met her halfway, she threw her arms around his neck, laughing. She pressed a firm kiss on his lips, and it grounded him to the here and now. For all he was confused about in his state of affairs, what he was absolutely sure of was that he wanted to be wherever this woman was. He surely wanted to kiss her again. This close, he could trace the gentle lines around her lips, because she smiled that damn much.

He could also imagine what else those lips could do.

"The meeting must have gone well." After one last squeeze to calm himself, he set her down, laughing.

"It went so, so well." Her excitement blew out in her words, chest rising with glee. "He said whenever we're ready to have his products, he'd do a special order for us. Can you imagine? Matching bandanas for parents and their pups? They're not currently in any storefronts, so if we go retail, Beachy would be the first. I told him I would send over the vendor contract later on today, when I get back into the office."

"That sounds exciting."

"It is. Now if only . . ." She bit her cheek.

"If only what?"

"If only we had a bigger space." She looked beyond him, to the beach, and shook her head. "Ugh. More serious stuff. I don't want to think of it right now. Did you take a ton of pictures?"

"I did." The way she pivoted gave him whiplash, but he relished it. She kept him on his toes; his spirit came alive with it. "It's just gorgeous here."

She tugged on his arm. "So . . . lemme see what you got."

"Oh, okay." He scrolled through his phone. "I really need to get a DSLR. This phone's not cutting it."

"But look at this one." She pointed one out from the gallery. "And this too." She had slinked an arm around his. "Jackson, you really have a talent. If you get a pro camera, does that mean you'll start doing pro work? Because I think you'd be great at it."

"Right. I'm nowhere that good."

Looking up at him with her deep-brown eyes, she added, "I mean it—don't sell yourself short. And you were amazing today with your feedback. I couldn't have done it without you." She beamed. "And now that I'm done with everything required, it's noodle time!"

Brimming with pride from her compliment, Jackson allowed himself to be dragged up the beach, but he thought twice about having to be out and about. They had two hours left on the road, not including short breaks and the ferry ride, and he didn't want to add to that. He wanted to be indoors, comfy, with Beatrice, to get to know her more, inside and out.

And as he watched her walking in front of him, sexy in her tight jeans, her exposed skin begging to be touched, Jackson's urge to be alone with Beatrice superseded food.

As she put on her leather jacket, he stepped in, clutching the two halves of the zipper pull. He connected the parts, pausing. "I have a proposition."

Her voice dipped. "What's your proposition?"

He zipped her up, admiring her fit. Beatrice in a leather jacket would always remain rent-free in his head. "How about we make the slow trek straight home and order in?"

"But the hand-pulled noodles . . ."

"Beatrice. The only kind of pulling I'm thinking of are your clothes. Off of you."

CHAPTER TEN

Hatteras, North Carolina

Current affirmation: I breathe through the unexpected.

Beatrice swooned. Literally. Heart thundering in her chest, and with the thought of them together and intimate, she said in a voice she didn't recognize, "Oh hell yes."

But shortly after the ferry ride, riding northbound on Highway 12, her mood plummeted. It had begun to sprinkle. And as she watched the occasional bead of water drop onto the leather of Jackson's jacket and streak down to its hem, all she could think of were her parents.

Marilyn and Joe Puso had died in a car accident in the rain. And while she'd never been triggered by storms as her brother Brandon still was, it didn't escape her that bad things happened on slick roads.

She tightened her grip around Jackson's waist, and she steadied her breathing. The last thing she wanted was to distract him, but her head swirled with images. Nervous energy skittered across her skin.

The bike slowed. She opened her eyes. Up ahead was a sign for Avon, which meant they were still about forty-five minutes from Nags Head, and in front of them was a line of red lights.

An accident. It had to be.

Then, the sky opened up, and rain came down in sheets. In front of her, Jackson's head swiveled.

She was getting soaked.

Jackson said something Beatrice couldn't discern; he squeezed her hand, bringing it up to his chest. Seconds later, he made a U-turn and took the first right to a covered parking area under a beach house. A house marker denoted that it was a bed-and-breakfast, and a neon sign hung on its front window read VACANCY. Best of all, it had an expansive wraparound porch.

She jumped off the bike and rushed toward the bed-and-breakfast's covered porch, giddy with relief. She removed her helmet. It had gotten dark, and the sounds of the road, the ocean, and the rain echoed into one chamber of chaos. "Oh my God. That was wild."

Jackson's helmet was off, and he ran his fingers through his hair. "I didn't expect for it to come down like that."

"Me either." Then hesitation descended. They were on private property. "Do you think they'll let us hang out here?"

"Probably not, but we can ask for forgiveness later. As soon as the rain settles and the accident clears, we can head down the road slow but sure. But right now? Being out there's asking for trouble."

She began to shiver at the thought, so she crossed her arms across her chest.

He rubbed her shoulders down. "Are you cold?"

"No, it's not the cold . . . that was a lot."

His expression fell. "I'm sorry. I've been riding for a while. I take it for granted that I know what to expect. I should have pulled over as soon as it started to sprinkle."

"Ahem," a voice said on their right, and Beatrice gasped, spinning toward it. It was an older, fair-skinned man with ruddy cheeks and facial hair. He wore a flannel and jeans. "Checking in?"

"Sir, we were wondering if we could hang out until . . ." Jackson gestured to the rain coming down in sheets.

The man winced. "I'm sorry, y'all, but no can do. We can't have loiterers, or people'll just be hanging out whenever they want, and we're really trying to run a good establishment."

"We can go somewhere else, Jackson," Beatrice suggested. "Maybe a restaurant down the road?"

The thunder answered her.

"I've got one room left," the proprietor said. "It's pretty and comfortable and warm. You guys are soaked, and it comes with complimentary robes and a food platter. So you can dry off and eat, and we can throw your clothes in the dryer. I've got a police scanner at the front desk, and I can let you know when the traffic clears."

Just then, another car pulled up, headlights dimming. The driver's side window rolled down, and a voice called out, "Still have room?"

The proprietor's gaze darted to Beatrice. She looked up at Jackson, who raised his eyebrows. "Your call."

She heaved a breath. "Getting out of these wet clothes sounds pretty good."

The proprietor waved the driver off. "Sorry, man, no vacancy."

Ten minutes later, Beatrice, with their room key in hand, climbed the staircase. It creaked with each step, the home showing the signs of wear, though it was neat and clean. Their room was on the third floor. Jackson followed behind, first grabbing water bottles from the kitchen.

After she stuck the key in the lock, the door opened to a heart-shaped bed covered in a red fuzzy comforter, with red and white pillows piled at the head.

Beatrice cackled at the gaudy furnishings.

"We should be getting room service soon . . ." Jackson's voice trailed off as he entered the room, stopping at the threshold. He was as still as a statue, jaw slackened. "That is . . . red."

Beatrice laughed even harder. She clutched her belly at what a weird day this had been, at the rise and fall of emotions she'd experienced even in the last hour. And how this man was giving her all the adventure and pivots and twists and turns that she thrived on.

And based on the mortified look on his face, he hadn't even been trying.

"We don't have to stay here if this is too uncomfortable," he offered. "There isn't even a desk where we can set down the room service."

She sat on the bed, bounced on it for good measure. "We can eat on the bed. No big deal, right?"

"Um . . . right." He piled the water bottles on the bedside table without looking at her. "Do you want to get out of your clothes first? So we can have them throw it in the dryer?" His cheeks reddened. "Not that I want you to undress or anything. I mean . . . you're just wet . . . from the rain."

Beatrice tried to disguise the whole situation with a giggle—Jackson had reverted back to his shy self—but as she went to the bathroom, goose bumps erupted on her skin.

The last time she'd been intimate with a man was . . . a long time ago.

Now that she was thinking about how long ago that was, it was really pathetic, because it wasn't for the lack of trying. It was just that as soon as she started to think that a relationship was going somewhere, it ended with unmet expectations.

She slipped her phone out of her soaked jeans. A slew of texts was on her lock screen. From her brothers, from Kim. A couple of pictures from Cathy of Roxy and her at the beach. Something about extra property, and Papadakis unhappy about being displaced, an update from Leila's camp.

Her head spun with information being pushed at her through the screen. Knowing that 100 percent of these people required a response ASAP, she wrote, copied, and pasted a generic response to all her messages: Got sidelined on 12 because of an accident on the road. Hanging out in Avon until it clears. Will respond soon.

Then, she worked at peeling off her clothes, which threatened to remain stuck on her body. Her nervous energy caused her to shiver as she donned the hotel's plush white robe, hands shaking while double knotting the ties.

Beatrice's phone buzzed with a text, like someone had heard her thoughts. The sender: Jessie Puso.

Jessie:
The rain is coming down hard.
Jessie:
If you're not on the road yet, wait a bit. The rain's pretty bad up here at the resort
Jessie:
Just LMK you're safe

Beatrice exhaled a long breath, letting go of the tension in her chest. It made no sense that a text from Jessie was exactly the thing to comfort her, as if she and Jessie were the way they used to be.

But it was.

Beatrice:
We got off the road.

Jessie:
And you're safe with him?

Beatrice:
Yes

Jessie:
Will you tell me where you are? Just for my nerves.

Beatrice sent her the B&B's location. And because Jessie was right there, at her disposal, and seemed to be a willing ear, she ventured another step.

Beatrice:

He's so nice. Like this could be something.

But I'm out of practice

Jessie:

<3 You deserve a good person

Jessie:

You don't need practice. You just need to keep your heart open

Beatrice's face warmed with Jessie's simple message, because she had been there through Beatrice's failed relationships. She knew that, at the heart of it, Beatrice had a hard time with emotional intimacy because she had lost enough people in her life. Beatrice could party with the best of them—hell, she was the party planner—but couldn't for the life of her get her own stuff straight.

Keep my heart open.

Beatrice:

Thank you

Jessie:

I'm a text away

She stuffed her wet clothing in the laundry bag and launched herself out into the bedroom.

Jackson had stripped out of his leather jacket, and he was kicking off his shoes. In his white T-shirt once more, just as he had been on the beach, he looked rugged, sexy, and absolutely snuggle-worthy.

When he looked up as she padded in, the heat of his gaze almost made her stumble.

Then, she noticed the bed. "Oh, you took off the red comforter."

His gaze darted to it, folded and placed on the ground. "It was . . . too much."

"Agreed. Well . . . your turn. In the bathroom. The laundry bag is hanging behind the door." Beatrice busied herself by getting on the bed and folding her feet under her. It felt a little awkward sitting there. Or maybe it was his vibe she was picking up? Whatever it was, she grabbed the remote control to distract herself. "I'll find something on TV while you change."

"Good idea." He passed her, keeping a hefty distance, and entered the bathroom. At the click of the lock, Beatrice focused on a good channel to pass the time.

Unlike Beatrice, Jackson was in and out of the bathroom quickly. In his robe, he hung the bag outside their door. Then he turned and cleared his throat. "Is it okay if I sit with you?"

"Yes, Jackson. Of course."

But when Jackson climbed on, it became all the more apparent how small the bed was, especially because of its shape.

As if reading her mind, Jackson asked, "How big do you think this bed is. A queen?"

"I'd say it's a half queen," she noted.

"Or a full and a half."

"There's definitely no room for the Holy Spirit."

He laughed. "I mean, it *is* the honeymoon suite."

"I think *suite* is pushing it."

There was a knock on the door, followed with someone saying, "Room service!"

"I'll get it." Jackson jumped up to answer, and after a brief interaction with the person outside, he turned around carrying a silver platter. He was also sporting a cheesy expression. "It's our complimentary food platter."

Beatrice could detect sugar straightaway. "Oooo, show me."

He set it down. The platter itself was heart shaped, with strawberries, melons, marshmallows, and other treats surrounding a bowl of warm chocolate.

"They also offered to come back with champagne, but I declined."

"Thank you. I actually don't drink."

"Ah. Okay." He looked behind him, at the TV. "Can I flip the channel?"

She handed him the remote. While standing, he switched to the news channel. Sure enough, there was a multicar accident on 12, and the live broadcast showed that it was soon clearing.

"Good thing we're here. It's still raining pretty hard," Jackson said.

Beatrice's tummy grumbled. "Do you mind if I get started?"

He did a double take. "Please, go ahead."

She took a bite out of the strawberry, and her eyes shut at its sweetness. "This is just so delicious. The strawberries are perfectly ripe." She tried the marshmallow next. "Oh my gosh, even better. How did they know that I'm a chocoholic?" And little by little, as her blood sugar rose, her spirits lightened.

Until she noticed that Jackson had not moved and was staring stiffly at a commercial on TV. "Jackson, do you want some?"

He put the remote control down on the bed next to her. "You know what? I think I'm going to hang out downstairs." He shuffled to the bathroom.

"Um." She frowned and went to the closed door. "What? Why?"

"I'm . . . it just might be better. I can . . . shoot. They have our clothes." Seconds later, the door opened to Jackson with a pained look on his face.

"Did I do something? What?"

His eyeballs rolled to the ceiling. "No. You didn't do anything at all. But with you in your robe and me in mine, and the strawberries . . . I . . ."

Then, like the sun's slow rise in the morning, so rose Beatrice's understanding. Her gaze dropped down to where his hands were clasped demurely in front of him.

A gasp escaped her lips. *Oh.*

♡

Jackson wasn't that guy—the guy who couldn't keep his emotions and libido in check. That guy who could put inadvertent pressure on a woman. That guy who wasn't respectful.

But here he was in a robe with a hard-on looking at this gorgeous woman who he'd imagined undressing and making love to more times than he'd like to admit.

"I know we planned for a night in," he jumped in to explain. "And I was ready for that, in your house or mine. But this room and that damn bed, knowing you're practically naked under that robe, and the noises you were making while eating . . ." He inhaled. "I didn't want to pressure you."

He braced himself for her reaction. A shove out the door, a right hook to the face, a tongue-lashing maybe (though the thought of her tongue wasn't helping the situation).

To his surprise, she took a step toward him, and then a second. Lips slightly parted, she grasped hold of his robe's knot, grazing his erection, and tugged him to her.

His knees almost buckled at the contact, at the sudden press of her bottom half to his. "Beatrice." He gripped her waist. His mind was already swimming, deep in all the things he wanted to do to her. But their secret . . . they had to talk about what this meant.

"Don't say let's go slow. Or that we need to talk. Or think about things. Because I don't want that." Her hands climbed the lapel of his robe, and with every inch, the desire in him heightened. "I want you to kiss me," she demanded.

Pros: Kissing her would please her. It's going to feel so good.

Cons: I might not want to stop when I start.

Jackson wrapped a hand around the back of her neck, and went for the underside of her jaw first. It had begged for his attention all day. He ran a tongue down the line of her jaw and then took her bottom lip.

She moaned into his mouth, and knowing that he was doing this, that he was giving her this simple pleasure, encouraged him to go further. "On the bed," he commanded.

She hummed a yes, and he led her, lips still locked in a kiss. Her hands worked quickly against the knot of his robe as they made their way to the bedroom, though he struggled with hers. Impatient, and after he helped her lie on her back, he spilled the front of the robe open to roam his hands against her silky skin, cupping her underwear-clad bottom. But it wasn't enough; he wanted to get closer.

"I double knotted it. I'll undo it . . . ," she said.

Jackson let up so she could work on her robe, and he shrugged off his. Below him, Beatrice smiled. "Hi. Look at you."

That appreciative look made him glad for every second he'd put his body through, but her progress had stalled on the knot. He took over the endeavor. "I want to see you."

Finally, thankfully, he loosened the damn thing, and her robe fell open in a lush cascade, exposing the curves of her beautiful body.

"Come here." She reached up with both arms. And when he obliged, falling into her kiss, it felt both familiar and new.

Beatrice wasn't shy in her foreplay; she was exactly as she was out in the world. Playful. Energetic. She roved her hands over his abdomen, testing his willpower by trailing her hand down under the band of his underwear, to where he was hard, for her.

Jackson gasped, loving the strength of her grip. "When you thought about me, did you think of this?" He palmed her breasts, caressing and licking, until she moaned. "The way you felt in my hands and in my mouth haunted me for days. My only regret was that I didn't get to hear you scream my name."

Beatrice sucked in a breath, and it was everything. "I did think of this. I've been thinking of this ever since our first date."

"No more thinking." He nestled himself in between her legs, enamored with the way her eyes fluttered with desire. "Just doing."

They picked up from where they'd left off in Vegas. They tumbled on every inch of the tiny heart-shaped bed, which creaked with each of their movements. And in between the occasional giggle at said creaking were the sounds of two people on the fast road to sex.

But the room phone rang, and it sliced the moment in half. They swiveled their heads to look at the phone on the bedside table. Of course it was heart shaped too.

"Should we get that?" she asked in between heaving breaths.

Jackson scoured his brain for an answer. All of him was mush, and it took a second to form words. "We should. Could be about the traffic."

"Right. We have to go home." She fell back onto the pillow, and combed her hair back with her fingers.

"Don't do that. I like you disheveled."

"Pilyo," she crooned, play-hitting him on the chest.

He arched an eyebrow.

"That means *naughty.*"

"Oh, yes, that's my new favorite Tagalog word." He bore down his pelvis against hers just to show Beatrice that he wasn't done with her yet, to her sudden gasp. Then, he called on his fortitude so he could detach himself to reach the bedside table, then hooked the phone receiver with a finger. "Hello." His voice was hoarse with misspent energy.

"Mr. Hill. It's the front desk."

"Yes?" Jackson nodded at Beatrice, to let her know that she'd been correct in her guess. She pressed her lips into a regretful smile, though she ran a hand through his hair. It was an intimate and sensual gesture, and he kissed the top of her nose. She smiled up in surprise.

"The traffic cleared. Just wanted to let you know. And the rain's stopped."

Jackson was distracted by Beatrice, who was tracing shapes on his chest, like she was leaving him a secret message.

"Mr. Hill?"

"Yes, cleared. Stopped. Thank you." Then he hung up, because Beatrice was now kissing his Adam's apple, and he was seconds from combusting. "Bea."

"Yes?" Her breath was hot against his neck.

"Road's clear. Weather's clear."

"Oh, that's great."

Except her tone didn't register as sincere.

"Should we go home?" He flipped her around so she was above him, legs relaxed on each side of him in an easy straddle. It was to get her to focus, though it worked against him because the view of her on top would absolutely be his undoing. "Or, should we spend the night?"

Jackson wanted Beatrice to make the call; he couldn't be trusted with this decision because his inclination at this moment was to cancel his entire week.

As she inhaled, her thoughts played across her face. Jackson detected the moment she decided because regret flitted in her eyes. "We should go home. Roxy needs me. I have work, and so do you. What do you think?"

"I think it's going to be painful to have to detach myself from you."

"We don't have to do that right this second. We can keep going." She dipped down and kissed Jackson's neck. The strands of her hair splayed across his chest, making him hiss with a growing hunger to be with her, and in her.

It made it hard for him to say his next words. He buried a hand in her hair, feeling the silky strands, coercing her to meet his eyes. He was desperate to be with her, but he wanted to do things right and make it the best it could be despite the circumstances. "When we finally make love, I don't want to be rushed. I want to take my time with you. I want to have my way with you and give you everything you need."

"Jackson, you saying that won't make me be more patient."

He laughed.

She plopped down to rest her chin against his chest. "I guess we have to be responsible adults. But maybe one more kiss?"

"I can do that."

It took another hour and at least two missed calls from his mother before they could extricate themselves from that heart-shaped bed, then another hour to get back to Nags Head. Beatrice picked up Roxy from his place, and he walked her back to her house, with a promise to text.

On cloud nine, Jackson floated through the front door to find his mother making tea. Tea, and it was after nine at night. Cathy Hill didn't take anything but water after dinnertime because it gave her heartburn.

"Ma?" He grabbed a soda from the fridge. Something told him that his constitution would need fortifying.

She gestured to the stack of papers in front of her—the printout from his Heart Resort research from a couple of nights ago. Then, she fished out a page and tapped a finger on Beatrice's picture. "I didn't mean to pry, but I read the words 'Willow Tree,' and curiosity took over."

His breath left his body. "What did you deduce?"

"Enough to know that your relationship with Beatrice is going to cause a whole lot of conflict." She shook her head. "What kind of luck is it to meet such an ideal woman, only for it to be . . . Jackson, dear God . . . she knows who you are, right?"

"She does." He leaned back against the counter and crossed his arms. Not out of anger but to hold himself. "She doesn't blame me for anything McCauley's done."

"And yet. You understand how this is a sticky situation."

He nodded.

Cathy shook her head. "I don't know about this. I was already worried about you working for that man, but with Beatrice involved . . . this is risky."

He looked at his mother intently. "Beatrice and I spent time talking about this, and we agreed to an arrangement, to keep things secret."

"And you're okay with that."

"Yes, for a little while. We're just getting to know one another." He pushed down the nausea that crept up from the pit of his belly. He had to trust Beatrice. And, their secret was temporary, and wasn't due to shame. "We're going with the flow."

"I've never known you to go with the flow. And what happens if your father finds out about this? Dillon can be vindictive. Obviously. It's right there in all those papers."

"He hasn't said anything about Heart Resort thus far, so that all might be in the past." Again with the nausea, because his father didn't have to have a reason to hurt people. Jackson was, after all, the example and product of it.

She grumbled. "I'm worried about Beatrice too. When her family finds out, they're sure to make her choose. And if she does . . . have you considered that maybe she might decide to choose her family?"

"I haven't asked her to choose."

"By simply continuing this relationship, you are making each other choose."

"That's enough, Ma." He braced himself against the countertop, to contain his rising temper. Cathy Hill always told the truth. She didn't sugarcoat the facts. And in this case, she was simply saying aloud what had become a thought spiral ever since he'd found out who she was.

He had to have faith. In Beatrice, in their relationship.

Dammit. He shook his head. "I'm sorry for snapping back. This is all going to work out, okay?"

"Okay." Cathy sighed. "Beatrice is a lovely woman, and you're *my* son. I just want the both of you to be happy."

He was grateful for the break in the conversation. "I *am* happy. What I am more of, though, is exhausted."

The kettle whistled, and she turned off the stove.

"You going to bed soon?" he asked.

"In a bit. I'd like to sit out on the balcony a few minutes."

He nodded. "Lonnie and I are meeting up in the morning. So if you hear me rustling first thing, it's why."

"All right, honey."

Jackson was midstride when his mother called his name.

"Jack," she said. "Whenever you see Dillon, please be careful? He's a charming man."

"I'm not easily fooled, Ma, but thanks." Then, he was promptly distracted when a text from Beatrice buzzed in.

Beatrice:
Got out of the shower and I'm sopping wet
Beatrice:
Giselle's coming over in twenty minutes. Wanna make out before she gets here?

Jackson spun around and beelined out the door, belatedly waving a goodbye to his mother, with sleep the furthest thing from his mind.

CHAPTER ELEVEN

Heart Resort, North Carolina

Today's affirmation: I am focused through distraction.

Chris called for a meeting early Monday morning, and while taking notes on her iPad, Beatrice squirmed in her seat, muscles sore from her and Jackson's long ride on Saturday.

She was also antsy. A slew of Beachy admin was waiting for her. Their socials, inquiries from vendors who wanted to work with them, and their burgeoning space had to be tended to. In addition to fulfilling subscription-box orders.

A notification flashed on her phone.

Jackson:
Free tonight? I miss my riding partner

She didn't hesitate in texting back.

Beatrice:
I miss riding too.

> **Beatrice:**
> And yes I'm free

Jackson:
Oh Beatrice. Pilyo

Her face erupted into flames, and images from the weekend rushed back, of the creaking heart-shaped bed at the B&B and their hot twenty-minute make-out session that had left her a flustered, bumbling mess in time for inventory. The weekend had felt like a long vacation, an escape from reality.

Jackson:
Don't tempt me to kidnap you from Heart Resort
Jackson:
Two days is too long

> **Beatrice:**
> I'm worth the wait.

Jackson:
I know you are. I waited five years.
I suppose I can suffer through another day

> **Beatrice:**
> I miss you though xoxo

Jackson:
That's it. I'm coming to get you. They'll let me in right?

She kept a grin from bursting forth. Sunday had been a wash in terms of their plans. Jackson had been caught up with work in the morning, and in the evening, Beatrice had been summoned to the resort by Izzy and Kitty for a movie night. She, of course, hadn't declined, but she'd ended up spending the night in her apartment.

Beatrice:
To hell with this rivalry!

Jackson:
To hell with it!

Beatrice pressed her lips into a line.

Beatrice:
Sigh. If only it was that easy.

Jackson:
😣

Jackson:
How about tonight at seven? I'll come get you.

Beatrice:
I'll be there with bells on.

Beatrice:
Or maybe nothing on.

She bit her lip.

Jackson:
Dang woman, you're going to kill me

"Ahem? Bea?" Chris's voice snapped her out of her thoughts. She looked up from her phone to her brother across the room, who was perched on his mahogany desk.

Faces were turned her way: Chris and Gil and their assistants. Kim, who was seated in the periphery of the room, answering emails on a laptop. And all wore serious expressions.

Her runaway libido ducked from his interrogating expression. "Sorry, can you repeat that? I was looking through my notes."

To her right, Gil snickered.

She rolled her eyes at him.

Chris sported a thin-lipped, deadpan expression. "Leila's camp contacted me yesterday, following up for more information about the retreat. Because you hadn't reached out yet."

"But"—her gaze darted between her brothers—"it's only been one business day, Kuya Chris. With our other clients, our response times vary between forty-eight to seventy-two hours."

"This is Leila, and my expectation was that you'd contact her right away, so . . . please." He looked at her pointedly.

She suppressed a sigh. "On it, Kuya."

"Which leads me to our next topic. Leila updated her numbers for her entourage, well more than we can accommodate on the resort since all the houses are full. And we heard that Papadakis was upset about being displaced, so we came up with a solution . . ." Chris stood and crossed his arms. "Gil?"

Gil nodded. "We have been in discussion about pursuing off-site quarters."

Beatrice frowned at the second time the word *we* was used. The word *we* was reserved for all the siblings. "Did I . . . did I miss a meeting?"

Chris's face remained neutral. "No. It was an idea that Gil came up with last night, and I agreed."

Gil spoke. "Time is of the essence. Heart Resort's capacity has been reached. And we think it's time to expand, into property management."

The room fell into silence, though an objection burst forth from Beatrice's chest. Her voice echoed when she said, "This is huge. A completely different business model."

Chris nodded. "Yes, and we'd like to move on it immediately. For now, we need a short-term solution to the lack of additional housing. It would have benefitted us, for example, when we had family members come for Brandon and Geneva's wedding. We could have given them a discounted rate, and then taken advantage of another source of income. Leila's entourage will need accommodations. In the long term, if her caliber of people become our clients, we'll need space for their assistants. It's also for clients like Papadakis, as Gil mentioned, who might want an optional experience and still partake in Heart Resort programming and amenities."

It made a lot of sense, so Beatrice took a breath to move past her initial surprise. "That means we'll need to hire more people to manage that off-site location. Who's the director in charge of that?"

"Brandon said he would spearhead it," Gil said. "He has a real estate agent contact who's available to show properties when he and Geneva return from their honeymoon."

Beatrice bit her cheek; so Brandon had already been consulted.

She of the four was last to know.

Which was fine, she guessed, despite the sliver of jealousy that had wriggled its way up her spine.

She shouldn't have been upset—she was the last person to demand transparency when she ran so much of her life independently. But to be left out felt personal. "What do you need from me for this project?"

"Nothing, for now. This was all just a major FYI to everyone in the circle. We won't be advertising a thing until we find a place that's suitable. What we do need is for you to deal with Leila ASAP. You've had the requirements a few days now, and we need actual movement on the arrangements. So . . . I'd like to be cc'd on all your correspondence," Chris added.

She frowned. "That's not necessary. I can handle her myself."

He shook his head. "Again, this is different."

"All right." Except the voice that came out of her was strangled. She gripped her Apple Pencil so the pads of her fingers were white, and she reminded herself to relax. This was her big brother's way of putting her in check, and she was going to allow it.

"Bea."

Chris's voice yanked her out of her silence.

"You look like you have thoughts on the matter."

"No, I understand." Her answer came swiftly and without hesitation, because she wouldn't let them see her flustered. "I'll reach out to her contact person ASAP."

The rest of the meeting finished up, and after, as their assistants left, Beatrice gathered her things, all with a knot in her belly. She was fretting over nothing, right? Yes, they'd always bickered among themselves, but they'd proven time and again that they had each other's backs. They were good.

"Bea."

"Yes, Kuya?" She lifted her face to Chris, who was sitting on the leather couch, an arm resting along the back. It was his relaxed look, which meant they were off the clock. Gil remained in the room and shut the door.

"I've . . . noticed."

She steadied her voice. "Noticed what?"

He looked down for a beat. "That you're barely here, and when you are, you've been distracted."

She plastered on a smile, though bitterness rose. She rolled her eyes at her middle brother, sitting silently in the corner. "Let me guess. Kuya Gil told on me."

"That's not fair," Gil said. "My concerns are legitimate."

Chris raised a hand to silence their brother, then turned to Beatrice. "I know there's conflict between you and Jessie and that's coloring his opinion. But today . . . I think there might be some truth to what he says." He leaned forward. "You take on a lot. It's what you do. It's how you thrive, and I don't want to squash your process. But what I'm getting from you is a different energy."

Beatrice relaxed, now hearing her brother's tone and seeing his expression. Unlike Gil, who'd come at her with a frontal assault, Chris was concerned, and for that she was thankful.

"My energy is different because it's scattered. There's a lot going on." Beatrice swallowed the lump in her throat, because there would be no avoiding this. "There's something I've wanted to tell all of you, Brandon included. I actually wanted to wait until he returned."

"I don't think stalling is going to help," Gil piped up.

"I'm not stalling." And yet, Beatrice bristled at the lie. She was the queen of stalling. So she started with their first concern. "I'm barely here because I've been spending time at Beachy or at . . ." The words lodged themselves in her throat. "My house in Nags Head."

Gil left the corner and plopped down next to Chris. "Wait a hot minute. You have investment property?"

She shook her head. "Not investment. Primary residential. It's where I've been staying."

What came were seconds of silence.

"I . . ." Chris frowned. "How long now?"

"A year."

"What the f—"

"I bought it on a feeling, Kuya. Like Heart Resort. The opportunity presented itself, and I didn't want to leave my inheritance just sitting in a bank. It's the perfect place. The sunrises are gorgeous. Mom would have loved it." At the hardened faces of her brothers, she cobbled together the speech that she'd planned time and again though failed to express. "I know I should have told you guys a year ago, but so many things were going on. And I wasn't really staying there all that much. But now that there's so much Beachy product, which is another thing I need to update you both about—the both of you and Brandon—the house has become one of my shipping locations, and sometimes it just makes sense for me to sleep there . . ."

Chris pressed his fingers against the bridge of his nose. "A year . . ."

"It sounds worse than it really is."

"No, it *is* worse," Gil remarked matter-of-factly. "A year is enough time and opportunity to tell us."

"I'm sorry. I didn't know how to approach this because Beachy's rolled up in all of it. Like I said, I started spending more nights there because Beachy is growing. Kuya Chris, you would be proud of it."

Chris bore the half smile of curiosity and weariness. "I am proud. I see what you and Geneva are doing. Eden says your ads are everywhere on Instagram."

"We also have twenty-three retailers that carry our housewares."

"That's great. And your subscription business is growing too."

"That's right. And we've got plans to expand—"

"Before you say anything else, Bea," he whispered, and a pause settled between them. She detected the beginning of her brother's judgment. He was everything but subtle. He approached everything on a straight road, the complete opposite of her.

So she knew what he was going to say next.

His voice was steady. "Am I shocked that you've had property all this time without telling us? Yes. Not going to lie; I'm hurt more than anything."

Guilt laced up her spine. "Kuya—"

"But." Chris shot Gil a look to mitigate a comment. "I've always said that I don't need to know about everything you're doing. I respect your privacy. And I'd hoped that in the last year, I afforded that. You buying property with your own money and not telling the family isn't a deal breaker for me. On the same token, I don't need to know about everything you're doing for Beachy, so long as you're doing what you need to do for the resort. Beachy is your business, literally, and not mine. But. I need to make sure you know what your priority is."

Gil crossed his arms in what she could tell was solidarity.

Chris continued. "Each of us has the entrepreneurial spirit. You especially. You've always had it. But this thing with Leila is a big deal. This isn't about one-upping another resort, though that is always on my mind, but it's to take Heart Resort, and us, to a level that will lead us to sustainability. If this was any other guest, we could drag our feet. We can make a few mistakes. We can lag on communication. We can even delegate communication with clients to an assistant—yes, Beatrice, I know about that too." His nose flared with discontent. "But this is Leila. Which means there's no time to be distracted. Got it?"

Beatrice nodded eagerly. "Of course. I'm going to give this my best."

He nodded. "Good. You have a gift, with people. You're the director of client relations because you have the ability to substantiate the cost of this resort. Customer service is above all, and you are the lead. And you're a natural at it. We're lucky to have you."

"I appreciate it, Kuya," Beatrice said, meaning every word. She liked being thanked and valued, but she braced herself for his final decree.

"All that to say, before expanding, really evaluate what that means, and if you, yourself, can handle it. And since Heart Resort is already expanding in a way, I'd like for your focus to be on Heart Resort's expansion first. We need you here. You are indispensable."

It was the final word, the last swing of the hammer. Chris's orders.

He was commanding her not to expand Beachy.

"I agree with everything that's been said," Gil added.

Great. "I guess I've got my marching orders." She stood to leave, stunned. His expectation was that Heart Resort would be her first priority. Because she was critical to their team. Which all made sense and yet left her incensed.

As she walked out of the office, Gil called out, "What's your house's name?"

Every home they'd lived in from when they were children had been named Puso. The resort's home and buildings were named too—and it had been Gil's idea, as part of continuing tradition.

"I don't have one yet," she said over her shoulder. Truthfully, she hadn't even thought about it—with her shuttling back and forth.

"That tells you that Puso and Heart Resort is still your home, Bea."

♡

With the wind blowing against his face, on a boat toward the next island to tour, Jackson pressed on the star icon on his phone screen to bookmark another federal job on the USAJobs website, this time for a project manager for the research and development department of the Veterans Affairs. It was for a job he wasn't quite sure he was qualified for, but he was at *that* point in this whole job-search process. Like throwing spaghetti against a wall and hoping something would stick.

For the record, he thought he would've been coasting by the age of forty. That life would've been set by now. But these days were proving otherwise; instead, he was discomforted by the unknown—namely, what he wanted to be when he grew up. What he did know: working for his father was not *it*.

It also wasn't lost on Jackson that if he no longer worked for his father, there would be a greater chance for him and Beatrice to be together. Being with Beatrice felt more right with each day, each moment, and even each text. And to think they hadn't yet made love. Yet.

At the thought, his body kicked on like a furnace.

As the boat slowed, Jackson's phone buzzed with an email—solicitation from a veteran-friendly university in North Carolina. "Part time to your passion," was what it read.

These ads had a way of finding him, much like how he had once had an errant thought about buying a newer helmet, and lo and behold, he'd been fed an ad on Facebook.

Usually, he didn't click on these university ads. He already had a bachelor's degree, and a master's degree in risk management sounded like the pits, to be honest. But the supposed soldier on the image—sporting a high and tight and wearing his camo uniform—had a camera strap around his neck, and Jackson's curiosity got the better of him.

The ad funneled him to East Carolina's art department, to the list of majors he could take. He snickered aloud. An art degree, at his age, and without having any real experience doing art?

"You're too old for this," he told the words on his screen.

"What's that?" Lonnie plopped into the seat next to him and peered down at his phone. He had the audacity to dress like a skipper—navy-blue polo, khaki pants, and a ridiculous skipper's hat, just for kicks.

Jackson clicked the screen so it went dark.

"Aw, is that on the down low too?" Lonnie chided. When Jackson stood—the boat had docked—Lonnie added, "Why so sensitive?"

"It's called privacy."

"We're brothers, though."

Jackson snorted, though a tiny portion of him wished that he could share more about his thoughts. But this was Lonnie, and only time would tell if he could be trusted.

Forty minutes later, after a very in-depth island tour, he and Lonnie stood with Peter at the rocky edge of the island. Across the sound was the outline of Duck and the occasional commercial fishing boat bobbing on the water.

"What do you think?" Peter prompted.

"It's great, except that it doesn't fit the minimum square-footage requirement," Jackson said.

"But it's private," Lonnie insisted. His brother picked up a rock and slung it across the water, and it skipped three times. "I think we should put it on the list for Dad. It's gorgeous here. And of all the island properties we've visited, this has the most promise."

"McCauley was specific," Jackson said. "He wanted at least a hundred square miles, and this is barely seventy-five square miles. Wild Oats is a hundred and fifty square miles, and the programs are packed. This place would barely fit the guests and the activities."

Wild Oats was a Willow Tree resort in South Carolina.

Lonnie chortled. "Oh, my dear brother. The most important criteria has everything to do with that up there." He gestured to the land formation just beyond the sight line. "Heart Resort."

Protectiveness, fear, and confusion rushed him and filled his ears. "What do you mean by that?"

"Why don't I leave the both of you to chat," Peter offered. "I'll get the boat ready for whenever you're done."

As soon as Peter's figure crested the hill and disappeared, Lonnie ran a hand through his dark hair. "Look, our father can say that this is for another adult summer-camp project, but I don't believe it."

"Why not?"

"Why not? Because." He did a double take. "Because he doesn't quit. When he sets his eyes on a target, he won't give up until he's shot it right in the bull's-eye. I bet he's setting up a couples resort."

"I don't understand this rivalry. At all." His chest was feeling all kinds of tight. It was followed by a sinking feeling that his and Beatrice's relationship was stuck, if not doomed, unless he did something about it. She'd put her trust in him, and he had to protect her.

His brother continued to explain the Heart Resort and Willow Tree turf war, all of which Jackson had researched. "But yeah," Lonnie said, "I bet there's more to this than what he's letting on."

"Well . . . we should go." Jackson wanted off this island. With the pier and that *something more* as his destination, he trudged toward it.

A call with their father would be his next step.

"Good idea. We'll need to lock this island down before someone else does." Lonnie scurried after him.

As they boarded the boat, Peter asked, "So, what do you think? Is this going on the list?"

"Maybe." Jackson avoided his brother's glare, but he had to do everything to direct their father away from Heart Resort. "What other options do we have for a private water view, with a total square footage of one hundred square miles?"

"I'll need to head back to the drawing board, but I'm confident I can find some options." He beamed. "You might even have better luck in isolated properties rather than stand-alone islands—there's just more inventory on the market."

"Our father wanted exclusivity." Lonnie took out his phone, sinking into one of the seats. He looked up periodically from texting as the boat backed up from the slip.

"I'll definitely keep that in mind as a priority," Peter said.

As the boat sped up, Jackson's belly twisted with nausea, but it had nothing to do with seasickness. He kept his gaze on the horizon to steady himself.

Lonnie moved closer to him. "Something's up."

"Nothing's up, Lon."

"You and your secrets, Jackson."

Secrets. That damn S-word. Jackson gripped the side of the boat. He'd prided himself on his transparency, his truthfulness. How had he gone from that to an NDA to a secret affair?

"Lon, do you think . . . that McCauley'll ever ease up on Heart Resort?"

He reared back slightly. "Why do you ask that?"

"Just curious."

He rubbed his chin with a hand. "Dad won't stop until he has the actual resort."

Goose bumps flourished on the back of his neck. "The actual land?"

"The land bridge, the buildings, all of it. And he doesn't care what he needs to do to get it, or who he needs to involve or pressure. My wife's brother works for Heart Resort, and Dad even tried to poach him—can you even? It's messy. That drama almost cost me my marriage."

"I'm sorry. I had no idea."

"Anyway, this rivalry isn't going anywhere. If anything, it's heating up. Nags Head is the Pusos' de facto hometown now, and you can assume that the people you or your mother meet either work or are friends with Heart Resort people. After that exposé, people are starting to take sides." His eyes widened. "Holy . . ."

"What?"

"Your NDA."

"What about it?"

Lonnie looked away with a stricken expression. "I hate to be the bearer of the truth, but I bet my life savings that you're here because no one knows you. Much easier for you to snatch up a sweet property for Willow Tree, right under the Pusos' noses."

I guarantee nothing is happening against Heart Resort. Jackson recalled what he'd told Beatrice that first afternoon. Had he unknowingly lied? Had he trusted his father too easily like his mother had all those years ago?

They were going at high speed back to the mainland, and Jackson looked off in the distance, at the beauty of the water, and he remembered a heart-to-heart conversation with his mother long ago. He'd been getting into trouble at school. He hadn't understood how he was living in poverty but his father wasn't. The internet hadn't been great at the time, but a thirteen-year-old in a library could do some damage. His father's last name had been easy enough to look up.

Cathy had said that she'd been swept up by the beauty of the Outer Banks as well as this magnanimous figure of a person named Dillon McCauley III. She hadn't bothered to ask him if he was attached. Nor had he thought to tell her that he certainly had been. She had trusted him. And when she'd approached McCauley with the pregnancy five months later, he'd all but rebuffed her.

She'd sent him photos of Jackson—he was a spitting image of McCauley—and every once in a while, McCauley had sent money, though not regularly. Otherwise, McCauley had been an absent father, until somehow, he'd found a way to get ahold of Jackson at his last duty station, offering him an olive branch and a job after retirement.

As if that was supposed to heal the previous three-plus decades.

Still, Jackson had trusted him.

He'd been glad to have been offered a job because he'd never gone without one since he was fourteen and biked his first paper route. And a part of him had wanted to circle the man and the family who'd all but shunned him, and to show them that he'd done just fine without them.

But what if he was being used?

Jackson was grateful for the wind and the whir of the boat's engine to distract him from the resurgence of his bitterness.

As they neared shore, his phone buzzed.

Beatrice:
I have to cancel tonight.

Jackson:
Bummer. Everything ok?

Beatrice:
So much Heart Resort stuff. Headed to Beachy but have to come right back here

Beatrice:
Spending the night with the fam

Jackson debated asking what was wrong. But maybe this was a good opportunity to take a breath, and instead of ringing up McCauley to talk to him about Heart Resort, he could ask him in person.

Jackson:
Reschedule? Tomorrow night?

Beatrice:
I hope so

Upon setting his feet on land and trailing after Peter toward his SUV, Jackson turned to his brother. "Wanna take a trip up to Carova Beach after we grab your car at Peter's office?"

Lonnie rubbed a palm over his brown hair. "This sounds serious if you're planning on dropping in on our father."

"Can I trust you, Lon?"

"Yeah."

"I'll update you when we're alone."

After all, Jackson needed someone who had his six. Lonnie had to be it.

CHAPTER TWELVE

Nags Head, North Carolina

Today's affirmation: I am nimble through obstacles.

After leaving a message with Leila's assistant, Beatrice headed to Beachy with a heavy feeling in her chest. She'd been caught off guard finding out that her brothers had planned something without her, and the more she sat with the knowledge, the more she grew uneasy. It should have been reassuring to her that they hadn't saddled her with more responsibility. But to not even have been consulted, and then to be scolded . . .

Okay, so she hadn't been scolded, but she'd been instructed. In one conversation, she'd felt both discarded and indispensable, and it had been a compliment sandwich that had given her indigestion.

But as she entered Nags Head, her spirits lifted. Her body relaxed, hands lessening their grip on the steering wheel, and she leaned back on the headrest. She could drive through this town's streets with her eyes closed. Here, she could get a little lost among the tourists, even among the locals. Nags Head, more than Heart Resort, felt like home.

She swung by the drive-through doughnut shop and picked up a dozen random assorted flavors before turning left off the main drag, to a bungalow-style home. After parking, she hopped up the stairs and opened the door, expecting to see the clutter that had built up in the last year.

She indeed saw that and more. Racks chock full of dresses were pushed up against one another. Shipping boxes, some still in their disassembled original states and others stacked high, were lined up against one wall. Tall counter-height tables that held two desktop screens sat buried in the corner.

Interspersed was the chatter of Giselle and the part-time staff. They were in an assembly line in the rear of the shop, with one of her part-timers, Jimmy, gathering the inventory, then passing the product to Kaylee, who compared it against the packing list, then passed it to Bree, who sealed the box and attached the shipping label.

"Good afternoon, team!" Beatrice cheered. "I've got treats!"

She was greeted with the same enthusiasm; it was a glorious sight to witness the teamwork and to hear the happy chatter, despite the sardine-packed conditions.

"Beatrice!" Her name was said in singsong and in the distinct voice of Fiona, her real estate agent.

Beatrice's shoulders slumped. This couldn't be good. Fiona was too busy slinging property to drop by for a social call.

"Fiona?" Beatrice called out, passing a display of herringbone throw pillows. She ran her hand across the fabric, and her insides trilled at the pattern and texture. It was the little things that made her glow with joy. And these days, it had everything to do with Beachy.

Scratch that. Beachy *and* Jackson, who she'd had to cancel on. But her brother had issued her a challenge, and at the moment, Heart Resort came first.

All her ruminations were momentarily swept away by the sight of Fiona coming forward from the racks of clothing, laughing. Though she was already dressed to the nines—Beatrice couldn't remember a day when Fiona didn't have a full face of makeup and a crisp professional outfit—she held dresses in each hand. Fiona's face was flushed, and her breathing was erratic, as if she were smack in the middle of Black Friday shopping. "There you are! Oh my gosh, how can you stand being here every day and not want to play dress-up? It's bad enough that you're a two-minute drive from the office. What a treasure trove."

"Trust me; I've tried on every single style and every pattern here. Have to make sure that it looks good, you know?" She hugged Fiona, attempting to infuse serenity into her voice, because she appreciated customers like her. "What brings you by? I mean, besides dresses."

"Right." She laid the dresses on one of the display tables. "I've got news from the commercial space on 12."

Beatrice grimaced. "Did someone already scoop it up?"

Of course the property had been snatched right off the shelf. It was in a prime location. It was move-in ready. She and Geneva shouldn't have waited too long—

"Actually"—her lips wiggled out a grin—"after we met the other day, I left a message with the owners to let them know that you were interested. They gave me a call today, and they are so motivated for you to take on the lease that they're willing to afford you a discount. One of the owners is a Beachy customer, and I quote, 'If there's anyone who I could envision taking on the space, it would be Beachy.'" She dug her phone from her pocket-size over-the-shoulder bag and thumbed the screen. "I've emailed you the copy of the lease."

"Wow. That's . . ." Beatrice was overcome with an emotion she couldn't place a finger on. Pride? Relief? Vindication? That what she was doing mattered, that it affected people. That maybe her idealism actually meant something. Her phone buzzed with Fiona's email, and she thumbed to it, and then to the attached lease. She read through the document as Fiona held dresses up against herself in front of the full-length mirror.

Beatrice's jaw dropped at the proposed discount. "Fi."

"I know." She nodded. "There *is* a stipulation. The offer stands until COB, which is"—she looked at her watch—"in a few hours."

Of course you're going to take it, her gut screamed, especially while standing in a shop that was bursting at the seams. But, there would be repercussions. It would entail buying themselves out of their current lease for the remainder of the year. There would be the moving expenses, and the money needed to remodel the new location.

All of which you are ready for, her gut countered.

There was also the crux: Both Gil and Chris had questioned her loyalty. Chris had directed her to make Heart Resort her priority.

Irritation swirled in her chest. Her only true responsibility *should* be to consult her partner, and no one else.

"Fi." She offered her a smile. "I'll need to chat with Geneva. Can you give me a few minutes?"

"Yes, of course." She shook the hanging clothing. "I'm off to try these on. If I don't see you when I'm done, just ring me up. I'm in the office the rest of the afternoon."

"Great." Beatrice headed to the back storeroom for privacy and dialed Geneva.

"Hello?" Geneva answered on the third ring, voice hoarse.

She shut her eyes. "Oh no. Gah, you're still asleep, or maybe something else. I'm so sorry if you're in the middle of . . . things, but this is so important."

"No . . . no, I'm awake." From her side of the phone came a rustle and a mumble. "We turned in late. The nightlife here is nonstop."

Guilt ran up her spine. "I would have just emailed you this information, but it's time sensitive."

"No, no, it's okay. I need to get up anyway. I'll make some coffee. But before you start, Brandon and I found this supercute housewares boutique, and it's a perfect fit for our stuff. I'll send you the info tonight. I already talked to the owner, and she knows to expect an email."

"Ah, that's awesome. I'll have Giselle send something over tomorrow."

"Okay." Her voice was wary. "What's up? You sound stressed."

"I am, but it's good stress."

"Is this about Jackson Hill?" she whisper-screeched. "I've been so tempted to call but didn't want to completely pry. And of course Brandon would get curious. Has it gotten hot and heavy?"

Beatrice gasped in jest. "I do not kiss and tell."

"Whatever! Tell me, tell me. Is your world completely upside down?"

"Honestly, that is probably the best way to describe it." Wincing, she hoped Geneva couldn't hear the lie in between her words. She'd *never* kept a secret from Geneva.

Geneva crooned. "So sweet." Then, a pause, when a low mumble sounded from her end. "Sorry to wake you, Bran. Yep. Just catching up on Beachy. Back to bed, babe." Rustling ensued. "Whoops, we woke the bear. We should get on about business."

Beatrice laughed and caught Geneva up on the lease, and the more she spoke of the possibility, the greater she was convinced. "The place on 12 is perfect, Geneva. Honestly, coming in here today, and even sitting here with all these boxes, proves to me that we've truly outgrown this location." On the other end of the line, her friend was silent, so Beatrice pushed through. "Financially, we can do it, and with the discount—"

"But have you discussed all of this with your brothers?"

"I updated Kuya Chris and Kuya Gil on my beach house and that we're growing, but no . . . not about *this*. This is our decision."

"Beatrice Cayuga Puso. There's no separation here. Yes, it's our decision, but you come as a package, and so do I now."

"If it makes you feel better, Kuya Chris said so long as I'm on top of everything at the resort, he doesn't need to know details on Beachy. And I am. On top of it."

Hesitation laced Geneva's tone. "I don't know, Bea."

"Look, our business decisions cannot take them into account. I started this company with my own money and effort. They can demand time from me, but they can't keep us from doing what we want." Saying it aloud filled Beatrice with newfound confidence, and Jackson came to mind. Their familial relationships shouldn't have bearing on their romance either. Neither one of them was at fault.

Geneva grumbled. "You Pusos, I swear. But . . . you're right, and sitting here letting time pass won't help the situation. In fact it might hurt us because 12 and Bryan is a sweet location . . . okay, I'm in."

"Yay," Beatrice squealed. "Watch out for the contract in your email to e-sign."

Shortly after she hung up, a knock on the door took Beatrice's attention.

Fiona stepped in with a Beachy bag and lifted it. "I think I just spent my last commission. All you need is jewelry!"

"From your lips to The Cathy Hill's ears. I'm hoping to carry her soon."

Fiona and Beatrice had similar style leanings, and Fiona's jaw dropped. "*The* Cathy Hill."

"Yup."

"I will be the first customer when that happens. Anyhoo, will I see you in my office?"

"Yes! I can sign my part, actually. Let's get it done."

"Perfect. I'll drive."

Beatrice, filled with hope and anticipation, followed Fiona out the door. She was going to do it. Beachy was expanding.

Next step: world domination.

She silently giggled at the rush of excitement.

Beatrice hiked a hand over her eyes. The sun was high against the bright blue sky, and there wasn't a cloud in sight. She jumped into Fiona's passenger seat. "So, how's business going? I didn't get to ask the other day."

"Doing well. The market's picked up, and there are so many folks wanting to move into the area."

"That's great. How's your new partner working out?"

"Peter's a nice guy. Super professional. He's new to the area, from Charlotte, but his contacts are definitely panning out—he has more corporate clients, some that are pretty hush hush, with NDAs, the works."

Beatrice grumbled, "What is it with those NDAs?"

"One thing I know is that those contracts are serious, and Peter somehow can manage it with ease. He hasn't even told me who his clients are representing, despite all the poking around I'm doing."

Beatrice detected something else to her tone. "Sounds like there's a *but* in there."

"Ha." She winked. "*But* . . . it's been an adjustment taking on a partner. You know me, Bea. I like the hustle of real estate, but I'm a little averse to change."

Fiona peered up ahead, toward the Outer Banks Elite Realty office, and parked. An SUV rolled up to park a few spaces down. "Speaking of. There's Peter in the SUV. He's with one of his NDA clients, and they've been quite high maintenance. Don't say I said that, though."

"Oh, you know me," Beatrice said.

"We're the same. Secret keepers."

The doors of the SUV opened wide, and a man stepped out and nodded at them.

"Peter." Fiona stepped out ahead and ushered her partner closer. "This is Beatrice Puso."

Peter wore sunglasses, which he removed while offering the other hand. "Peter Holshbach."

"Nice to meet you."

"Great to meet you." He glanced briefly at Fiona. "Headed out? Or coming in?"

"Coming in. You?"

"Same. Great day so far." At the sound of car doors closing, he turned. Bodies were exiting the vehicle.

Two men, and one of them was Jackson.

Her Jackson.

Her body hummed, in tune with his presence. And the way he was striding toward her—he was like an animal on the prowl, his eyes never leaving her face.

Belatedly, she remembered that they weren't supposed to know one another, and she plastered a generic smile on her face. But other thoughts descended in rapid succession.

Peter was representing Jackson. Jackson was at a real estate office. Therefore, he was looking for property.

For what? And why?

She was saved from her tide pool of thoughts by Peter, who said, when the men neared, "Fiona and Beatrice. You'll need to excuse me. We've got something to hash out. Great to meet you, Beatrice."

"Same, Peter." Beatrice grabbed Fiona's hand. "Back to Beachy."

Because she had to get out of there.

"What? Bea, are you okay?"

"I need to go now. I'm sorry."

"Of course."

Finally in the moving car, Beatrice clutched her belly, unable to catch her breath. This was all levels of awful.

Willow Tree was, without a doubt, gearing up to ambush Heart Resort.

♡

Jackson drummed his fingers against his thigh. He was sitting in the passenger seat of Lonnie's Lexus and looking out the window as the horizon sped past his view. The sky was gorgeous, but he couldn't enjoy it, consumed by the current text conversation he was having with Beatrice.

His phone buzzed in his hand.

Beatrice:
Are you really not going to tell me
why you're working with Outer Banks Realty?

> **Jackson:**
> I have an NDA

Beatrice:
Seriously?

> **Jackson:**
> Seriously

Beatrice:
Because if Willow Tree is putting up a
couples resort in the area, I need to know

> **Jackson:**
> Beatrice, please.

The phone rang in his hand. The caller was Beatrice, so he sent it to voice mail with a wince.

> **Jackson:**
> I can't talk right now

Next to him, Lonnie hummed to a country song, as if he didn't have a single worry in the whole world. "So are you going to tell me how the hell you're involved with Beatrice Puso, or will I have to listen to that thing buzzing all afternoon?"

Her name coming out of Lonnie's mouth snagged Jackson's attention like a fish on a hook, but he forced his body to not react. "I've no idea what you're talking about."

He cackled. "Please, brother. *That* was Beatrice Puso—every self-respecting Willow Tree employee has memorized the Pusos' faces, and I saw the way she was looking at you. She all but lit up in your presence, and you were grinning like a fool."

Jackson grumbled, because there was no use lying. "You're not going to say a damn thing about Beatrice while we're at Grandview."

"Whoa. Do you think that low of me to believe me a snitch?" He shrugged. "Okay, so normally I would have thrown you under the bus, but since you pulled me out of my funk that one day, I figure I owe you one."

"You're such a ray of sunshine, Lonnie."

"I'm just keeping it real. McCauley genes aren't soft by any means. You should know."

That stunned him. "I'm *not* like the both of you."

"You might have grown up on the opposite side of the emotional tracks, but believe me—I see it. You have an edge too."

Jackson huffed and turned away from his brother. For all his faults, he would have never, ever left his own family to fend for themselves. But he had to keep focused. The purpose of this trip was to find out his father's plan for Heart Resort.

"What I don't understand is why? You aren't half-bad looking, and far from being a loser. You've got a lot of things going for you—why did you involve yourself with a Puso? Of all the families and tourists in this hell of a place."

"I met her in Vegas years ago . . . and she's currently my next-door neighbor." He glanced at Lonnie in anticipation of his reaction.

Sure enough, it was as if he'd been given a treasure trove of gold. He gasped in glee. "No freaking way. That's, like, what movies are made of."

"If only." Because at least he would be guaranteed a happily ever after.

Jackson had never believed in fate. He'd chalked up living next to Beatrice as coincidence. But surely their paths hadn't crossed for them to simply walk away from one another. Were they supposed to give it up for the greater good of their families without a fight?

But a fight meant that there would be a winner and a loser.

"And I thought *I* had drama."

Oh God, this *was* drama. Jackson groaned. "What the hell am I supposed to do, Lonnie?"

"This all boils down to how much she means to you. Wait . . . scratch that—what you mean to one another. Because if she doesn't think this is going anywhere, then why burn your bridge with Willow Tree?"

Why indeed?

Because this bridge was never his in the first place.

Because he didn't want to be on this bridge at all.

Lonnie opened up the sunroof, and the sounds of traffic filtered in, pulling Jackson from his thoughts. Then, Lonnie picked a playlist on his phone that was semipleasing for the next several minutes, and Jackson was distracted enough to relax into the passenger seat.

His phone buzzed with a text from the Marcus-and-Gavin group text: Update? How's it going?

Jackson:
It's going, but it's haywire

Marcus:
?

Gavin:
I'm afraid to ask

Jackson:
Long story. Will call later. What's up?

Marcus:
Got orders

Gavin:
Excuse me? Do you mean Army orders?

Jackson:
Hold up. What happened to your plans?

Marcus was at twenty years and was in the works to drop his retirement paperwork. There should have been no new orders.

Marcus:
Opportunities came a knockin, and I answered

Jackson:
Where's it to?

Marcus:
UNC. They need an instructor for ROTC.
Gavin:
How much time does that add?
Marcus:
2 years. But I'm thinking of going back to school, and so is the wifey, so this might work out.

Jackson blinked and then reread the text. Apparently, he and Marcus were on the same wavelength.

Jackson:
That's great. Happy for you
Gavin:
So long as it's what you want, then congrats
Marcus:
Don't you both still have your GI Bill?

Jackson:
Yeah

Gavin:
Yep.
Marcus:
Go back to school with me
Gavin:
That's a hard pass

Jackson:
What, you want me to pack your lunch too?

Marcus:
Smart ass.

Marcus:
Think about it you two

Jackson shook his head. Even if he had wanted to go back to school—which, okay, he could admit he was curious about—what would he even take up? The things that interested him wouldn't make him any money. He'd never been pretentious; he'd never felt the need to have a ton of letters behind his name. He'd been fulfilled with the uniform he'd worn and the rank he'd earned.

"What?" Lonnie asked.

"What do you mean, what?"

"You just shook your head."

"N . . . nothing. Just texting."

"Well, get ready for some real-life confrontation, because we're here." Lonnie flipped on the blinker to turn right, east toward Grandview, his father's beach home.

Except it wasn't the average beach home. It was a sprawling raised mansion, inspired by Spanish renderings with curved archways and dark wood trim. It had also withstood everything the coastal storms could muster.

Jackson snickered at the monstrosity, which had been his exact reaction the first time he'd rolled up a couple of weeks ago. He'd halted his motorcycle at the edge of the driveway, stunned at the opulence and angered at how he and his mother had lived. Financial insecurity had been a reality in their lives.

The food stamps. The free lunches. None of this was to be ashamed of. He was a product of his environment. He'd become a soldier because of it, and in turn he'd helped his mother right back. Together, and with a supportive set of friends and his grandparents, they'd made it. No one could take that away from them.

But you couldn't blame a man for getting a little pissed.

Lonnie parked next to a Benz—their father's. He cut the engine. "So, I would appreciate it if you didn't say anything about what I told you the other day, about me and Heather. I told Dad that Heather and the kids are on an extended vacation."

He looked at his brother. "Now it's *you* who thinks low enough of me to assume that I would spill something that was obviously private."

"I'm just saying. Dad can sniff stuff out. It's his superpower. He just knows." Lonnie spoke to the windshield, as if Jackson wasn't sitting to his right. "I couldn't get away with anything, and, well . . . I guess that means you need to watch out too. I don't know. I'm getting used to you, Jackson, and I . . . kind of want you around."

Then, Lonnie got out without fanfare.

Was that . . . his brother being nice?

Jackson slipped out of the car and followed Lonnie up the stairs to the front door, where he pressed the doorbell.

Darlene Klinger, Grandview's household manager, opened the door with a smile. With her silver hair piled upon her head, she was a petite and matronly White woman with a British accent. She was clever, sharp, and kind, and on day one, Jackson had figured out that she was the captain of this house's ship. They'd hit it off immediately. While everyone looked upon Jackson as an enigma, the hidden son, Darlene had welcomed him with open arms.

"Boys." She backed up, holding the wooden door open. "This is a surprise."

"Where is he?" Lonnie said without preamble.

"Mr. McCauley is in his bedroom study."

Lonnie stepped ahead.

Jackson held back for a beat. "How's it going, Darlene?"

She shrugged. "Same ol', same ol'."

"How's the old man?"

"Grumpy, as usual." Her eyes lit up. "But your timing is impeccable. Landon's getting started with dinner prep. Will you be joining us?"

"You're asking me if I want a five-star meal? Absolutely, we're staying. Thank you."

"You're always welcome, Jackson."

He took the stairs by two, catching Lonnie halfway.

Lonnie snorted. "Kissing her ass?"

"Not even close. It's called respect. It would behoove you to show her a little."

"She never really liked me. She didn't like my mother either." He climbed the rest of the way up, and Jackson followed, holding the slick wooden banister. The stairs curved until they reached the second floor, where the railing looked over the foyer.

"Dad?" Lonnie knocked on the lone heavy pine door to the left of the stairway before walking in. Their father was sitting on the other side of a large desk. On the tabletop were stacks of folders; at the head was an in-and-out box. Next to him, bent and holding out a folder for McCauley to sign, was Cole Ricci, a marketing executive.

The marketing executive, from what Jackson remembered from the media he'd read, who'd egged on Heart Resort on social media.

Jackson's stomach soured; as Cole passed him on his way out the door, Jackson could barely keep from snarling.

After being prompted, he and Lonnie took the two seats in front of the desk. Everything, absolutely everything, in the office was a luxury item. From the premium leather seats, to the carved wooden desk, to the antique books that lined the shelves behind their father. No expense had been spared.

Dillon McCauley III was broad shouldered and large everything. Thick neck, big hands, a sizable girth. Standing, he was six feet three and towered above Jackson's six-foot frame. In his sixties, McCauley had the presence of a linebacker and the matching attitude. Hell, Jackson didn't know what his teeth looked like with the way he kept his lips pressed into discontent.

Jackson wasn't scared of him, but he was intimidating.

"This is a surprise. What's gone wrong?" McCauley looked up briefly from the paperwork he was signing.

No salutation, not even a courtesy smile. This was where Lonnie got it from.

"Nothing's gone wrong," Lonnie said, presumably trying to ease the tension. "We actually found a place that you might like."

"You've been at it for almost two weeks. All that time, and only one choice?"

Lonnie's face reddened. "We wanted to make sure it fit your criteria. And it's near everything you need."

"That so?"

"Yes, sir. It's on the Roanoke. Though it's smaller than you asked for."

His lips curved in disapproval. "So it's not perfect."

Jackson jumped in. "Lonnie and I have hit the road—we've toured all the island and peninsula properties, and nothing is as close as this." He might have not agreed with Lonnie about the island, but at that moment, his brother needed the backup. Thinking on it now, he found it ridiculous to ask for perfection when it was impossible to achieve, especially with the parameters they'd been given.

Leaders who asked for perfection weren't looking for the truth. They were encouraging people to lie, to blow smoke up someone's behind. And that wasn't how Jackson ran his life. No lies.

Usually.

"Here's more information." Lonnie handed McCauley the real estate listing and the seller's brochure.

Silence ensued as McCauley read through the stapled packet. After minutes passed, he lifted his gaze, and his eyes darted between the two of them, assessing. "How close to Heart Resort?"

There it was. Jackson held his breath.

"Enough that you can see the outline of the peninsula," Lonnie said.

McCauley grumbled in thought. After a brief moment he said, "All right. I want to see it the day after tomorrow. You may go."

That's it? Jackson frowned at the dismissal—they'd driven over an hour and a half for a ten-minute meeting—though he did as he was told like a good soldier.

But when the office door closed behind them, Jackson regretted not speaking up. He'd been flustered. He turned to Lonnie. "I need to know what his intentions are for Heart Resort."

Lonnie shook his head. "You're really willing to risk getting into it for Beatrice? Do you like her that much?"

"Yes." The answer roared through him as definitive as the ocean's waves. But it wasn't just about Beatrice and the fact that she'd been able to touch his life in such a short time—this was about him too. Lonnie could have done the property search on his own. What was Jackson's real purpose?

"Well, good luck." His brother wiped the sweat off his brow, obviously affected by their father's presence too. "Meet you downstairs when you're done. A beer's sounding good right about now." Lonnie turned and jogged down the stairs, leaving Jackson alone in the hallway.

As the seconds passed, Jackson began to lose his nerve. He hadn't planned out what he was going to say.

Turning, he encountered a door to his right, and it was slightly ajar. He peeked in. The room was shadowed with heavy plants, custom furniture, and what felt like secrets lurking in every dark corner.

It was a library, with built-in shelving filled with books, as opulent as McCauley's office.

Jackson's eyes wandered, catching on a photograph against the back wall. Though a little too far for him to discern the subject, the outline was of a heart turned on its side.

Heart?

His breath hitched. *Puso.*

He entered the library, drawn to the photograph. It focused as he neared; the frame itself appeared to be antique. Sure enough, it was a black-and-white aerial photo of an island. An inscription was written on the bottom right side. 1921. Below it: McCAULEY ISLAND.

"You're still here." McCauley's gruff voice startled Jackson, and he spun.

He swallowed his nerves, belatedly soaking in the island's name. "Yes, I wanted to speak with you privately. About what I'm doing here."

An eyebrow arched—and for a beat, Jackson thought he was looking at himself in the mirror. An older, wrinkled, cold version, and yet so definitively his DNA. "You signed the contract. You're representing me by purchasing land for a project."

"Right. An adult summer-camp resort."

"That's what I told you."

"But why? Why the NDA, and why right here, in the Outer Banks? Why me and not Lonnie? And now that I'm hearing more and more about it, what does this all have to do with Heart Resort?"

Jackson realized now that he should have asked these questions sooner. That perhaps, despite his age, he was the most gullible person he knew.

McCauley pointed to the photograph. "See this? McCauley Island was a true island at one point, but with how the earth shifted, it's considered a peninsula now. Currently, it's named Heart Resort."

"I know that much."

"Did Lonnie tell you the history of the island?"

"No."

He snorted. "I'm not surprised. That son of mine tries but can't quite take the ball to the end zone. He was lucky to marry Heather; she's his saving grace, and he'd be a smart man to keep her happy and not drop the ball like he did while offering on that island. It was for sale about seven years ago, and I relied on my boy to handle the purchase. To my detriment."

Jackson tried to piece this information together with what he currently knew, but he was still confused.

As if reading his mind, his father sidled up next to him and presented him with a book. It was leather bound, and within its black pages were sepia and black-and-white pictures tacked with photo corners. Jackson spied the dates—the book started in the early 1910s.

"The McCauleys originated from Dublin and immigrated through Ellis Island, first landing in New York City and then making their way down south. Brutal times they were, but when World War One called, my great-grandfather, D. M. one, was drafted. After the war, he returned to North Carolina with enough money in his pocket—and a motor for a mouth—that he bought himself a piece of land no one wanted. McCauley Island. Wasn't much back then, but he built on it, tried to live on it, only to abandon it to some city transplants in the fifties. Since then it was passed down from one family to another, and it was called different names; at the same time, tourism in the Outer Banks grew. Meanwhile our family was managing family resorts, the old-school kind, all the while not knowing there was an actual island that once had belonged to us.

"I myself didn't know about the island until it came up for sale. I caught wind of it, and I did a little poking around, and lo and behold. The previous owner had died, with the whole thing already set up commercially. It was meant to be. Or so I thought, until Lonnie screwed that up. He underestimated the Pusos, who came in and robbed it from under our noses."

Jackson felt a rush of protectiveness over his younger brother. But he didn't want to interrupt McCauley in what felt like an honest moment. Curiosity had him hanging on to his every word.

"I had high hopes." McCauley ran a finger down an edge of a sepia photograph. "I had already started to dream about what it would become. A resort on a heart-shaped island. It felt . . . perfect. It doesn't belong to us right now, but I haven't given up." He shut the book with one swift movement, his shoulders expanding. "My boy, what *we* are, besides cutthroat, is patient. And one day, that peninsula is going to belong to us once more—if not in my lifetime, then I trust that it will be in yours. Because I don't have much time left."

"What do you mean?"

McCauley went to the desk at the corner and rifled through one of the drawers. He handed a folder to Jackson before he sat on one of the leather sofas, grunting. "Take a seat."

The folder was cold against Jackson's palm. After he sat, he opened it to typed notes with McCauley's name on top. There were figures and abbreviations, some Jackson recognized. "Your medical records?"

The man nodded.

Jackson flipped through the records, though he couldn't make sense of it all. Then, slowly, words popped out at him. Cardiac. Chronic. Congestive heart.

"Congestive heart failure?" Jackson looked up at McCauley, now picking up the slight sheen of his skin. What he had interpreted as a tempered, flushed appearance looked to him now as the face of a man who was living with a chronic condition.

"I was diagnosed almost a decade ago, and it's catching up to me. The thing about mortality is that when you're faced with it, everything becomes crystal clear. What one wants, simply, is the ability to live in the quiet and the peace. I'm not looking to expand into the adult summer-camp resort space, and not even the couples resort space like everyone thinks I am. I'm looking to make an upscale senior vacation community. Somewhere where there is absolute privacy. Somewhere *I* would love to live, with everything ADA compliant. Not only is it needed, with our increasing population made of baby boomers and Gen Xers, but it will make us a ton of money. McCauley Island is perfect for it, though I'd demo that whole setup they have and start from scratch."

"But it belongs to Heart Resort. How do you plan to do that?" Jackson's voice was a squeak, his concern restricting the full intensity of his words.

"By building around them. By growing our own business; by being patient for the moment they falter, and we'll be right there to take it from them. Right now, they're on a high. They've reached the top of the game. But we've been in the game longer, and we know that weathering decades of business came with resilience, which they haven't proven. And because we built a senior community, they won't consider us a threat. You're here as an extra precaution—no one knows you as a McCauley." He linked his hands together. "But we are, and we always will be here. They're maxed out at Heart Resort. Which means that's it for them, unless they expand. We aren't going to let them if we can help it. Then, when they get tired of playing, we'll be right there to buy them out."

"We?" Jackson was slowly putting all the pieces together.

"You. You're my son. The rightful son who should be running this business. Not Lonnie. I've watched you for years, from afar. It's why I hired you, besides the fact that you could move around the Outer Banks without anyone recognizing you. I wasn't sure if you would take the job, but you've been here almost two weeks, and I already can see what kind of man you are."

"And what's that?"

"Smart, strong, levelheaded, logical. Exactly the kind of person to run Willow Tree."

Jackson's throat clogged with emotion, with both trepidation and thrill. With fear and wonder. Was his father asking him . . .

"Jackson, I want you to stay, permanently. I might not be a great father, but I'm a pretty damn good businessman, and if there's any person I could give this place to, it would be you."

CHAPTER THIRTEEN

Heart Resort, North Carolina

Today's affirmation: I will focus.

Despite the bright smile of Ava Wutuku, Leila's executive assistant, on video chat, Beatrice could barely keep her own on her face.

She was exhausted, having worked late on her to-do lists for both Heart Resort and Beachy, and from her rough night of insomnia waiting for Jackson to text back.

Even now, she had to resist the temptation to ensure that her phone's ringer was on and turned up, that she had reception. She was so consumed that she wasn't tracking what Ava was saying.

Thank goodness for Kim, who was taking copious notes. Taking lead, actually.

From under the table, she felt a gentle nudge against her shoe, and Beatrice stirred to present.

Ava was speaking. "We'd love to schedule a video chat for Leila to meet you and the rest of your team in a few days." She looked down at her iPad. "Leila relies heavily on her gut before she commits to events or projects, especially in this case, since this is a vulnerable situation."

"Oh, of course." Beatrice forced herself into the moment. "And we want to make sure she's comfortable."

"Great. I'll get back to you on the date very soon."

After a round of thanks, Beatrice shut her laptop screen and looked across to Kim. Eyes rounded, clearly overwhelmed. "This is. A lot," she squeaked.

"My notes are a mess," Beatrice said. "Thank you for nudging me back there. My mind is all over the place."

"That's what I'm here for. Are you . . . okay?"

"Yeah." She offered her as sincere a smile as she could give and shook herself back to business. "It *is* a lot. But we have our systems in place. We're doing more hand-holding because she's Leila, but she's coming to us because of exactly what we do. We're great at this."

"Right; you're right." Kim pressed her hands against her planner page. "Okay. We have a little more than five weeks—we can do this. On top of everything else."

"Of course we can," Beatrice affirmed, though judging by the way Kim was gripping her pen, there was more going on. Beatrice linked her fingers together. She understood it could be intimidating sitting across from a boss. "Kim? Is something else going on?"

She blew out a breath. "I'm getting married."

Beatrice had a thing for the M- or the W-word. *Marriage* or *wedding*.

Oh, who was she kidding? She loved anything that involved a celebration, a reunion, or a party. In a second she was on her feet and rounding the tables, just in time for Kim to stand and receive her hug. "Oh my gosh. Congratulations. I'm sorry; I didn't even ask if I could throw myself at you. And who are you marrying? And when? Sorry, is that too forward?"

"No, no it's not." Kim's face softened. "I'm marrying my college sweetheart, Heath. He's in Raleigh. We've been long distance since I started working here. All that to say, we planned to marry with the justice of the peace around the time of Leila's stay."

"Ah." Beatrice smiled. "Not to worry. You don't have to be here for her arrival. The lion's share of your work should be done by then."

"I know . . . it's just . . . I have five weeks to find a cute dress and do all the plans and . . ." She pressed her hands against her chest. "You don't need to know about this. Sorry, this isn't your problem. It's not even a problem. It's a good thing."

"Of course it's a good thing. But a wedding is still a lot to plan. Do you have help?" As she said it, Beatrice winced at herself. Because she hoped both that Kim had help and that she didn't, because would she want to help plan another wedding?

Heck yeah!

"I do, sort of. My best friend, Lucy, is coming a week before the ceremony. She lives in Florida. I mean the point of marrying with the JOP was not having to plan a million things, but I still feel like it's a million things."

"Because this day will be the most special ever, no matter how big or small it is." Beatrice looked at her watch. There was a laundry list of things on her docket. None as fulfilling and as happy-making as helping Kim, though. And frankly, Beatrice needed a mental break and distraction from how her love life had imploded in one fell swoop. "We've got an hour and a half before I'm needed at Beachy. Wanna go to Kitty Hawk Bridal? They've got all kinds of dresses, some super simple that you might love."

"Oh . . . I don't know . . . we've got so much work."

"We can discuss clients on the way to the bridal shop. Heck, I'll drive, and you can do email." They walked out of the headquarters office and encountered Eden Chan Puso, Chris's wife. She was Filipino Chinese, and her dark hair was windswept, her cheeks pink. "Hey, ladies."

"Hey." Beatrice noticed Eden slinging her beach bag around her shoulder. A Beachy beach bag, which made Beatrice beam. From inside peeked her noise-canceling headphones, which only meant that she was dictating her next romance novel. "What's the amazing Everly Heart up to?"

Her smile turned mischievous. "I can't say yet."

"Oh, c'mon, a hint?"

She tapped her chin. "Hmm . . . it's about a guy and a girl who fall in love and—"

"Eden!" Beatrice playfully shoved her sister-in-law. "What's the point of having a romance author in house if you can't tell us about your next book?"

"Patience, dear reader." Eden threw her head back in a laugh. "Where are you both off to?"

Beatrice nudged Kim with an elbow.

"I'm getting married." This time, Kim said it more confidently. "Beatrice is taking me to Kitty Hawk Bridal."

"Oh, really?" Eden's voice was beseeching and wistful. "Can I come?"

"Really?" Kim's eyebrows rose. "Yes. Of course. I mean, this is . . . amazing, that you guys care."

"If there's a family that loves weddings, it's the Pusos." Eden grinned. "Give me a sec, and I'll switch out my purse."

A little more than a half hour later, Beatrice was standing behind Kim and gazing at her reflection in the long mirror. Kim was wearing the second dress in her lineup of five—the first had been an immediate no—and she exuded an unbridled joy.

It never got old seeing a person feel good in the clothing they were wearing. "What do you think?" Beatrice fluffed the skirt so it fluttered around Kim's legs.

"I just love it. And Heath. Heath is going to love it too. This is it."

The bridal assistant, who was wearing black, appeared. "That was a lightning-fast decision."

"All the magazine and online articles were right. When you know, you know." Happy tears had sprung to Kim's eyes. "Thank you. I needed this, and you just understood. I was so worried how to get it all done, and here we are, one step closer."

Beatrice offered her hand. "I'm honored to help."

But the words boomeranged back to pierce her heart. She'd had a hand in everyone's weddings, in baby showers, in birthday parties. She coordinated, she remembered birthdays, she scheduled the family photos. And the only man thus far who she could see herself participating in these same activities with was one she couldn't bring home.

Because his family had almost destroyed hers. His family could still do so.

And he was pulling away.

"Let's seal the deal, shall we?" The bridal assistant helped Kim off the dais and then back to the fitting room. Thank goodness, because Beatrice needed a breath.

She clicked her phone awake—still no new notifications from Jackson. Frowning, she went to her messages, in case she'd missed a text. Alas, there were none.

She read through their texts from last night.

Beatrice:
Why didn't you pick up?
Beatrice:
When can I see you? I'm heading back to
Nags Head tomorrow night

Close to midnight, he'd finally answered.

Jackson:

Sorry I was in the middle of work

Jackson:

I'll be back tomorrow night too

Beatrice:

Should I be worried?

Beatrice:

Where are you?

Jackson:

Please trust me

The mere fact that he hadn't confirmed where he was meant that it involved Willow Tree.

Foreboding clogged her chest. His texts had been vague. But she had to trust him, right? So much was lost over text, and assumptions could only lead to misunderstandings.

From afar, Eden gave her a curious smile and, being an intuitive person, took Beatrice's side. "That was nice of you to bring Kim here."

"Aw, you know I'm always happy to."

"I know you're always ready to help someone, but *happy* might not be the right word."

She looked into her sister-in-law's curious gaze and understood that Eden wasn't buying it. Eden was sharp.

But Eden was loyal to Chris, which meant Beatrice couldn't divulge her secret. At least not all the way. Beatrice walked to the reception area and lingered in front of a veil display, examining the intricate lace. Eden followed. "I was just wondering . . . this whole rivalry with Willow Tree. Where does it really stem from?"

Eden's shoulders slumped. "Oh no, is my husband starting all that again? I thought that he was starting to let it go—"

"No, no, he's . . . he's been good." Chris and Eden's past marital problems had been in part because of Chris's conflict with Willow

Tree and Dillon McCauley III. "But with the talk about Heart Resort expanding, I wonder if the drama will heat up again."

"Do you not agree with the expansion?" Eden searched her face.

"No, that's not it. I guess I'm just anticipating what this will all mean."

"Yeah . . . honestly, I'm not sure. Chris told me of one interaction he had with Dillon McCauley, which I assume is where their story began. But . . . I suspect it has everything to do with the resort's location. Chris had mentioned once that Willow Tree wanted the peninsula."

"The actual peninsula?" Beatrice's heart thumped against her chest cavity. "I didn't know that. I thought the competition was more territorial, more theoretical, I guess."

"You know your brother. He kept it to himself because he wanted to protect all of you." Eden's gaze darted over Beatrice's shoulder, and her face lit up with a smile. From the dressing room emerged Kim. She was back in her work clothes, and across her arm was her dress, which she paid for at the register.

"I'm so happy," Kim said as they all walked out of the bridal shop. "You don't even understand. Like a whole weight has been lifted off my shoulders. I haven't made a ton of friends since I moved here, and I've felt a little lonely." Then, she startled, backtracking as she opened the back door of Beatrice's Tesla. "Not that you guys are my friends. I mean, you were kind enough to take me here—"

Beatrice held the door open to halt Kim's train of speech. "Kim, what's important to you matters to us too."

"You do know that she's vying for an invite to your ceremony, right?" Eden said wryly before getting into the passenger seat.

"Don't scare her." Beatrice slipped into the driver's seat and then buckled up. "I still haven't told her that we have to approve her fiancé." She winked at Kim through the rearview mirror as she backed out from the space.

They cruised to Highway 12 with the windows down. Not as many tourists on a random Tuesday, and Beatrice took in the quiet. The weather was perfect, the wind cooler today, and she stuck an arm out and spread her fingers.

Right then, Beatrice craved that extrasensory experience to calm her spinning mind. Perhaps nothing was wrong, and she'd simply jumped to conclusions. Maybe there was a perfectly good and innocent explanation as to why Jackson was at Outer Banks Realty. Just because Jackson had not texted since last night didn't mean Willow Tree was conspiring against Heart Resort. And no, Jackson was not purposely keeping a secret from her. She herself wasn't perfect at communication, right?

Damn secrets. Like stray hairs after a haircut that wouldn't wash out—they just got more inconvenient and irritating.

God, I miss you so much, Mom. Beatrice yearned for her mother; she longed for sage advice, for wise words, for perspective. For her mother to hug her and rub her back. On what had been Beatrice's bad days, she used to lay her head on Marilyn's lap, and Marilyn would stroke Beatrice's temple gently with a thumb. It would still her nerves, ground her to the moment, and aid her to a restful sleep. Then, she'd wake up feeling that much better.

What she would give for a repeat of those moments. Heck, a sign that her mother was around. That Beatrice wasn't alone in her thoughts.

The ring of a bell took Beatrice's attention. She turned her head to the left, to an actual, literal sign: Cathy Hill, riding her bicycle, ringing her bell to pedestrians in her way.

Beatrice reacted instinctively, passing Cathy and turning right at the first gravel parkway. To Eden's and Kim's confusion and questions, she said, "Wait right here. Give me . . . like ten minutes."

Beatrice exited her car and stomped across the gravel. Rocks lodged in her sandals, but she hardly noticed with Cathy in her sights. Then, she stepped in front of the bicycle.

It halted with a screech.

"Goodness, dear." Cathy Hill was fifties chic, with a scarf holding back her hair and large dark glasses on her face. She wasn't wearing a helmet, but Beatrice held back in saying so, even if it was killing her.

"Hi, Cathy. I . . ." It was only then that Beatrice realized how frazzled she must look, and that she hadn't planned on what to say. So she blurted out the first thing that came to mind. "I wanted to mention that we signed the lease for the new shop. We're actually getting keys tomorrow. And if you're still interested in bringing over some jewelry, I'd love to sit down and chat about it."

"How exciting, and absolutely. Thank you. Anytime you're free, I can be free. But . . ." She took her glasses off her face. "Is there something else, dear?"

Beatrice cleared her throat, nodding at a family of five that walked around them, each with an ice cream cone in their hand. Her next thought was chicken-and-waffles ice cream, and Jackson. And how he'd asked her to trust him. They'd made a promise to be honest with one another, above all. She eked out a smile. "Nope . . . that's it."

"All righty. Well, I'd better go. Don't want my heart rate to get down too low." She raised an arm to show off her activity tracker. "Just got this nifty thing. Me and my girlfriends formed one of those accountability groups, and of course, I've got to win."

Beatrice cackled. "Go you."

"That's right. I *will* go." Her grin was wide and bright. "But let's get together soon. I do miss that Roxy of mine. You and Jackson have both been quite busy. I'll be glad to have him home tonight, and I know he's eager to see you. Around nine?"

He's eager to see me. Beatrice's shoulders sagged with relief. Cathy's words were the reassurance Beatrice had been craving all day. "I can definitely come by. Thank you."

As she watched Cathy ride away, Beatrice was only then able to breathe.

Thanks, Mom.

♡

McCauley's voice had resonated in Jackson's head the whole way back to Nags Head, along with the facts that ticked off in sequential order.

McCauley was chronically sick.

McCauley wanted to expand Willow Tree.

McCauley had targeted and would continue to target Heart Resort.

McCauley wanted Jackson to be part of Willow Tree.

McCauley had called him *son*.

For four decades, Jackson had waited for some kind of validation that he belonged somewhere. Now, he had it.

But he knew what being a McCauley represented. It meant unyielding loyalty, more binding than any NDA. In the twenty-four hours that he and Lonnie had spent with their father, finding out the full scope of the business—the massive responsibility of managing hundreds of people, the sheer amount of money he would be dealing with, and the inherent mission of expanding—he'd learned that there would be no in-between. He was either in, or out.

Pros: Take my rightful place in this family.

Cons: Lose Beatrice and possibly my mother in the process.

His mother had been right. There would be a choice, and his proposal had come earlier than he'd expected. And while his choices were binary, he *did* conclude that there was hope somewhere in the middle.

If Jackson took his rightful place, then he would be afforded more choice.

If he made certain choices, he could shape Willow Tree's trajectory.

If the trajectory changed, then perhaps the Heart Resort rivalry could be over.

All of this—this information—was why he couldn't text Beatrice back. Not only was he not in the position to tell her everything because of the NDA, but he didn't want to jinx this hope, not until he was sure what was possible could be real.

After Lonnie dropped him off that night, Jackson paced the bottom of Beatrice's back steps where the sand met the concrete. He hadn't formulated how he could explain that he was considering joining Willow Tree permanently.

He couldn't believe he was even thinking about it.

"Jackson?"

He turned at the sound of his name, and from the darkness came Beatrice. She was wearing a green summer dress with thin straps. It was cheerful and soft; it was everything she was.

They hadn't seen each other in two days, and he'd missed her.

I don't want to miss her.

"You're a sight for sore eyes." He felt his body exhale and took her into his arms. "I was just on my way up."

"Your mom—she told me that you'd be home at nine."

He kissed her hair, and her scent flooded him with comfort. "She just left on a walk with a new friend she'd made. Which means she should be gone for a while."

"Ms. Cupid strikes again." She half laughed, then stepped back. "We . . . need to talk."

"We do. Do you want to come in?" He gestured up to his house.

"Sure."

Jackson led her up the stairs. Once they were in his house, alone, the vibe intensified.

"I'm sorry I was vague, Bea," Jackson started as Beatrice grimaced, saying, "I know I shouldn't have demanded for you to go against your NDA."

And dammit, every part of Jackson went to mush. All the anger and angst he'd felt about Willow Tree and all the confusion about what he wanted to do made way for this unbelievable tragedy of a family situation he and Beatrice hadn't asked to be a part of.

He shook his head, laughing.

"What's so funny?" She stepped up to him.

"This whole thing is so messed up." He set his hands on her shoulders, and the contact allowed him to breathe. She calmed him, as if she transferred her joy and optimism like diffusion. "I got the family history straight from the source."

"I've been told that Willow Tree wanted the peninsula . . ." She searched his face. "You don't have to say a word. But I just want to know if he still does."

Jackson thought through the channels of his NDA and, after a long pause, decided to tell the story a different way. "Did you know that Heart Resort was once named McCauley Island?"

"It used to belong to your family?" At his silence, she leaned a forehead against his chest for a painful moment. After, she looked up at him, resolve in her eyes. "Well, it's ours now, and it's going to remain ours."

"I know."

"But he's not going to stop, is he? He's going to keep expanding and wait for the moment to come take it."

Jackson dropped his gaze, unease growing with the accuracy of Beatrice's statements. She made everything sound infinitely worse.

"And you're going to be a part of it." She stepped back.

"No." He sought to pull her back. "I won't."

"How is that possible? Because I can't *not* be a Puso."

"And I'm forever a McCauley, but it doesn't mean that the future has to play out the way we think it will."

His family name came with wealth. It came with prestige. It came with people, a team. A household that was permanent, a family history that he could trace back to Dublin, Ireland. He hadn't thought he wanted any of this growing up, but now it had been offered to him on a silver platter, for the taking.

This should have been an easy decision.

But he couldn't allow Beatrice and her family to be collateral damage.

"What does that even mean, Jackson? You work for him now."

"But I'm not working against Heart Resort. And I'll do everything I can to keep Heart Resort safe." Even if it meant finding property for his father as far away from the Outer Banks as possible. Even if it meant working around the rules of the NDA and compromising with his father. He was willing to do whatever was necessary.

But he didn't want to do it while hiding their relationship in the shadows.

"Beatrice, Lonnie knows about us. My mother knows. Soon, others will know: your family, mine. I'm not sure it's feasible that we keep us a secret. And in all honesty, I don't want to keep this quiet. I would rather live in truth than pretend. I would rather know what we're up against. But we need to stand together."

He saw the scenarios play themselves out in her eyes: of them telling their families, of enduring their criticism. There would be consequences.

Beatrice was quiet for an unbearable amount of seconds. Because what he was asking her was to admit that he was worth it. That they were worth it.

She seemed to take a step back, during which Jackson's heart fell.

Then, as if changing her mind, she walked squarely in his direction and threw her arms around his neck.

"Okay," she said before kissing him roughly.

"Okay. Okay." Relief pulsed with each beat of Jackson's heart. He backed her against a wall, trailing his tongue on the underside of her chin. She tasted like lemons, quenching all his doubts, and he couldn't get enough of it.

They were doing this.

"Where?" Her voice was clear and serious.

"Top floor." Jackson locked the front door with a flick of his finger and tugged her down the hallway and up the stairs. They stumbled against furniture and bumped walls, unwilling to stop kissing. He didn't want a second where his lips weren't touching hers.

It took effort and too much time, but they reached his bedroom, the turret room, circular and banked by windows, facing the water. He shut the door, making sure to keep the rest of the world behind them. The real world, anyway, not this corner of their own universe, where it was just them and the beach and the dark sky.

She walked backward, unzipping her dress, nimbly fingering the thin straps off her shoulders. It was sexy and innocent all at once, and when the dress billowed to the floor, exposing skin and lacy underwear, his body ignited with need.

"We're doing this," he reminded her—he reminded himself—as he tugged off his shirt.

She unbuttoned his shorts and shimmied them and his underwear down, eyes never straying. "Yes, we are." Her lips parted minutely as she inspected him, and this show of desire set him on fire. The only thing that kept Jackson from going into a frenzy was understanding that beyond this lust were the consequences of their chosen actions.

She rested her hands on his pecs, and he gripped her waist; her skin was burning up, and he wanted to bask in all of her despite their problems. To Jackson, this simply felt right. Except . . .

"Beatrice—"

She pressed a finger to his lips. "I'm not afraid. Are you?"

"No. But . . ." He rubbed a thumb against her cheek and inspected the line between her eyebrows. "This is the first time."

"First time?"

"That I'm seeing you frown, for real. And I hate that I'm causing this." As he said it now, his need turned down to a low simmer.

She held on to his wrists. "It's not you causing this. It's everyone and everything else." She got on her tiptoes and kissed his chin, trailing her lips down to his Adam's apple. "You . . . you make me happy. You make me forget. You make me feel good."

He groaned against the hunger raging anew through him and caught her bottom lip with his teeth in a lust-filled moment. How he wanted to just take her freely and without consequence. "I wish . . ."

But he wasn't sure what he was wishing for. Were they not who they were, they would have never reunited. Their story would have ended in Vegas.

"Me too," she said as if reading his mind. She fell back on her heels and looked up at him through her long lashes. She pulled him forward to the bed. He kissed down her torso while peeling off her clothing, and with the moon a spotlight, they explored each other's bodies.

Jackson could have been content with that the whole night. But this moment felt like a long-awaited reunion after a deployment, with the combination of newness and familiarity. It felt right, and perfect—serendipity and the luck of Vegas rolled into one. So immense, despite having not yet had sex, that he was sure *she* was the woman he was going to spend the rest of his life with.

He'd said those words to himself that night in Vegas, and it hadn't made sense then, and it shouldn't have made sense now. Love, he'd learned, took time. It took a lifetime. And sometimes it didn't stay—his first marriage had shown that.

It was too early, right?

He pulled away for a beat, breathing in the warm air around them. He needed to calm his head, his heart.

"Jackson." Beatrice's voice knocked him out of his ever-pervasive thoughts. She was looking at him seriously and intently. "What's wrong?"

He fingered the hair out of her eyes, their faces close. Touching his forehead against hers, he slowed his ragged breath. "You make it hard to think."

She giggled. "Being naked doesn't help the logic."

"No. It sure doesn't."

"What are you thinking about?"

"That this matters to me. That you matter to me. I wanted to go slow, but I don't think I can, not with you."

"Good. Because I don't think there's anything more right than you and me."

The emotion that welled up inside him brought all his carnal tendencies to the surface.

All Jackson had ever needed was an intention, a promise, a commitment, and he would reciprocate. And Beatrice's words, her confidence in them, were enough.

He rolled on top of her and took her mouth wholly while she ran her fingernails down his back. He rocked between her legs until she groaned his name.

"Please," she whispered in his ear.

He wanted to give her everything she asked for, so he sheathed a condom and settled in between her legs. Eyes on her, he entered her gently and, with her encouragement, increased his pressure, his speed. He watched her every expression. He wanted to make it perfect; he wanted to make this all about her. Her climax became his priority and his mission.

After, he fell asleep with Beatrice breathing deeply in the crook of his arm, only for his eyes to fly open in the middle of the dark and foreboding night.

CHAPTER FOURTEEN

Current affirmation: I speak my true emotions.

It was déjà vu of their Vegas night when Beatrice heard her phone buzzing somewhere in the dark bedroom, and she once more contemplated not opening her eyes at all. Maybe if she shut her eyes and ears hard enough, she could keep the rest of the world away. She didn't want to leave this, or leave Jackson. She wanted to protect them exactly as they were.

Because they'd done it. They'd made love, and what should have been an unbridled joy carried the hard truth that someone was going to get hurt.

"Bea." Jackson's voice was gruff and comforting, and the sound of it sent a measure of peace. She felt his lips against her eyelids; he kissed each gently, making her giggle so that she couldn't *not* open her eyes. And when she did, she was met by handsome and sexy Jackson smiling down at her in this crooked way. He was too cute for words—his hair was floppy and irresistibly youthful, though the lines around his eyes emitted maturity and wisdom.

And he surely had proved it in the way he'd handled her body, with full control and confidence. That and with this big open heart—that was how Jackson made love: with care, with steadfast attention, and with the intent to make her happy.

"Hi." Her voice croaked.

He kissed her on the nose. "Your phone."

It stopped buzzing, a blessed silence. Seconds later, a text came in. She turned to the side, away from the noise. "Ugh. Reality calls."

He faced her, propping a hand against his temple and sporting a matter-of-fact expression. "Tell me more. About your reality. What are we up against?"

Beatrice straightened in bed, pulling the covers across her top. She wished it didn't sound like it was them against the world. "I'm . . . Mom, for the lack of a better term. Ate Eden, Kuya Chris's wife—she's begun to take the role. But I am still . . . I don't know . . . my siblings might look to Kuya Chris for tangible decisions, but they rely on me to make things okay."

"You're the keeper of the peace?"

"No, that's Kuya Gil. Brandon's the joker. I'm the vibe, I guess. Much like when you see a little kid fall, and the parent says, 'You're fine, no blood!' And the child completely believes that parent. That's me, that . . . parent."

"And you say that with a smile."

"I mean, yeah."

"And who takes care of you?"

She breathed out a long deep exhale. It was a question she asked herself a lot these days, now understanding what it felt like for someone to think of her. "My siblings watch out for me too. But everyone's married. Gil's even getting back together with his ex." Then, she shook her head. "These aren't complaints. Just facts . . . how about you? What's your reality?"

"Oh, do you mean besides having a ruthless businessman of a father and a half brother who gives me whiplash emotions?"

"Yeah, that's all." She laughed, and it felt good to do so. Because this topic was so . . . serious.

"Well, like you, there are expectations. And the tricky part is maneuvering around it. I hated McCauley all of my life because of his absence . . . but now he's here, and I don't know what to do with that."

Hate was such a strong word—it was a word Beatrice's mother had reminded her to avoid. But she didn't ask him to reconsider; the hurt was evident on his face.

"We should make a plan," he said now.

"A plan is good." She sobered. "Because we had sex."

"We sure did." His face changed, and he waggled his eyebrows.

She pushed him playfully, though admittedly it eased the worry that was starting to build in her chest.

He peered at her. "What? Seemed to me you enjoyed it."

"More than enjoyed. I want to do it again and again." A swirl began in her core, and she inched closer to him so their torsos touched. She lifted her face up for a kiss and reveled in the slow way his tongue explored her mouth. Then, as naturally as the kiss had begun, it ended with Bea gently creating space between them. "I just meant that we've, you know, upped the ante . . ."

But Jackson shifted, and the sheet draped lower. Beatrice spotted the treasure trail that led down below, and her imagination continued past the sheet blocking the rest of her view.

He tilted up her chin to his mischievous grin and dropped a peck on her lips. "And?"

Face burning, she bit the inside of her cheek. "Sorry, not sorry. Got distracted."

Then, her phone buzzed, cutting out the last of the playfulness.

"Shoot," she said.

His expression changed. "Bea, you said you weren't afraid. Neither am I, and I think we should tell everyone."

Beatrice's heart swelled with Jackson's bravado, but she had to be honest. Now, in the calm, with a clear head, what thrummed through her was fear. "I need time to tell my brothers."

"How much time?"

"I don't know. But soon? I'm showing them the new Beachy tomorrow. We signed for the larger space."

He beamed. "What? Congratulations."

"I meant to tell you first thing, but . . ." Grinning, she swept her eyes over their bodies. "But anyway, I'm surprising them with that news. So, first things first."

A frown crossed his face. "They don't know?"

She paused. "Not exactly. They know we're expanding, though. I've also told them about my Nags Head house."

Jackson was quiet as he examined her face.

"What are you thinking about?" she asked after a pause. His expression was unreadable.

"I just . . . don't understand how you've been able to keep this all hidden. I don't like to keep secrets from people, Beatrice. It's lying."

"A secret isn't synonymous to lying. And sometimes, secrets are necessary, don't you think?"

"Not unless it's top secret government information—I prefer to be transparent. I lived so much of my life as a secret. My mother was kept a secret . . ."

Defensiveness rose from within her. Families were nuanced, and their situation was especially complicated. "I'm sorry that happened to you, Jackson, but it's not always black and white. As someone who's kept so many secrets for solid reasons, and even for others, I take offense. *You* have an NDA you're working with—you yourself aren't being a hundred percent transparent." Beatrice tried to infuse a lightness into her voice, though her tone rose to a soprano.

"Hey." His hand ran down the length of her body and ended at her waist. He gripped it, easing her temper. "You're right. Look, I'm willing to keep us on the DL for a little while. It will give me some time to decide how to tell McCauley. Who knows? Maybe there's even a way we can massage things?" His voice trailed off.

And just like that, Jackson defused the situation, and Beatrice softened in his arms. His words caught up to her. "Do you mean mediate? Because if we can do that, it would be so much easier."

"*Mediate* might be too strong a word. McCauley isn't made for mediation but for winning."

"How about peace?" she whispered. "Peace between them, for us?" It sounded good; it sounded normal and so functional, and optimism sparked inside her. "Kuya Chris turned over a new leaf since Heart Resort Exposé; he hired a larger staff. He hasn't quite been as competitive. He may be open to it. Can you do that with your father?"

Beatrice had been as surprised as the rest of the family that Chris had passed some of the reins to Gil. At the thought of him, and then Jessie, Beatrice felt another pang of guilt. Who was keeping secrets that could break up the family now?

"McCauley and I *have* spent a lot of time together the last couple of days, and he seemed . . . willing to get to know me."

That was curious. "You're getting along?"

He rubbed the top of his head, fingers pushing back the strands of hair. Only part of it stayed up, the rest draping down across his forehead, and the intimacy of witnessing this small detail squeezed Beatrice's heart. His gaze was in the distance, like he was composing sentences in the air.

"Growing up, I felt incomplete despite having Mom as a constant. And lately he made me feel like I was part of our family history. I didn't expect it, to be honest. And I'm not so sure if I should believe it, or trust it. But it made me think that I can have control about what happens in the future, for Willow Tree." His gaze seared into her. "It gave me hope, that maybe he'll think twice about whatever he was planning on doing if he knew that I found you . . ."

At the pause, she asked, "You found me . . . what?" The breath had left her lungs. He was looking at her so intently that she wholly empathized with the story of his plight. Of this young boy needing his father. Of finally being acknowledged, and the hope that they could be a family.

He ran his fingers through her hair, pushing the strands away from her face. "That I find you beautiful, astonishing, remarkable. And that I hope he doesn't do anything to hurt the person I have the most massive crush on."

Beatrice couldn't keep her smile from bursting forth, because he'd nailed on the head the exact emotion she felt for him. He was a massive crush that gave her mini explosions of giddiness. When she was around him, she wanted to squeal. In him, she saw the future. At this moment, she envisioned them standing together against the expectations of others, fully in love.

In love?

Was this love? Beatrice loved people; she cared for them inherently. She gave herself to them in the things she did. She said it freely.

This felt like more.

Beatrice hugged his chest. For his honesty, for his admirable ideals, for believing in them. But also for what they would need to do to make this right for them. "We'll figure this out."

"We will," he reassured her.

From downstairs came the sound of the door closing, bringing forth the reality of here and now. "Oh my gosh, what time is it? Your mother. She lives here." Had she come home in the middle of them having sex? Had she heard them?

After he looked at his phone, he kissed her. "It's just shy of eleven. And my mom's bedroom's on the first floor. She texted while you were asleep. She saw your shoes at the front door."

She slapped her palm against her forehead. "This is so embarrassing. She knows I'm here."

He laughed. "It's all right, Bea. We're grown, and she understands that."

"Here's another Puso fact. It doesn't matter how old one is. If my brothers saw your shoes at the front door, you'd better believe they would've come knocking."

He shrugged, grinning. "I suppose if I had a sister, that might change the conversation a little. But you . . . you can stay. Will you?"

"Yes." The answer was swift, though with the talk of reality came thoughts of her ever-pervasive responsibilities. "I take it back—let me check my phone. Geneva gets home today, and with all the stuff with Beachy, she might want to chat." She spotted the phone on her side of the floor, grabbed it, and checked her notifications. "Looks like Geneva's dropped off stuff from her trip. And"—she pursed her lips regretfully—"I need to work for at least a couple more hours. Is it okay if I take a rain check?"

"Absolutely. How about tomorrow night?" He tucked her into him so that their legs scissored together. She reveled in his strong hold, in what physically felt like protection, over her. As he pressed his thigh between her legs, her eyes shut in pleasure.

"That's too long from now." Her voice came out husky, lust ramping up. She wanted him again. But as if the world was conspiring against her, her phone buzzed. She groaned.

"I'll be counting the minutes."

"One more kiss for the road," she said, lifting her lips to his. Then, with what felt like absolute anguish, she peeled herself away from him to dress. After, she helped him make the bed, fluffing the pillows so they were straight.

It was a small glimmer of domesticity that made her suck in a breath. He straightened the final corner of the comforter and stood to his full height. "Ready?"

"Yep."

At his front door, she wrapped her arms around his waist. "So . . . ," she prompted. "We're going to do this?"

"Yep. You talk to your people. I talk to mine. Maybe see where they're at. Find out if a truce is even possible." He laid his hands on her shoulders. "But whenever you're ready to tell them, I will be."

She heaved a breath at that one obstacle and avoided his eyes to slip on her shoes.

"I'll walk you home," he said.

"You don't have to. I'm so close."

"Still." He bent down to kiss her. His lips were featherlight.

"Okay."

Five minutes later, Beatrice entered her beach house. She was the epitome of the heart eyes emoji. As Roxy sniffed her legs, Beatrice leaned back against the door.

"Why hello, Cinderella."

Startled, Beatrice jumped. "Holy mother of . . ." She pressed a hand against her chest, turning to the woman lying on her couch. Her already lifted spirits soared. "Geneva!"

Geneva sat up in time for Beatrice to tackle her back down. "Oh my God. I feel like I've been gone for a year." She laughed.

"It felt like a year. Why didn't you say you were here?"

"I wanted to surprise you." She gestured to the beach bags next to her. "Pasalubong."

Beatrice squealed at the prospect of gifts. They both hefted the bags onto the kitchen island. Beatrice unloaded mugs, and magnets, and a whole lot of Asian snacks while Geneva nuzzled Roxy.

"So I couldn't help but stop at the Asian market," Geneva said.

"You know I never pass that up either. I don't take it for granted."

With a hand in her bag, Geneva paused. "Guess what else I have in here? Not from Nashville, an FYI."

"What is it?"

She pulled out her iPad. Then, a pin-striped fabric swatch and Geneva's well-used ring of paint swatches.

Beatrice clapped and hooted.

"After that final contract came through, I was hit with a dose of inspiration. I couldn't help but work on the new Beachy design while on our honeymoon. Honeymoon? What honeymoon? Though . . ." She looked off into the distance, wistful.

Beatrice grimaced. "No romantic details about my baby brother, please—that is just . . . gross."

"Sorry." She sighed. "Anyway . . . what do you think so far?"

"Well, I love this. All of it. And I trust you inherently," Beatrice declared, running her hand over the fabric.

"Good, because I went ahead and planned the initial schematics of the layout." Geneva turned on her iPad and, after a few taps of her Apple Pencil, brought her to a screen that had a top-down view of the space with the finished decor drawn in. Beatrice could imagine the complete picture. The space was going to be warm, inviting.

"Oh, Gen. It already looks so, so good."

"Also, I solidified dates for the movers—though to save money, we should try to move some of these boxes ourselves. Shouldn't be too bad with your brothers helping."

Someone else can help us, Beatrice almost said. Instead, what came out was, "Great. I'll let them know tomorrow when I surprise them with the new Beachy."

"Are you kidding me right now—" Geneva started.

"Before you freak out . . . I didn't want to do it until the lease was signed, and now that it's come through, it's full speed ahead."

"Um . . . okay." Geneva still looked incredulous, turning off her iPad. "Because Brandon knows, though I've sworn him to secrecy. And I hate that."

"I promise. It's the first thing I'm going to do tomorrow."

"Okay."

"But, speaking of secrets . . . I've got something a little more complicated to update you with."

"Oh God. Does this call for dessert?"

Beatrice headed to the freezer and took out Geneva's favorite ube-flavored ice cream, pulled a spoon from the drawer, and handed it to her. "You should sit."

"Oh, this must be serious."

"It is."

Her best friend hopped up on the counter seating. After a sizable spoonful of ice cream, Geneva inhaled. "All right. Hit me."

Beatrice blurted out the words before she could think twice. "Jackson Hill is the son of Dillon McCauley the third."

Another spoonful stopped halfway to Geneva's mouth. "He's a McCauley?"

With the words said aloud, Beatrice's worry was reinforced. She leaned her elbows against the countertop and cradled her head. "He's a McCauley."

"No." She set down the spoon. "So you met a McCauley in Vegas five years ago?"

"I know. It's unbelievable."

"Beatrice, I'm so sorry."

Her friend was pitying her because she had come to the same horrible conclusion as Beatrice had—that, dammit, this wasn't fair.

Then, Geneva frowned. "But wait. I heard a man's voice outside. And with you coming in here all in a daze. You were just with him. So you're still together?"

Beatrice nodded, feeling Geneva's judgment. "I really like him, Gen. More than like, I think. There's just something about him. It feels like I've known him forever, like he's always been a part of my life."

Geneva reached across and held her hand like only a mother would. (And between the two of them, sometimes Beatrice felt like she was truly younger compared to serious Geneva.) "But what if the attraction is more because you can't have him?"

"I thought of that too." She shook her head. "But I felt this same connection in Vegas. I felt it when we saw each other for dinner. And the more we spent time together . . . like at Ocracoke—"

Geneva frowned. "So you knew back then?"

"I found out before our chicken-and-waffles-ice-cream date. Since then, things have become serious, and we're trying to find our way around it."

"Find your way around?" Geneva sat back.

"Yes. Because is Jackson culpable? Am *I* culpable?" She gestured at her computer and her journal, in which she'd scribbled illegible notes, and shame rode up her spine. "I deserve a PhD in stalking. I looked up everything about him, about Willow Tree."

From social media accounts, to genealogy, to Facebook, to online white pages, Beatrice had traced Jackson all the way back to when he'd entered the military. Yep, she'd found his picture from basic training, fresh faced in a uniform that didn't have a rank, hair shaved into a buzz cut. "He only started working for Willow Tree earlier this month. And he hasn't been a part of that family at all. Not his entire life."

"And yet," Geneva interrupted, "you know how Willow Tree has been terrible to Heart Resort."

"That wasn't Jackson."

"Beatrice." Geneva's voice was firm. "He *is* Willow Tree. Just like *you* are Heart Resort. It's the thing I've been telling you all along. There's no separation of family and work. It's all intertwined."

Beatrice's cheeks went aflame; Geneva always had a way of bringing her back down to earth. "Why does this happen to me?" Beatrice whined. She knew she sounded like an immature brat, like someone who had the worst lot in life. Yes, she'd been through rough times, but so much of her life was good. "I've got the worst luck." Beatrice headed to her love seat and plopped down.

"First of all, it's not about luck." Geneva grabbed a sparkling water from the fridge and handed it to her. "It's about timing and circumstance and facts."

"Basically luck." Beatrice snickered. "I want this to work, Geneva."

"It won't work." Geneva sat down next to her. "Beatrice Cayuga Puso."

That got Beatrice's focus. "Yes?"

"I see you trying to justify this. Heart Resort Exposé was a mere six months ago. There's absolutely no way that you can be with him. Not even an iota. Not unless you want to split from Heart Resort and your brothers. And I won't let that happen."

"I know. I know. I know." She said it three times to get it into her head that yes, she understood the consequences.

"You still don't sound convinced." A snort came from Geneva. "Beatrice . . . from one friend to another. Heck, one sister to another, woman to woman? What the hell is going on with you?"

"You're sounding like Kuya Gil."

"Am I? Then maybe that means you should listen." She heaved a breath, and her expression softened. "I'm sorry. Look, I'm worried, okay? I'm worried that with all your juggling and keeping secrets, you're losing your way. That you're actually willing to turn your back on your brothers for a man who you barely know? It was a Vegas affair. A motorcycle ride and a make-out session. Is that worth a family fight? I know this sucks. But I have to be honest, Bea . . . I'm not sure if I can back you up on this. I love you, but you need to know where I stand. The best thing is to talk to Jackson and end it."

Beatrice absorbed Geneva's words, knowing that it took so much for her to say them. And yet, what Geneva hadn't experienced as an only child was that Beatrice was the priest to whom everyone confessed everything. Beatrice supported others' dreams before her own.

She was indispensable, as Chris continued to remind her.

For once . . . for once, Beatrice wished that she could make mistakes and not be judged. To have the freedom to find out what was right for herself, to be with Jackson because she wanted to. Because it was what her heart wanted.

Selfish. Beatrice wanted to be selfish.

And who was Geneva to say how Beatrice felt about Jackson? This was Beatrice's love life. *Her* life.

"I just sense . . ." Beatrice landed on the final truth, then tried again. "I think I could fall in love with Jackson. I've never felt that before. But you're right. I have to end it."

That last sentence came out of her mouth because it was something she thought she should say, because that was what a loyal sister did. But she hated it. And she wasn't sure she believed it.

"I'm sorry, Bea." With open arms, Geneva hugged Beatrice with a sister's strength, and Beatrice had no choice but to succumb. But she couldn't relax in Geneva's arms.

♡

After dropping off Beatrice, Jackson was in his head as he trotted up his beach house stairs. His thoughts spiraled around Beatrice, Heart Resort, Willow Tree, and his father. So much so that when he entered and found his mother propped up on one of the kitchen stools, he jumped back in surprise.

"Goodness, I didn't think you were up."

"I couldn't sleep." She tightened the knot of her robe.

"Oh, God. I'm sorry . . ." His neck burned with embarrassment and especially at the knowledge that he'd bragged to Beatrice that it was all right that she'd spent part of the night.

"Oh, no . . . that's not what I'm talking about. You're a grown man, and you can very well have anyone over you wish." She hopped off the stool and filled the kettle with water.

Tea again.

"Mother?"

"Jack, you're an expert on risk management. I was wondering how often a person should reevaluate their risk?"

Jackson couldn't discern Cathy's tone. "It depends on the activity. If it were high stakes such as life and limb, shelter, safety—I would say often."

She clicked the stove on, then set the kettle on the grate. "Where would family and love fall in there?"

Jackson leaned against the counter on his elbows. "Something tells me that this doesn't have anything to do with The Cathy Hill coming out of retirement."

She turned. "No. It has everything to do with this gut feeling that you and Beatrice are getting serious. And with you spending the night at Grandview, with *that* man—well, it's worrisome. I'm concerned that you and Beatrice are in over your head. Yesterday she and I ran into one another, and I could just tell that her feelings for you run deep." Her unsmiling blue eyes bored into him. "I don't know what I'm saying here, because I love—*love*—that you and Beatrice found one another. But the pain that's sure to follow is going to be immense. I don't even want to sugarcoat it."

The last thing Jackson ever wanted to do was put his mother under any kind of stress. It had been unavoidable with him being in the army; an army parent was a role he himself wasn't sure he could do. So he wanted to ease her worry. "Spending the night at Grandview was about me finding out more about myself. And yes, it was to figure out how Beatrice and I are going to manage what we have. But I had to try to figure out what that means. Wouldn't you do that too, especially for someone who was important to you?"

Her eyes glassed with tears. "That's the thing, Jackson. I did that. And the door was slammed in my face. And it was by the man who has gotten under your skin."

Jackson shook his head. "He was always under my skin, Ma."

She came around the island and laid her hands on his forearms, squeezing. "I just want to protect you. Always have. Always will."

"I know." He wrapped his arms around her.

CHAPTER FIFTEEN

Today's affirmation: I take advantage of every opportunity.

After a walk-through of the empty shop on 12 and Bryan, Beatrice stepped out of the double doors.

Fiona dropped keys into her open palm, then slipped her sunglasses over her face. "Congratulations, my friend."

People sidestepped them on the sidewalk. Cars honked in the distance, music emanated from open car windows, and all of it was a symphony of triumph to Beatrice's ears.

Welcome, world, to a bigger and better Beachy.

"In a week and a half, these doors will open to the public." Beatrice gripped the keys, the jagged edges a reminder of the responsibility of a bigger lease. It had never been more apparent to her that adulting meant having multiple emotions exist at one time: excitement, and apprehension, and hope. "Not a moment to lose."

"Are you doing a grand reopening?"

"Nope, it's going to be an open house. Beachywarming." Saying it loosened her chest, and she smiled. "What do you think?"

"I think it's a fantastic idea. You can count on me to be here to support." Fiona threw her arms around Beatrice. "But work calls—I'd better run." She opened her car door. "Are you going to start moving in today?"

"I've got a first load in the car, and Geneva's at old Beachy packing up. My brothers are coming by in a bit, and I'm giving them a tour. It's going to be a surprise."

"Aw, how sweet. I love how you guys are so close. Makes me wish my family lived nearby. Almost." She winked before getting into her car.

"Thanks for coming in early to meet me."

"It worked out. Happy moving-in day!"

Beatrice watched the back of Fiona's car as it exited the parking lot, anticipation rising despite the layer of exhaustion that comprised her current physical state. She hadn't been able to sleep after her chat with Geneva last night; if Geneva's reaction to Jackson's identity was a taste of what her brothers would exhibit, Beatrice was in trouble.

Antsy, Beatrice commenced on doing an initial cleaning. She swept and wiped down counters and windows, because it made her feel better. For extragood vibes, she plugged in a diffuser with ylang-ylang and jasmine essential oils.

She proceeded to bring a first load of boxes from her car, which was parked in the employee space in the back, when a booming laugh reached her ears. She looked up from the trunk, toward OBX Diner, the restaurant adjacent to Beachy. OBX Diner was never without customers—another boon for Beachy—and currently a group of people were heading inside.

Beatrice spotted Jackson. He was hard to miss with his straight posture and tousled hair. All at once, her body hummed, dousing all her worry like water over a campfire.

Yes, it had been only a little more than a week, but it felt as if she'd lived alongside him ever since the first day they'd met, and she simply was lacking the details of his life and vice versa.

She shut the trunk and readied to yell his name, but her voice strangled in her throat. The person next to him, she recognized now, was his half brother, Lonnie. The other, Peter Holshbach.

Which left the last man in their group. He was taller than the rest of them, wider, and imposing.

Dillon McCauley III.

Beatrice kept an eye on the group as they entered the restaurant, heart pounding. In fifteen minutes her brothers would be arriving. For Dillon McCauley III and Chris to cross paths would not be a great way to start any of their days. She rushed into the shop and texted Jackson.

Beatrice:
I saw you walk into OBX diner

Beatrice:
I'm here at the new Beachy

Jackson:
I thought you would be at Heart Resort still?

Beatrice:
Schedule change. My brothers are coming in abt 15 minutes. Just a warning

Jackson:
All good. Still waiting for a table.
Won't be seated for 20 minutes.
What is it with this restaurant?

Beatrice:
Locals know the good places.

Jackson:
What are you doing?

Beatrice:
Just cleaning up

The chat went silent, so Beatrice jumped onto her email to distract herself from her current worry. It was a jumble in her inbox, so instead, she called her assistant. "Hi, Kim, I figured a phone call would be easier than answering all the emails. Can you give me the TL;DR?"

"Yep. First thing: Leila sent over a date when she wanted to meet. I followed up with the rest of the team, and as soon as I get a consensus, I can set it on your calendar. Second: The property search for Heart Resort's secondary location has begun, and there's a request for you to come along with the rest of the team. Third: All incoming guests have been sent their welcome packets. I did receive a couple of questions I wasn't sure how to answer. One was about access to cell phones when it comes to babysitters, and another about switching homes. Fourth: We received two complaints from current guests who felt like their cabins could have been bigger."

Heart Resort's amenities included sleek tiny houses to encourage togetherness.

Beatrice groaned. "It's called a *tiny* house . . ."

Kim chuckled. "You might have to answer that email."

"I'll do better than that. Go ahead and offer them a one on one with me either at Hapag on the deck or on video chat."

"Okay. Will do."

Beatrice rubbed her temple as the information she received found slots in her already full brain. "But thank you, for all the work you've done. You are so on the ball. And speaking of . . . how are you doing, future bride? What's next on the list to plan, and can I help with any of it?"

"Aw, should we talk about it now?"

"Sure, why not? A little bit of wedding talk can soothe the nerves." *Mine especially,* Beatrice thought.

"I'm searching for an after-ceremony dinner venue. But I'm not familiar with local places."

"Ah—easy peasy. I'll send you a list of my favorite spots, and you can see if there's a fit."

"Oh, thank you."

A knock startled Beatrice, and she almost dropped the phone. She looked across to the front doors, to a person leaning in, hands cupped to look inside.

Her insides lit as bright as the noon sky. As she walked to the front door, she said, "Kim, I'll call you back."

Jackson stepped in as soon as the door was unlocked, and he scooped her up in a kiss. Eight hours had been too long for him too, apparently.

Beatrice giggled against his lips. "How'd you get away?" she asked after he set her down, hands pressed against the rough weave of his Henley. Goodness, she had never considered a Henley a sexy garment, but here she was.

"I said I had to take a phone call. It's not uncommon for that crew, so they didn't even think twice. I practically ran over here."

"Is that why your heart's beating so hard?"

"No, it's because of you."

Her belly did that thing again, where it swirled with joy. "You know exactly what to say to a girl."

"To you, you mean." He bent down and kissed her once more, leaving her breathless. "I should go, right?"

Alerted to the time, Beatrice widened her eyes. "Yeah, you probably should."

"All right. See you tonight. I should have some alone time with McCauley today. Nervous to see your brothers?" He locked his arm around her neck and kissed her hair.

"Yep, but I'll be fine." Her voice came out as a squeak. "Right. You should go. The last thing I want is for them to roll up on you, and your father comes out of the restaurant to look for you, and it turns into a western shoot-out."

Jackson half laughed; then he stiffened. "That's not funny, is it?"

"Nope." Beatrice all but pushed him out the door after one last kiss. Then, inhaling deeply, she straightened her clothes. She had just reapplied her lip gloss when Chris's Suburban pulled up in front of the shop.

Her nervousness spiked when her brothers exited from the vehicle. Each had their distinct expressions: Chris as suspicious, Gil as curious, and Brandon as flummoxed. What was similar among them was that all three were wearing their Heart Resort polos.

She looked down at her clothing—she was in a Beachy dress. Whoops.

She met them halfway, on the sidewalk. Brandon overtook his brothers with a mischievous smile on his face, undoubtedly reading her mistake and knowing what this meeting was about. He bum-rushed her with a hug. "Hey, Ate Bea."

It was exactly what she needed. "Hey." She girded herself and swallowed her fear as Chris and Gil approached.

"What's this?" Chris asked. "What are we doing here?"

"I'll show you." She opened the door and led them inside, silent except for their ominous footsteps. "I want to welcome you to the new Beachy."

"New Beachy?"

"Remember last week when I told you that Geneva and I were going to expand? This was what we were talking about. An actual retail space."

Gil's eyebrows rose. "I thought that we decided that you wouldn't be—"

"Congratulations, Ate," Brandon interrupted, easing the tension in the room. "I think it's great. It's wise not to have all of your eggs in one basket. Dresses and housewares, subscription and retail and wholesale. Right, Kuyas?" His eyes darted to both of their brothers.

She appreciated Brandon's attempt at peacemaking, but she could see the trepidation on her older brothers' faces. Chris was especially silent.

That was good, right? He hadn't blown up right away, which meant that, perhaps, he would be open to the new Beachy as well as Jackson.

Beatrice swallowed a lump in her throat.

"This is huge, Bea. Congratulations. But what does this all mean, for Heart Resort?" Chris finally said, looking around. "You'll be taken up moving into this new place and managing a larger operation." He flashed their brothers a look. "Especially at a time when the resort is expanding."

"I can do both," she declared with a smile.

Until you can't, her conscience nagged. *Until you have to finally make the choice. With Jackson too.*

Beatrice pushed her conscience into a make-believe closet and locked the door. One thing at a time.

Gil made a noise to emphasize his doubt. She shot him a look. For a brother who used to be pretty neutral about most situations, he sure didn't have her back at the moment.

"Do you doubt me?"

Gil stuffed his hands in his pockets. "Look, it's not me who's forgotten to wear the proper uniform. It's a normal workday for you, and yes, we're here at your request, but have you been doing Beachy work all morning? Or resort work? Seems to me you're moving further away from the business rather than closer. Even Bran here—"

"Hey, don't drag me into this. I'm glad for Ate Bea," Brandon interrupted.

"Thank you." At least she still had Brandon on her side.

Chris's alarm blared on his phone. "We can talk about this later. Let's head back to the resort. We have our meeting with our real estate agent to go over our wants and needs for the secondary location. He has potential properties lined up."

"But, we don't technically have anything to talk about since this is Beachy business."

"And yet, I feel like we do," Chris said pointedly to her and Gil. "Hop in the Suburban with us. One of us can bring you back here later on."

"With all of you attending, why do I need to be there? I could be . . . working on work."

"Already shamming," Gil said.

"Always complaining," she cheered.

"Tension's rising," Brandon sang, moving past all of them out the front door.

"Enough, you two." Chris rubbed his beard. "I can't believe I'm even mediating. We're grown. Anyway, Bea, I want you there. It took all four of us to decide on Heart Resort, and it will take the four of us to decide what properties match with our needs. But, Gil, drop it."

Gil raised his hands as he headed toward the door. "You got it."

Once alone, Chris turned to Beatrice. "The both of you are getting to be too much."

She shrugged. "It's not me who's always raring for a fight."

"But you don't deescalate either."

"I can try, but he needs to also." She heaved the heaviness in her chest away, then noticed they were out of hearing range from her other brothers. *Now's the time to bring up Jackson.* Now was Beatrice's opportunity. "How are . . . you and Ate Eden doing?"

"Good. Fine." He frowned. "Why, did she say something?"

"No, not at all. Are you . . . feeling at peace with how the business is going?" She cleared her throat, fully understanding that she wasn't being smooth at all. *Get to it, Beatrice.* "And how are you with all that stuff with Willow Tree?"

He counted out his answers using his fingers. "I'm feeling pretty good. Gil has really stepped up. As you can see, I'm playing less of a bad cop. It's also given me more time with Eden, which ultimately has helped us. But Willow Tree? I might not be fussing over them, but it doesn't mean I hate them any less."

She internally gasped. "Still hate, huh?"

"I never forget, Bea. They've been quiet too, which is a little unnerving. Mike, whose sister is a McCauley by marriage, doesn't have much to report except that the guy's long-lost son is back."

"Long-lost son?" The words barely escaped Beatrice's constricted throat.

He snorted. "A spare heir, I guess. Luckily there are four of us. I say bring it."

"Yeah, bring it," she whispered, full of dread.

There would be no way for Beatrice to broach the subject of Jackson except to come right out and say it. There would be no easing in of the truth. Whenever she finally told her brothers, she'd have to be prepared for the worst-case scenario.

And that was not this second.

Chris led the way outside, but before Beatrice opened the passenger door of the Suburban, he pulled her back by the elbow. "For what it's worth, Bea. Even with all the changes, and perhaps some transitional things you need to work on, I'm proud of you. I know our parents would be so proud too. Especially Mom. You know she'd be at Beachy every chance she had. She would have been your best customer."

"Thanks, Kuya." Her face warmed with the beginnings of tears, though she blinked them back. But it was probably more likely that their mother was turning in her grave for the secrets she continued to amass.

♡

McCauley was spitting fire.

"This island is too damn small." McCauley's voice echoed across the sound—Jackson bet the fishermen out on the water had heard him.

"This is the best option we have." Lonnie was trying to explain one more time. "Unless you want to look beyond the Outer Banks."

"No."

They were getting nowhere. They'd toured a total of five islands and peninsulas today, two of which were repeats of the other day, because McCauley had been dissatisfied. Hours had passed, and now rounding the afternoon, they were no better off than they had been this morning.

Correction: they were getting nowhere when it came to properties, but Jackson was getting somewhere with his father. McCauley was listening to him. The day had been filled with details, from construction to finance to marketing, and though none were his expertise, Jackson had been able to volley ideas and provide feedback.

Admittedly, Jackson was basking in all of it. He knew it was a slippery slope; he couldn't get too attached, knowing that he would soon talk about Beatrice. But here, at this moment, he belonged in a way that he'd never felt before.

"There are . . . other options," Jackson offered, to lead his father a completely different direction. Overnight, Jackson had scoured through land listings as far south as Myrtle Beach and as north as Maryland. If he couldn't halt McCauley from purchasing land, he could at least increase the distance between the two resorts. "But I do believe that no matter what you choose, there will be some sacrifice in other areas."

His father had begun a slow march to the pier, where Peter Holshbach was waiting for them. He gave Lonnie a side-eye. "*Now* do you understand the secondary and tertiary effects of decisions? It's not just what happens immediately after a failed mission but all the consequences years down the line. It was a small ask to keep an eye on a property and properly bid on it. God forbid. McCauley Island slipped right through our fingers."

Lonnie looked stricken at their father's rant, which started and ended in a huff. McCauley climbed onto the boat and sat in one of the captain's chairs in front in definite avoidance of the both of them.

Ouch.

Lonnie's neck flushed a deep red.

Jackson empathized. Squad leaders, platoon sergeants, and commanders had raised him with sometimes harsh words.

But a surprising protectiveness rose within him. Lonnie was a pain, but he was his little brother.

Jackson made his way to the front of the boat, and took a seat in front of his dad. If he was really being given this opportunity to be someone in this family, in Willow Tree, he might as well continue to speak up.

McCauley spared him only a moment's glance. "What is it?"

"Peter has some alternate locations, but they're not peninsulas or islands."

He shook his head. "I want privacy."

"I understand. But there's also accessibility to consider. It could be an easier and faster start-up because it's a mainland build."

McCauley was still looking off in the distance, deep in thought, so Jackson decided to come at it from another direction. "To have a private but mainland property would still be unique. We'd have to parse out cost, ultimately, but for the kind of project you're thinking of, accessibility will be so important. Isn't that what we want for our guests?"

At the word *we*, Jackson felt a tinge of nausea in the back of his throat; on the other hand, his father pursed his lips in approval.

"*We*. So you've given it some thought."

"It's hard not to think about it," Jackson said truthfully. The day had gone so well that at times, he had to remember that he wasn't supposed to like the guy. It had been everything about the man: the slow roll of his words, his sharp wit, and seeing Jackson himself in him.

He's a charming man. His mother's warning wormed out of his subconscious, and he refocused his intentions. Beatrice. Heart Resort.

"It's easier to think about staying because I met someone here," Jackson said.

"Really? A local?"

Jackson nodded.

"You like her?"

"I do."

"Does she know you're a McCauley? She's not some gold digger, is she?"

Jackson snorted aloud, though he trod around his questions with care. "She's an entrepreneur, and she's part of a couple of businesses."

And then Jackson saw it, a quirk in his father's lips. It could have been from amusement, or pride, but it gave Jackson hope. That maybe all of it would work out.

"Have Peter line up some beachside properties for the day after tomorrow. We still need at least ten units, private beachside access, and all that. The same other criteria applies."

"Great." Jackson was eager for space, and he hefted himself to his feet. As he headed back to his seat, he noticed Lonnie's brown eyes trained on him.

An hour later they arrived at the real estate office. McCauley entered his privately driven SUV and bid them an understated farewell—he was staying at another one of his properties in Duck. Jackson had been prepared to walk home since the vibe between him and Lonnie had been tense on the ride from the dock, but he was offered a way back.

As soon as they both shut the doors of the vehicle, Lonnie spoke. "You've only been here two weeks, and he's already taking your advice, not mine. He barely spoke to me today." He snorted. "Little does Dad know that all that kissing ass is you trying to curry his favor."

"I don't know what you're talking about."

"Come on. You're not that slick. This has everything to do with Beatrice Puso. It's going to be a hell of a day when it all comes out that you've been with her. The only thing worse than that is staying with her."

Jackson bit his cheek to keep himself from snapping back. Lonnie wanted a rise out of him, but he wasn't going to take the bait.

"Or maybe it's not about Beatrice but you sliding into the business like I originally thought. Spending the night up at Grandview the other day . . . it had to have been that he asked you to stay, for good." Lonnie did a double take. "Or maybe it's a combination of both?"

Lonnie's perceptions were so close to the truth that it rendered Jackson unsteady, and it took him too long to generate a comeback. "You should be thankful that I stepped in to take the heat off of you about Heart Resort."

"Heh. Good one. But I don't need your help, Jackson."

"Noted."

They rode in silence a few minutes, soon reaching Jackson's house. Seeing the beach just beyond the windshield had a slight calming effect, though Jackson was still bothered. His motivations were feeling slippery in his hands.

He turned to Lonnie. "Look, I don't want to fight."

Lonnie twisted his hands around the steering wheel. "Things aren't sitting right with me, and I don't like it."

It was the closest to an apology for the both of them, and Jackson was going to take it. "See you in a couple of days."

"Yep."

Jackson stepped out of the car and watched his brother drive off, a hand in the air in farewell. His head and heart burgeoned with confusion at how he'd gotten swept up with McCauley. And now, looking up at his beach house, he wasn't in the mood to face his mother.

He texted Beatrice, as he'd promised he would.

Jackson:
I'm back from work. You on HR or here?

Beatrice:
I'm at old Beachy

Jackson:
Good to have company?

Beatrice:

I just sent everyone home. Want to help me pack?

Jackson:

At your service. I'll be there in 10

It took only eight minutes on his bike, and after the short ride, Jackson felt slightly better about his day. He knocked on the back door, belatedly realizing that he looked a little rough from the boat ride and, simply, from all the thinking he'd done.

The door opened to Beatrice's smiling face, her hair in a bun with a bandana tied around it. She was wearing a Beachy apron, and her cheeks were sun-kissed. She had zero makeup on, giving him a glimpse of the future, of waking up next to her on any given day, and all at once he allowed his body to relax.

"Hey, Jackson." Then her expression changed. "You all right? Come in."

He walked into a mess. Stuff was everywhere. Clothing in plastic bags, boxes like a haphazard tower in one corner. He spotted a desktop computer on a table buried in the clutter. "I'm fine, but are *you* all right?"

"Oh this? This is just the beginning. It always gets worse before it gets better. And, this is nothing compared to what's out in front. Now that is *whoa*."

Jackson knew that Beatrice was talking about decluttering and packing, but somehow she got to the heart of what he was thinking. He grimaced at the truth of it all.

"You look like you're going to be ill, Jackson."

"Not ill. Just . . . it's been a day." He offered her a smile. "But we can talk about it later. I came here to help. So point me to . . . um . . ." He turned in a circle, unsure where to start. He was usually good at this, at determining hot spots and putting everything in its place, but today had felt upside down and sideways.

"Here. Come here." She waded through the inventory of clothing and cleared a box off of a padded chair—he hadn't even seen it—and pointed right at the seat. "Sit."

He raised an eyebrow. "Why should I sit? You should sit."

"Nope. My store. My rules. Sit."

"Fine. But not for long." He plopped down on the wing chair, and the cushions caught him expertly. As he sank into its softness, he exhaled.

"Nice, right?"

"Very nice."

"Okay now, make room." Then, Beatrice sat down on his lap, wrapped her arms around his shoulders, and squeezed.

It was a hug amplified, and while technically he was holding her, she was, in fact, cradling him. So much so that he shut his eyes and willed this obtuse emotion off his shoulders.

"It feels like you had a day like mine." When she spoke, her voice vibrated throughout his body, and he felt grounded for the first time today.

"It was full of . . . stuff."

"Do you want to tell me about it?"

Beatrice was smart not to push the nondisclosure; still, Jackson tiptoed around the showings. "Technically, it was great. McCauley and I are seeing eye to eye on things. We're getting along."

She lifted her face from his. "That's awesome."

"I know, but my past younger self feels betrayed by how happy my current adult self is by this."

She fingered the strands of his hair. "You can't be upset with yourself today for being surprised at a good thing because of something that disappointed you long ago. People can change."

"Do they?" He looked up at Beatrice, at the optimism that clearly made her who she was. She was the kind of woman who had to make an effort to frown. Her default expression was pleasant, with a hint of a smile.

"I hope they do. Can you imagine what my brothers and I could hold over each other's heads? So much. We're a big family, and what comes with that are these massive personalities. We've made mistakes. Lots of them." She fixed his collar. "I'm thinking of this a little selfishly. If you and your dad are getting along, then maybe peace *is* possible."

"I mentioned to him that I was seeing someone."

Surprise flitted across her face. "So fast."

"Yeah." Jackson then thought of Lonnie and the tension between them. He heaved a breath. "How about you? You seem chipper. How was today with showing your brothers the new shop? Did you get to broach them about us?"

"Today was a mixed bag. My brothers were congratulatory but not ecstatic about the new Beachy." She looked down at her lap for a beat. "I knew they weren't going to be thrilled about the shop, but I guess I wished they would have been."

"They'll come around. They were probably just surprised. It's a huge, great thing you're doing with expanding. That shop is perfect. Seeing you inside it today . . . it felt like you were always there. And I mean, you need the space."

"Thank you. I needed that. I mean, Geneva and the team and I pump each other up, but hearing it from someone who isn't part of the business itself is nice."

"If you ever need any help . . . ," he hedged, not wanting to infringe on her time and space, "I enjoyed helping you out with Breezy Bandanas. Business is interesting, and seeing what you do behind the scenes would be fun. Or, I can help you move boxes too. Either way."

"You're hired right now. Right this second." She hugged his neck like a vise grip, and he didn't dare complain because he didn't want her to let go.

After she eased her hold, she said, "I did mention Willow Tree to Kuya Chris."

"Oh?"

"My brother's still not a fan."

Damn. Jackson's body slumped with the news. "And by *not a fan*, you mean . . ."

"He used the H-word." She pressed her lips into a half smile of embarrassment. "I'm sorry."

"You don't have anything to apologize about."

"I . . . wish we could just skip this whole thing of telling them."

His ears perked at the sudden doubt in her tone. "What do you mean by that?"

Then, his mother's words returned to him: *Have you considered that maybe she might decide to choose her family?*

"That I wish we could keep it all separate. It's just so good the way it is, and so much less drama. Why *can't* we just go on with our lives and be neighbors? Honestly, I'm irritated that we have to get their permission. We should do what we want to do."

"You . . . don't mean that, do you?" The idea that they would have to prolong a secret relationship felt like he'd rolled in mud. And the way Beatrice was speaking, in her casual tone . . .

"Part of me does."

He adjusted her on his lap so that he could look at her squarely. "You know I can't do that, right? I'm not going to be the other man."

She laughed. "Being the other person isn't the same as the secret person. We'd be exclusive but have secret rendezvous away from our families. It could even be exciting."

He was getting confused, and trailing behind was a swirl of anger and worry. Was she joking?

Her face softened. "Jackson. Babe. You look like you've turned to stone. Of course I'll tell my family. You are important to me. I care about you, about us. It's just going to be harder than I expected, and I wish it wasn't so."

"Okay." And yet, why did she look almost green at the gills?

"But until then, I guess that means we get to sneak around some more?" She leaned her forehead against his, and strands of her hair cascaded around his face. She pressed her lips against his firmly, though chastely. It was just the exact kiss he needed, solid and confident, and it made up for his sudden insecurity.

He tucked her hair behind her ears. "Whenever, wherever."

She bit her lip in a mischievous smile, eyes darting around her.

He grinned. This woman.

But he . . . he was a man who stuck to deadlines and timelines. He linked his fingers with hers and kissed the top of her hand. "How about this. You tell me what we need to get done tonight here. Then we can call your bluff."

She brightened. "You don't mind? Not exactly the date you were probably expecting."

"Not a single bit. We have time."

CHAPTER SIXTEEN

Today's affirmation: I have a firm grasp on time.

Jackson had been wrong. Beatrice was, in fact, running out of time. It was going to take longer than anticipated to get the shop ready for Beachywarming.

"Okay, so give it to me. What do we need to do to make it happen?" Beatrice asked. It was the next day. At the new Beachy, she and Geneva were sitting cross-legged on a sheet on the floor with their devices spread out like they were having a picnic. In the background were the sounds of the Beachy team unpacking.

"We have to work around the clock. The good thing is that all the display shelves and tables are on the way, so those will arrive on time. But we'll lose at least today and tomorrow as the paint dries." Geneva gestured to the painters unloading their trucks out front. "Which means that we'll be working nonstop on the lead-up days." She met Beatrice's eyes. "This also means you'll need to take time off from Heart Resort."

Beatrice's answer was swift. "I can't."

"You're not even going to consider it?"

"Gen. I literally stood here yesterday and told my brothers that I could handle both jobs. Tomorrow we're looking at properties with the whole family."

Her arms shot out to the sides. "And yet, we have a Beachyversary to celebrate. You're my other half. We are one whole brain. I need you. Obviously, we'll have to do our duty tomorrow, but after that I need you here."

Beatrice pressed a palm against her forehead. The pressure. She was feeling it from everywhere. Her conversation with Jackson last night had been the straw that was starting to bend her back, though not quite breaking it. The face that he'd given her when she'd suggested they remain a secret awhile had been what had shocked her the most. Yes, she had been joking, but he'd been on the verge of getting upset at her. They'd made love after he'd helped her pack up, and nothing had seemed amiss by the night's end, but it had been clear that his patience was running thin too.

Her initial declaration of "I am not afraid"? It had been said in haste. Because she was definitely afraid.

Along with this fear was an irritation. She should be able to do what she wished, from expanding her business to dating whomever she pleased.

"I can see what I can do," Beatrice said now. Her business partner was expecting a solid CEO answer.

Her face softened. "Good. All right. Let's clear this spot and help unpack."

Beatrice's phone buzzed as they cleaned up.

It was Jackson.

Jackson:
Right outside your door

"I need to take a call," Beatrice said as Geneva walked to the back. She hustled to the front windows and peeked out. Jackson was parked under a tree, somewhat shaded by its overhang. Sitting on his motorcycle and in full gear, helmet on but visor up, he oozed sex appeal.

Jackson:
Safe to come out?

Beatrice:
be right there

And with one last look over her shoulder to make sure the coast was clear, Beatrice bounded outside and darted to his motorcycle.

He stayed seated on his bike, though his helmet was off by the time she reached him, and seeing his smile was a delicious jolt to her system. She wrapped her arms around his neck. "Hello. I missed you."

He planted a kiss squarely on her lips, while his left hand held her waist in place. "I missed you too. I haven't seen you all day."

"I know. Texting just doesn't cut it. What are you doing out?"

"Running an errand for Mom, doing a pickup at the craft store, so I thought I'd stop by. She's working her butt off. You should see the house. The entire first floor is her studio."

"I love that. I can't wait to see what she makes for us."

He gestured to the shop with his head. "How's everything going?"

"It's going. Lots of work up ahead. I'll be on the clock till bedtime, just like last night. I may need your help again." She entwined her fingers in his hair, relishing the thought of once more ending the night with him.

His eyes flashed. "I'm at your beck and call."

Loud conversation from the painters at Beachy brought their minds back to the tasks at hand.

"Back to work, boss lady." He let go of her waist and squeezed her hand.

"You too. The Cathy Hill awaits. I'll see you tonight." Then, after they shared one last kiss, Jackson donned his helmet and set off out of the parking lot.

Beatrice watched him go, heart squeezing at his thoughtfulness, when the sound of an engine and a honk made her jump. It was a Jeep with its top down. Brandon.

"Ate Bea!" Brandon waved before parking the Jeep.

She came up to the driver's side. "Hey. What are you doing here?"

"Just dropping food off for Gen. Dim sum." He lifted two pink boxes from the passenger side. "Who was that?"

"What do you mean?" She began to sweat. "Let me help with those boxes, Bran."

"No worries; I can handle it." Brandon hopped out of his truck. Then Beachy's front door opened, and Geneva exited. The two greeted each other with a kiss. "Food for you, babe."

Geneva was positively glowing. "Thanks, babe."

It was the perfect segue for Beatrice to head back inside. "I'm going to leave you two lovebirds alone."

"Nooo." Brandon's answer was protracted. "Who was the guy on the motorcycle? I saw you kiss him." Then, he looked to his wife.

Geneva's expression was undoubtedly judgmental, though she didn't respond.

"Ate Bea?" His shoulders slumped. "Aw, c'mon. You won't say? It's me . . . Bunso . . . your favorite baby brother. I know you like to keep things private, but I need to get you back for all the crap you've given me through the years about everything. Who is he?"

"Oops, will you look at the time." Beatrice glanced at the phone in her hand. "I've gotta run." Lifting two fingers into the peace sign, she turned to head back inside.

"You do understand that he's got to pass our test, right?" her brother called from behind. "He's got to pass Friday dinner!"

"Bye, Bran."

Beatrice didn't take a full breath until she walked into Beachy. Time was undoubtedly running out.

215

♡

"He said that?" Jackson laughed as Beatrice recounted her conversation with her brother Brandon. Lying down on reclined deck chairs at his beach house after working at Beachy, they held hands while looking up at the clear night sky. From inside came the echoes of another jazz playlist his mother had on loop as she worked.

"I know, right? As if I gave his girlfriends a hard time."

"Mm-hmm. You sure? You probably interrogated those poor girls."

"I wasn't *that* bad." But at Jackson's dubious expression, she admitted, "Okay, fine, I was, but someone had to uphold the standard. And I wasn't just that way with him but with Kuya Gil and Kuya Chris too. We're lucky to have Ate Eden around. She's amazing."

"Then there's Jessie."

Beatrice had mentioned Jessie a couple of times to Jackson. "Yeah. My jury's still out on Jessie."

"How does Gil feel about that, now that they're getting back together?"

"Of course he doesn't like that I haven't drunk her Kool-Aid. But someone has to remind everyone what she's done."

"That's . . . pretty harsh, don't you think?" He was looking at her sternly, though he kept his voice neutral. Admittedly, he was taking all this personally, though he wasn't angry. "If people judged my mother in the same way you're judging Jessie, then there would be no room for forgiveness. And didn't you say that you believed that people could change?"

Her face stilled. "It's just that she let everyone down."

"But maybe Gil did too."

Her chest rose and fell as she took a deep breath. "Yeah."

He tugged her hand, for her to look at him. "Are you upset at me for saying that?"

Her lips pursed for a moment. "No, not upset. Just . . . you called me out."

"I called you in." He offered her a smile. "There's a difference, and it's because I care about you. A lot."

"I care about you too."

Jackson loved this. This spending time, the conversations, the discussions. The ability to talk through exactly what he was thinking. "Was Geneva upset knowing I was there today?"

"I'm not sure. The day was so hectic that work took priority. I'll follow up, though."

"Well, your family sounds like a lot of fun in general."

Her smile made it up to her eyes. "They are, actually. At the very end of the day, you can count on them for anything."

"I can't wait to meet and get to know them."

"Same." She nodded. "Soon."

It was a relief to hear those words. Hiding in a shadowed corner of the parking lot earlier today had not been a good feeling. He would have liked to meet Brandon today. Did Jackson understand why they needed to keep their relationship a secret? Yes. Had it been only a short time since their relationship had begun? Also yes. But they'd agreed to come clean to their families, and it was taking longer than he'd expected, and he couldn't explain the shame it brought up. He felt it, though, deep in his bones.

He focused on the stars in the sky, on what he could tell was the Big and Little Dippers, and breathed positivity into his thoughts.

"Jackson." She turned onto her side.

He did the same. "Yeah."

She scanned his face. "Thank you . . . for talking things through about Jessie. And for not being angry for associating Cathy with all of it. I'm trying."

"I know you are."

"Also." She paused, swallowing. "I know we've spent only a few days together, but I wanted to say that, well, I—"

"Knock knock." A man's voice filtered up from the back stairs, and Jackson shot to his feet. Next to him, Beatrice sat up.

"Who's there?"

"Lonnie." His brother reached the final step to the balcony, and his gaze landed on Beatrice. "Holy shit . . ."

It put Jackson on edge immediately. Lonnie had been unreliable throughout their entire working relationship, and after their last conversation, Jackson wasn't sure what he was capable of. Over his shoulder, he said to Beatrice, "I'll be right back," and he brushed past Lonnie, gesturing for him to follow him down the stairs.

"Are you freaking joking right now?" His brother's laugh was wicked and grating, trailing them as they made it down to the sand. "I mean, I know I gave you a hard time yesterday, but I didn't *actually* think you were stupid enough to keep this going."

"Just . . . be quiet."

"No, I will not. Jackson. *Jack.* I know you haven't been around long enough, but you can't do this."

Very few people called him Jack. It was a nickname reserved for people who cared about him, who were a part of his life. Hearing it out of Lonnie's mouth raised his hackles. "You're not going to say a word."

Lonnie raised his hands in the air. "I won't. I wouldn't want to be involved in this. If it were up to me, I'd rather not even see this. To witness is to be culpable, and I value my hide."

"I'm planning to tell McCauley. I almost told him the other day. I'm just waiting for the go-ahead from her."

"And how's that going?" At his silence, he nodded. "Right. Of course she hasn't told her own family because this is a crap situation. Because you're not supposed to be together. This isn't romantic, man. This is a plain old tragedy. I just hope that it's love and it's worth it."

"She's worth it."

Realization flitted across his face. "Hold up . . . let me get this straight. You're risking your entire legacy, she's risking her family, without the L-word. This is wild."

"I'm not talking to you about this." Jackson didn't want to hear it anymore. Every relationship was different. They progressed in their own ways. What he felt for Beatrice was intense and real. Was it love?

Maybe.

Yes?

But he wasn't going to discuss this with his brother.

Have you considered that maybe she might decide to choose her family?

"What do you need, Lonnie? What are you doing here?" he spit out, chasing his mother's words away from his conscience.

"I wanted to come by and see if you were free to grab a beer."

He peered at him. "That all?"

"Yeah. But you're busy, so . . . I guess I'll head out and grab a drink myself."

"Alone?"

"Yeah. See you tomorrow." He turned to trudge through the sand. There was a slight hunch to his shoulders, and he'd stuck his hands in his pockets.

Jackson made it halfway up the stairs before listening to his conscience. He'd been taken care of by strangers throughout his life. Lonnie was his actual brother, and Jackson literally had nothing to hide from him.

So he yelled out into the beach, "Hey!"

Lonnie turned around. "Yeah?"

"Want some tea?"

CHAPTER SEVENTEEN

Today's affirmation: I remain calm through emergencies.

"Have you all noticed our family never moves around in small numbers?" Beatrice looked at the reflection in the rearview mirror and marveled that every seat was taken in Chris's Suburban.

Chris snorted and glanced at Eden, who was sitting next to him in the passenger seat. "Who needs kids when I have all of you back there?"

It was the next day, and the family was gathered to look at properties for the second Heart Resort location. They were currently en route to the fourth property on their list.

Sure enough, Brandon and Gil were in the third row bickering about baseball, with Geneva in between them mediating. Next to Beatrice was Jessie, and to her surprise, it was significantly less awkward between them. With Jackson's words in her ear, and with the small ways that Jessie had been there for her, she checked herself and her attitude.

"So, what's next on the docket?" Eden asked.

Brandon spoke up. "This next one's a fixer-upper. A set of bungalow beach houses in Salvo. They're all first row, and super private. Though the listing price is well below our budget, this is going to be a complete redo."

"Salvo? That's far." Beatrice glanced at the passing view. They'd been up and down Highway 12 all day.

"It's only twenty miles from the resort," Gil said from behind.

"Right, but that's twenty miles from the hub. Should we be needed in either place, that's a twenty-minute commute." She shifted in her seat, uncomfortable with what felt like haphazard plans. "This feels so fast."

"It feels fast because you haven't been thinking about it as much as we have," Chris pointed out. "Much like we thought it was fast for you to move shops."

At her husband's comment, Eden clucked in disapproval.

"It's not shade," Chris reiterated. "You've been thinking of expanding for a while, and it totally made sense, right?"

"You're right," Beatrice whispered back, though his words sure did feel like shade. But she wasn't going to object. Yes, there had been a couple of tense moments in the last day, but her brothers seemed to have moved on from the Beachy expansion.

With the thought of Beachy, she glanced at her phone to check for any news from Giselle. As she half listened to the conversation in the truck, she checked Beachy's socials and then hopped over to Heart Resort emails. Kim had plugged in Leila's video chat appointment on her calendar.

To her personal email address, she received another email from Kim. It was an e-invitation that contained an animated graphic with the words: You are cordially invited to celebrate the nuptials of Kim Jones and Heath Davis.

"Eeee!" Beatrice squealed, clicking yes immediately.

Eden turned, grinning. "You must have just gotten the invitation."

"Yes, I have. Wait, when did you all get yours?"

"Like three days ago!" Geneva laughed. "Are you just getting around to your personal emails?"

Her cheeks burned with embarrassment. "I mean, yeah. Seriously, my inbox is a mess."

"You're a busy lady. I bet you have emails coming from everywhere," Jessie remarked. "And I don't know about you, but I hate email. I think I have about ten thousand in my inbox."

"Yep. At least."

Eden turned once more, eyes round. "I literally just shivered. I'm an inbox-zero kind of girl."

"Uh-huh. Me too," Geneva added.

"Wait a sec," Chris interrupted. "Kim? As in Kim Jones, your assistant, is getting married? Where have I been?"

The car exploded in conversation that took random turns until Chris slowed. They were at Salvo, an even smaller beach town about ten miles south of Rodanthe. It was quaint and quiet, with abundantly fewer people milling about.

They parked and filed out of the Suburban. Sand whipped in all directions from the gusty wind.

The resort's real estate agent, Dave Disick, had parked behind them and stepped out of his car. He was a young man—he looked to be in his early twenties, Black, and preppy in his khaki shorts and button-down shirt—but was already making a name for himself. Chris liked him because he was savvy and assertive.

"The property should be up ahead to the left. Let's come at it from the beach to see what it looks like," Dave suggested.

As they shuffled through the beach-access path, Beatrice yawned, and she pressed a hand against her mouth. Last night had been long, though wonderful. It had been an awkward introduction with Lonnie, but once she'd understood that he hadn't taken part in any of Willow Tree's antics, she'd felt much more comfortable. For that short amount of time in Jackson's beach house, with all of them drinking herbal tea, it had felt like they were in their own little world. A world where she was her own person.

"You're over here smiling to yourself," Geneva whispered next to her. "Let me guess who you're thinking about."

Her tone had a layer of snark, and Beatrice was wary. "I know you don't approve."

"I approve of your happiness. It's him I don't approve of. I take that back. Not him but his family."

"So basically him."

"It's different, and you know it." She sighed, wrapping an arm around her. "I'm trying to be open minded, okay? What are you going to do?"

"What else? I'm going to tell my brothers."

"Really?" She held Beatrice back by a hand. Her lips lifted to an approving smile. "When?"

Her head spun. "I don't know. Today? Tomorrow? I'm looking for the right time." All Beatrice knew was that last night had also given her a glimpse of what it was like to live their relationship out loud. And she wanted more of that, despite the terror that continued to shoot through her.

"I'll be here for you when you do."

"Thank you. I'm going to need all the luck."

"Honestly, the fact that Jessie's back in the family is a good sign. This might work out better than you think. Speaking of, with the two of you interacting a little on the way here—that's good, Bea."

"I'm trying."

They'd gotten closer to the surf, and Dave turned, presenting the group of homes like a prize. "Twelve bungalows. Though still a public beach, it's near isolated. There's barely a soul around."

Beatrice squinted at the houses. Each of the four in front of her was nearly slouching, with half the siding either damaged or terribly soiled. "I'm not a designer like you, Geneva, but this doesn't look great."

Geneva hummed, head tilted to one side in assessment. "There's work to be done—that's for sure. But can you hear that?"

Beatrice grinned, understanding. "Just waves."

"Yep. Let me get to Bran, toss some ideas around."

"Okay." Beatrice watched her friend sidle up to her brother and slip an arm around his. He turned to her in the most natural way and kissed her on the temple. It was sweet and organic, and, by God, Beatrice wanted that.

Still, Beatrice knew that it took time and determination to make a relationship last. Geneva and Brandon had had their share of ups and downs. One of their downs had taken Geneva away from Heart Resort for months. Chris and Eden had once been on the verge of divorce, and Gil and Jessie had actually done so.

Was Beatrice ready for that? Was she ready to weather the ebb of telling her brothers about Jackson? Would she be able to admit that when she was with Jackson, Beatrice noticed nothing else? That with him, she felt like she was invincible, like forever was a possibility when her entire life had shown her otherwise?

A text buzzed in, and Beatrice warmed upon seeing that it was Jackson.

Jackson:
Just thinking of you.

Beatrice:
Same.

Jackson:
I'm going for it today. I'm telling him.

Beatrice:
Me too.

Typing it out fortified Beatrice, and she felt a rush of strength. She would tell Chris first after tonight's Friday dinner.

Jackson:
It's going to be ok. Their issues are not ours.

Beatrice:
Their fight isn't ours either.

Dave led their group up the stairs to one of the homes.

"Is this even safe?" Jessie said aloud, and giggles skittered through their group.

"Still, the potential . . . ," Dave remarked, as expected.

"Um," Beatrice objected, wary of the squeak of the floors when the last of them entered the house. "We also should have probably worn masks. Can you smell the mold?"

Jessie shot her a look that read "Right?" like they were back to their former friendly ways, and Beatrice had to bite her lip to keep from grinning. It was an expression just between the two of them, from their private conversations about the silly things in life. There'd been days when Jessie would spend more time with Beatrice than she did with Gil. After their parents had died, Jessie had taken care of the family; she'd cooked the meals, cleaned the house, made sure Beatrice had showered and dressed.

"Okay, okay, so there will be some things to fix. And this house is by far the worst of them all. But location, right? The owners are eager to sell. And this beach makes you feel like you're at the edge of the world. The air, the water. The sand."

A memory flew in, of one of the first times their family had vacationed in the Outer Banks, when Marilyn Puso had gleefully run to the back deck of their rented beach house, arms wide open.

Then, at that moment, Beatrice heard the name of the property in full clarity. It burst from her lips. "Sagana."

Gil met her eyes. "Abundant. It's perfect. I vote yes with Beatrice."

His declaration took her aback. She didn't remember the last time they'd agreed on something. "You do?"

"Yes, I do. And, the price is right."

"I want to tour all the houses," Brandon said. "Add up totals and see if it makes sense and what the owners are willing to concede to."

The team split, some going with Dave to walk through the other homes, and some opting to stay behind. The shuffle of bodies left Beatrice alone with Jessie.

"Do you want to walk down to the water's edge? And have a quick chat?"

"Okay," Beatrice squeaked and cleared her throat. She felt her heartbeat in her ear, a true sign that things were getting serious. Thank goodness for the brisk wind to keep her breathing, because she would have passed out. This was why she ran from telling the whole truth, despite her strong opinions. At the heart of it, she didn't like conflict.

They reached the edge of the surf, where the sand was packed and walking was easier. "You're a hard woman to get alone. So thank you for staying," said Jessie.

"It's fine."

"Beatrice, I have owed you this conversation for months now, and I guess I haven't had the courage to tell you . . ." She halted, which gave Beatrice no choice but to turn. Jessie had stuffed her hands in her jean pockets, and the collar of her shirt folded and flapped in the wind. "I should have told you that I had wanted . . . that I want . . . to come home. To you all. To Gil, to my girls, to your brothers, to Eden and Geneva, and to you. I made a lot of mistakes, and Gil and I had, and still have, a lot to work through. It's going to take a long time to repair what we both have done. But I love him. And we're giving each other a second chance. I hope that you can give me a chance too. Because I miss you."

Jessie had jumped right into it. She was so the opposite of Beatrice in that respect. While Beatrice procrastinated and skirted around the truth in hopes to ease it in, just to keep everyone happy, Jessie just toppled down all her walls, leaving Beatrice completely exposed.

Beatrice had always known she was loved. But when you lost people who loved you once, the pain was overwhelming. And losing Jessie, who she'd clung to after her parents had died, a woman who she'd considered her big sister in every way, had been unbearable. Was it fair to say it had felt like Jessie had died?

Unmet expectations. It was what got her time and again.

Tears sprang to Beatrice's eyes; those tears had been lying in wait behind the anger that had kept them at bay, though the wind swept them away. "I was so mad."

"Me too." She toed a shell in the sand and wiped her cheeks with a hand. "I was mad at myself for a long time. It was so painful to leave you. You're my family, more than anyone." She lifted her gaze to the middle distance. "I'm fighting for this marriage, Bea. I never expected nor do I expect now for you to take sides. But I wanted you to know that my love for you as a sister never went away."

"Are you and Kuya out of the woods?"

She shook her head. "No, we're not. This stuff doesn't correct itself overnight. But I believe that the core of me and Gil, of what kept us together long ago? It's still there. We go to therapy. We're trying to find our way as individuals, because that's what happens when you're together so young. You kind of meld into one another and forget who you are."

"But you're trying."

"We are. You can't get rid of me yet. My only plans are to be here with Gil, work on being a mom to Kitty and Izzy. Keep doing freelance stuff. Watch out for you so you don't wear sandals on motorcycle rides."

At the mention, and remembering her and Jackson's ride and their B&B encounter, Beatrice couldn't help herself; she burst into a laugh-cry. Those felt like much easier times. "God, that seems so long ago."

Voices came from inland. Another group seemed to be inspecting the houses, and she and Jessie began casually walking toward the car. Closer side by side, their arms accidentally brushed one another. Jessie wasn't physically affectionate except to her daughters, and this proximity was a sign. It was the beginnings of peace.

"Did something come from that trip?" Jessie asked.

"Actually? Yes." She bit her lip to keep her smile at bay.

"Will we get to meet him?"

"Maybe," she said offhandedly. She and Jessie were close enough to the group of people, and the way they all stood niggled at her instincts. Beatrice noted where her family was located. Gil was in the car, and Chris, Brandon, and Geneva were with Dave, walking from one of the homes.

Her instincts careened her forward to intercept her family.

"What's up?" Jessie chased after her.

"I'll explain later. Just help me, please, or you're going to meet him much sooner than we planned."

Because that group? It was led by Peter Holshbach, and with him were Jackson, Lonnie, and Dillon McCauley III.

♥

Jackson's spirits plummeted as soon as he saw the stretch of beach and the unending sky above it.

Now this. This property had potential. But Salvo was too close to Heart Resort, just twenty miles away.

"Aw, no, I'm not so sure about this place." Lonnie shook Jackson out of his thoughts, and he turned. Lonnie was pointing toward the houses. "The siding has to be done on all the buildings. You can see the porch and the railings are lopsided. These houses might have so much damage that we'd have to rebuild them from the ground up."

"Agreed." Jackson nodded at his brother. Solidarity shone in his eyes. After their night hanging out at his beach house, he and Lonnie had turned a corner. Without discussing it, Jackson knew that Lonnie would try to protect Heart Resort, too, for him.

Their father grumbled, hiking a hand above his eyes. He squinted at the homes. This was the third set of properties they'd seen this morning. They were at the end of Peter's list.

Jackson was ready to propose viewing properties farther away from the Outer Banks.

"It doesn't get as busy here in the summer," Peter supplied. "It's truly a hidden gem."

"Look at those massive beach houses, though." Lonnie gestured at the multifloor homes just to the left of the farthest bungalow. "Those could easily house up to twenty people at a time. It could be party central."

"Trust me when I say it's like this throughout the summer," Peter argued. The guy seemed to be eager to sell. "And everything is piped and wired. Great access to the main road for all your supply needs as well as your employees."

Jackson glanced at his father and caught his eye. *This is not it* was what he tried to channel.

McCauley returned a deadpan expression. "Give me the stats on this place?"

Peter went on, and once more, he discussed the terms of the sale, and as he did so, Jackson's eyes wandered to the horizon. For a beat he missed his friends. They would've discerned what he was trying to say. It was the kind of bond forged not only by time but through proximity and trust. They could have had conversations without saying a word, punctuated by a laugh, accentuated with a nod or the shake of a head.

He just didn't have it with McCauley.

Not yet. Give it a chance.

He had forty years of a chance.

His phone rang in his pocket, and it thankfully dragged him out of his thoughts. His emotions were everywhere today. After last night's evening with Lonnie, his mother, and Beatrice all in one house, it felt like a kind of breaking of the cycle. But being with McCauley this morning was a reminder his father was still intent on keeping the cycle going.

A sudden thought inhabited Jackson's mind: McCauley was sure to retaliate after he found out about Beatrice.

His heart thudded a foreboding beat.

"You gonna get that?" McCauley said.

Jackson fiddled with his phone and answered it, stepping away from the group.

"What are you doing here?" breathed a woman's voice.

He took the phone from his ear, looked down at the screen, and then returned it. "Bea. Hey."

"Move them toward the beach. I can't keep my siblings away for long."

"What are you talking about?"

"Don't act obvious, but we are literally a block from you. See the group? It's the whole Heart Resort team."

Jackson tilted his head slightly to the right, and sure enough, a gaggle of people was exiting from one of the homes. "Got it."

He hung up, sauntered back to his brother's side, and crossed his arms to emit serenity. He waited for Peter to finish his sentence.

A gust of wind flung sand into Jackson's eyes, and he blinked against the grains. As his vision cleared, he saw Beatrice walking their direction, accompanied by two men in black shirts. Her brothers. And the fourth . . . the fourth he didn't recognize from the website, though he had a stapled paper in his hand, much like Peter had. It must've been their real estate agent.

The moment brought Jackson to when he was ten, riding his BMX bike down a steep hill for the first time, truly behind the curve on how to turn or stop or slow down, and knowing full well that he was seconds from crashing.

At any second McCauley was going to see them. But at the last minute Beatrice stopped her brothers, and they huddled.

It bought Jackson enough time. "How about we take a stroll down the beach? Get a feel for how isolated it really is. Then we can decide if the rebuild is worth the location."

"Good idea," McCauley said. "I'd like to know how far my clients have to walk before they have to see a nonclient."

Jackson wheezed his gratitude, toddling behind the group. After they reached the surf and turned, he was relieved to find that Beatrice and her family had made their way to an SUV with its headlights on.

"Oh dang. Round two," his brother said, sidling up to him, the volume of his voice just loud enough for him to hear.

He felt his body give, finally understanding what his brother was implying. If that other guy with Beatrice's group was a real estate agent, then both businesses were looking at the same property.

No.

His phone buzzed in his pocket. A text from Bea: Are you here for these homes?

Jackson:
I have an NDA, Bea.

A trio of dots appeared, then disappeared, and then appeared again. It reflected the conundrum he was feeling at the happenstance and how horrible this whole situation was.

Next to him, Lonnie snickered. "Dad would have a heyday knowing his public enemy number one was within his eyesight."

"And it's exactly why you won't say a thing."

"I wouldn't. I kind of like Bea." He gestured to his father, who was in deep conversation with Peter. "But Dad seems to have a lot of questions about this place. I'd venture to guess he's interested."

Dammit.

His phone buzzed.

Bea:
Seriously what are you doing here?

Think, Jackson, think.
Was there another location they could revisit?

And then he remembered the for-lease sign on one of the build-ings on Ocracoke Island. "Peter, are there more options for us to take a look at?"

Peter frowned, confused.

Go with it, Jackson attempted to channel.

"Um." Peter cleared his throat. "There are always other places."

Jackson spoke with what he hoped was an encouraging smile. "I was at Ocracoke Island the other day, and I remember a for-lease sign on a first-row commercial property. I don't know how I forgot about it. I know it's outside the target area, and we wouldn't own the whole island, but it's even more private than this. There's a ferry to deal with, but it's a reliable form of transportation." His gaze darted among the men in the group. "It might be a good idea to take a look at it before we put in an offer on this place."

"Hm. That would be interesting." McCauley rubbed his chin with a hand.

"How about we break for an early lunch? Top off, then head down before we make any real decisions?" Jackson said. All the while, his phone buzzed in his pocket.

"Lunch does sound good right about now." McCauley laid a hand on his belly, reliably.

Peter plastered on a hesitant smile. Inside, Jackson wished he could give the guy his commission for all his trouble. "I know just the place for lunch. There's a sit-down barbecue joint in Waves we can head to. That'll give me time to ring up the place in Ocracoke."

"We'll need the sustenance." McCauley rested his hands on Jackson's and Lonnie's shoulders. "Today's the day we can finally seal the deal, my boys."

My boys. The term twisted Jackson's stomach.

With the way things were going, Jackson risked being called a slew of other names by McCauley and, worse, by Beatrice.

CHAPTER EIGHTEEN

Current affirmation: I am clearheaded and logical.

Beatrice:
What are you doing here?
Beatrice:
Please tell me you're not bidding on this place too
Beatrice:
I think we're putting in an offer
Beatrice:
NVM. Brothers aren't convinced
Beatrice:
You left me on read. Why haven't you answered?

Beatrice stared at her unanswered texts. Her whole family was at Friday dinner at Salt & Sugar, their weekly destination, but she couldn't concentrate.

While the vibe *around* her was relaxed, the vibe in her *body* was topsy-turvy. There was a whole hurricane going on in her brain. She was spinning stories in her head of the worst-case scenario of why Jackson's people were at Salvo—that they were there to put a bid on it too.

It was one thing for her to tell her brothers about Jackson's relationship to Willow Tree, and another to make this announcement while Willow Tree was in active competition with Heart Resort.

And why wasn't Jackson texting back? He was surely trying to douse his own fire around him, but she wanted an update. It had been hours. Enough time that the Heart Resort team had viewed a couple more properties.

With worry bubbling through her, she scooped dinner into her mouth by the spoonful, and not surprising, her stress level dropped a smidge. All her comfort foods were at the table: sinigang na hipon, llempo, and inihaw na bangus. And boy did she need the comfort.

Next to her, Geneva groaned.

Beatrice could swear that her friend was turning green. "Are you okay, Gen?"

"Yes? No? No, I think no."

"Bathroom?"

Geneva nodded fervently, standing. Beatrice followed to the stares of their family.

Tonight, their party was seated indoors. The restaurant's lights were dim, and Beatrice navigated around occupied chairs to the bathrooms tucked into the silent hallway. The shadows cast by the overhead lights made Geneva appear sullen.

"What's going on, Gen?"

"I feel . . . weird."

She shook her head. "Weird? What do you mean, weird? You never say something is weird."

Her friend was the more logical of the two of them, and she didn't use words like *weird*.

So this in itself was weird.

"Are you and Brandon okay?" Beatrice asked—because what else could it be? So she rushed through a speech that she'd never thought she'd present. She had been their wedding planner, after all, and part of her preparation had been to have all the speeches handy. "It's totally normal to feel a little claustrophobic at the beginning of a marriage. So many things are going on, with the business and all the plans—"

"It's not . . . that." Her words came out in pained snippets. "I think I'm . . ."

Geneva brushed past her and rushed into the bathroom, the door to which was ajar.

Then, she bent over the toilet and heaved.

Beatrice rushed to hold back her hair. "Oh dear. Oh gosh." She rubbed her back. "I'm here, Geneva, I'm here." She reached out with a toe to shut the door, though it closed only partway.

"This is so gross . . . I'm sorry, Bea." Her voice echoed as she spoke into the toilet.

"Don't be sorry. You and I have been through worse. What did you eat for lunch? Maybe it has something to do with that?" Beatrice discussed all the possible reasons why Geneva was sick to fill the silence in between her heaving. "But you'll be okay. I'm here. I'll take you home. I just need to grab my keys."

Finally, there was a pause in Geneva's heaving, and she sat back on her heels. When Beatrice saw that she was finally composed, she offered her hand and lifted her to her feet and to the sink.

Beatrice looked at her friend through the reflection in the mirror. She took in the dark circles under her eyes and what she now realized was a fuller profile.

The realization was like an unveiling of a statue. A tug, a pull, and then a total exposé.

"Geneva?"

Geneva was washing her hands, and soap bubbles foamed in the sink. "Yeah."

"Are you?"

"Am I what?"

"You know," she whispered. "Pregnant."

"Why are you whispering?"

"I don't know." She cleared her throat. She knew she was being silly. To Beatrice, Brandon was still a teenager. Somehow, in her brain, she was able to skip the whole sex thing.

She was truly becoming like her mother, and she wasn't sure how she felt about it.

"But do you think?" Beatrice asked once more.

Her friend was taking too long washing her hands, and that was an answer in itself. "You *are* pregnant," Beatrice said.

After shutting off the faucet and drying her hands, Geneva bit her lip and nodded. Then, a smile spread across her face. "We found out about a month ago."

"Oh my gosh! Congratulations!" Beatrice wrapped her arms around Geneva's body and squeezed her as hard as she could tolerate. "A baby. I'm going to be a tita again."

And yet, Beatrice found herself holding back in her joy. Geneva had known she was pregnant a month. Four weeks, and not one word to Beatrice.

"Bran and I decided to keep it on the DL, because of all the things that could happen, you know?" Geneva's voice was hesitant. "Jessie had a miscarriage between Izzy and Kitty. And Eden had an ectopic. Did you know?"

"No, I didn't." Insecurity rose in her chest, though not stemming from what she didn't know about Jessie or Eden. Those were intimate losses, and while she would have wanted to have been there for them, she understood. This was about her best friend keeping something from her, deliberately. And . . . "You told Jessie?"

"I did. I . . . I had some spotting the first week I found out, and I was so scared. It was a brief moment in time. I think you were staying at your beach house when it happened."

"Oh, of course." Beatrice shook her head, reminding herself that she was being foolish. Her evolving relationship with Jessie didn't mean that Geneva had to feel the same way about her. And yet, was she the last to know?

Was she losing her best friend? Was she losing touch? Gil had insinuated enough that Beatrice was being a flake. Geneva didn't approve of Jackson. And Beatrice was sometimes a little flighty.

All these damn secrets.

"Hey." Geneva tugged her by the wrist and woke her from her thoughts. "I'm sorry I didn't tell you earlier. I wanted to wait a couple more weeks, just until we heard the heartbeat. We've been holding our breaths, and I have been so emotional." Her gaze dropped down for a beat. "Which is probably why I've been a little hard on you when it came to Jackson. Everything's coming at me so fast, and sometimes I can't think straight."

Beatrice hugged her friend to keep her from having a full-on meltdown. With it, she willed her mixed emotions away. It hurt to have not been in the know. She felt left out. Her cheeks burned with what she realized was a boomerang of what she'd done to her brothers. Of what she was doing to them now, being with Jackson and knowing full well that it would bring conflict.

She hadn't been forthcoming herself.

As Geneva sniffled, Beatrice admonished herself. *Stop it, Bea.* This was not her moment. This was Geneva's, and she had to be strong, for her. "I'm so, so happy for you." She smiled for her friend's benefit. "And I'm so excited. I'm going to buy all the best toys, and outfits, and accessories." An idea descended, chasing away the last bit of darkness in her heart. "We can offer children's wear, Geneva."

Geneva cackled. "One thing at a time. First, we have to move into the store."

She held up a finger. "Right. Of course! But then children's wear."

When Geneva laughed, Beatrice relaxed. They were okay, right?

They were okay.

"We should head back out there," Beatrice said. "Ready?"

Geneva heaved a breath. "I think so."

Beatrice opened the door and stepped out but noticed that Geneva hadn't followed. Her friend was biting her bottom lip, and a shadow passed across her eyes. "I'm sorry, I just got a whiff of . . . I don't know, but . . ." She backtracked and stood next to the toilet, bending over. "No, dammit."

"Ladies, are you okay in there?" A man's voice boomed into the small room.

"Oh God, I'm so embarrassed," Geneva growled.

"Yes, we're totally fine," Beatrice said, looking up belatedly to a barrel-chested man at the threshold. He had a toothpick sticking out from his mouth.

Red flags flashed before Beatrice's eyes. Dillon McCauley III.

"Pardon me . . . ," he said, then halted, his eyes registering her face. Did he know who she was? Had he scoured her picture as the entire Puso family had memorized his?

Next to her, Geneva raised her head from the toilet seat. "Oh my God. When it rains."

♡

From the rear walk-up window of a pop-up restaurant called Tacos by the Beach, Jackson grabbed a mint and stuck it in his mouth, crunching without tasting it. His body was on high alert because Tacos by the Beach was a stone's throw away from Salt & Sugar. From where he stood, the restaurant's side parking lot was in view, and it was packed with vehicles.

What were the chances that the Puso family was here for their Friday dinner? Did they eat this late in the evening? Would they be driving up anytime?

Damn Peter and his foodie proclivities. Of all places to suggest to McCauley, who loved Mexican food. Jackson hadn't been able to get a word in for another suggestion after Peter had talked up Tacos by the Beach. Jackson hadn't wanted to protest hotly in fear that McCauley would see right through him.

It had been about ten minutes since McCauley had left the eating area behind the food truck to take a call, and Jackson was counting every second. They'd toured three more properties after Salvo and lunch, and all had potential, but none had been like the Salvo property, which had the best price and location. But how to dissuade his father when Salvo was most ideal?

"Breathe, Jack. You look like you're about to hurl," Lonnie remarked under his breath as Jackson sat back down at the picnic table. Peter was sitting on a different bench with a phone against his ear.

Jackson swallowed the shards of mint and looked at his watch. Time felt of the essence. It was killing him to ignore the burning texts from Beatrice in his pocket, but he hadn't wanted to cause panic. He also hadn't wanted Beatrice to lose faith in him for being unable to somehow protect her family.

Jackson would do everything in his power to give her good news, but nothing could be done when his father wasn't around.

"He's been on that call awhile," Jackson growled.

"He's probably talking to some key players." He opened his mouth to say more, but his buzzing watch snagged his attention. "Shoot. It's Heather. I'll be back." He took the call and headed toward the edge of the parking lot.

Jackson couldn't sit any longer, so he meandered to the other side of the car. He was expecting to hear the sound of his father's voice, but when he rounded the corner, there was no one there. McCauley wasn't on the other side of Tacos by the Beach, nor was he in the vehicle. Each step Jackson took as he looked for McCauley was ominous, and a rush began in his ears that he knew wasn't from the wind or the waves.

"Peter!" Jackson called out. "Do you know where McCauley went?"

Peter was texting and didn't look up from his phone. "Restroom."

No. Jackson was already moving to the restaurant. "I'll, uh, grab him to make sure he's good to go."

He approached the nondescript building, noting an SUV parked in front. Was it the same one that had been at Salvo? Next to it was a white Tesla.

Shit.

Jackson pulled the restaurant door, and bells rang above him. Inside, the dining room was dimly lit, with music playing in the background. Twinkle lights hung from above, and the chatter of diners filled the quiet moments. And though he'd eaten a full dinner, Jackson's mouth watered from the smell of garlic and onions.

Two guys with Heart Resort shirts walked past, toward the other side of the restaurant. And now closer, one looked super familiar. Dark hair, dark eyes, with a slim build. But what snagged Jackson's attention were the aviator glasses tucked into his shirt. From his knowledge of the "About Me" page of Heart Resort's website, he deduced that this was Gil.

But there was more.

Jackson never forgot a face; it was a handy talent to have with all the places he'd lived while in the military.

He'd seen Gil sometime in his life. But he just couldn't nail down when.

Gil must have felt him staring because he looked at Jackson and then did a double take.

The bells above the door rang again, and it brought Jackson back to the present, to his very urgent problem. Of the Puso family here in this restaurant, where McCauley could be.

Lonnie was at his side. "Did you find him?"

"Not yet." Jackson moved toward the hallway before he registered it, with Lonnie at his heels, and sure enough a group had congregated in the small space. Among them, he spotted Beatrice with an arm around another woman's shoulders.

"Bea," he called out, and faces turned his way, including McCauley, who returned a stunned expression.

Dammit. Jackson was too late.

Beatrice walked toward him, eyes as serious as they could be. They questioned him as to why he hadn't texted or called; they were asking him what he was doing there. She took his side.

"Hey, you're . . . the guy from Vegas," Gil said, eyes darting from his sister to Jackson.

"You know each other?" Beatrice asked.

"Yes . . . he . . ." Gil's voice trailed off, from which Jackson's memory filled in the rest of the silence. That night, Jackson had had two encounters—one with Beatrice, and another with a man who'd needed a little bit of assistance.

What were the odds?

"Yeah, I remember." Jackson pointed at him, infusing casualness. No one needed to know the circumstance. "We hung out a little, and you insisted on taking a selfie together."

"Dang, you're basically part of the family." Lonnie snickered.

The hallway went silent, and heat rose in the tiny space. His immediate worry was Beatrice, that he'd failed her. He gently took her by the elbow and out of the hallway, to the foyer.

The rest of the group followed them.

"Well, Dillon McCauley, we meet again," came another voice, from a stern-faced bearded man. Bodies parted to make way for him, and though he was half a foot shorter than McCauley, he looked equally intimidating.

McCauley took the toothpick from his mouth. "Christopher Puso."

The rest of the dining room seemed too quiet.

"You don't have enough establishments to go to that you have to come to the only Filipino restaurant in town?" Chris asked.

"I didn't realize that there were limitations as to where I can eat."

"That's funny, because you surely try to manage where we try to do business." An eyebrow arched. "That was you. In Salvo."

"I had a feeling too, when I saw your big group come through." McCauley snorted. "Can't get anything done in this place without someone finding out." His eyes darted briefly to Jackson.

The tension—the implication that he'd broken their NDA—was suffocating. Jackson was speechless.

"Wow. Small world, right?" Beatrice's voice was airy and artificially cheerful. "Everyone, this is Jackson Hill. We met in Vegas, the night before your wedding, Kuya Chris. What a total coincidence."

"He also assisted me that night," Gil said.

Chris eyed Jackson, as if prompting him to say something. Jackson was being given the floor. And in any normal situation, he would have been on it. But the commotion, and then Gil, and the mixed groups, and the past and the present all confounded him. Jackson came up blank.

Then, Chris nodded at Gil, a vague and strange response to the moment.

Jackson was flummoxed. He wasn't sure what that nod meant, but it was enough of an opportunity to do the easiest thing, and that was to get his father out of there. Because doing this in public, no matter what was going down, would not be wise. "It's time that we go," he said, catching McCauley's eyes. To a frowning Beatrice, he said, "It's good to see you, Bea."

"Wait." She dipped her face to him. "We should just tell them all now."

Pros: We finally tell everyone the truth, all at once. It will all be done with in one fell swoop.

Cons: McCauley could take the advantage and cause a scene. This could go from a quiet altercation to another public slaying, though this time in real life.

Cons: I didn't plan for this.

Jackson shook his head decidedly. "I'm sorry, Bea. Gotta go." It was the safest course of action.

He turned away from Beatrice's incredulous expression and walked out. Jackson hoped that the rest of his group would follow him, and thank goodness, they did. The air outside had never felt so good because he was a second from passing out.

He was trailed by Lonnie's nervous laughter. "If I didn't know better, that Christopher Puso was going to take your head right off, brother."

While climbing into their vehicle, as Jackson was still contemplating why Chris had deescalated the situation, McCauley said, "Jackson, you've got a lot of explaining to do about that girl in there."

"That woman," he corrected.

"Is she the woman you talked to me about? The one you're seeing?"

He avoided his father's eyes. "Does it matter?"

"Yes, it does." McCauley stood at the open door of the truck, blocking light from the outside. "It matters to her because she's the one who's going to have to deal with the aftermath after we do what we need to do. And it matters to me because you signed a nondisclosure."

"Which I did not breach," he declared. "I don't break my commitments."

"We'll see about that."

CHAPTER NINETEEN

Current affirmation: I allow others their opinions.

Beatrice was numb all over.

Outside on the gravel parking lot, where the family congregated after a quickly ended Friday dinner, it was unusually silent as they stood in a haphazard circle, shadowed by the setting sun. Beatrice's exhausted and impatient nieces were sitting in one of their cars, on their devices.

If only Beatrice could have done the same. What she would've given to be able to escape from this situation, to hide out and sleep this entire week away.

Because had Jackson really done what he'd done?

Here Jackson was, a man who she'd thought she could count on, and he hadn't stood up for their relationship. He'd scurried away. He'd given a flippant apology and straight up walked out of the restaurant.

This wasn't happening to her.

"Beatrice?" Chris's voice made her turn. He was perched on the Suburban's bumper next to Eden. Brandon had his arms around Geneva. Jessie stood off on her own while Gil paced.

She rested her eyes on Brandon. "So I guess he didn't pass Friday dinner."

Brandon returned a sad smile.

Chris stuffed his hands in his pockets. "So, what's the deal with you and Jackson? The real deal."

Beatrice told him their story, starting with Vegas. They listened as she disclosed leaving her phone number under the hotel door, and meeting Cathy, who had led them back together. "We had something well before we found out who we were, and we thought we could get past it. We thought we could convince you and Willow Tree to get along and we could be together." She tucked her flyaway hairs. "Our plan was to tell our families today. Though not exactly like this."

"I'm sorry, Beatrice." Eden approached her and wrapped an arm around her shoulders.

She sank into Eden's hold. "And I can't believe you knew him too, Kuya Gil."

"He was kind enough to say that we 'hung out,' but he took me out of a sticky situation in Vegas. It makes it more disappointing that he acted like such a coward."

Jessie hissed a rebuttal.

"It's okay." Beatrice knew that she was on thin ice with her siblings, no matter how disappointing this was for her.

"No, it's not," Jessie looked pointedly at Gil. "What you need is support, and not judgment."

"Thank you." Beatrice nodded at Jessie, grateful for her help. She turned to Chris. "Are you . . . are you mad, Kuya?"

"Because the resort's public enemy number one was on our turf? And pretty much made it clear that he was planning on staying? No." He winked against an errant beam of light that burst through the clouds. "It's all par for the course. I can guarantee he's going to put an offer on Salvo. Now especially, knowing that we want the place too. But the fact that you were with Jackson and didn't come out with it right away . . . it's feeling so déjà vu. You keep withholding information, Bea."

"Because an omission is still a lie," Gil declared.

"My God, Gil. It's more nuanced than that. Of course they tried to see how they could work around it. It's obvious they've fallen for one another. They can't help that their families don't get along," Jessie snapped back, gaze settling on Beatrice.

"Have you fallen for him?" Chris asked.

"Yes," Beatrice admitted. "Obviously he didn't feel as strongly."

His face softened. "Obviously, if he can't stand there to take the heat, he's not for you."

She nodded. And yet, Jessie's words about nuance also remained. What had she been expecting? A declaration of their relationship? A stance for the Pusos when he had been thrust into his own family just this summer? Most of all, Beatrice wasn't perfect. She had her own courage to work on. She might have been ready to tell her family today, but yesterday and the day before, she hadn't been, when he was.

They'd never even told one another that they loved each other.

Oh, Mom, my heart. It hurt. It hurt all over.

"It's time for us to head back to the resort." Chris dug his keys from his pocket. "It's been a long enough day. Coming with us?"

"I need to pick up Roxy. And I've got a whole list of things to do for Beachy."

"I'll check in with you tonight. But don't forget. Monday we meet with Leila via video chat."

"Yep, it's on my calendar."

Chris opened his mouth to say something else, then seemed to decide against it. He climbed into his Suburban. After final hugs from the rest of the family, Beatrice was left alone in her car, sitting in the parking lot.

It's obvious that they've fallen for one another.

Jessie's words replayed themselves in her head. She thought back to how their relationship had been intense from the start. Had she been a fool all this time? Had she misinterpreted every interaction and every sentence?

The shock of rejection slowly uncovered itself, and anger emerged. She texted Giselle. Can you keep Roxy an extra half hour? Gotta get something done.

Giselle:
Of course. Meet you at Beachy whenever!
I'm still here and she's keeping me
company while I print labels.

Beatrice:
TY

Then, Beatrice drove her Tesla as fast as traffic allowed to her Nags Head beach house. Parking under her home, she spotted Jackson's motorcycle. She took his stairs by two, heart in her throat.

She didn't have a speech prepared for this. In her short drive, she'd felt a range of emotions, from anger to pain then incredulousness. Because it still didn't escape her how little she knew of Jackson. Beatrice and Geneva were like sisters, and she'd never thought Geneva would keep a pregnancy from her.

Unmet expectations, all of it.

She knocked on his front door. The lights were on, though no one answered, so she rounded the house to the balcony. She peeked over the railing, as if she could spot him in the dozens of beachgoers. Maybe yesterday . . . maybe yesterday she could've done it. But now?

"Beatrice."

She startled at the sound of her name coming from her balcony. Jackson raised a hand. "Stay there," she said before she jogged back down the stairs.

He was at the top of her stairs waiting for her. For a beat, she swooned. His hair was damp, and he'd changed into a thin gray T-shirt, the cuffs of its sleeves settling perfectly on his biceps. It was unfair how breathtaking he was, because she was supposed to be mad at him.

Stop it, Beatrice scolded herself.

"I'm sorry I froze." His eyes were pleading, and he took a step forward. From this far away Beatrice saw his sincerity.

"You didn't freeze. You ran. We had a chance to say something, to just get the truth out there, and you bailed."

"I didn't know that you were going to be there—"

She interrupted the start of his excuse. "You would have, if you had texted back."

He ran his hand through his hair, eyes darting away for a beat. "I know. I wanted to . . . I don't know . . . make it better before I did. And I was caught off guard. All I could think of was to get McCauley out of there."

"What do you mean, make it better?"

He shut his eyes.

"Your father's going to bid on the property," she concluded. At his silence, she shook her head. Chris was expecting Willow Tree to make an offer, but she'd held out hope that it wouldn't happen. "He can't bid on that property. Heart Resort wants it. Can't you do something about that?"

"The mere fact that you think I can change an entire system that existed before me is laughable, Beatrice. I just got here. I don't even know where I stand now. But please . . . forgive me."

"And where would that leave us if I did? You said just now that I was foolish to think we can change an entire system. Do we continue on as if everything around us isn't on fire? Our families are going to fight for the same property, and then what?" She looked down at her feet, realizing the truth of what was in front of her.

Their lives were incompatible.

"What are you saying?" he asked.

"I had always considered myself smarter, a little wiser, when it came to relationships. For a long time, I was good at being on my own, of not taking anyone too seriously. But somehow, you'd gotten to me, Jackson."

"Bea, I feel the same way about you. Which has made all of this just . . . confusing."

"It wasn't confusing to me at that moment when we were in front of everyone."

His expression fell, and Beatrice looked away. God, sometimes she wished she could say something scathing and not feel bad about it, but here she was. Feeling guilty that she'd hurt him. "Look, we didn't think when we got together that our families would be each other's nemesis." Saying the word made her snicker. "Maybe I just expected too much from what could've been. Maybe I read too much into us, because I was convinced we were meant to be."

"Don't say that," he interrupted her. "I wanted to tell our families a long time ago, Bea. I wanted for us to tell them from the start. I froze—that's all."

"It's not *all*. There's a reason it happened, Jack." She leaned a hip against the railing for support, and she shut her eyes for a brief moment to gather her strength. "Our loyalties are to our families, and it must remain with them. Or, there's pain. Our fault was that we assumed we could change everyone else. After we found out about who we were, we should have just stopped this. I shouldn't have opened that door back up. I shouldn't have asked you to keep us a secret. I shouldn't have asked myself that either." She swallowed back the nausea building inside of her. "Because you and I are over."

"No." His voice cracked. "No, Bea. I love you."

Beatrice's eyes filled with tears. They came from a place she didn't go to often. Admittedly, she let the good things in life supersede the sadness and disappointment. It was what was expected of her, and it was easier to live looking at the bright side. It was easier to sometimes ignore the truth.

One of which was that she was falling for him too.

Jackson stepped up to Beatrice and cupped her chin gently. He swiped her tears away with a thumb. "Are you hearing me? I love you. I felt it before today but thought it was too early to say. It's why I was willing to keep us a secret. I wanted it to work. I believe in us."

His words made it that much more painful for Beatrice to finally say the truth. She was learning the lesson all the couples around her had learned. "I love you too, Jackson. But . . ." She heaved a ragged breath. "It's just not enough for us to love each other, to want to make it work, or to believe. It's not even good enough that this might have been coincidence, or meant to be, or that we thought we were lucky. Not in our real lives." Beatrice took both of Jackson's hands into hers and squeezed them.

Jackson gasped. "So that's it? We're just supposed to walk away?"

"Yes . . . and I'm going in. I've got a full night at Beachy. Let's end it here, where we can still be cordial, okay? We've got a long road. We're neighbors, and there's The Cathy Hill to contend with." She smiled, hoping that he wouldn't contest. Beatrice had to save her heart and her spirit for what would come.

"If that's what you want."

"It's what I want."

He nodded, finally, and lifted Beatrice's hand to kiss it.

Then, he turned and walked down the stairs.

When the sound of his footsteps faded, Beatrice choked out a sob.

♡

Jackson wiped his errant tears from his cheeks, admonishing himself. Cordial? Could he really remain cordial with Beatrice after everything that had happened between them? He'd told her he loved her. She'd said she loved him back.

Jackson gazed up at the inky-black sky dotted with stars and searched for the hope he found in its beauty but found none.

How was he supposed to move on?

Jackson's phone buzzed in his pocket. It was Marcus, separate of their group chat. Jackson had texted him and Gavin after returning from Salvo in a fit of desperation. The text chain had been an epic show of his guilt and fear—from losing Beatrice to losing himself.

Marcus:
You okay?

Jackson:
It's over

The phone rang in his hand a second later. He contemplated not answering it. He knew what would greet him on the other end of the line; Marcus, if anything, knew when to rally the troops.

He winced and took the call anyway. "Hello?"

"Jack." The caller's voice was soothing and strong. It was the voice of the person who'd seen him at his romantic worst. It was the voice of his friend, his ex-wife.

"Hi, Emily."

He heard her exhale. "Marcus told me everything. I'm sorry."

"Can't seem to get it right, Em." He half laughed. "My first wife left me for my best friend because she said I didn't love her the right way. And the woman I fell in love with just told me that love isn't enough."

"Hey," she objected with sarcasm in her voice. "I didn't leave you for your best friend. I got tired of playing second to the memory of a Vegas fling . . . and anyway, didn't it work out for the best?"

He rubbed a hand against his hair. "For you, I guess."

"For you too. You got your chance with Tricia. *Beatrice.*"

It should have been awkward, for Emily to be with Marcus. But it was far from it. Emily was a veteran, and after filing for divorce from Jackson, she had been stationed—where else—where Marcus was stationed. They'd become friends, and one thing had led to another.

Jackson hadn't stood in their way when they, together, had revealed their attraction for one another. Apparently, Marcus, the guy who'd been hell bent on staying single, had met his match.

"And look what happened, with me getting that chance, Em. I'm standing here in the dark, alone, a hot mess, and I can't do anything about it."

"Anything about what? What happened between you and Beatrice? You and your father? Or between Willow Tree and Heart Resort?"

"All of it."

"I doubt that. This isn't a tragedy that's already been written."

"For a woman who's with the love of her life, you sure have a lot of opinions." He feigned nonchalance. It was the only way he wouldn't once more break down into tears. "Besides, she and I can't just step away from our obligations."

"Why not? Let's take you—you lived a whole life without your dad."

"Right. But it's different now."

"It is, because you found someone incredible. And I'm not talking about your father. When we were married, I remember wishing that you would look at me the same way you looked when you'd recall *Tricia*."

"Gah, I must have been horrible." He scrubbed a hand down his face.

"Not horrible. Just misguided. But I was the same. I didn't quite want to face that we both wanted different things. Anyway, this isn't about us. This is about you, and getting back up, and not giving up. You're still there."

"I don't even know what to do next."

"Remember when we went to counseling? Our counselor told us that what brought us to the marriage might not be the reasons why we stay. Jackson, you went to the Outer Banks for a reason. What reasons will keep you there? You have a choice. She has a choice. This isn't the end of it if you choose each other."

Emily was an expert at burying the lede, and it jabbed against his gut. All this time, he had been concerned about Beatrice choosing him, but it was he who was confused. He had run away from the restaurant confrontation not because he hadn't wanted to cause a scene but because he had been hesitant. He had gotten attached to McCauley, to this potential of a family, despite his best efforts.

"Jack?"

"I'm here. I think . . . I think I should go for a ride. Gotta think."

"Okay . . . don't forget to wear your reflective gear."

"Of course. I'm always safe."

"Check in with Marcus when you get back?"

"I will. Thank you, Em."

After Jackson hung up, heart heavy, he grabbed his gear and jogged down the stairs. He willed himself not to look at Beatrice's carport area, and instead focused on his ride.

His bike was a beauty, gleaming even in the shadow. He rolled it out from the darkened corner, then stepped onto the pedal to start it.

The bike growled, vibrating through his body. There was no room for anything in his chest when he rode. No regret, no anger, no what-ifs. Just the idea of the journey, because not even the destination mattered. On his bike, he hoped to be able to breathe.

He cruised, past pedestrians, past golf carts that had somehow found their way to the road, past bars and restaurants and souvenir shops, making random turns to keep things interesting.

Then, he stopped at a light, and when he looked up to the right, he caught sight of a parked white car in the new Beachy parking lot. A woman popped out from the driver's side. It was Beatrice—of course it was Beatrice. It was as if his body was primed to seek her out.

Even if she was a Puso.

He was bum-rushed by a set of emotions in his moment of inattention—or, better yet, his moment of distraction. Anger at this entire situation, and absolute regret.

It wasn't fair. He'd done everything right. He tried to do everything right, and yet, nothing came easy. Damned when he felt nothing; damned when he did. Damned when he avoided risk; damned when he jumped in with both feet.

He swung his wheels to turn right at the light—he was going to speak to her again. The move earned him a honk from another vehicle, and he drove into the parking lot.

He parked under the shade of the same tree from yesterday. A U-Haul took up space in front of Beachy's windows, below the new signage that had gone up above the storefront.

They were moving in. *They* meaning Beatrice and another woman with curly red hair—Giselle, he assumed. Beatrice jumped into the truck, joining her, and with raised pleasant voices they brought boxes into the shop.

Beatrice sounded like she was completely fine, as if they hadn't just broken up.

What was he doing there? This was a mistake.

The boom of thunder brought his gaze upward, to cloud cover that had rushed in in the few minutes he'd been there. These damn unexpected storms.

The two women were tag-teaming a box, barely out of the truck when the first droplets began to fall. Jackson lowered his visor and held his bike upright. The smart thing to do was to head back home.

But there were the boxes lined up on the sidewalk, and Jackson could never leave when someone needed help.

It began to rain as he walked up to the U-Haul, meeting Beatrice at the open door. When she saw him, her expression fell.

It was a stab to his heart. He'd elicited the opposite behavior just yesterday.

She was damp from the rain; strands of her hair were plastered to her cheeks. "What are you doing here, Jackson?"

"I saw that you needed help, so . . ."

After a beat, she handed him the box she was holding. "Okay." She gestured to the woman behind her. "This is Giselle, my office manager. Giselle, this is Jackson."

"Nice to meet you. Well . . . I'm gonna . . . head in." She scurried into the store, no doubt not wanting to be in the middle of their drama.

But Jackson snapped to it. He brought boxes in from the sidewalk and assisted Beatrice in locking up the truck.

All in all, it probably took fifteen minutes, but Beatrice's silence made it feel like it was a lifetime. He'd gotten used to her filling up the lull with her small talk and ruminations about everything.

After they were done, Beatrice walked him to the front door. "Thank you. I appreciate you helping us out."

"Yeah, of course."

"Was there another reason why you're here?"

"I was just out for a drive and saw you. I wanted to come in here and say . . ."

She looked into his eyes. "Say what?"

"That we should . . ." And still, he couldn't put into words what he wished they could do. Run away? Fight the system? Be their own people? They were words of the naive.

"Okay then . . ." She gathered her hair over one shoulder. "If you'll excuse me. I need to clean up around here."

"I can stay and help," he said desperately.

She popped the door open. "Thank you for everything, Jackson. But I'll take it from here."

CHAPTER TWENTY

Today's affirmation: I take care of me first.

Beatrice was running late. If she left her Nags Head house right now, she could walk in thirty-five minutes before the meeting with Leila, which was ten minutes after Chris had mandated for her to be there. He was going to be ticked. But she had taken her time with her hair today. Though she felt wrung out, she wanted to attempt to look decent. Her phone had been blowing up all weekend from everyone, all in concern. Her doorbell hadn't stopped ringing from a random sibling coming by, and she wanted to appear better. Present, despite a weekend of moving into Beachy. Joy, even when she missed Jackson with her every fiber. Optimism, despite the dreary, overcast day.

She inspected her beach bag and counted off her necessary items: planner, sunglasses, granola bar, bottled water. Then, she grabbed Roxy on her leash and walked down the stairs, only to see Cathy on the phone, pulling out her bicycle.

Beatrice waved out of politeness, though she rushed at cramming everything but her phone into the trunk of her car. It was hitting her again, this wave of regret that her relationship with Cathy might have to change too. She had no issues with carrying The Cathy Hill in the shop, but she'd need to tamp down her growing attachment to her.

Cathy waved back and hung up the phone. She wore linen pants and a flowing shirt. Around her neck was a gorgeous shell pendant, and as she walked her direction, Beatrice could not help staring at her chest.

"That pendant is . . . magnificent," Beatrice said.

"Oh . . . this?" Closer now, Beatrice noticed Cathy's flustered expression and bloodshot eyes. "Yes, um. I have one just like it going into your shop."

"That's wonderful." Beatrice heaved a breath, relieved that she was still game to stock the store, but her attention turned to her apparent worry. "Everything okay?"

"No. It's Jackson. I think he has food poisoning. We had take-out last night, and I passed on the slaw because it smelled suspicious, though he'd had practically a container by then. He was on the toilet pretty much all night." She winced. "It's been rough. I called his doctor, and he sent meds to a pharmacy just down the street."

"I'm so sorry to hear."

"I'm about to bike over to grab it. It has to be me since I'm in his records. But I don't want to leave him. Can you . . . can you watch him for me?"

"Oh . . . um." She stilled.

Cathy shook her head. "I know things aren't the way they used to be, so I hate to ask. But mama's intuition, you know? I haven't seen my son sick in years . . ."

"He might not want for me to . . . I don't know, see him like that."

"Dear, my permission is all you need."

Beatrice hadn't been there for her parents when they had passed, and she carried the regret of that still. She'd thought . . . had she been around for them to hear her voice, would they have tried to pull through? Could she have said something to console them?

Since then, she hadn't been able to turn away from anyone who was sick.

"All right, I'll stick around. Let me lock up my car."

She hugged Beatrice. "You're a lifesaver."

"When was the last time he threw up or . . ."

"It's been a couple of hours. Then again, he hasn't tried to eat or drink since then." Her eyebrows drew down in worry. "I'll be back in fifteen minutes. Twenty, tops."

As Beatrice watched Cathy bicycle away, she sent her brothers a status update: Running late, will be there before time. Kim is up to date.

Then, Beatrice gripped Roxy's leash and looked down at her for moral support.

Roxy's head tilted to the side.

"You're right. He'll appreciate the both of us being there."

And yet, her heart beat as loud as the bass from the party house at the end of the street. They'd declared their love and broken up anyway, and how sad was that?

Beatrice picked up Roxy—instantaneously feeling better—and walked up the stairs and through Jackson's front door.

All the first-floor windows were open. Unlike her frigid beach house, theirs was just shy of cool with the breezy crosswind. The curtains fluttered, and the sound of jazz filtered through the space. Beatrice didn't know the musician.

She did, however, recognize the man lying on the couch. His eyes were shut, and he was shirtless and wearing joggers. An arm was slung across his forehead.

"If I stay absolutely still, then the world won't move," he said.

Beatrice's heart squeezed. Jackson was in agony. In her arms, Roxy fussed, so she set her down.

And her dog, the traitor she was, jogged straight to her favorite friend. Roxy propped her front paws on the couch cushion and licked Jackson on the chin. Startled, he opened his eyes, then softened at the sight of her dog. He turned ever so slowly toward Beatrice, and there went her heart.

It was a puddle of goo.

Because his eyes sparked with what looked like relief.

"Hey." He swallowed, and his Adam's apple bobbed. "You just missed my mom. She's gone to . . ." He turned a mild shade of green.

"Nope. I'm here for you. Do you need anything right now?"

He shut his eyes as if in concentration. Then, after a pause, he said, "I don't know. I think . . . I think I'm thirsty? But I'm afraid to drink."

"How about just wetting your lips with some ice. That might help. But it's a good sign that you're thirsty." She rushed to the kitchen and filled a glass with ice from the refrigerator dispenser, then set it on the coffee table.

Jackson looked at the glass desperately; it was out of reach.

"Do you mind if I sit next to you?"

He half laughed. "You're asking me if I mind? When it's you who might mind sitting next to me. I'm not exactly fresh."

"I don't care about that," she said, meaning it. She perched on the couch cushion next to his hip. She offered the cup. "Do you feel like trying?"

"I think?"

"Do you know that you actually only need about an ounce of liquid an hour? So, not even a shot glass worth."

"Okay." His face contorted into a grimace. "Damn coleslaw . . . maybe I shouldn't think about it."

She laughed. "No, you shouldn't. Think of lazing around in the waves, and soaking in the sun. Breathe, now."

Beatrice watched his eyes close; his chest rose and fell with every deep breath. Then, he nodded, indicating he was ready.

She handed him the glass of ice. He tipped the glass, and the ice bopped his upper lip.

Well, that didn't work. "I'll feed you the ice," she decided, already fishing the little bits out and dropping a couple into his mouth. "That's good, Jackson. We can try again in an hour." She cleared her throat, realizing that she wasn't going to be here in an hour. "Or, you can try whenever Cathy gets here."

He lay back down. "Thank you, for coming. Am I keeping you from something?"

"I've got things covered. Not a big deal."

"It *is* a big deal because we're no longer exactly . . ."

"No, we aren't. But, I still owe you, Jackson. For the hard time I gave you the other night, you still helped me with those boxes. You have helped me in so many ways. Ways I didn't even know about, like with Gil." She looked down. "He told all of us what happened. That's kind of wild how you met so long ago too."

"What happens in Vegas, am I right?" He snorted. "Consider our debts canceled out, with you just being here, and bringing that dog of yours." He glanced at Roxy, who was perched on the back of the couch like a cat. "Thank you."

"Well, you're not rid of me yet. I'm not leaving until The Cathy Hill gets back."

"I love that you call her that." He snorted, eyes shutting. "It's just one of many things I love about you."

She knew this was sickness talking. Sickness and gratitude. But inside, she also reveled in it, that he felt for her the same way she was feeling for him, despite what was going on between their families.

Loving him wasn't the problem. She'd been drawn to him years before. It was that she wasn't sure how to stop loving him, or how to love him along with her family.

"I wish it were easier between us," she ventured, feeling brave because he wasn't looking right at her.

"Same." His voice was a whisper. "Because I think . . . I think it could be forever."

Forever. It was a wish said in her dreams. It was the promise of all the weddings she'd planned, of all her expectations met. It was the thing she felt for him. "Jackson? What did you say?"

She wanted to hear it again, because *forever* was different from love, wasn't it? *Forever* meant commitment; it meant staying.

Beatrice nudged Jackson gently, but he'd fallen into slumber.

♡

Jackson awoke from a dreamless sleep, though he wasn't sure how long he'd napped. The last twelve or so hours had been a lucid dream, starting with that first trip to the porcelain goddess that had nothing to do with a party but with coleslaw he'd been so intent on scarfing down.

There was a thin sheet on him. Carefully, his eyes slid to the coffee table, where half a glass of ice water dripped with condensation, and then to the dog that was sitting so properly with its pink tongue sticking out, watching him.

Roxy.

The rest of the morning came back to him in a slow clip. Of Beatrice coming by, of looking up at her beautiful face. Of the comfort he felt knowing that she was there. "Bea?"

"Jack? Hey." Her voice was soothing; she came around from behind. "You had a good fifteen-minute nap. How do you feel? Need to go to the bathroom?"

"No?" He wasn't sure at the moment, nor did he trust his body, which was feeling all sorts of things. Dizziness, headache, blurred vision.

Regret.

Love.

Still, he sat up, using his elbows to prop himself. His eyes crossed for a beat but righted themselves.

Nope, nothing was coming up his esophagus. "I think . . . I'm okay."

"Here, I'll help you." She steadied him by the shoulders, lifting him to sit. She inspected his expression. "Okay still?"

He nodded; he keyed in to his body, and how close he was to Beatrice, that she was touching him. "I think I do need to go to the bathroom."

"Can you make it? I can bring a bucket over."

"No, not that."

Her face registered. "Oh."

"No . . . not . . . that either. I just want to brush my teeth. I feel really disgusting."

"Understood. I'll help you."

"I'm twice your size, Bea."

She rolled her eyes. "First of all, that is a major exaggeration, and second, you should know that Filipino nurses are on the forefront of inpatient care—many help people who are actually twice their size. You're just a few inches taller. And I'm not planning on carrying you there, just a little prop. Okay? You know what they say: the bigger they are, the harder they fall."

"Yeah, okay," Jackson agreed, but only because he knew that she wouldn't quit.

After a deep breath, Jackson heaved himself to standing. He felt the blood rush down to his feet—it was really an odd feeling—and he steadied himself with an arm around Beatrice's shoulders. He was shirtless, and she was so close, and he couldn't even enjoy it because he was so focused on keeping upright.

"Got it?" she asked.

"Yep." He moved his legs. He could feel them, and his toes. He shuffled one step and then another. "I'm good from here."

"Okay." Still, Beatrice followed closely behind while he made his way to the bathroom, to the sink. He was surprised to see his phone on the windowsill. He must have placed it there during one of his runs to the bathroom, and he'd completely forgotten about it.

He made careful work of brushing his teeth, then ran a wet hand through his hair. He looked ragged. Dark blue under his eyes, sunken cheeks with a greenish hue to his skin. What a difference twelve hours made. He'd seen his share of patients coming into hospitals looking like they were at the brink of death and then walking out with pink on their cheeks.

It made him more grateful for caregivers at the bedside and for Beatrice, who was standing outside the door.

His phone buzzed on the sill, and curiosity piqued. He was like Pavlov's dog to the thing. It could've been nothing—an email notification from the motorcycle shop in town that he'd subscribed to. But it could also be his brother or father updating about the Salvo property.

Everything hinged on his father's decision, and Jackson had been working nonstop behind the scenes so his father wouldn't bid on Salvo. He'd been sending him property listings; he'd attempted to speak to his father's inner circle. Jackson couldn't just sit here and allow his father to act without his intervention. He wouldn't be able to live next to Beatrice and simply pretend that they were *just* neighbors. He loved her.

He finished up brushing his teeth and washing his face. Then, after drying off and rolling on deodorant, he shimmied to the sill, his surroundings tilting with each step. Finally, he swiped the phone from the sill, seeing the notifications from his brother.

Lonnie:
how are you feeling?
Lonnie:
dude you alive?
Lonnie:
Dad wants to make an offer. Check your email for the details

And the most recent:

Lonnie:
If you're still down for the count
I'll have to be the one to call Peter

Jackson's thumbs flew over his keyboard.

Jackson:
Just got up

Lonnie:
Damn. Sorry man.
Lonnie:
want me to do the deal?

Something inside Jackson seized. This was an opportunity.
He would stall.
A knock sounded on the door. "Jackson?"
"I'm coming. Just drying off." His voice was hoarse, and his throat was dry and in pain.

Jackson:
No, I'll do it. Give me a few minutes.

Lonnie:
OK. Keep me posted.

He stuffed the phone in his pocket and put a hand on the door-knob. After one last look in the mirror and a sigh at how pathetic he looked, he opened the door.

Beatrice was on the other side of the threshold by a foot, and her worried expression flipped a 180. "Hey. You're looking better already."

He took a step, and the ground moved at his feet, so he reached out to her. "Looks like my body's objecting to that statement."

She slipped her arms around his waist and held on. He wrapped an arm around her, cringing at how awful he must appear.

She smiled up at him as if reading his mind. "You're fine. I promise."

So he told his body to relax a little, and her arms firmed up their hold. He willed himself to feel every step, to savor this moment despite his unsteady body and heart, and as soon as the couch was within reach, he contorted himself to sit.

"I'll bring over some crackers. Test that belly." She picked up the sheet and the pillows that had fallen off the couch.

The sight prompted such an overload of gratitude that as she straightened, Jackson grabbed her gently by the wrist. "Beatrice."

She smiled, allowing herself to be led to sit. "Yes."

"You're being so nice."

"I'm being a good neighbor."

Is that all? he wondered, though he wasn't sure if he wanted to know the answer. He forged on, not wanting to waste this moment as he had the other night at the new Beachy. "I know that what's happened between us hasn't been great. But meeting in Vegas . . . maybe it was meant to be."

She peered at him, and her lips quirked into a smile. "What are you saying, Jackson Hill? Mr. Dress Right Dress?"

"That maybe if we hadn't met so long ago, I would be withering away, suffering on my own right now. I wouldn't have gotten to know Roxy and learned the difference between a maxi and an A-line dress. And did you know that there are a dozen different pliers for jewelry making? I know because the last couple of days, The Cathy Hill put me to work. Apparently I looked hapless." He knew he was rambling, but he couldn't help himself. "I guess what I'm trying to say right now is I wouldn't have all this had we not met."

A real smile grew on her face, and the sight of it . . . he swore it made him feel like he was all the way better. "Oh, Jackson. The things you say when you're not feeling great. It's . . . to be honest . . . sweet."

"And doesn't it feel like our paths were meant to cross? I mean, I even met your brother. That's all got to mean something, right?" His mouth continued to move, like being sick had unlocked the dam that had held his innermost thoughts back. "I looked for you after Vegas. I only had your first name, and I looked you up on Facebook, and boy was that a fail." He shook his head. "I'm sorry. I don't know what's come over me. I just feel like this can't be it for us. How could we come together after five years and be done after two weeks?"

"Jackson." She looked down a beat. "For what it's worth, I will never see fried chicken or waffles or vanilla ice cream, or a combination thereof, without thinking of you. But, that moment at Salt & Sugar? It was the most uncomfortable situation I'd ever been in. It wasn't because of who we were. Ultimately, we're adults, aren't we? We can choose who we want to be with. But ideally I want to be in a relationship where we're not fighting each other's family while trying to work on ourselves. When you walked away . . ."

"I'm sorry. I'm so sorry."

"I know you are. But I can't forget it—not now, at least."

He nodded. "I respect that. And I respect you coming over to help me." He hoped that she could hear the sincerity in his words. But something Beatrice had said caught up to Jackson. "What did you mean, the things I say when I'm not feeling well? Did I say something while I was half-asleep?"

Her cheeks reddened. "It's nothing."

Feeling a rush of exhaustion, he leaned back on the couch. "Please tell me."

She cleared her throat. "You . . . you said that it could—"

The door opened with a slam, startling them both. Beatrice all but leapt to the other side of the room, picking up a random cup.

His mother walked in with a paper bag cradled in her arms. "Oh my gosh. I'm so sorry that took forever. They said the prescription would be ready, and by God, they damn well lied."

"Let me help you with that, Cathy." Beatrice grabbed the bag and padded to the kitchen, then unloaded the contents. Beatrice avoided Jackson's eyes, but when he slid his gaze to his mother, Cathy gave her son a slow and meaningful wink.

"So, what did I miss?" Cathy asked.

CHAPTER
TWENTY-ONE

Current affirmation: I have boundaries.

When Cathy got going with her storytelling, there was no way to halt it. She was a speeding train without brakes, and for all of Beatrice's attempts to get out of the conversation, Cathy would jump in with another random tale.

"Wow. That all happened when you were out?" Truly, Beatrice was amazed at how the woman attracted commotion. And despite the ticking clock reminding her about her upcoming meeting, she stalled to find out how her tale ended.

Or maybe Beatrice didn't want to go to this meeting. Admittedly, she'd enjoyed the last thirty minutes with Jackson. He might have been the one who needed the TLC, but it was Beatrice who'd experienced a little bit of closure.

As Cathy segued down a tangent, Jackson pressed his fingers against his eyes. It took everything in Beatrice to not laugh. "What's wrong, Jack?"

"Oh, he's probably just embarrassed because I talk too much," Cathy said.

"That is an understatement." He groaned.

"Listen, buddy, I can dump this Pedialyte down the sink."

As they continued to banter, Beatrice's heart broke a little at how she missed her parents, and that she had so much to fix with her brothers. That was the thing with secrets. When you kept them *for* others, your own circles weren't affected, but when they were yours, they drove a wedge between you and the people you loved, even if they didn't know it.

And she didn't want to be that way any longer.

"You're lucky you have one another," she said now. "My mom, she would do this thing." She laughed to herself, right before shyness overcame her. "Sorry."

"No, I want to hear more." Jackson's voice was warm and inviting. Cathy perched on one of her stools.

Beatrice sat back down; had she really thought that she was leaving right that second? She could spare another couple of minutes.

"Okay, um." She cleared her throat. Usually, it was easy for her to talk about her parents. Despite her cluttered life, her memory was precise, especially when it came to her mother. But right then, she felt more vulnerable than ever. "We had these family parties—they were large, and full of party crashers. It was a free-for-all. Anyway, my mom and my aunties would sit around a table and gush about how amazing their children were. But my mother, she was just so . . . ready. She was competitive. She always got the last word in." As she spoke, she conjured a slideshow of images of her mother and aunts. "When I watch you banter, it reminds me of how life used to be."

She squirmed in her seat. There was competition between their families. Beatrice rarely divulged her innermost thoughts unless people were meant to stay, and they weren't.

A calendar notification chirped from her phone, and after glancing down at it, she gasped. If she didn't leave now, then she would miss the meeting.

Standing, she said, "I've got to run."

Jackson shifted. "I can walk you . . ."

"No, no worries." She bent down to hug him and, in doing so, realized that probably wasn't the best move. It had been an automatic gesture. She straightened. "I'll check in with your mom to make sure you're doing well." Then, with a final wave to Cathy, she said, "See you."

Then she hightailed it out the door with Roxy.

The fresh air snapped Beatrice back to the present, to reality. She'd gotten caught up in there. Correction: she'd let herself get caught up in the comfort of their company.

Jackson's words returned. *I think it could be forever.*

But she couldn't forget that there was more to their relationship than the two of them. And *thinking* was not the same as knowing, or being.

"Ready to get back to work, Roxy?" Beatrice peeked at her notifications; they were in the dozens, all from her brothers. She winced in anticipation of their disappointment.

And when she got down the stairs, she found that parked behind her space, blocking her Tesla in, was her brother's Suburban.

Oh no.

"There she is," Gil's voice echoed from above.

Her brothers were at her front door.

"What are you guys doing here?" she said with as much casualness as she could muster.

"Let's talk inside," Brandon suggested. "I'm melting in this heat."

She climbed the stairs and opened her door. Brandon and Gil walked in, but Chris gestured for her to enter first. "I . . . was just on my way to Heart Resort. What happened?"

Brandon moseyed around her living room. Gil picked a spot on the couch and sat. Chris was still at the door.

Three brothers and one sister. Though outnumbered all her life, Beatrice had never felt in the minority. In fact, since their parents had passed, she'd taken the role of speaking in proxy for them.

But right then, she knew her brothers were united in their thoughts. Chris moved to the window, as if he wanted feet away from her.

"Leila canceled. In the last minute," Gil said. "Good thing, because you flaked."

"Look, Kuya Chris, Kuya Gil, Brandon. I know this looks really bad."

Gil piped up. "What part? That you had a thing with a competition's son without informing us? Or that today you were willing to blow off an important meeting to be with him?"

It was more like help care for him, but the details didn't matter. Beatrice went to the kitchen island and leaned against it for support, for what she knew would be the conversation where none of them would walk away unscathed. They'd reached the edge of their patience, and she'd pushed them there. "I can explain."

"Please do." Chris's face was morose. "I keep thinking it's going to get better. I keep thinking that this is the end of your secrets. I want to support you, Bea, but you're making it hard."

Silence permeated in the room. It was heavy and thick. She had no more excuses or passes she could cash in to ease her brothers' anger. And frankly, she didn't know if she wanted to do that any longer. "Jackson needed help, and I chose to help him. He needed me, and I felt like things were covered at Heart Resort just in case I didn't make it on time. Kim has been working with me for a while, and she's capable—"

"But that's not the problem, is it? The issue is about giving us your word, your dedication."

"I wasn't finished," she said. "I was also going to say that I was tired. We moved all weekend, and I slept in. And I did my hair. To take care of myself."

"It's nice. I like it." Brandon pointed to his own head in a whisper. "But I agree with them, Ate Bea. We're supposed to be a team."

"Thank you, and I know. Which brings me to the thing I haven't been able to tell you."

"Goodness, what more?" Gil rolled his eyes.

"I want to do Beachy full time."

Gil's mouth opened, but nothing came out.

"So this is not about *him*?" Chris asked.

"No." She swallowed her fear. "But being with him, and losing him, made me understand how much I want to lead my own way. To make my own choices in my career."

Gil shook his head and stood in a huff, stuffing his hands in his pockets. She looked to Brandon, whose gaze was rooted to the floor. Then to Chris, who seemed to be blowing air out through pursed lips.

"Is that your decision?" Chris asked with a deadpan expression. "Are you giving your notice?"

It felt like someone had taken the area rug underneath her and pulled it; it rendered Beatrice unsteady. She hadn't thought this far ahead. Her psyche hadn't allowed her to see beyond her revelation. Perhaps it had been protective, like when she'd rushed through the darkest climax of Eden's romance novels to get to the happily ever after. In her vision, she went straight to being that small business owner, wearing her own dresses and managing her beautiful, bright storefront.

She stuttered her next words. "A . . . am I being f . . . fired?"

"Directors don't get fired. They resign." Chris's voice was cold and cutting.

"Kuya Chris, that's harsh," Brandon hissed; then to Gil, he pleaded, "Kuya Gil."

Gil faced her now. "If Beatrice wants to stay, she'll say so."

The weight was thrust upon her once more, and it sat against her chest. To deny it would be foolish; four out of four of them knew the truth.

Taking this first step would change everything; this she understood in her bones, which was why she'd avoided this moment for a year.

"What I want," she started. "What I want is to step away from Heart Resort."

Jackson:
Is there an offer on the Salvo property?

Peter:
Not at the moment, but there's rumor of serious interest.

Jackson:
Is it from the Puso family?

Peter:
Honestly I don't know. But if I had to guess? Yes

Jackson's phone rang in his hand, and Peter's name appeared on the screen. He put it up to his ear and, without pleasantries, asked, "Do you know about the drama going on?"

"I do now. Fiona caught me up."

"So you see what kind of a predicament I'm in." Jackson didn't say any more and let the truth settle between them. "I don't know what to do." Jackson stood from where he was on the couch, and shuffled in a mild haze to the front deck through the living room, away from his mother's humming from the kitchen table. He hated sounding confused and undecided. People usually came to him for advice.

But in this case, what was right for him? Why was he still here? And what did he want? When Jackson stood next to his father, he belonged. With him, he would have what could be an infinite amount of opportunities. His future would be set, and so would his mother's.

Then there was Beatrice, who embodied love. Commitment. He'd seen it earlier today; he felt it inside him. But she'd said she wanted the ideal relationship without the strife of family issues, and would the Pusos ever accept him? Even if her family took Salvo, could she forgive him for not standing by her at Salt & Sugar?

He risked losing Beatrice either way. Which left him to make this decision for himself once more. For what he expected he wanted out of his life. For what he thought was right.

When Jackson walked out onto the balcony and looked down at the alleyway that led to the parking spaces under the homes, he noticed a Suburban parked adjacent to Beatrice's house. He frowned. Beatrice had left his place twenty minutes ago.

"I can't tell you what to do." Peter snatched Jackson out of his thoughts. "This . . . this is complicated, but it all comes down to a simple step. You can make an offer, or you can wait it out. I can only contact you ASAP when an offer does come in and hope we can get the upper hand."

Jackson shut his eyes. "How long do you think I have?"

Peter blew out a breath. "I don't know. Maybe end of day? But we'll need to be ready before that. Jackson, I can't tell you how much better it will be for our offer to come in first. Depending on how high the offer is, the seller might just snatch it up and not entertain others."

Jackson heard the plea in his voice. Peter wanted to make the sale, and Jackson was keeping him from doing so. Still, it was a chance. "All right. Give me an hour. Two at most."

"Okay."

Jackson bid Peter goodbye and hung up, just as a guy entered Beatrice's balcony with a phone against his ear. He wore a ball cap and a black polo. Then he turned, seeing Jackson.

Brandon.

He leveled Jackson with an expression he couldn't discern, though it neither offended nor intimidated him. He was being examined—he knew that—and for a beat he was regretful that he looked so shabby.

Brandon took the phone away from his ear, then pointed it at him. "Feeling better?"

The question was a surprise. He'd been expecting a threat. "Better. Thanks to your sister."

He nodded. "She's great."

He's shy was what Beatrice had told him once about Brandon. So Jackson simply said, "She is."

Brandon dipped his chin to his chest. "Hey, listen."

"Yeah."

"I probably shouldn't be saying so, but . . . things went south just now. Scratch that—south in some ways but maybe a good thing in the end? Beatrice was always the one to keep us together and, well, with her business, and everything else . . ." He had to know that Jackson would understand that he meant *him*.

"I should come over. I caused this. I can explain and make it better."

Brandon shook his head. "No. We're headed out, and she . . . told me to come out here to tell you that she doesn't want to see you."

"She told you that?"

He nodded. "She said that it wouldn't affect The Cathy Hill. But she wants her space. So don't text her, or call her."

Jackson nodded, understanding what Brandon was saying. "Is she okay?"

"I think? You know Bea; she can appear fine, even if she really isn't. My wife's meeting her at Beachy, though."

A bit of relief settled in. "Oh . . . okay."

"I've got to go. Good luck, man." Then Brandon turned and entered the double doors, leaving Jackson on his side to mull over his next move, which would unequivocally be the most important.

Even if he and Beatrice were over, it didn't mean that he shouldn't still do the right thing.

He dialed his father's number as he walked into the house. He hobbled upstairs to his bedroom and into his closet.

McCauley answered after the first ring. "Son, any news on the property?"

He turned on the closet light. "About that. Are you convinced that Salvo is the place for the next Willow Tree investment? We could take the next week and search for more areas. Properties come on the market all the time."

"I'm absolutely sure. Might I remind you that it was you who suggested Salvo in the first place. Though, I have a feeling that this has something to do with that little girl."

"Please don't call her a little girl."

"Son, we're not going to mince words here. Make the offer."

Jackson shut his eyes and pressed his fingers against them. He was tired, so tired, from being sick, and from playing this game with himself.

Because this was what this was about. Not McCauley, not even Beatrice. But himself.

He had convinced himself that he needed this—his father's approval.

"Jackson." His father's voice softened. "I know I haven't been a good example when it comes to relationships. But our business . . . our work . . . is important. This g . . . I mean young woman's got your mind twisted up. It feels dangerous and sexy being with someone whom you know is forbidden. But it isn't real. Think of it logically. Parse out your choices. You know the right thing to do."

He was interrupted by a knock on the bedroom door, and he turned to see his mother come in. "Jack, you should be laying down. You're in no situation to be up and about, not until you have had at least a meal."

He turned away from his mother, hoping that she would get the hint, while McCauley droned on about Beatrice and the Pusos.

He tried to stay focused on his current logic. "This isn't just about her."

His mother turned him by the torso. "Who is it?" she mouthed.

He shook his head at his mother. Then, to McCauley, he said, "I think we should meet and discuss this."

"I've got too many things to tend to here in Grandview." McCauley's answer was a growl.

"Then I'll come to you."

Cathy waved a hand in front of his face, but Jackson refused to meet her eyes. After he hung up, he resumed grabbing clothes from his closet.

"Where are you going, son?"

"I need to meet with McCauley."

"I refuse to let you get on a bike right now, Jack."

Right. His body had a slim chance of keeping upright. Jackson thumbed to his brother's last text. "I'll ask to borrow Lonnie's car. Or Peter's. Someone."

"No, you're not—"

He braced his hands against the doorframe, frustration coursing through him. "Mother. Please. For once, I don't need your opinion on this. I'm forty years old, and I can choose to see my father if I want to." He inhaled deeply to stave off a wave of nausea.

"You didn't let me finish. I was going to say that you're not going without me. You need a driver. And, you need backup, even if all I do is sit in the car. You need your six covered."

His lips curled up into a smile. She was an army mom through and through. "Do you promise to be good?"

"Cross my heart."

CHAPTER
TWENTY-TWO

Current affirmation: I stand on my own two feet.

As soon as Beatrice parked her Tesla in front of Beachy, Geneva was at her driver's side window, arms crossed and with a crestfallen expression.

Beatrice gathered herself as she got her things together. Now that her side hustle was her real full-time job, there was no time to lose. She had to work her business like her life depended on it. And she was going to start by getting out of the car with dignity.

But she couldn't keep it together once she opened the driver's side door and stepped out. Her whole body began to shake from relief that she still had a friend in Geneva, and from the belated realization that most everything in her life had fallen apart.

"I'm so sorry, Bea." Geneva's face crumpled as she hugged her. "I heard, about everything."

"I . . ." The faces of her brothers flickered through her memory—of their simultaneous shock when she'd agreed to step down from her position. Her voice croaked out her next words. "What if this fails, Gen? God, what if we don't get everything ready for Beachywarming? What if it all goes down the drain and I risked everything for it? And with Jackson. I love him, and I don't know how I'll ever stop."

Geneva stepped back. "I don't know how I can help with Jackson. But I'll be here for you no matter what. I know I haven't been there as I should. After Brandon and I got married, I wanted to . . . I don't know . . . side with him, protect him against everything. I thought that meant telling you what I thought right and wrong was, when it's you who has to make that decision. I should have realized how much he meant to you, Bea. I'm your best friend, and I should have *seen* it. So, I'm sorry," Geneva said.

"I'm sorry too. I put you in a situation to cover up for me, which was wrong. I'm going to be a better friend too."

They hugged a final time, after which Beatrice inhaled a cleansing breath. Then she wiped her tears from her face.

"Are you ready to go in?"

Beatrice nodded.

"Good, because I can *also* do something about Beachywarming." Geneva led her by the hand through Beachy's doors. "And I've got a crew who love us and Beachy and who want to help us."

Beatrice was met by all the women in her life: Fiona, Eden, Giselle. Jessie. Even her Heart Resort assistant, Kim. *Former* assistant, because she had a sneaking suspicion Kim would be rightfully taking her place at Heart Resort.

"All right, everyone, we know what to do, right? We've got five days." Geneva clapped. "Let's start on our checklist."

The shop became a flurry. Giselle called out directions. Music sounded through the space from the Bluetooth speakers. Boxes were sliced open.

It was exactly what Beatrice had needed. Work. Something tangible when she couldn't discern what she was feeling. Creating and building something when parts of her life had crumbled. For the moment, she grounded herself rather than looking for signs, because it was this moment that mattered, wasn't it? It wasn't the past, or the future even. It was now, being around these women who supported her.

Her heart hurt—she was starting to sound like Jackson.

During a break, and as she sipped water, she looked across to Jessie, who was arranging dresses on a hanger. Beatrice had noticed that she had remained focused, though she hadn't socialized with the others. That had always been Jessie—she handled life with a kind of stoicism and no-nonsense attitude, and Beatrice had looked up to this supermom.

But Jessie wasn't at all a supermom. She was, in fact, very human, and Beatrice had punished her for it.

As Geneva passed by with a clipboard, Beatrice held her back by the elbow. "Hey, did you ask Jessie to come out?"

"No. She overheard me talking this over with Eden, and she arranged a babysitter for the girls so that she could help. Nice, right?" Geneva flipped the paper up on her clipboard.

"I should talk to her."

"You should." Geneva smiled. "On the drive back from Salt & Sugar on Friday night, she gave Gil an earful. I'd never seen her so angry."

Beatrice nodded and headed in Jessie's direction, but as she neared, she began to lose her nerve. She meandered to the nearest clothing rack and fiddled with the dresses, though they were already arranged correctly.

Because the truth of the matter was that it was Beatrice who had been the jerk. An utmost jerk, and hypocritical at that. At least Jessie had come out with her affair immediately after it had happened. She hadn't tried to hide it, while it had taken too long for Beatrice to fess up.

Jessie had been a mirror for all of Beatrice's indiscretions, and while Beatrice had been unnecessarily unfair to Jessie, it wasn't so the other way around. Jessie had always been kind.

So she gathered her humility and brought herself to Jessie's side, clearing her throat. "Um, thank you, for coming in to help."

Jessie kept her gaze on the rack. "I'm honored to be here. I hope . . . I hope I'm not overstepping."

"You aren't at all. Many hands mean light work," she said casually, and as she repeated those words said by Jackson several days ago, her heart broke a little more. But she pushed it aside; she had to do better, starting right now. "And, thank you for sticking up for me. For helping me the other day to distract everyone. And you were great, too, with Heart Resort Exposé. I don't think I mentioned it."

Her face lit up. "It was an honor to do that for Chris and Eden. It was a transformative experience for me too."

Jessie needn't say any more about that. The whole family knew that working on the exposé had been the first step in her reconciliation with Gil.

"Listen, I know that I haven't been the best to you," Beatrice started.

"Bea—"

"Let me get this out. I know I haven't been fair to you. At all. Even as you kept reaching out, like at the beach, I don't think I really listened. I don't think I really understood."

"Understood what?"

"How much you were torn between what you wanted for yourself and for the rest of your family. When you and Gil divorced, all I thought about was what I was feeling when . . . when I could have been there for you despite it. I'm so sorry, Jessie. I was an awful friend. A more awful sister, because I shouldn't have shut you out. I chose to forget the fact that you're such a good mom, and an even better sister to me." Tears had gathered in Beatrice's eyes. "Even throughout all this. Even when I haven't been either."

Jessie drew Beatrice into her arms. It was the first hug they'd had in over a year, and it was comfortable, familiar, and true. It was a big sister's hug. A mother's hug, really, in Jessie's sure, fearless grip. It was a hug that said she would never leave Beatrice, no matter how much she pushed her away.

Finally, after gently letting go, Jessie said, "I regret having that affair, but I don't regret the things I learned about myself and about what I need, and what I have to improve. One of those things is not to keep stuff to myself. I used to bottle it all up to be the perfect wife. I wanted you all to think I had it all together. I was a farce, though."

Everything Jessie was saying hit Beatrice in the heart like tiny arrows. She'd often felt like she was carrying the weight of the world, that she had this image to protect and a role to play. "Secrets have a way of coming out."

She smiled. "They do. But when you let them go . . . it's a relief. There's work to be done, but you become a little more honest with yourself. And then you come to a point where you can accept yourself, who you want to be, and who you want to be with.

"Your brothers will come around," Jessie continued. "They're in shock, but they love you. And for all the bluster of Pusos, one thing I've learned about you guys is that at the heart of your relationships, there's room for grace and possibly forgiveness. I mean, I was lucky enough to be married into it. And with Jackson . . . whether or not you get back together . . . you were so lucky to have felt that deep, earth-shattering love. It's what we live for, as humans. It's what maternal love is like—it's what you feel for your brothers, too, and why this is so painful. It stems from the same place. But I'm here with you, for when you need me." She held out a hand. Not in a handshake but in a "Skip down the road" offer. In an "I'm with you" declaration.

The store seemed to brighten. As if the clouds had parted above her, and beyond them was a sliver of light from the sun. It wasn't quite the perfect horizon that Jackson loved to photograph, but it was the start of it.

Beatrice took her hand. Of course she did. This was her Ate Jessie, after all.

♡

Jackson was even sicker after their drive to Grandview because his mother was a daredevil in the driver's seat. And now, parked in front of the home, he rolled down the window to breathe in the fresh air.

"By God, that is hideous," Cathy commented, eyes on the front windshield. She raised her glasses and then set them back on her nose to peer at the home. "In any way you look at it. You sure you don't want me to walk you up? Will you even make it that far?"

"I'll be fine, if I can get the nausea in check."

She cringed. "Are you sure it's just the coleslaw?"

He thought twice before he answered and decided to stay silent. He honestly didn't know. On the drive, despite all the swerves and twists and turns, he couldn't arrive on what to say to McCauley. The pros and cons continued to war inside of him.

As hideous as Grandview was, the person in there was his father. His *father*, his DNA, the person he'd wished for at every turn of his life, even under the resentment that he'd built over the years. That push and pull of being wanted endured despite the pain of the truth of who McCauley was. It had plagued him his entire life.

Jackson needed to deal with it once and for all.

He needed to be free from it, from him.

"I know I said that I wouldn't ask questions or make any comments about your involvement with Willow Tree and your father. But I am going to make a statement." She turned in her seat and reached out to touch his shoulder. "I'm proud of you. For everything you are and what you stand for. Even through decisions I didn't understand, and the hills that I wish you didn't have to climb. Because you're willing to make the decision, the call. And yes, the risk, even if you wish you didn't have to. Jackson Hill, my son, I want you to never have to compromise who you are, so whatever you're deciding to do here, I support you. One hundred percent."

"What if it means working with McCauley permanently?"

"Then you work with him, and I'm going to make sure I'm there to protect you."

"What if it means starting over?"

"Even if it means starting in the negative. Besides," she added with a gleam in her eye, "life is about that, you know? We go forward and backward, left and right."

"I spent the last twenty years moving forward."

"Then I think it's quite all right to pull over if you want to, don't you think? Take a look at the map. Or, I don't know, tear the map up and just go."

"That sounds frightening."

"I know. And exhilarating." She laughed.

"You and Beatrice are so alike."

Her face softened. "It's why I adore her. But this is not about her and you. This is about you and this decision you have to make." Her voice dipped. "Speaking of the damn devil."

Jackson peered out the window to the shadow approaching them. His father was driving up in a golf cart.

"Don't get out of the car," Jackson instructed Cathy. The idea of the two seeing one another catapulted him outside, nausea be damned, to get this conversation over and done with. There was no singular way that he would put his mother in a situation to be face to face with McCauley. He didn't know what she was capable of.

And this had to be his fight, his conversation.

He willed his legs to go and imagined that the ocean air was a salve to his nausea. He took deep breaths to stave off the gurgling in his belly and approached McCauley, who stepped out of the golf cart.

"I saw y'all drive up, and you were just sitting there. I don't have a lot of time." He looked beyond him. "Who's in the car with you?"

"My mother."

"Cat," he whispered. Then, as if he'd been startled to the present, his eyes cut to Jackson. "What do you need?"

"I'm asking you, in person, to consider another property. Something else. Someplace else." He swallowed the pride that threatened to surge out of him. Because it shouldn't be hard to be decent; Jackson shouldn't have to beg for it. "Please. If not to keep the peace between Willow Tree and Heart Resort, then for me."

"Did you really drive up here to question my decision?"

"Yes, sir. Respectfully." He clenched his hands into fists to keep himself upright and focused. To hold on to the optimism that McCauley would listen to him, that he would consider his opinion in this. That he would find Jackson important enough to do this one thing for him.

McCauley's face hardened. "Here I thought we got to a point, Jackson, that we understood one another. I thought you and I . . . were cut from the same cloth—to not let a woman come in between an important decision, in between family. But maybe I was wrong."

Jackson knew—he knew in his logic, in the synapses in his brain, that his father was being manipulative. That whatever this man was saying was part of a plan. That, in his power and greed and his experiences in between, McCauley was who he was before, during, and after Jackson. Cold, calculating, and charming.

But damn did it sting. Jackson forgot all about his nausea, inconsequential now to a realization that this was the reason why his mother had kept him away from McCauley.

Jackson was not like his father. And that was all right.

"I was wrong, too, for thinking that we were more like each other. For wishing for it." Jackson winced at how he'd ignored all his mother's warnings. His mother, who had never, ever failed him. "And I'm pretty damn lucky that I'm *not* like you. I don't want to be. I always said I would never turn my back on family, and by God, I can't believe I almost did," Jackson said. "I'm not going to put in the offer."

"If that's your decision." McCauley guffawed, jaw working. "You had to know that if you couldn't do the job, Lonnie could do it just as well, or anyone else on staff. You can turn in the beach house keys to Lonnie. I expect you out of there by the end of the week."

Jackson thought of his mother, her things, her artwork laid out. And that Beachywarming wasn't until the weekend. His heart broke with what they would have to do—to have to relocate. To have to look in the mirror and know that he was unemployed, without a home, and unmoored in the truest of ways. And he'd lost Beatrice anyway.

He swallowed his father's cold ultimatum like shards of glass. "Got it."

McCauley's eyes darted down, and then up to Jackson's face. Then, he turned and climbed back up into his golf cart. "You sure?"

And unlike how he'd felt accepting this job from McCauley a little less than a month ago, Jackson said, "Positive."

"What's your plan B, then?"

Jackson didn't owe his father a follow-up. And he himself wasn't sure, but he looked up at the sky, at the expanse of it all, and felt something come upon him. A sliver of bravado. That there was more for him to do and, maybe, to learn. "I don't know. Maybe go back to school?"

McCauley snorted. "Good luck to you."

"You too, with . . . everything."

After a nod, his father turned on the cart and executed a sharp U-turn.

Jackson watched Dillon McCauley III, his father, drive away, closing the door that he had previously propped open with his one wish for what he'd thought was normal.

Then, he walked back to the car, where his mother was waiting for him.

CHAPTER
TWENTY-THREE

Today's affirmation: I step out in confidence.

In the afternoon the day before Beachywarming, everything was set to go.

Beachy was ready, and Beachy was beautiful. It was exactly the way Beatrice had envisioned it: full of light and beautiful things. Racks of colorful dresses inhabited the floor space. Against newly painted walls were modern shelves filled with specialty home items. From the ceiling hung a brilliant crystal chandelier, so extra that it made her and Geneva giggle whenever they looked up at it. In the middle of the shop was a setup for their preferred spotlight vendor—which currently was The Cathy Hill.

And tomorrow, the shop would be full of beautiful people.

Had Beatrice said *beautiful*?

Beatrice was so proud; she'd put all of herself into the shop. Admittedly, in the beginning, she had worked her butt off to try to stave off the feeling of emptiness. But that desperation had become something else.

The practice of work had saved her, as it had done in the past. It had given her a connection to her purpose and, after that, to everything else: the spiritual, the emotional, the logical. It had reminded her that what Jessie had talked about—this deep, earth-shattering love? She had that for Beachy too. Not for what it was in a material sense but for what it embodied. This was from her heart, her hands, and her mind.

Beatrice had let everyone go for the afternoon; she picked up her dustrag. She hated dusting with a passion normally, but these days, all she could do was clean. Her house was spotless, and Beachy was apparently dustless, but she was going through the motions anyway.

Everything was in place. All the vendors had been verified: the catering, the music, the photographer, the local artists like The Cathy Hill.

For the millionth time in the last week, Beatrice's heart hurt, and she let it flow through her instead of pretending it didn't exist. She would no longer hide from the truth of her and Jackson's situation: that they both always had a choice. That she was sad about it—that she would be sad for a while.

They always had a choice. Five years ago and anytime thereafter. And for them to be together, they would need to choose each other above their family situations. To get him back—because she believed in the possibility that there would be a third time for them—that was what she would have to do. And unlike how she'd tackled her problems in the past—in a chaotic, close-your-eyes-and-jump-in-with-both-feet way—she realized that she would need to tackle this process in order.

Which meant starting with herself.

Then with Beachy.

Then with her family.

And *then* Jackson, if he'd still have her.

It was the purest form of adulting and accountability—in understanding the present situation as it was, in truly deliberating all her decisions.

It was about being honest with everyone but absolutely with herself first.

A knock sounded on the front window, and her breath hitched. Outside was a man. A man who she hadn't had the courage to speak to since last week. He raised a hand in a hello.

Beatrice walked to the door and unlocked it. Bells rang as the door swung open. "Kuya Gil."

Her brother was impeccably dressed, clean shaven, and well groomed. Being with Jessie looked good on him. "Hey. I'm here because it's Friday."

"I know it's Friday."

"Are you coming to dinner?"

"Am I still invited?"

His shoulders slumped. "Beatrice."

"I honestly wasn't sure. We all haven't exactly spoken."

"You haven't been by your apartment on Heart Resort."

"It doesn't make sense for me to go there since I don't work there anymore."

"So that's it? You no longer come to Heart Resort because you don't work there?"

This kind of talk was exhausting. "Kuya Gil. I can't with the banter. Not today."

He heaved a breath. "I guess that means we can't sweep this under the rug like everything else?"

She shook her head. "Too bulky. Hard to hide."

"I remember when you used to hide your hard-boiled eggs in the basket of pandesal."

The memory flew in, and Beatrice smiled. "I hated the yolk with a passion. But Mom believed in those eggs. 'An egg a day keeps the doctor away.'"

"I went to school and said that once, and my friends trolled me for weeks."

She laughed at the thought until silence settled between them once more.

His gaze dropped for a beat. "I miss you, little sis. You're the glue, you know? Business . . . it brings out stuff. Maybe the worst in people. It certainly brought out something in me that I didn't like, because I wrapped up all the personal things between us and struck back. I'm sorry. I was wrong. I wasn't being the big brother our parents tried to instill in me."

This olive branch took all the fear and animosity out of Beatrice. She immediately hugged her brother around the waist; it was all she'd needed, to be met halfway. "I did the same thing—I kept putting that thing with Jessie between us, and now I get it. Now I know. Two people can try to keep everyone else out of a relationship, but the fact of the matter is that no one else has the choice but them. That even if so many people are rolled up into it, it's really not any of their business. You and Ate Jessie needed to have the freedom to figure things out."

"Ate Jessie, huh?" He'd caught the change. "She did mention that you two are talking."

Beatrice stepped back and grinned. "A little bit here and there. It's getting better."

"Do you know what else will help? More time together. With all of us. Come to dinner. We're all waiting for you."

She couldn't contain her smile. "Okay. I'll go grab my stuff."

Gil headed outside while Beatrice scuttled to the back room. With a finger on the chandelier light switch, she took in the total view of Beachy in the way she imagined it would look in a professional photograph. Atmospheric, romantic, hopeful. It was glorious, and it set off a memory of Beatrice shopping for homecoming dresses with her mother, of Marilyn Puso's almost superhuman endurance to find just the perfect dress. How many times had her father simply waited for them sitting on a bench somewhere with shopping bags at his feet? Too many.

Beatrice warmed at the thought.

Her mother *was* here. She would always be here.

Then the crystals of the chandelier shook from the AC turning on, and light twinkled like stars. It reminded Beatrice of the night when she and Jackson had looked up at the sky. The night she'd almost told him she loved him.

Everything reminded her of Jackson, but nothing more so than the sky, the stars, the horizon.

Jessie had been right. Jackson had been her deep, earth-shattering love. And she was glad to have had it, if even for a short time.

Beatrice shut off the lights and turned on the alarm, and as she exited the door and locked up, her phone buzzed in her purse. She fished it out as she crossed the parking lot.

It was the family group text.

Chris:

You won't believe it, but Salvo is ours. I'll tell you more when you get here. Still getting info.

She jumped into Gil's minivan; Gil was in the driver's seat thumbing his screen. "I don't understand. We went into escalation, but Dave was sure Willow Tree would beat it," he said. "I mean, this is great. But what the hell happened?"

"What the hell indeed," she whispered.

The fifteen-minute drive was filled with a cycle of silence and neutral questions on topics that didn't delve into anything about love, or marriage, or Heart Resort.

But it was a start.

When they rolled up to Salt & Sugar, Chris was standing in the gravel parking lot with Brandon. "Oh, this is serious," Beatrice mused. A nervous giggle escaped her lips.

Chris didn't wait for Gil to press on the emergency brake. He all but opened Beatrice's door. "Willow Tree backed out."

"What?" Beatrice was hearing things, because Willow Tree never backed down.

"They rescinded their offer."

"Is this a trick?" Gil asked.

"Whether or not it is, we're being sent the paperwork to sign tonight."

"Oh my God." Beatrice pressed a hand against her thundering heart. Only one person could have made this happen. *Jackson.*

Chris gestured with a head. "C'mon, we can talk about it more in the restaurant. Let's put some food in you, Bea. You've worked hard getting Beachy together, and we've got a lot to discuss in regards to Jackson Hill. I have a feeling that he's involved."

♡

A crash sounded from the kitchen, and Jackson jogged in from the bedroom. "Everything okay?"

His mother was on her hands and knees picking up broken shells among wire and large beads and broken glass. "Yep. Just a little accident."

Guilt pierced his heart. He weaved around their half-packed suit-cases and her carefully wrapped projects to reach her and bent down. "I'll clean this up."

"I'll get the dustpan and broom." She stood with a groan.

Jackson grunted. He hated this. He hated all of this. He'd messed up. For the last couple of days, in between finding a decent hotel to stay in, which was near impossible, he'd been mulling over in his head what he could have done better. When could he have made better choices and decisions? How could he have handled McCauley to have lessened the pain and inconvenience of being thrown out?

"Dammit." A glass shard pierced his skin, and he hissed from the pain. He stood to grab a paper towel and pressed it against his thumb. The throbbing was minuscule, but a wave of sadness came over him, slow and all-consuming. At how much he'd gained in three weeks, and at how much he'd lost in one afternoon.

Worse, he'd gotten the taste of what life could have been. To have been accepted into his family. To have found love.

"Oh, my dear." His mother arrived at his side, and she rested a hand on his back.

"You must have thought that I was so stupid coming out here thinking I could have something with McCauley, and then falling for this woman so quickly."

"Do you want an honest answer?" She gave him a side-eye.

He guffawed. "As if you're capable of anything less."

"Then . . . I wasn't surprised. Everyone has their path, Jackson. Finding your father and then being with him was always a part of yours. And falling for Beatrice, well . . . she's not hard to fall for. Just as you're not so hard to fall for either. Yes, it felt fast, but I'd like to think it's been in the works well before you even knew one another."

"That's silly."

"You keep saying that, and it's okay."

"The worst of it is still coming. Lonnie told me Salvo's in escalation, with Willow Tree in the lead. Whatever chance I had with her is gone."

He'd caught sight of Beatrice occasionally, driving in or out of the carport, or walking Roxy to the beach. In all times, he'd scrounged his brain for an apology for Willow Tree, for his father, for his family. In all times, he'd failed, because what could he have *really* said? That he was sorry for the hostile takeover? If it hadn't been for Jackson, McCauley would have never considered Salvo. It was Jackson's fault. Jackson's. Fault.

And at the end of it all, he had been given specific instructions to give her space. He had to respect and accept it.

A knock sounded on the door, and Jackson looked down at his mother questioningly.

She shrugged. "I'll grab it. You get a Band-Aid. They're under the kitchen sink."

When he returned to the living room, Lonnie was at the threshold.

"Hi, Ms. Hill." He nodded at Jackson. "Hey."

"We have until tomorrow to hand you the keys, Lonnie. Close of business. That means five o'clock." They really didn't have much to pack, but he didn't want to rush. And he simply wanted to have a little bit of control.

"I . . . I know. But I thought . . . why not give you a hand?"

"So you can rub it in?"

His mother tsked as if they were toddlers. "Take it outside, boys."

"Let's do that." Jackson gestured to the back door, curiosity surging through him. Lonnie dipped his chin down at Cathy. It was more respect than he'd expected from his brother but not enough to let his guard down. "Why are you here?"

"I know you have your U-Haul and everything, but I brought my truck and an extra pair of hands. Look, I heard about what happened between you and Dad. Alls I got to say is that I'm not him. I know that sometimes I act like him, and that maybe I take his side. But with this . . . I want to help, somehow. Willow Tree isn't just Dad, you know? It's me, and Heather and my boys. And you. Because you're a McCauley."

"Nah. I'm just a Hill with some McCauley in him."

"Okay then. That's fair. But that McCauley in you—it's the same as me. And, I dunno, I just want to try, with us. When Dad goes, there's me and my family and then what? Willow Tree? What does that even mean? I don't want that. These last few days . . . I guess I missed you. It's nice, to have a brother."

Part of Jackson wanted to throw himself at the guy. Because this was exactly what he had been waiting for. For someone to say that he was family. In the way Lonnie was saying it now, he could tell that it was sincere.

But . . .

"Look. I'm not asking for us to share bedrooms or anything. I just want to be here for you, even as a driver. Let me help you bring stuff to your hotel tonight."

Jackson took a deep breath. He could do that. "It *would* make things go faster." He offered his hand.

Lonnie's face broke out into a smile, and he pumped his hand. "Yeah, great. Put me to work."

CHAPTER TWENTY-FOUR

Current affirmation: I tackle every task with precision.

With a covered dish of chicken adobo and garlic fried rice in hand, Beatrice left Friday dinner with one thing on her list, and that was to talk to Jackson. To thank him for what he'd done, with the dish as an olive branch.

And more . . . if he would allow it.

But when she arrived at his beach house, the lights were off. The bicycle she'd lent Cathy was in her own parking space. There wasn't a motorcycle, or a moving truck present. When she climbed the stairs and peeked in the windows, there were no signs of life.

She let out a breath of disappointment. He was gone.

Of course, she knew he wasn't all the way gone. Cathy would have said. Beatrice had texted with her today about Beachywarming. The lovely woman Cathy was, she hadn't pressed about Beatrice's relationship with Jackson. But she had let her know which hotel they were staying in, and that after the event, they would be getting on the road to San Diego.

"It's time for me to go back home and revive The Cathy Hill," she'd said. "I'm reopening the studio."

Still, Beatrice had to see Jackson in person. It couldn't wait. Tomorrow would be too busy, and every second was one more she could speak to him. Their relationship had been the kind that hung on urgency. Every day in the Outer Banks with him had been another rung up or down the ladder of their relationship. She couldn't take this night for granted.

The streets were busy as she drove toward their hotel. She spotted the small U-Haul from Highway 12 parked in a corner space, next to a trailer that she presumed would be for Jackson's motorcycle, but there was no bike to be found. Which meant he wasn't in. After circling the block once more, she pulled off with the engine idling, mollified and humbled.

It felt like a sign; she felt acceptance in her bones. Her whole body went slack, and she sobbed. She'd shed tears all this week, but this was a free flow, in the dark, in private.

This was the last loose end to tie up, and she'd thought . . .

She'd thought that she would get her happily ever after like the rest of the family had.

But maybe, maybe this was where her story had to end. Her growth was with herself, because loving oneself had to be the first step. And she had Beachy. Beautiful Beachy, which was her message to the world.

"You know what? It's fine," she said aloud. Because it was. It truly was.

She would still miss Jackson—she would still wonder—but she would come to accept the situation.

She looked down at the covered dish. It would be a shame if it went to waste. She decided to text Cathy anyway: Hey, I've got leftover Filipino food. Are you up for a quick drop off? I'll be in the parking lot for about ten minutes. If you don't text back, no worries. I'll see you in the morning!

She drove up to the hotel lot and parked next to the U-Haul, and she looked through her emails to pass the time.

After ten minutes passed, Beatrice buckled her seat belt and started the car. Then, her phone buzzed.

Cathy:
I'm up, but not dressed. You're welcome to come to my room. Room 103.

♡

"Wow." Jackson had just gotten off the phone with Lonnie, who'd relayed the most recent news. He looked over at his mother, who was texting on the hotel bed.

"What is it, Jack?"

"McCauley pulled out of the Salvo deal."

"Hm. That's great."

But her tone was suspect. There was not a stitch of surprise in it. "Mother?" He came around to her side of the room and perched on the radiator, crossing his arms. "Did you have anything to do with this?"

"Why would you say that?"

"Because . . . you just seem so calm . . ." But he shook his head; perhaps he was wrong. Would his mother have really gone out of her way to speak to McCauley after years of zero communication? "You're right; never mind. I guess I'm just shocked."

McCauley played to win, and the idea that he'd backed out on something that could have been a clear and easy win . . .

Jackson breathed out some of the tension that he'd been carrying. Though a part of him wondered what had made McCauley change his mind, he also didn't care. What was most important was that the Pusos were no longer McCauley's target. Jackson could drive away from the Outer Banks tomorrow afternoon with that heavy brick of responsibility off his shoulders.

The heaviest, of course, was losing Beatrice, and getting over Beatrice. He hoped that the West Coast beaches would give him the healing he needed, that helping his mother fix up her art studio would help him figure out what he wanted to be when he grew up.

His phone rang once more, this time with an area code he didn't recognize. It was late, and surely it was spam, but he didn't want to miss an important phone call. Could've been potential employers. Or schools. An opportunity. Could've been Beatrice, calling from another phone because hers just happened to be out of commission, and she'd meant to call earlier.

Hey, a guy could dream.

"This is Jackson Hill."

"Jackson, it's Christopher Puso."

"Um . . ." *Stunned* was a mild description of Jackson's reaction. "Hi."

"I'm probably the last person you expected on the other line, but I wanted to say . . . thank you. For whatever you had to do regarding the Salvo property. We e-signed paperwork tonight. It's the future site of Heart Homes."

"In full disclosure, I don't know how that happened either."

"Well, I'm sure you had a hand in it. Your father is . . . committed and dedicated to his work, and it had to have been something personal and drastic to change his mind. Anyway . . ." His voice trailed off. "The relationship between you and my sister. I . . . I acted out of anger. I put her in a position that I regret. But, I want to apologize to you. And I want to thank you, not only for Salvo but for being there for Gil in Vegas. Gil told me about you so long ago. When I realized it was you at Salt & Sugar, I didn't properly acknowledge it, and I should have. I guess I . . . was having a hard time reconciling everything."

The look Chris had given him at Salt & Sugar—that was what it was. "I . . . you're welcome. It was so long ago."

"It's not my place to tell Gil's story, but sometimes it takes one thing to change a person's life. And you were that thing."

Despite not knowing all the details, Jackson understood the sentiment. One singular thing, one moment, one uttered word could alter the course of one's life. One night in Vegas irrevocably changed his, after all.

"I hear you're off to California." Chris filled in the silence.

"I am. To help get my mom settled."

"Good luck with everything."

Jackson continued to look at his phone screen seconds after Chris had hung up. "That was interesting," he said to his mother, smiling. He had accepted that he was leaving ash and dust from his short time in the Outer Banks, but he wasn't. Not totally. It gave him some hope that maybe a relationship with the Puso family could be built. That maybe he could return whenever Beatrice was ready for him.

A knock sounded on the door, and his emotions whiplashed once more to curiosity. It was late, and there were too few people who knew they were here.

"Did you ask for room service, Ma?"

"Hmm?"

Jackson was already walking to the room door, and he opened it to Beatrice carrying a covered dish.

He blinked. And blinked again from the rush of déjà vu at seeing her right in front of him. He'd wished for this in the last week. "Bea?" He bent down to scoop her into his arms, belatedly realizing that he probably shouldn't.

But Beatrice had leaned toward him, and their arms and bodies collided in a half hug. It was awkward but comforting. He caught a scent of her shampoo, and it encapsulated him with relief.

A nervous giggle escaped her lips. "Oh my God."

At the same time he blurted out, "I'm so sorry."

"No, it's fine." She stepped back; her cheeks were pink. "I didn't see your bike out there . . ."

"I had it serviced . . . I'm picking it up in the morning." He shook his head, still confused. Lonnie, Chris, and now . . . "How did you know where I was?"

"Excuse me; pardon me," said a squeak of a voice. His mother sidestepped past them. "I'm going to grab some ice. I'll be right back. Though, take your time." She patted Beatrice on the forearm, taking the dish from her.

Then, with a gentle push so Beatrice was inside the room, Cathy closed the door behind her.

"She did it again." Beatrice's eyes glassed over, and a smile broke out on her face.

"She did," was all Jackson could say. The sheer sight of Beatrice had seized his entire body. "What are you doing here, Bea?"

"We just had our Friday dinner, and I had extra food, and I thought you both would be hungry . . ."

"Thank you, but that's not what I mean." Jackson half laughed. Because she was, as usual, so damn sweet. Her presence had brightened this drab room up, and he felt light on his feet.

"I'm here because your mom told me that you were leaving for California, and I just couldn't let you go without saying goodbye." Her gaze dropped to the carpet, and then back up to his face. Her expression crumpled. "Dammit, Jackson, it's been an awful week. I know I told Brandon to tell you to give me space, and you have every right to tell me to go."

He grasped her hand. "No. I don't want you to go."

Her eyes rounded. "Really?"

"Bea. I understood why you asked for space. All this—us? There are no instructions for this. I'm glad you're here."

She squeezed his hand and nodded. "I missed you. Everything was against us, Jackson, and I let myself believe that we didn't know each other enough, that I had to play a specific role in this family, that I needed buy-in from them as to who I choose to love. But when you were sick, you said that you thought it could be forever—"

Jackson's face warmed. "I really had loose lips when I was delirious with food poisoning."

She cackled. "Yes, but it made me think long and hard about what that took. And I'm ready for it. I love you. I . . . I know we have a lot to work on. But . . . can we keep in touch?"

It was the same question Jackson had asked Beatrice in Vegas, before she'd walked out the door. So reminiscent, along with the dish she'd brought over, and the way they couldn't stop touching one another, that it felt so right, and meant to be.

This time, though, Jackson didn't push the notion away. Because he was starting to believe it.

Jackson lifted her chin with a knuckle and hovered his lips over hers. He paused for her consent, and she gave it when she tilted her face upward, rising on her tiptoes. Their kiss was short, chaste, and sweet.

When she opened her eyes, Jackson grinned down at her. "Can I speak now?"

She nodded.

"This week was the worst without you, Beatrice, but it wasn't all your doing. I almost lost myself trying to be the person my father wanted for me to be. But I know now that it's because I need to make decisions, about what I want to do with my life. I don't know what's up ahead for me. And I think . . . I think I want to take my time to find out what my next step is. But you have brought so much joy into my life. Optimism. Hope. And I want to discover all of it with you."

She threw her arms around his neck. "Really?"

"Really. You don't mind having me as a tagalong?"

"No way. Never." She pulled his neck down, and he obliged, eager to capture her mouth with his. They kissed fervently, pressing their bodies together.

He never wanted to let her go. Emotionally, that was, because he still had one more thing to do. Keeping his hands on her waist, he set her down. "I have to take my mom back to California."

"I know you do, and I want to visit you, if time allows. I want to make this work. For whatever you need, whatever job you take. Although . . ." She bit her bottom lip, eyes lighting up. "I've always got room for a superorganized, detailed thinker on the Beachy team."

The thought of being able to work with Beatrice every day made him laugh out loud, not because it was funny, but because . . . wow . . . it could be an option. "Are you serious?"

"As a chicken-and-waffles ice cream cone."

"I love the idea."

"Good. Now can I ask a question?"

"Anything."

"What happened with Willow Tree?"

"I told McCauley that I wouldn't put in an offer on Salvo."

She covered her mouth with a hand. "Who made the offer?"

"Lonnie."

"So you had nothing to do with him pulling his offer?"

"Nope."

"Then who . . ."

The door beeped and unlocked, opening an inch. "Are you decent in here?" his mother crooned.

Jackson's gaze locked onto Beatrice's. She arched her eyebrows in true understanding.

"The Cathy Hill," they said together.

CHAPTER TWENTY-FIVE

Las Vegas, Nevada
Five Years Ago

Today's affirmation: I will keep my people together.

Beatrice scrolled through her texts as she exited the elevators at the MGM Grand, still with a smile from her little rendezvous with Jackson, and halted at the words on the screen.

Geneva:
Gil is missing

Her jaw slackened, and she halted in her tracks, which garnered a slew of curse words from people who were walking closely behind her. Someone shoulder checked her, and her tiara tipped forward on her face. She got caught in the whirlpool of casino goers passing like schools of fish, and all she could think of was Jessie and their two little girls, Izzy and Kitty.

Jessie was going to roast Gil if he messed up one more time.

And Beatrice was going to take her turn at him if he decided to show up drunk to their eldest brother's wedding in the morning.

>**Beatrice:**
>Where was he seen last?

Geneva:
Aladdin.

Aladdin had been the group's second stop for the night.

>**Beatrice:**
>OMG that was four hours ago

Geneva:
everyone assumed he was with Jessie
Geneva:
but he's not. Eden got a text from Jessie
ten minutes ago asking where he was

>**Beatrice:**
>crap

Why, why, why? She was having a great night. Everything was going to plan. This event was so important, and it had to be perfect. Adding Eden to the family was symbolic that despite the loss they'd endured, the family would continue to grow. This marriage signified hope.

But it would be a hot mess if Beatrice couldn't locate Gil soon.

>**Beatrice:**
>okay let's get a search party together

Geneva:
before we do, how was that guy?

Beatrice's face warmed with the memory.

Beatrice:

sighhhhssss. He's perfect. I hope he calls me

Geneva:

he would be a fool not to

Beatrice:

I guess if it's meant to be . . .

♡

"The rideshare is, like, a minute out." Jackson peered at the headlights of oncoming traffic, marveling at the packed streets. Despite the night sky, the billboards, building lights, and passing cars lit his surroundings brightly. To his buddies Marcus and Gavin, he said, "We need to look for a white Camry."

"I can't tell makes and models of vehicles. What's the license plate?" Marcus asked.

But as Jackson started to read the plate number off of his app, he heard someone yelp. He turned to the noise, at first unable to discern where it had come from—the wide sidewalks were that congested—when a flash of white caught his eye.

A guy was on the ground, and he was surrounded.

"What's up?" Gavin, curious, turned to where Jackson was looking. "Oh, crap."

"Car's here," Marcus said.

"Hold the car, Marcus," Jackson said before rushing to the person's aid. The people around him had dispersed, leaving the guy, wearing all white and a condom lei and aviator glasses hooked onto his shirt, lying on the ground. Jackson helped him to standing. "Hey, are you okay?"

The guy's clothing was crumpled, and his pants were covered in dirt. As he brushed them off, brown streaks bloomed on the fabric. He was a mess; it was an unfortunate sight. "They tried to take my wallet. But you chased them away."

"Oh damn."

"Iss okay," his voice slurred, and it was only then that Jackson picked up the strong smell of liquor. This guy was out of it. Big time. "And I still have my phone." He produced his cell phone with a magician's flair, and he laughed. Apparently, this was all so funny.

"Great. Should you call someone?" Jackson gently led him to a bench, which was shockingly free.

"Nahh." He shook his head, plopping onto it. "I'm in big trouble. Drank too much."

"Oh, I see." Jackson's heart went out to him. And if there was one thing he'd learned in the army, it was that sometimes you had to get a little creative to get the work done. "How about *I* call someone."

"Oh sure." He stuck the phone against Jackson's chest.

"Jack!" Marcus called from the car.

"Almost there!" To his surprise, the phone was unlocked. With a few swipes, he clicked on his messages, to a group chat that was labeled "bros & sis." A slew of messages waited for him, and sure enough, with a quick glance, Jackson deduced that the guy had gone MIA. Jackson dropped a pin of his location. Then he said to the guy, "Now I want you to stay right here, okay? Don't go anywhere."

"Okay."

Thank goodness, he was amiable enough.

"Wait, can I get a selfie?" He grabbed onto Jackson's shirt.

He hesitated at first, then relented. "Yeah, okay." He leaned next to the guy's face as he snapped a picture. "I wish you luck," Jackson said, walking backward before his friends dragged him into the back seat of their rideshare.

He felt a slight sting of worry. While the car idled at a long stoplight, he turned and saw a curly-haired woman throw her arms around the guy.

Jackson let out a breath.

Hopefully it would all work out.

CHAPTER
TWENTY-SIX

Five Weeks Later
Southern Shores, North Carolina

Jackson washed his hands and looked at his reflection in the mirror. He readjusted his bow tie and said, "I will use my voice."

He winced at his weak attempt. So, he tried once more. "I will use my voice."

This time, his voice echoed through the bathroom, earning him a look from someone walking in. But he didn't care, because these affirmations Beatrice had turned him onto were working, for the most part.

Today would be another test.

With one last look in the mirror, Jackson walked into the lobby and toward the conference room, passing the signage on the tripod that read JONES-DAVIS RECEPTION. Just beyond the double door threshold was a party. On the dance floor were people doing the soul train. Servers dressed in black picked up cups from tables. And Beatrice, his Beatrice, shot by, a vision in lavender.

"I thought this was supposed to be intimate," a voice said. Jackson turned to see Gil with Kitty, his youngest daughter, on piggyback. "Isn't that what Kim and Heath wanted?"

"*Technically*"—Jackson used air quotes for the word—"they wanted the ceremony to be intimate, but somehow Beatrice convinced them to go all out for the reception."

He snorted. "That's what they get for working with Beatrice Puso. It's never, ever intimate or small. It's go big or go home. Speaking of home." He nudged him with an elbow. "Is everything set?"

The thought of it made Jackson's heart skip a beat. "Yes. It's set. And . . . thank you. For everything."

"No need for thanks, Jackson. I've never seen my sister as happy as she's been these last few weeks. It's good to know that there's one more person who's by her side. Strength in numbers, especially when it's family. And I'm glad it's you."

Jackson's neck heated at the implication that he was family. After he'd returned from California, where he'd stayed a short two weeks, he put in an offer on a modest third-row beach bungalow in Nags Head—which he planned to name Sunset. Sunset, to match Beatrice's beach house's name: Sikat ng Araw, for the sunrises she watched from her living room window. Only a row would separate them as they got to know one another; the short distance would also allow each other space and privacy whenever they needed it.

For now.

His army pension would take care of Sunset's mortgage and allow him to save money while going through a photography and graphic design course. He was also Beachy's newest hire doing the back-end processes: managing inventory and processing orders. It had been a massive set of risky decisions in such a short amount of time, but for Beatrice, he had been willing.

"It's time." Gil yanked him from his thoughts as the cake was rolled in on a cart.

"The cake, Daddy. Get closer!" Kitty yelled.

"All right already." Gil took steps forward but, with a final look back, said, "I wish you luck."

"I'll need it." There went his voice, another squeak.

Jackson watched as the bride and the groom cut their cake, and one of the catering staff sliced up the rest of the cake and placed it onto plates. Geneva handed him a slice with a nod. "You've got this."

"Thank you." He scanned the room.

She gestured to the right. "There she is. Go get her."

Jackson didn't need to be told twice. He took long strides toward Beatrice, who was chatting up one of the servers. But when they locked eyes, her smile grew.

His heart went into triple time. These moments were what he lived for. It wasn't the hoopla, or the grand gestures, but the sincere acknowledgments, the small tokens of kindness. Like Lonnie's invitation to dinner so he could meet Heather. His mother's random emails.

Beatrice's megawatt smile.

"Oh, cake. Thank you, baby." She kissed him on approach.

That too—being called *baby*. Kissing without hesitation.

At the moment, though, Jackson couldn't get a word out. He could only watch as Beatrice poked at the cake. "What the heck?"

People gathered around them. Giselle showed up with a phone, with his mother on FaceTime.

"Jackson?" She let out a nervous giggle. She dug the fork around, unearthing a miniature velvet cinch bag stamped with The Cathy Hill. She held the plate still and looked up at him with doe eyes. "*Jack.*"

And jeez, when she called him Jack—he couldn't get enough of it.

He plucked the cinch bag from her plate while someone took the plate away. With shaking hands, Jackson loosened the bag and shook out a velvet box.

Beatrice gasped. "Oh my God."

"I told The Cathy Hill that your lucky number was three." Jackson opened the velvet box to reveal a ring with a setting of three diamonds. "I know it's only been two months, but to me, our love began over five years ago, when we took a bet on each other. I love you, Beatrice. I want to spend my whole life with you. I'm not a superstitious man, but even I know that my lucky streak began on that night." He took her left hand and got down on one knee. At the crowd's gasp, he presented the ring. "Will you marry me and—"

Then Beatrice, being Beatrice, fell to her knees, wrapped her arms around his neck, and kissed him to silence. He couldn't even get the last of the question out.

"Yes, Jack, yes. I'm the lucky one," she said into his ear, as the room erupted into applause. "But, who's going to plan our wedding?"

♡

ACKNOWLEDGMENTS

Like Beatrice, I too believe in a little bit of the woo-woo. It's part of my foundation, coming from a spiritual family and stemming from my Filipino culture. And I am fully aware that so many things in our journey cannot be predicted, no matter how much I try to wrangle the future with my planners and calendars and productivity tools.

Due to the combination of blessings, luck, serendipity, coincidence, and fate, I have had the most amazing people by my side in the writing of this book. Editor Lauren Plude, who challenged me to up the ante of Beatrice and Jackson's stakes and saw the heart of their romance and their individual personalities. Agent Rachel Brooks, who infused such confidence in me through every email and phone call that it dashed away any of my doubts. The entire Montlake team, to include Jillian Cline, Mindi Machart, Karah Nichols, Patricia Callahan, Stephanie Chou, Elsa K., photographer Regina Wamba, and cover designer Eileen Carey. My author sisters #girlswritenight: April Asher, Annie Rains, Rachel Lacey, and Jeanette Escudero. Tall Poppy Writers. The ever amazing #batsignal crew: Mia Sosa, Tracey Livesay, Nina Crespo, Priscilla Oliveras, and Michele Arris. #5amwritersclub. And special thanks to Racky, the bunso of our family, my "baby" brother in Alaska, for all of his guidance on proper motorcycle etiquette. All mistakes concerning all this are mine! (I'm a total wuss when it comes to riding a motorcycle—though I would consider a three-wheeler.)

Greggy, Cooper, Ella, and Anna—you are the motivation behind this writer! I hope I've encouraged you to seek your passions! Greg, you are my bestest friend and the greatest partner! 143.

And you, dear readers and influencers and reviewers, who I hear from on the daily through my socials and emails: thank you! I'm bolstered by your feedback and enthusiasm, and your belief in these characters, and in me. I'm grateful for the support.

EXCERPT FROM *WHEN JASMINE BLOOMS*

CHAPTER ONE

Louisburg, Massachusetts
Two years ago

Mothers were meant to be strong.

They were meant to be strong, and brave, and intuitive.

Leto, the Virgin Mary, Mother Earth, Gaia, the triple goddess—they were idyllic representations of motherhood. Powerful and nurturing. Decisive and protective. They hovered in the background, boosting, prompting, encouraging their children, the main characters of stories.

These offspring would blossom from under their tutelage so they could take their rightful places in the world, and for and through them, life would continue.

I carried this privilege on my shoulders, on my soul, with such bound and determined gratitude. Child-birthing and child-rearing books had taken up permanent residence on my bedside table from the moment my husband Quinn and I decided to be parents. When that dream came true and we had four little women under our care, my focus—my life—was to be exactly like the mothers I'd read about.

Early motherhood hadn't been without its insecurities. Dealing with four definitive personalities had driven me to scour those aforementioned books, consult message boards, and aspire to be those deities of motherhood. Without my own mother to look up to, I sought mother mentors in my surroundings and from parenting groups, blogs and social media experts, and literature.

Decades later, I'd done it. My husband and I had done it; we'd completed the enormous task of parenthood. Our children's bedrooms were guest rooms, our dishwasher only ran once every couple of days, and just two pairs of house shoes resided next to the front door.

We had thought we could take a breath.

But no one—not a single person—had prepared me for this.

Scratch that. One mother had, though I hadn't listened.

Standing in the study, in front of the blazing flames in the fireplace, I ran a thumb against the dark brown leather of a book in my hand. The divots of the embossed leaves and the crevices of the title felt like craters against my skin. *Little Women.* This book had guided me throughout my life, its characters known to me as if they themselves were alive. Meg, Jo, Beth, and Amy—I had been each of them at different phases in my life, finding comfort and similarities in their mannerisms and goals.

Then, one day, Marmee had taken center stage. Marmee: the mother, the strong, the brave, the intuitive, modeled after Abigail Alcott, who had been the epitome of resilience and the mother of Louisa May Alcott. My sights had reset, and for twenty years, I found confidence and comfort in her stoic and loving nature. She was the mother I'd aspired to be. Marmee had been a military wife, and she'd made a life helping others, just like me. She'd had a husband who loved people, as my Quinn did. She'd had four children.

She'd *had* four children.

A tear slid from my cheek and dropped onto the leather and streaked down the cover.

I had read this story so much that the pages were yellowed and wrinkled and annotated. The contents were all but memorized and imprinted in my brain.

And yet, despite my having reread this story—and in this same study—the tragedy of Beth's death, as large as it was on the page, hadn't settled in. Marmee had lost Beth, but my eyes had glazed over the words; I'd turned the pages without pausing to consider what that had really meant to the family, to Marmee.

And now I knew why.

It was because Marmee had simply moved on after a brief bit of mourning. The page turned to a new chapter. The story ended, and that was that.

The dam holding back the rest of my tears burst, and a sob lodged itself in my throat. In this book, there was no resolution to the worst thing ever to happen to a parent—which was to outlive their child.

And what was I to do with that? What use was this book?

How had Marmee been able to open her eyes each morning knowing one of her babies was gone?

How would I?

An hour remained in my Libby's funeral reception, and the house, called Sampaguita, was full of strangers. My husband and girls were shell shocked—they were statues in the flow of well-wishers, devoid of their usual cheer and sass. Which left me, because of my position and my status, to rally.

Mothers were meant to be strong. But what did that mean right now, for me?

I gripped the book tighter, knuckles turning white.

One thing was clear, though: This book? It failed me, except to make it perfectly clear that in grieving their children, mothers did so alone. Mothers moved on to take care of everyone else. It was their role, my role, to keep the world going.

After a final look at the book, I tossed it into the fire. It roared as the pages and leather singed and curled into the flames.

Much like my heart, it turned to ashes.

* * *

Cold fingertips against my wrist snapped me out of my haze, and I blinked to a woman speaking in front of me, and her mumbles turned into actual words.

". . . was the best baker in the neighborhood. I'm sorry for your loss." The woman had a downturned expression. She was White and looked to be in her thirties, with the faintest of wrinkles on the sides of her mouth.

We were introduced a while ago by Libby herself, though at the moment her name had escaped my memory. Then again, all my senses were muted; my body was numb, vision hazy at the edges despite my overconsumption of coffee.

Still, I pressed my lips into what I hoped was a smile. "Thank you for coming."

"Of course. I just can't believe this. I remember when Libby . . ." The woman continued, and the sound of my daughter's name on her lips flooded me with pain. My body tensed, eyes shutting ever so briefly so my lungs remembered to expand and contract. In and out, fill and empty. Carbon dioxide for oxygen.

There had been so many stories today, stories that were meant to be reminiscent and lovely. Stories meant to console, to bring joy. But all of it had had the opposite effect on me. Each memory had left me with regret for all the things I hadn't done, with desperation to change time.

I let my gaze travel throughout the room, using the drone of the woman's voice as a means of escape, to the indoor jasmine plants growing next to the windows, the macramé wall hangings. The old family photos on the wall, intermixed with local artists' work, hung by Libby after Quinn and I moved out of the house years ago to downsize.

How this home had changed since we'd moved to Maryland—it still took me by surprise. These walls had been a witness to the fights, the laughter, the wishes, the stories. We'd named it Sampaguita for the national flower of the Philippines. Although Arabian jasmine did not grow in the United States, wild jasmine bordered the property; it had always filled the air with such an intoxicating scent that when the girls used to come in from playing outside, their clothing and skin had smelled of it. And it was only fitting. The blossoms of the sampaguita reminded me of my little girls, each one unique and delicate and hardy all at once, with qualities comprising a smattering of both my Filipino and Quinn's Scottish roots.

My eyes landed on Quinn, standing among a group of men, sipping on a whiskey, a hand in the pocket of his slacks. He was nodding though his expression was blank. Then, as if sensing me, he turned his face. Despite his sad smile, he was gaunt, with bluish half moons under his eyes.

He hadn't slept; then again, I hadn't either. While Quinn had paced the house, my sleep, or lack of it, had been riddled with dreams of Libby playing her piano. Running in the backyard chasing the neighborhood stray cat. Sprinkling flour over a mass of dough.

My husband's attention slipped away to someone speaking to him, and I sought out my girls. It was an unbreakable but necessary habit, to count my people like we were in a crowded amusement park. We were an unwieldy bunch, an overfull suitcase of personalities and priorities and demands. If we didn't watch it, a moment's inattention could lead to someone getting lost or in trouble.

I counted them off in my mind's checklist.

Mae, beside the buffet with an empty dessert plate in her hand, next to her husband, John, heads bent down as they negotiated dessert with their three girls.

MJ, sitting in an armchair, legs out and crossed, fingers clasped on her lap. Across from her was Quinn's aunt Anne Frasier.

Amelia in the crook of her fiancé Theo's arm.

Libby.

Where's Libby? My gaze darted in between and among faces for my thirdborn, for my tall child with Quinn's chiseled jaw and high cheekbones and introversion that one could feel in her vibe.

Then, after a beat, a brick-heavy realization descended over my already weary body.

Libby was gone.

She's not here.

My breath left my body, and my eyes filled with tears, though the outpouring was interrupted by a nudge against my hand.

". . . if you could sign." Something cool was placed upon my open palm, and it startled me back to the present. I blinked my way to the woman's face, whose mouth seemed to be moving quickly, making shapes. Her dark eyes widened with excitement.

Focus, Celine. This time, I forced myself to key in on actually trying to understand what this woman was saying. After inhaling a gulp of stagnant air, I asked, "What's that?"

"Can you . . . sign it?" She gestured down to the thing in my hand—a book. My book, my debut, published earlier this year. *It Will All Be Okay* was a mothering book, not unlike the ones I had consulted all those years ago. A self-help title, with its purpose to help others harness their passions even in the thick of motherhood.

It had flopped—according to my standards, at least—making mediocre sales.

But Louisburg was anything if not loyal. A half hour west of Boston, this town was proud of every single celebrity it produced, to almost ridiculous lengths.

So ridiculous that this woman had brought my book to my daughter's funeral reception to have it signed.

What kind of person would do that?

In my silence, the woman's smile faltered. "I'm such a fan. I listen to your podcast and follow you everywhere on socials. Knowing how much you accomplished being a mom and an entrepreneur. You inspired me to create a business plan. I wanted to come to one of your conferences, but it's just too much with the three kids. You know how it is. I can't get away."

Her words passed like the horizon outside of one's windows when driving down the highway, swiftly and lacking purchase.

The last thing on my mind was work.

Celine Lakad-Frasier Inc. had no place here. Hell, it was due to what I had thought was my calling that I hadn't gotten to Libby on time.

Who did that? Who didn't rush to their child's side when they called? Me.

"Oh, well . . . okay." I accepted the pen that the woman was holding out to me. This woman had been Libby's friend, and it was easy enough.

The woman opened the book to the title page, and I tipped the pen against the top of my name and scrawled my signature.

The sound of the piano took my signature's trajectory to the bottom and off the page. I spun to the instrument, a gifted hand-me-down from Theo's grandfather, our next-door neighbor, parked in the corner of the family room.

A young man was sitting on the piano bench. The fallboard was raised, exposing the white keys. Behind him were two others, neither of whom I recognized. He ran a finger gently against one of the white keys, and he pressed one down. Then another and another.

The notes came together into one of Libby's most favorite pieces to play.

A shiver ran through me, catapulting me away from the woman; I haphazardly handed her back the book. Crossing the room took too long, and as I did, the vision of my little girl tapping "Chopsticks" on a toy keyboard rushed to the forefront in my memory.

How joyful she had been. The piano had dashed her insecurities, and on it she'd learned to succeed and fail, to love and become frustrated, to negotiate and to win.

And this piano was sacred.

The young man's face lifted at my arrival, expression falling. "Oh, I'm sorry . . . Libby and I, she gave me some lessons—"

"No one plays this piano," I said, my voice cracking. I set a hand against the fallboard, a threat—to his fingers, to another story about Libby.

What was worse than losing a child knowing you could have done something about it? It was losing a child whom you'd lost touch with, a child who had a whole life you didn't know anything about. But this piano was undoubtedly Libby, Libby in the way I had known her when we had lived in the same home.

It worked, and the man jumped out of the chair in continued apology, the group scuttling to the corner. Quinn approached me, body hovering above mine. He was just over six feet tall, and he blocked out the light of the low ceiling, though it cast a halo around his reddish-brown hair. "Celine?" Worry laced his tone.

In my periphery, Mae, MJ, and Amelia watched me intently. Though in their twenties, they still took note of my actions and reactions. It was both a mother's privilege and a burden to be on a pedestal. It was also a blessing and a curse to be a public figure. And rolled together, that put me under a microscope.

There could be no tears here, no outbursts. I couldn't slam the fallboard shut, nor could I scream from the top of my lungs. Not in front of these people and especially not in front of my children . . . what was left of them.

With a final look at the keys, I lowered the fallboard. "I . . . I'm fine. I'm sorry . . . it's just . . . this was her most favorite thing."

A mumble of an apology came from the young man, and Quinn eased the moment by leading him to the buffet table and plying him with a plate of pastry.

I was left staring at the closed piano, and the decision came to me.

Locking it up was the only solution. I grasped the end of the brass piano key sticking out from the hourglass keyhole, and I twisted it to the right.

A click followed, securely locking the fallboard in place, easing the tension in my chest. I hadn't been able to protect Libby, but I could very well protect her piano.

ABOUT THE AUTHOR

Photo © 2020 Sarandipity Photography

Tif Marcelo is a veteran US Army nurse and holds a BS in nursing and a master's in public administration. She believes in and writes about the strength of families, the endurance of friendship, and the beauty of heartfelt romance—and she's inspired daily by her own military hero husband and four children. She hosts the *Stories to Love* podcast, and she is also the *USA Today* bestselling author of *In a Book Club Far Away, Once Upon a Sunset, The Key to Happily Ever After,* and the Journey to the Heart series. Sign up for her newsletter at www.TifMarcelo.com.